DRAGONFIRE

'One of our agents is missing,' Harris said. Salvage.

'You want me to find him?' Sawyer asked finally.

Harris looked directly into Sawyer's good eye for the first time. He was keeping it under control, but Sawyer could sense the desperation underneath. Harris hated his guts. He had called Sawyer in not because he liked him but because his career was on the line.

'I want you to replace him,' Harris said.

'Who was it?'

Harris shook his head. 'No need to know.'

'What's the mission?' Sawyer asked at last.

Harris leaned forward, his forearms on the table. His eyes were very blue and very cold.

'We want you to start a war.'

Also in Arrow by Andrew Kaplan

Hour of the Assassins
Scorpion

DRAGONFIRE

Andrew Kaplan

ARROW BOOKS

Arrow Books Limited
62–65 Chandos Place, London WC2N 4NW

An imprint of Century Hutchinson Limited

London Melbourne Sydney Auckland
Johannesburg and agencies throughout
the world

First published by Century 1987
Arrow edition 1988

Printed and bound in Great Britain by
Anchor Brendon Limited, Tiptree, Essex

ISBN 0 09 947980 X

To those for whom Southeast Asia
was more than a place on a map
and
to Justin, age 3. I really like you too.

Because Thou Lovest the Burning-ground,
I have made a Burning-ground of my heart –
That Thou, Dark One, haunter of the Burning-ground,
Mayest dance Thy eternal dance.

– a Bengali Hymn

ACKNOWLEDGEMENTS

This book was written in the south of France, a fact which created its own peculiar set of advantages and difficulties. My thanks are therefore due to a number of people who assisted in the early proofing and word processing of the manuscript, particularly Jake and Susan Lowe, Colette Stoltz, and the people at Fortune Systems International in Monte Carlo, especially Eva Ehojoki and Brooke 'Pete' Taylor, President of Fortune Systems International. It should also be noted that without the unwavering support of my agent, June Hall, and my wife, Anne, this book would not exist.

Chapter headings and symbols are quoted from *I Ching*, Sam Reifler, Bantam Books, 1981 ed.
  Bengali hymn quoted from *The Religions of Man*, Huston Smith, a Mentor book, New American Library, 1961 ed.
  Security regulations of Tuol Sleng prison quoted from *National Geographic Magazine*, Vol. 161, No. 5, May 1982.

AUTHOR'S NOTE

The symbols and sayings that begin each chapter are taken from the I Ching, the Chinese Book of Changes. The I Ching is almost as old as China itself. The version that has come down to us was used as an oracle by the Mandarins of the Chinese court and it is still widely employed by fortune-tellers throughout the Far East. Hence it provides a unique window on to Asian thinking.

The Book of Changes originally evolved from a simple yes-or-no oracle based on tortoise-shell patterns, in which a solid line (———) indicated yes or Yang (crudely translated in the West as the masculine force), and a broken line (— —) indicated no or Yin (the opposing or feminine force). But the need for greater subtlety was felt early on, and first a second and then a third line was added to form a trigram.

Each of these three-line trigrams (eight combinations are possible) came to represent a unique aspect of the world, such as Heaven (☰), thunder (☳), fire (☲) and so on. In addition, each trigram is associated with specific symbolic attributes. For example, the trigram for marsh and mist (☱) also represents happiness, pleasure, magic, destruction, sensuality, youngest daughters, the animal character-istics of the sheep, the colour blue, autumn, the direction west, etc.

However, the I Ching is concerned not so much with things as they are (which the Chinese considered illusory) as with things in the process of change; hence the name, Book of Changes. Each line may change from Yang to Yin or Yin to Yang, and each trigram may combine with another to form a six-line hexagram.

Normally, the first statement of the prophecy describes the configuration of this hexagram. For example: 'The wind blows above the earth' means that the hexagram consists of

1

the trigram for wind on top of the trigram for earth. The remaining statements are prophecies which may sometimes seem obscure but which would have been perfectly clear to a Chinese courtier. For example, the statement 'The man places mats of white grass beneath objects set on the ground' is a warning to take extraordinary precautions.

There are sixty-four possible hexagrams (eight squared). The ancient Chinese believed that these sixty-four hexagrams encompassed all of human experience.

In the plain between the hills of Kulen and the giant lake called the Tonle Sap, the ancient Khmers of Cambodia built a vast complex of temples, of which the most famous is Angkor Wat.

The temples were an attempt to create in stone a kind of map or enormous scale model of the Hindu universe, but after the Hindu deities failed to protect the city from a disastrous Cham invasion in the twelfth century, the pragmatic Khmers dedicated their new temples to Buddha. However, many of the existing temples retained their old pagan and Hindu associations.

One of these, the Phimeanakas (completed circa A.D. 1000), is located within the Angkor Thom complex, north of the temple of Angkor Wat. The ruin is a single pyramid made of laterite; the tower has not survived. According to legend, the structure was built upon the site where an early Khmer king, acting to protect the kingdom, had nightly congress with a dragon goddess (in some versions a giant serpent) in the form of a beautiful woman.

The Khmers believed that the goddess could not be destroyed except by her own dragonfire, the only weapon that could harm her.

PROLOGUE

They were friends once. The kind of special friends the men of the hill tribes call 'death friends' to distinguish them from those with whom one merely shares rice and talk. Nearly two decades later the fact that they had known each other at all became a critical element of the Dragonfire operation, as the affair came to be called within the National Security Council.

Locked inside the 'Black Vault', the innermost sanctum within the CIA complex in Langley, there actually exists a photograph of all of them together. All except Pranh, who snapped the shot. Of course, no photograph of Pranh himself was ever needed because there was a time when, under the name Son Lot, you could find his face on posters plastered all over Cambodia.

Still attached to the photo is a yellowing label typed by some long-forgotten army S-2 intelligence analyst. It reads: 'US Special Forces advisers attached to the 11th ARVN Ranger Battalion. Parrot's Beak sector, Cambodia. 5 June 1970.'

The photo itself is black and white. It shows four young men sitting in relaxed poses atop an armoured personnel carrier. They are wearing camouflage fatigues dappled by the sunlight and are cradling their weapons with the casual ease that comes with long familiarity.

One of them, Parker, is caught in the act of flipping his cigarette in the direction of the camera. He seems tanned, even cocky, wearing the kind of cynical sneer that only the truly innocent are capable of.

In the middle is the agent later known only as Sawyer. The photo is the sole physical evidence he ever existed because after Dragonfire his personnel file and all cross-references to his real identity were purged from the data

5

banks of the CIA's Cray supercomputer. In the picture he is shirtless and so lean you can almost count the ribs. His green beret is draped over the muzzle of a captured AK-47 and he is squinting in the strong sunlight. He still had two good eyes then, before the eye-patch that was to become his trademark, and looked like a young Jack Kennedy.

Next to him is Harold Johnson, nicknamed 'Brother Rap', holding up a fist clenched in the Black Power salute. He sports a sparse nineteen-year-old's moustache, a Black Power shoelace bracelet and love beads; the words 'Born to Kill' are painted in white letters on his helmet liner.

Squatting near the machine-gun mount is Major Lu, wearing green fatigues and over-sized aviator sunglasses that make him look as the Buddha might look if he had been turned into a frog.

It was an ordinary photo. It captured only their faces, not their souls.

On the day after it was taken their friendship was torn apart for ever.

PART ONE

The dragon lies hidden in the deep.

CHAPTER 1

The deep yawns above the thunder.
Whoever hunts deer without a guide
Will lose his way in the depths of
   the forest.
The superior man is aware of the
   hidden dangers.

She was dressed in silk, red and gold, and on her head was a gold crown spiralling to a point like a temple chedi. She stood alone in the spotlight, one foot gracefully raised in the classic lakhon dancer's pose. Her left hand gestured downward in a rejection of passion, as it will in the final dance on the last night of the world, when the stars fall from the sky and the mountains are engulfed in flame. Her right hand was upturned, signalling the acceptance of her lover and the primordial thrust of his desire. Her face was exquisite, her dark eyes impassive.

Now the rhythm of the pi-nai and the drum grew more insistent. She began to move her hips, swaying to and fro as though summoning an invisible lover. Two slave girls rushed from the wings and began to unwind her sarong. She wriggled out of her clothes in waves, like a snake moulting its outer skin, until she stood completely naked. She bowed in a gesture of submission, her slender body glistening with sweat, her bud-like breasts heaving, her buttocks moving in an enticing motion old as time.

The stage was wreathed in smoke from the joss sticks, mingled with the fumes of opium and tobacco. The smoke twisted and swirled in shafts of light like a living thing.

The drumbeat quickened as the slave girls threw off their

robes and stood naked but for big leather phalluses strapped to their loins. A collective male sigh escaped the audience. The drumming mounted to a crescendo as the two slave girls took turns at playing the male. Their bodies tangled together, passion ripping through them. The drums went wild as they climaxed with savage cries, their black hair flying as they whipped their heads back and forth, then sank gracefully to the floor, limp and spent.

The crowd of Asian businessmen, sprinkled with the occasional serviceman, roared its approval. Green twenty-baht notes were tossed on to the stage. Smiling, the dancers came to the edge of the stage to pluck notes from upstretched hands using only the muscles between their legs.

In a dark corner booth two men who had been engrossed in their conversation glanced over towards the stage. One was a portly, greying Asian in a blue silk suit obviously made by a Hong Kong tailor who knew what he was doing. The other was a tall Occidental wearing the safari-style khakis inevitably affected by American officials and journalists in Indo-China.

'There is true seduction of Asia,' Vasnasong said, gesturing at the naked dancers. 'The promise that you can do anything . . . absolutely anything.'

Parker raised his eyebrows. 'Are you talking about sex or power?'

'They are intertwined, like Yin and Yang. True power is ability to indulge every desire, every whim, no matter how bizarre. Is that not ultimate aphrodisiac?' Vasnasong smiled.

'I thought you Buddhists frowned on sex.'

'Although, like most male Thais, I spent time as naga, I am far from being bhikku monk. Besides, Lord Buddha did not teach physical passion bad. Only that to pass beyond suffering, you must also go beyond pleasure. Only then comes profit,' Vasnasong replied, his eyes twinkling.

Parker jumped at the conversational opening. Otherwise they'd be here trading Chinese fortune-cookie talk all night.

'Speaking of profit, of this thing with Bhun Sa, can it be arranged?' he asked.

Vasnasong sighed inwardly. Such rudeness was typical of a farang. Americans were the worst. Always in such a hurry that they heard only the words, never the nuances between the words where conversation really takes place. So be it, he thought. With such a one subtlety is meaningless anyway. But first he would exact a tiny revenge.

'Do you desire? It is house speciality,' Vasnasong said, indicating the spicy water-beetle paste with his chopsticks. He had seen that the farang was disgusted by it by the expression on his face when it was served.

Parker shook his head. Smiling, Vasnasong shoved it insistingly towards him and was secretly delighted by Parker's obvious discomfort as he attempted a small, polite nibble.

'Delicious,' Parker said insincerely.

'Ah, yes.' Vasnasong smiled.

'Does that mean it can be arranged?' Parker said, looking around anxiously as though he was afraid of being overheard.

'Mai pen rai.' Vasnasong shrugged. 'In Bangkok, Hawkins-khrap, anything can be arranged – for a price.'

Hawkins was Parker's cover name.

There was a burst of applause and Parker glanced towards the stage. In the spotlight a voluptuous woman was seated in a hanging bamboo basket, her naked bottom protruding from a hole in the basket. To the accompaniment of raucous cheers from the audience, she was slowly lowered on to a sailor who had volunteered from the audience.

Parker nodded and leaned forward across the table. 'How soon can I get up-country to see Bhun Sa?' he whispered. No one could hear him in all the audience noise. On stage the sailor slowly twirled the basket. The woman revolved on his erection like a top.

Vasnasong looked curiously at the farang. 'Have you ever been in hill country of Golden Triangle, Hawkins-khrap?'

'No. Why?'

Vasnasong laid his finger alongside his nose in a gesture of warning. 'The hill country is most dangerous place, Hawkins-khrap. Most dangerous. And of all the hill people Bhun Sa may be most dangerous,' Vasnasong said uneasily.

'Yeah, well, the world is full of tough guys.' Parker shrugged. Did the prick think he was dealing with a Boy Scout? he wondered.

Vasnasong smiled politely. What was it his honoured father used to say? 'To reason with a fool is as to belch into the breath of a typhoon.' He plucked at a morsel of lemon chicken with his chopsticks, then genially raised his glass of Mae Khong whisky. 'Then may you meet only good and overcome all your enemies, Hawkins-khrap,' Vasnasong toasted, and they both drank.

'When can I make contact?' Parker said hoarsely, choking back the whisky. Mae Khong was guaranteed by the manufacturer never to be more than two weeks old.

'Tonight. Very soon,' Vasnasong said, consulting his gold Rolex. 'And now,' he added, delicately faking a yawn, 'a thousand pardons, but I am old man and my bed calls.'

'Wait a minute,' Parker began angrily. He started to grab at Vasnasong's sleeve but instead found the torn half of a red hundred-baht note being pressed into his hand as part of a handshake.

'A beautiful girl will have matching half. Follow her and you will find what you seek,' Vasnasong whispered and stood up. He glanced around, as if nervous for the first time, but all eyes were on the stage and the squealing basket girl.

Parker surreptitiously felt for the ·45 automatic in the holster nestled in the small of his back. 'See you soon.' Parker grinned, his fingers touching the gun grip.

'Sawat dee khrap,' Vasnasong said, pressing his palms together in the wai sign.

A burst of applause came from the front, distracting Parker. The basket girl and the sailor were gone, replaced by a pretty girl who looked as if she had barely reached her teens. She was trying to do something obscene with a snake.

When he turned back, Parker found himself staring at the most beautiful woman he had ever seen, standing where Vasnasong had stood just a few seconds before. It was like a conjurer's trick, and for a moment Parker couldn't believe his eyes. He was spellbound. He couldn't take his eyes off her.

She was tall for an Asian, with straight black hair that fell below her shoulders and dark almond eyes luminous with mystery and passion. They reminded him of the eyes of an ancient queen painted on the wall of a four-thousand-year-old tomb he had visited once in Egypt. She wore just a touch of lipstick and eye shadow on that exquisite face and smelled of jasmine. Her sarong was white silk, embroidered with

12

gold and somehow tightly moulded to her body in a way that was at once modest yet dazzlingly sensual.

She smiled, revealing captivating dimples and perfect white teeth and, like any bar girl, asked him if he wanted a good time, number-one time. But she was no bar girl. He was sure of that. His throat had gone dry and he had to swallow before he could ask her how much.

'Tao rye?'

'Nung roi kha,' she replied, asking for the hundred.

As if in a trance, Parker handed her the torn half of the hundred-baht note. She unfolded another half and matched the two pieces. She looked around once to make sure no one was paying too much attention to what was, after all, an everyday transaction. All eyes were on the snake dancer.

'You follow,' she whispered in English and ducked through a bamboo curtain that led to a side exit. Parker tossed a bill on the table to cover the drinks. By the time he reached the alley outside, she had already disappeared.

The alley was dark and strewn with garbage. But just a few feet away Patpong Road was bright as day from all the neon lights. Parker hesitated. She had vanished as if she were a dream, or maybe one of those spirits the Thais built those little dollhouses for in the corner of every dwelling. Then he thought he caught a faint whiff of jasmine lingering in the hot, sticky air characteristic of the nights before the southwest monsoon.

It's no dream, he told himself. She's your only link with Bhun Sa, so don't let her get away.

He ran out into the street. Traffic was heavy all along Patpong Road. Three-wheeled samlors, cycles and motorbikes narrowly weaved between the honking cars, barely scraping through by inches. Asian and European men, civilians and servicemen from half a dozen countries, prowled the sidewalks, while girls in tight slacks and Western jeans called their siren song from brightly lit entrances to the bars and massage parlours. Rock music in a dozen languages blared from open doorways. Street vendors sold cigarettes and picture postcards from their top trays, pornographic photos, Thai sticks and black balls of opium and hashish from the bottom trays.

At first Parker thought he had lost her in the crowd. Then

he saw men staring after someone near the Silom Road intersection and just caught a glimpse of her white sarong rounding the corner. Ignoring Langley rules about never calling attention to yourself while on a tail, he ran after her. Rounding the corner, he was in time to see her duck into a side street near the corner of the Bangkok Christian Hospital.

She was very quick and very good, he thought, settling into a normal walking pattern about a hundred yards behind her. Even just walking, she moved with an animal grace that was incredibly sensual and, despite all his training, he found he couldn't take his eyes from the teasing sway of her skin-tight sarong.

She moved nimbly down side streets and darkened alleys, slipping between noodle stalls lit by kerosene lamps, a white figure flitting ahead of him in the darkness like a ghost. He knew he should contact his case officer to let him know he was entering the red zone. They had drilled that into him a hundred times. Always keep control posted. Better to miss an opportunity than to lose communication. But how, without losing her? She has to stop some time, he thought, reassuring himself. When she did he would find a phone before he made contact.

At the next corner she paused to study the posters outside a movie house showing the latest karate epic from Hong Kong, glancing out of the corner of her eye to see if he was still with her. He made no effort to close the distance. He was grateful for this time to catch his breath. And he had to make sure they weren't being followed.

He studied the reflection of the street behind him in the darkened window of a closed goldsmith's shop. Traffic was bumper to bumper even at this late hour. Shoppers were filling wicker baskets in the fluorescent glare of a nearby market. At a sidewalk restaurant a prospective diner was sniffing at a cauldron as the owner held up a live crab for his inspection. Everything seemed normal enough except . . . Parker suddenly felt a terrible urge to urinate. His mouth had gone dry. *He was being watched.*

A big-muscled Thai in a suit that looked as if it had been made for a much smaller man stood patiently waiting at the Number 71 bus stop. He wasn't looking at either Parker or the girl. But the buses in Bangkok didn't run after midnight.

14

There was another possible bulldog leaning against the noodle stall ahead. Also Thai. It looked like a front-and-back tail. They were boxed in.

And was it his nerves, or did the passenger in a passing dark-blue Nissan sedan take an excessive interest in him? The look had been held just a fraction too long, he decided. That meant they were mobile as well.

Parker thought about aborting. There was sure to be a public phone back at the hospital on Silom Road. And what about the girl? Had she spotted the tails? He tried to think of a way to signal to her, but it was too late.

She had started moving again.

He had no choice. He decided he would have to follow.

If only he knew where she was headed, he could try to flush the tails, he thought. She was heading south towards the Sathan Nua klong. Which way would she go when she reached the canal, left or right?

Then it hit him what she was up to. There was a water-bus dock near the Convent Road intersection. She had seen the tails. She was going to make a run for it on the water.

If he could eliminate at least one of the tails, they could still make the rendezvous. Assuming he was right, that is. If he was, the lead tail would stay with the girl, the second would peel off with him.

There was only one way to find out, he thought, as he came abreast of the movie-house ticket booth. He acted as if he were going to continue after the girl, then turned, bought a ticket from a sleepy-eyed young clerk and hurried into the darkened theatre.

The tail would expect him to go out of another exit, according to standard flushing procedure. Instead he took a seat in the last row near the aisle. When his eyes had adjusted to the dark, he could see that only a few seats were occupied. Being able to see better than the tail, whose eyes would have less time to adjust, should give him an extra edge, he thought. He slipped the ·45 automatic from its holster and clicked off the safety catch. He watched the curtained entrance while glancing at the movie out of the corner of his eye.

On the screen the Chinese hero, clad in a black karate outfit, was spinning in the air, kicking out with devastating effect against at least a hundred white-suited adversaries from the karate school of a mad scientist. The sound-effects man must have gone crazy because every blow sounded like a car crash. The kicks sent the hero's opponents flying like ten-pins despite missing them by at least a foot. All in all, one against a hundred seemed like a pretty fair fight, and Parker was wondering what the hero would do if he was in Parker's spot when the curtain parted and the second tail burst in.

As he headed down the aisle, glancing left and right, Parker slipped behind him and, grabbing the back of his jacket, jammed the muzzle of the ·45 into the Thai's broad back.

'Hold it, buster. Yoot!' Parker hissed.

The big man hesitated. Parker felt the Thai's muscles tense in preparation for a move and viciously jabbed the gun into his kidneys.

'Don't try it,' Parker whispered.

The Thai barely flinched. But at least he stopped moving.

Parker prodded the man ahead of him back up the aisle and then to the small toilet cubicle off the threadbare lobby. The toilet itself was a foul-smelling hole in the ground, where flies buzzed noisily. A single, naked yellow bulb barely lit the darkness.

'Take off your belt,' Parker demanded and, when the Thai's pants were around his ankles, used the leather belt to tie his hands behind him.

'You no understand,' the Thai began.

Parker never let him finish the sentence. He cold-cocked the Thai with the butt of the Colt, hitting him behind the right ear with all his might. The Thai sank to his knees and Parker hit him twice more on the head. The man sprawled unconscious over the filthy hole, his face in the muck. Parker didn't wait to see if he was still breathing. He had more important things to do.

Parker raced out of the movie house and down the street towards the klong, ignoring the astonished glances of passers-by. He had to catch her.

There was still a crowd on the Sathan Nua landing and at first he thought he might still be in time. But it was too late. The sleek white water-bus, jammed tightly as a rush-hour subway car, was already pulling away from the landing.

Even if he could get through the crowd, it was too far to jump and the gap of water was widening every second.

He stood there panting, watching the water-bus pull away. He searched for her face in the crowd. He caught a glimpse of her looking back at him from the railing. It was a strange look. He tried to read her expression, but it was too dark, the moment too fleeting, to see anything clearly. But it was her all right. There was no mistaking the white sarong or that exquisite face. Further on down the railing he thought he saw the lead tail.

Parker tried to decide what to do. Then he noticed a cluster of hang-yao, long-tailed water-taxis, moored to the bank near the landing. Parker motioned to the first driver. He showed him a purple five-hundred-baht note and a minute later they were on the klong, bouncing in the wake of the water-bus.

As they sped along the klong, getting wet from the spray thrown up by the water-bus, Parker tried to figure it out. They had to reach the next landing at New Road before the water-bus got there. But it was all happening too fast. The girl. The tails. Who sent them? Vasnasong? Bhun Sa? Or someone else? It made no sense. The mission had barely started and already it was coming apart. None of it ever made any sense and he remembered something Jack had told him long ago, back in Da Nang.

They were having rum-and-cokes on the veranda of the Grand Hotel, looking out at the lights on the fishing junks bobbing on the c ly slick that was the Tourane river. Around them grunts fron the American Division sat around the tables drinking and openly shooting up skag bought for two bucks a vial just outside the base gate. The street boys and whores swarmed around the grunts like moths around a lamp, filling the air with cries of 'Cheap Charlie' and 'Fi' dollah' and 'You numbah-ten Charlie'. He had been complaining, Parker remembered. Nothing was working. Not their rules, their strategies, their technology. Nothing.

'You have to remember, this is Asia. Things are different here,' Jack had said.

Parker felt a sudden longing for the green Virginia country-side outside Langley. The rolling hills, the white picket fences, the *cleanness* of it. How sane it was; especially compared with the squalor, the unending noise and intrigue, the sheer misery of Asia. He'd been out here too long. This would be his last mission, Parker decided.

A change in the growl of the hang-yao's engine brought him out of his thoughts. They were coming into the New Road landing. The water-bus had just tied up and begun to unload as the hang-yao bumped against the bank. Parker was on his feet even before the driver could tie up. There was no time to waste. He had to catch her before she got off the boat.

Teetering like a man on a tightrope, he leaped from the prow on to the wet bank. His foot slipped and he had to scramble up the bank on all fours. By the time he was able to turn around passengers were already streaming off the water-bus, mingling on the landing with the crowd that was trying to board.

He couldn't find her in the crowd. He stood there searching until his training suddenly brought him up short. He couldn't be so damned obvious. Get cover and scan, he told himself.

He stepped over to a noodle stand on the quai and ordered a bowl of kow pat. Leaning against the stand, he casually turned and began a methodical scan of the landing, quartering the crowd in the market area, those heading for New Road, then the landing area and those still on the water-bus. She wasn't in the crowd moving towards the bright lights of the New Road or in the market. He began to panic. He couldn't find her. But it was impossible. He couldn't have missed her. She had to be there.

Think, dammit, he told himself. What do you know about her, beyond the fact that she's beautiful? His mind raced. Her connection with Vasnasong? Bhun Sa, maybe. She's fast. A pro, spotting the tails like that and making for the water. A pro, under surveillance. What would she do?

She must have changed the image, he thought. Unconsciously he hadn't been looking for her but for the white sarong. He repeated the scan of the landing area and this time he spotted her quickly. She had thrown a red silk shawl over her shoulders to cover some of the white and break up the image. She was a pro, all right, he thought.

Parker nibbled idly at the kow pat as he watched her head away from the New Road and towards the market stalls and sampans along the banks of the Chao Phraya river. He got ready to follow her, but something in the back of his mind was sending him a warning signal. There was something wrong. There was . . .

She was no longer under surveillance. The lead tail had disappeared.

There were only two possibilities. One, her change of image had worked and she had lost the tail or, two, the tail had been switched and someone new was now tailing her.

He had to choose one. He decided she had lost the tail for two reasons: because he couldn't spot any sign of the opposition now and because he wanted to stay with her. He wanted it!

He followed her as she weaved among the market stalls, moving purposefully as though she were nearing her destination. She paused by a fish stand for a final check. Half hidden under racks of dried squid, hanging like sheets of red parchment, she glanced back to make sure she hadn't lost him.

Parker took the opportunity for a final check of his own. He could see the lights along the Thonburi side of the river winking like fireflies as the boat lanterns bobbed in the wake of the river traffic. The silhouettes of tall palms and temple spires could be seen dimly against the electric haze of the city lights. The steamy night smelled of mud and fish piled up on the river quay. There was no sign of the opposition.

Why not?

There was no time to come up with an answer. She was moving again.

She made her way along the embankment where the rice barges and the sampans were tethered. They had left the market area and it was darker here. The only light came from the kerosene boat lanterns. Then she stopped.

Parker waited. It was quiet but for the gentle lapping of the water, the occasional creak of a boat, the distant sound of a radio. And, from somewhere nearby, the scent of a burning joss stick.

She had come to two sampans lashed together, tethered by a short rope to a stake on the muddy embankment. They were set apart, away from the other boats closer to the market area. There was no one on the decks. They floated a

19

few feet offshore, with water on all sides, so that no one could enter or leave without being seen or heard. From a security aspect, whoever had set this up had chosen well, Parker thought.

She glanced, for the briefest second, back towards Parker, then, with a slight tug on the rope, lightly leaped across the few feet of water on to the deck of one of the sampans. She hopped over the gunnel on to the other sampan and disappeared under the thatched arch that served as a roof.

The sampans looked deserted and oddly menacing. Nothing ventured, nothing gained, Parker told himself as he pulled the ·45 automatic from his holster and cocked it. He took one deep breath, then moved.

In seconds he covered the dozen or so strides to the bank and leaped on to the deck of the sampan where the girl was. The deck bobbed under him as he ducked under the thatched roof, the ·45 in the two-hand firing position.

Parker stared at the interior of the sampan, unable to believe his eyes. His hands dropped uselessly to his side. Thunderstruck, he looked around in a daze. It wasn't possible, he told himself. Yet, impossible or not, it had happened.

The cabin was empty. The girl had vanished.

But there was no place to hide, he thought, as he began to poke around. There were no signs of a struggle. The interior was lit by a Coleman lamp and he found an American filter-tip cigarette with lipstick on it still burning in an ashtray on a low wicker table.

Parker felt as much as heard someone behind him. He whirled around, his gun ready, but there was no point to it. There were two of them. They carried Chinese-made SKS carbines and had him neatly bracketed between them. Even if he got one, the other would surely get him. They were young and they had that mindless, wild-eyed look of itchy-triggered adolescents that in Asia means that they might kill you even if ordered not to.

One of them shouted something, and although Parker didn't understand the language he was using, there was no mistaking the meaning.

Parker dropped his gun.

One of them sneered, then kicked him in the stomach. As he doubled over, gasping, they knocked him down with the

20

butts of their rifles. Parker curled into a foetal position as they began a merciless beating but, at a barked command, they stopped as suddenly as they had started.

From his position on the deck Parker could just make out a figure in the doorway, the face hidden in shadow. He struggled to a sitting position. There was a sharp pain when he moved, and he wondered if they'd broken a rib. He started to wince, then stopped himself. Never show weakness to an Asian, ran the Langley credo. Bad face. Instead always take the initiative.

'What's the meaning of this outrage? I'm an American official and I demand . . .,' Parker began.

The shadowy figure brushed aside his tirade with a flick of his finger as if it were a fly. The two guards grinned at him like gargoyles.

'Few things are more ridiculous than someone in your position making demands,' the figure said in excellent, though accented, English.

'Where's the girl?'

'She served her purpose. Now you will serve yours,' the figure said.

The voice was oddly familiar. Where had he heard it before? What the hell was going on? Parker wondered. Still, he had to try to establish some kind of control over the situation before it was too late. He licked his lips; they felt like sandpaper. He was suddenly very thirsty.

'Both the American government and General Bhamornprayoon are fully aware . . .,' Parker began again.

'Ah, a general,' the voice mocked. 'I too am a general. There is no shortage of generals in South-East Asia,' the figure said as he stepped into the light.

When Parker saw the general's face he knew at once, with an overwhelming sense of sadness and certainty, that this truly was his last mission. He would never see the green hills of Virginia again because, even after all these years, he immediately recognized the man in front of him.

'Hello, Pranh,' Parker said.

CHAPTER 2

Water tends to move earthward
away from heaven above.
In a situation where there is
   strife
the man knows how important first
   steps are.

Sometimes an entire era can be evoked by the name of a local watering hole. The Deux Magots in Paris. Harry's Bar in Venice. The Caravelle in Saigon. And Houlihan's in Bangkok, Sawyer thought.

From the outside it hadn't changed much since the rowdy days, when B-52 crews from bases with names like Udorn, Ta Khli and U-Tapao had nightly mingled with wild-eyed Marines on R 'n' R, light-fingered bar girls and Chinese black marketeers who could sell you anything, including the contents of the overnight bag you had left back at your hotel. In those days Houlihan's had been a kind of discount store for used intelligence, low-grade stuff like the locations of military units and MACV leaks to journalists. Sawyer remembered how Barnes used to say that information was Houlihan's third most popular commodity after sex and dope, in that order.

'What about booze?' Parker had demanded. He was falling-down drunk at the time and pronounced it 'boosh'. A Marine sergeant at the next table, thinking Parker had said 'Buddhists', yelled out 'Fuck the Buddhists!', at which point the girl in his lap with the see-through blouse tried to scratch his eyes out, starting a riot that almost closed the place down.

'Ah, booze, the stuff that takes the suffering away. Whisky is the Catholic version of Buddhism, you might say. Not even a distant fourth,' Barnes had replied, ignoring the mayhem around them and talking in a deep County Cork brogue that lacked nothing despite the fact that he wasn't Irish and had never spoken that way before.

Houlihan's.

Although the 'H' in the neon sign was out, which meant that it was safe to approach, Sawyer lingered near the noodle stall on the corner.

He watched the three-wheeled samlors and motor-scooters put-putting through the traffic, looking for anyone who spent more time gazing at Houlihan's than at the mayhem of traffic around him. There were always a few low-level agents on scooters patrolling the red-light district, the grunts of the intelligence business. He took his time to check the windows and roofs of every building with a view of Houlihan's entrance. Safe was always better than sorry, he thought, remembering with a little inward grin Koenig's famous dictum about how paranoids would make good agents if they weren't so trusting.

The afternoon sun sent ripples of heat through the gasoline haze. The air felt thick and greasy. It lay over the city like a pool of stagnant water, smelling of Prek-kk-noo pepper and burning joss and diesel fumes, the scents that, even if you were blindfolded, would tell you you're in Asia. The neon lights from the bars and go-go joints, the cars moving in bumper-to-bumper convoys like schools of fish, the goggle-eyed tourists glancing left and right as they moved slowly through the oppressive heat made Sawyer think of an aquarium. Soi Cowboy was a living exhibit of man's underside, Sawyer thought, and he wondered why he had been stupid enough to come back to Asia.

What was it the Japanese said? 'Every man must climb Mount Fuji at least once, but only a fool has to climb it twice.' What does that make me, he asked himself as he crossed the street to Houlihan's, having verified that there was no outside surveillance.

Inside the bar it was dark and cool as a cave. The meeting had been timed for the late-afternoon lull, and the place was almost empty except for a couple of bored bar girls plying drinks to a bleary-eyed British sailor and Barnes himself at his old stand behind the bar, polishing a glass and listening to the kick-boxing returns on the radio.

One of the bar girls got up from the table and started to come towards him, and the Vietnamese words for 'Beat it', 'Di di mau', almost popped out of his mouth. The feeling of *déjà vu* was very powerful and he had to remind himself that the war had ended a long time ago. He hadn't thought the memories would be so strong. Sweat began to prickle along his entire body. But he should have expected it, he reminded himself. Memory is stimulated by environment. If you want to remember long-forgotten scenes from your childhood, go back to the old neighbourhood. He shook her off and headed for the bar.

Barnes looked up as Sawyer approached, but his face showed no sign of surprise or even recognition. He was still a pro, Sawyer thought, as he ordered a beer. He wondered if Barnes had recognized him right away, or had he changed too much? Sawyer stared at his own reflection in the peeling mirror behind the bar. He was wearing civvies now: a short-sleeved shirt and light-coloured tropical slacks. That was different. And the black eye-patch, of course, which made him look like a cross between a pirate and a shirt ad. But the dark hair and the aquiline looks hadn't changed. Nor the odd green colour of his good eye. Perhaps the lines around the mouth, he thought. Older, more cynical. He wondered if the idealistic young soldier he had been would like how he had turned out. Somehow he didn't think so.

Well. He shrugged mentally. They had all changed.

He watched Barnes draw the beer with those big, beefy hands that, according to legend, could squeeze coins into lumps of metal. He noticed that Barnes still wore the same hai-huang amulet on a CIA gold chain around his neck, breakable into separate links for instant currency. But Barnes had aged, he thought. His close-cropped hair had gone completely grey. His skin had also gone elephant-grey. His eyes had a disconcerting glaze; the pupils were pinpoints and Sawyer wondered what Barnes was smoking these days. Looking at him, it was hard to believe that, in his time, Barnes had been one of the greats. They'd called him 'Mad Max' in those days, because he had once charged his jeep into an NLF village armed only with GVN propaganda leaflets and, as he put it, 'a ·45 in my jockstrap'.

In those days everyone in 'Nam with a 'Get Out of Jail Free' card knew Barnes, Sawyer remembered. An ex-Marine sergeant, Barnes was one of the CIA's early counter-insurgency agents. He had earned his spurs in the Philippines doing what the Company used to call 'agitprop', which was a euphemism for a campaign of sabotage launched against the Hukbalahaps. That was back in the early Fifties when Barnes, working for the already legendary Colonel Ted Lanigan, helped to engineer Magsaysay's election. When Lanigan became CIA station chief in Saigon in '55, Barnes went with him.

Some of Barnes's feats in those days became CIA myths, like the time when Barnes managed to contaminate the oil-supply depot in Hanoi and ruin the engines of almost every truck and bus in North Vietnam. Later, after using massive bribes to subvert the Hoa Hao and Cao Dai sects, Barnes ran a double agent who led the Binh Xuyen, Bay Vien's bandit army, into an ambush, thereby bringing Ngo Dinh Diem to power in Saigon. 'After Dien Bien Phu and the Emperor Bao Dai abdicated, Saigon was like a whorehouse without a madam. The Colonel and me, we *invented* South Vietnam, for Chrissakes,' Barnes used to proclaim to sceptical newcomers sucking down gin-and-tonics at the Caravelle. Whether it was true or not, Sawyer knew for a fact that Barnes was the point man who, seven years later, launched the CIA-sponsored coup of Generals Don and Minh that finally toppled that same Diem and the rest of the notorious Ngo family.

By then Lanigan was long gone, replaced by Donaldson and Secretary of Defense McNamara's new-style paramilitary CIA teams, whom Barnes used privately to call 'McNamara's Ragtime Band', and even Barnes began to lose the faith.

There was a tinny growl from the radio as the crowd cheered. They must be broadcasting live from Lumpini stadium, Sawyer thought.

'May one purchase an Elephant lottery ticket here?' Sawyer asked Barnes, beginning the series.

According to Langley, the sequence was required even

between agents who already knew each other in order to verify that both were legitimately involved in the operation.

'You get better odds on the sporting wagers,' Barnes replied.

'Who is favoured in the main event?'

'Samsook, the Tiger of Raiburi, is unbeatable at four to one,' Barnes shrugged.

'Yet even the unbeatable can be beaten.'

'The will of heaven is inscrutable,' Barnes grinned, letting Sawyer know that he recognized him by the twinkle in his eye.

He leaned confidentially across the bar. 'Watch your ass on this one, Brother Jack,' he whispered.

'Jai yen yen,' Sawyer agreed. Literally translated, the Thai saying meant 'heart cool cool'. To master one's emotions was more than a virtue in Asia. It was the only way to survive.

But Barnes still looked troubled. 'I mean it, amigo. Asia's not what it was.'

'What is?'

Barnes nodded. He looked as if he wanted to say something more, then his face brightened artificially. 'Shit. Here comes the fucking Nippo Leather set,' he whispered *sotto voce*, a big shit-eating grin on his face.

'What'll it be, gents?' he called out loudly, moving to serve a pair of Japanese businessmen sporting the ever-present cameras dangling around their necks like tribal folk emblems.

Sawyer hesitated, to make sure no one was paying any attention to him, then went through the beaded curtain and up the stairs to Room Five, as indicated by Barnes – 'four to (or plus) one'. Most of the girls hadn't shown up for work yet and the corridor was empty. The unmistakable scent of opium seemed to permeate the walls and the sound of a pi-nai came from behind the door. Sawyer knocked four times, then once and went in.

The room smelled of stale perfume and sex and bamboo from the matting on the wall. Over the empty bed in the corner was the inevitable calendar picture of the Swiss Alps that for some reason every bar girl in Asia seemed to cherish.

Harris was already waiting.

He glanced ostentatiously at his watch to remind Sawyer

that he was late, then seemed to think better of it and gestured for him to sit down. Sawyer sat at the rattan table and Harris poured them both cold glasses of Singha beer from sweating bottles. As a professional courtesy Harris had let Sawyer sit where he could watch the door. But he played it by the book, turning up the pi-nai music on the radio and running the tap in the sink. The plumbing chug-chugged like a boat engine that wouldn't start, then settled down to a slow gush of tobacco-coloured water.

Harris mopped his forehead with a soggy handkerchief. There were big sweat stains under his arms and Sawyer felt a secret delight at his discomfort. They couldn't stand each other. Being American males, their mutual dislike was manifested by elaborately disguised attempts at sincerity.

'How's Rio? They still have those sexy cariocas in those teeny string bikinis?' Harris asked, putting the kind of leer into his voice men use when they want to prove they're one of the boys.

It was a lie, of course. Rio was for the record. In fact, Harris had yanked Sawyer from the Managua operation. Brazil was the official cover because of Congressional resistance to anti-Sandinista operations in Nicaragua.

'Either the girls are getting bigger or the bikinis are getting smaller,' Sawyer replied, grinning back at Harris. It was a game anyone could play.

Of all of them Harris had changed the least, Sawyer thought. He still had the fair hair, tennis-court tan and the kind of clean-cut features that ad directors have in mind when they call for a 'Young American Executive' look. A little sleeker, maybe. In his designer-label tropical suit Harris could have been taken for a diplomat or a successful businessman. In fact, he was the CIA's Deputy Director for Covert Operations, and it was said that he never asked a question to which he didn't already know the answer. It was also said that he never told the truth unless he thought no one would believe him.

'Do you like "Sawyer"?' Harris asked.

He was really asking if the cover story was acceptable. It was light cover designed basically for initial entry, not deep penetration. Sawyer was supposed to be an American Red Cross representative here to co-ordinate support for the refugee camps near the Cambodian border. They had supplied him with the usual documents, marked-up and smudged work papers and so on. More than adequate for an initial scrutiny or airport check. All genuine: the Company was always good that way. The cover name 'Sawyer' had been supplied by the computer back at Langley, and Sawyer suspected that the program was running through a children's literature database because his name came from Mark Twain and Harris's code name for this op was 'Tin Man'.

Sawyer shrugged.

'If it's not OK, give me a day and I can change it,' Harris offered.

'It's OK.'

'How was the flight?'

This kind of solicitude was way out of character for Harris and it irritated Sawyer more than Harris's usual know-it-all smirk. Sawyer suddenly felt like a mischievous kid about to kick over the milk pail. Anything to get Harris out of his 'Pass Lady Bracknell the cucumber sandwiches' mode.

'I hope you didn't drag me all the way to Bangkok with a Cherokee just to make small talk,' Sawyer snapped.

A Cherokee code in a cable was the highest urgency level for open communications and, because of it, Sawyer had left an operation in pieces; Ricardo would have to scramble on his own. Langley rules and nobody likes it, and during the long flight hours Sawyer had entertained himself by thinking up a dozen different ways to nail Harris's balls to the wall unless he had a damned good reason for it.

Harris flushed, though Sawyer couldn't tell whether it was from anger or embarrassment. 'We have a little problem here,' Harris admitted.

'First the Cherokee. Now this.' Sawyer gestured vaguely at the room, because the fact that they'd had to use such a well-known location for the rdv meant they'd had to set things up in a hurry. 'You're beginning to worry me, Bob. What happened? Somebody get it caught in the zipper?'

Harris winced. He obviously disapproved of Sawyer's lack of Company style. But he didn't object. That worried Sawyer even more.

He studied Harris carefully. Harris was an actor, he

reminded himself. He didn't feel emotion. He used it. If he was acting now, it was because something had gone wrong.

Even Barnes had warned him about this one. And Harris had flown out from Washington to brief him himself. That meant they were blown.

Basically there were three kinds of mission failure: counter-penetration, public exposure and the blow-up, which was the worst, not only because you also got the first two and more but because the whole thing had fallen apart and the opposition was waiting to pick off anyone coming over the wall.

Salvage operations, as they were called, had almost a hundred per cent mortality rate, and the Langley wisdom was that the only way to get rid of an agent that was surer than a Mafia hit squad was to send him out on a salvage mission.

'It's salvage, isn't it, Bob?' Sawyer asked quietly.

Harris was good, Sawyer thought. Instead of looking at Sawyer, he lifted his glass and studied it with the calculated intensity of a college Hamlet contemplating Yorick's skull. When he put it down Harris was careful to keep both hands in sight. He must've gotten that from my file, Sawyer thought with a little inward smile. 'Never make any move that might represent a threat to the subject. This agent is dangerous at all times, with or without a weapon.'

'Like I said, Jack. We have a little problem here,' Harris admitted at last.

Understatement was Harris's style, like the British habit of calling World War Two the 'late unpleasantness', and hearing Harris admit to a little problem was the worst sign yet. Sawyer felt an icy shiver slide down his spine. When he was a child they used to say that when you got that feeling someone had just stepped on your grave.

'I'm listening,' he said.

Harris took his time, as if telling Sawyer wasn't a foregone conclusion. It was a little like watching a woman who's already invited you into her bedroom and changed into a sexy negligée debate with herself as to whether she is going to do it or not.

'One of our agents is missing,' Harris said.

Salvage.

29

'You want me to find him?' Sawyer asked finally.

Harris looked directly into Sawyer's good eye for the first time. He was keeping it under control, but Sawyer could sense the desperation underneath. Harris hated his guts. He had called Sawyer in not because he liked him but because his career was on the line.

'I want you to replace him,' Harris said.

'Who was it?'

Harris shook his head. 'No need to know,' he remarked primly.

In a way Harris was within his rights, Sawyer reflected. A case officer was supposed to give an agent only enough data to do his job and not to encumber him with information that might distract him or, worse, fall into enemy hands.

Except that Sawyer wasn't having any of it. It was bad enough to walk into a minefield, but he was damned if he was going to do it with his eyes closed. He finished his beer and stood up. Over his head the ceiling fan revolved slowly as the world, barely stirring the air.

'This isn't a briefing for CTP trainees, Bob. You don't want to tell me who it is, replace him yourself,' Sawyer said.

Harris reddened. Sawyer wondered if he hadn't gone too far. Then he told himself that with someone like Harris there was no such thing as too far.

Whatever Harris's real reaction, he obviously thought better of it. His smile reminded Sawyer of the kind of smile an attorney whose client has been caught cold on tape might use when he tells the jury it was police entrapment.

'It was Parker. Mike Parker. Running under the cover name "Hawkins". He seems to have vanished into thin air,' Harris said carefully. He concentrated on pouring the rest of the beer into his glass.

Sawyer felt the sudden urge for a cigarette. He hadn't touched one in ten years and all at once the craving had returned.

'I believe you knew him, didn't you?' Harris asked a shade too casually, as if he hadn't gone over Sawyer's file with a fine-tooth comb before setting this up. As if Cambodia had never happened.

The sounds of the pi-nai on the radio faded like dying hopes in the hot, still air.

'In the Parrot's Beak. I remember that real well,' Sawyer said.

'Things are different now,' Harris said, disapproval in his tone, as if memories, like warranties, were supposed to expire after a certain length of time.

Neither of them said anything. Outside they could hear a furious street argument in singsong Thai. A woman cried out and the arguing was drowned out by the sound of a samlor with a bad muffler roaring by.

Harris waited, like a good salesman who knows that once he's made his pitch he has to let the customer argue himself into the deal. From somewhere came the tinny wail of a Chinese love song and for no reason it reminded Sawyer of a line from Kipling. Something about 'a fool who tried to hustle the East'. And he knew he was hooked and that that son-of-a-bitch Harris had known it all along. Because it was Asia. Because he had left a part of himself here. Maybe the best part. Asia. Like a schoolboy picking at a scab, we just can't leave it alone, he thought.

'What's the mission?' Sawyer asked at last.

Harris leaned forward, his forearms on the table. His eyes were very blue and very cold. 'We want you to start a war,' Harris said.

CHAPTER 3

A fire beneath the open sky.
The superior man distinguishes
things according to their kinds
and classes.

The dragon sailed slowly across the sky, its long red tail
unfurled like a banner. It was a big male, a Chula, although
so high up it was hard to tell how big. When it turned back
towards them they could see a smaller female Pakpao caught
in its bamboo talons. Far below it a second female kite, a
petite Pakpao with a silvery tail, darted through the air
currents like a fish desperately fleeing the inevitable. She flew
into, and then broadside to, the wind, flaring to throw him
off, but the Chula was not to be denied. He came around in
ever-tightening circles until the Pakpao had nowhere to go
but up or down, riding the thermals like an elevator. Even
then he waited, hovering high above her, unmoving, his
paper wings and tail fully outstretched, as she began her last
pathetic ascent.

The swoop, when it came, was hard and fast. The Chula
dropped nearly a hundred feet in a few seconds and, just
when it seemed he might miss the Pakpao altogether, his
handlers brought his nose up sharply, snaring her with the
bamboo hook. But the Pakpao suddenly somersaulted in the
same direction. The tail, its embedded razors glittering in the
hot sun, whipped across the Chula's main control string. All
at once she was free, soaring high in triumph as the big
Chula tumbled out of the sky like a broken thing. It fell for
what seemed like a long time before finally smashing itself
on the muddy surface of the river.

The elegantly dressed guests assembled on the terrace of the hotel broke into loud applause and, as the triumphant Pakpao team bowed and scrambled for coins thrown down to the quay, everyone began to move back under the gold-coloured awning. Above the murmur of voices and the tinkle of cocktails Sawyer could hear the god-awful voice of the Swiss Chargé d'Affaire's wife, the one in yards of rose tulle that made her look like a pink chicken, wondering if it was over and who won.

'Wonderful performance. Wonderful,' the American Press Attaché gushed. He was a moon-faced little man named Schwartz, with the small feet and odd dancer's grace fat men sometimes have. 'It's the Thai national sport. They take their kite-fighting very seriously here,' they overheard him explain to the local stringer for an international news magazine, whose only previous interest in sports had been watching naked women wrestle in mud. Schwartz's round, sweating face was beaming as he passed by, oblivious to the look thrown at him by Sir Geoffrey Hemmings, the British Consul. They all watched Schwartz two-step over to the Press table to make sure their glasses were filled and that they got their handouts.

'Extraordinary kite fight, that. In the end the female does a flip-flop and destroys the male. Almost a metaphor for the battle between the sexes, mightn't one say?' Sir Geoffrey asked, a polite smile failing to mask the wicked gleam in his eye.

'Don't be boring, Geoffrey. You think you're being provocative, but you're not. It's just boring,' Lady Caroline said, touching her tongue to her lip to check her lipstick.

'It's not boring, dearest. It's small talk. That's my job,' he said wearily and Sawyer caught in his voice the dead echo of a theme replayed over and over again in a marriage.

'Small men make small talk,' Lady Caroline retorted, turning back towards Sawyer. 'I take it you're a British subject too?' she asked, brushing close enough for her breasts to graze his arm. The gesture was deliberate and she meant her husband to see it. Not that anyone could have missed it. She was wearing a white silk number cut so low it would have been considered obscene if it hadn't carried the label of an Italian designer, the cost of whose creations could pay off the national debt of a small Third World country.

'No, American actually,' Sawyer replied. He hadn't meant to say 'actually' and just threw it in at the last second to be consistent with the British character she had just bestowed upon him.

'American. Ah, that's so much cleverer to be these days,' she said.

'For God's sake, Caroline,' Sir Geoffrey sputtered and for a moment they were all embarrassed for him.

'Don't swear, Geoffrey, dear. You might be overheard and the Thais take offence so easily,' she said, reddening. It made her look younger and Sawyer could see how pretty she must have been once. She was still attractive, with the kind of well used yet sleek blonde lines that immediately suggest images of thoroughbred horses and fast white yachts and shuttered afternoons with a tennis instructor. She reminded Sawyer of the few women in his past who he had known from the first were out of his league. And because he had known it, and maybe they did too, and because he was younger, he had treated them badly, worse than he had ever intended to. Oddly enough, that only made them want him even more. As he watched Lady Caroline bring her admittedly superb breasts to bear on him, he wondered with a touch of sadness if those women in his past had also finally gone sour, like wine kept in a bottle too long.

'You're looking at one of the great triumphs of modern technology,' Barnes had said, pointing her out when they first arrived. 'Lady Caroline Hemmings. Aged fifty and not a wrinkle or a stretch mark anywhere. You name it. Eyes, chin, hair, tits, thighs, ass – there isn't a part of her that hasn't been redone at least once. There are whole Swiss plastic surgery clinics named after her.'

At the moment Barnes was leering expectantly at her like a man about to hear the punchline of a dirty joke, but she ignored him entirely to concentrate on Sawyer.

Sir Geoffrey coughed politely as though about to say something and Sawyer decided that he was the diffident sort who would always do that. Except that his shyness might have been what the Company tacticians called 'misdirection' because Sir Geoffrey was also the local head of MI6 and was rumoured to have worked once with Sir Robert Thompson's tough counter-insurgents in Malaya.

'You, uh, mustn't mind Caroline,' Sir Geoffrey explained. 'And please don't flatter yourself into thinking she's flirting with you personally. The only requirement she's ever had for anyone is that he wear a pair of trousers.'

There was a burst of laughter from a nearby group and the small Thai orchestra in native silks started up an excruciating rendition of an old Beatles song. For an instant the jangled rhythms and Asian quarter-tones took Sawyer back in time to that French cabaret on Tu Do Street in Saigon and he almost missed the look that passed between Lady Caroline and her husband.

'Don't apologize for me, Geoffrey. Besides, it's all bloody nonsense. There isn't a farang man worth having in this whole bloody town.'

'What about slant-eyed men?' Barnes put in crudely.

Lady Caroline smiled the kind of smile the English upper class reserves for members of the lower class who don't know their place.

'Don't be silly, darling. Asian men all have such tiny cocks,' she said, nimbly plucking a glass of champagne from a tray carried by a white-coated waiter as she waltzed over to another circle of guests.

The three men were left standing there, each with his own thoughts, or maybe they all shared the same uncomfortable male thought. They sipped their gin-and-lime drinks, avoiding each other's eyes.

Sawyer watched Lady Caroline work the room. She was good, he thought, noting the way she deftly flirted with what passed for the cream of Bangkok society: diplomats, Western businessmen, wealthy Thais with political connections and the occasional Chinaman who was just too rich to ignore. She was talking to one of them now, a pudgy old owl in gold-rimmed glasses, sweating in a grey silk suit. He was beaming at Lady Caroline like a Chinese Santa Claus, and next to him was the inevitable dough-faced wife, a relic perhaps of the Chinaman's earlier, poorer days. He looked ordinary enough, but there was something about the Chinaman. An air, generals have it, of being able to order a competitor ruined, or a village destroyed and not lose a minute's sleep over it. He would hate to ever owe the Chinaman any money, Sawyer thought, nudging Barnes. A hint of people instantly available at the snap of a finger. It was the kind of hidden power that a good head waiter can smell in a second. Spies too, if they're any good, Sawyer thought, nudging Barnes.

'Who's the slope with Lady C.?'

'Vasnasong. Muchee squeeze. Import–export. God, I hope that old bag doesn't come over,' Barnes muttered under his breath, while grinning like a banshee across the room at the Swiss Chargé d'Affaires wife who was headed their way but fortunately veered off towards a locally prominent silk merchant distantly related to the Thai royal family.

Sawyer nodded. Import–export was the classic cover for smuggling in every river port in the world. In Bangkok that meant jewels, rice and opium. And even more profitable cargoes, like arms and people. He glanced at Vasnasong with heightened interest and for a moment their eyes met across the room, neither of them showing anything more than polite curiosity, and then both turned away. But something bothered Sawyer. Something about the name. Then he had it.

'What is he, Max? Teochiu?' he asked Barnes.

Barnes winked. 'Head of the class, amigo. He's a Chink, all right. Got to be to do import–export in this part of the world.'

'Then why the Thai name?'

'Daddy was a Thai. Momma-san was Chiu Chow. They say he started as a coolie.'

'How does a coolie get so rich?'

'How does anybody become rich?' Barnes shrugged, as if the making of wealth was a mystery he wished he could solve.

Sawyer was about to reply, then thought better of it. Instead he nodded and went over to the bar to get his drink freshened, telling the bartender not to put in the ice cubes. It was best to get his stomach acclimatized gradually to the bacteria here, although if the bugs in Central America hadn't finished him off, nothing would. Leaning back against the bar, he casually checked the room one last time. The diversion would come any time now.

When he came back Sir Geoffrey was still watching his

wife with an opaque expression that couldn't be read, the kind of bland look honed at a thousand committee meetings, and Sawyer wondered what the bitch had on the old boy. Was it a little slant-eyed moose in a Silom Road walk-up with pink-flowered wallpaper peeling from the places where the roaches have eaten away the paste? Or maybe he liked young cowboys and a touch of leather. Whiff of the old public school, maybe. Whatever it was, watching the two of them was a little like catching a glimpse of something in an apartment window across the way that you wished you hadn't seen.

'One shouldn't, uh, take Caroline the wrong way. She's . . . um, well, there's more to her, you know. She, um, set up this whole benefit thing for the, uh, Cambodian refugees. She cares a great deal for the, um, refugees,' Sir Geoffrey sputtered.

There were dark circles under his eyes. They gave him a kind of sad dignity. Sawyer almost felt sorry for him until he remembered who Sir Geoffrey was and wondered how much of it was real.

'She's obviously a woman of, uh, deep passions,' Sawyer said carefully, as Barnes snorted into his gin-and-lime, trying to stifle his laughter. But the look Sir Geoffrey gave them was no laughing matter and Sawyer wondered, not for the first time, what the hell he was doing there.

It wasn't his line of country at all. Too public. Harris might as well have taken out a full-page ad in the *Bangkok Post*, he thought irritably, feeling very exposed. As if to underscore the feeling, he spotted Schwartz hovering like an anxious hostess over a well-known American network television anchor passing through on his way back to New York from Beijing. The anchorman wore an Abercrombie and Fitch safari suit, the one with the big bullet loops over the pocket in case you ran across a charging elephant – *de rigueur* for American journalists in the tropics. Sawyer knew he had stopped off in Thailand only for a quickie 'Starving babies in refugee camps' on-the-scene exclusive, but still it made him antsy.

Mind you, the charity thing went with his cover as a Red Cross representative, he told himself, remembering the Farm doctrine that cover isn't a story. Cover is who you are. He remembered how Koenig used to say that it was the Eastern Europeans, clinging to dog-eared identity cards, who understood cover best because in the Soviet bloc you literally are your papers; without them you don't exist. He saw Schwartz glance surreptitiously at his watch to make sure that he got the anchorman to the massage parlour on time and felt marginally better. That meant the diversion would come at any moment now and they could get down to it. But Harris had been right about one thing. They were on very thin ice.

'You have to go carefully,' Harris had stressed in that steaming whore's room over Houlihan's. 'Very carefully. There are a lot of sensibilities here. Especially with the Thais.'

At that moment Harris was lounging back in the wicker chair like an undergraduate; his feet, crossed at the ankles, were pointed towards Sawyer.

'You know, you really shouldn't point your feet at anyone, Bob. The Thais consider it a mortal insult,' Sawyer observed.

'I'm not interested in native superstitions,' Harris snapped, unaware of any irony. But then, after an uncomfortable moment, he uncrossed his legs and leaned forward. The sweat stains under his arms had grown almost to the hem of his jacket. A bead of sweat dangled from his chin like a wart and Sawyer watched it idly, wondering when it might fall.

'Christ, doesn't it ever cool off in this fucking place?' Harris wondered.

'This is the cool season,' Sawyer lied, enjoying Harris's discomfort.

Harris nodded as if filing the information as an item for his expense report. He motioned Sawyer closer. It was an old-fashioned precaution, meaningless if the room had been bugged, Sawyer thought. As Koenig used to say, 'There's no such thing as safe communications any more. They've got bugs today that can pick up a cockroach's fart from a mile away.' But then Harris was a headquarters type, the kind whose idea of danger was a cutting remark at an embassy cocktail party, and the very fact that he was out here was more important than anything he had to say. It meant, as Harris himself put it, that it was a 'political matter'.

Harris tapped his finger on a local guidebook resting on

thè table. On the back cover was a crude map, and his finger touched the area near the Thai–Cambodian border.

'Three weeks ago a report surfaced at the NSC,' Harris began, shaking his head to indicate that he wasn't about to reveal the source of the report. But Sawyer knew that, as a matter of policy, the fact that the National Security Council had met and acted upon it meant that the data must have been independently confirmed, usually by a second source.

Harris looked around uneasily at the dingy room as if half expecting to see enemy agents leaping out of the cracks in the wallpaper.

'God help us if this place has been bugged,' he muttered. Sawyer understood his uneasiness. Harris was, in the jargon of the trade, about 'to drop his pants'. But this was more than standard paranoia. If Harris was worried about a safe house rdv being bugged, then he was as good as saying that it was a kamikaze mission, the kind where they show you your body bag even before you go out. And the very fact that Harris was lifting the edge of the curtain this way meant they were desperate.

'Maybe you'd better tell me what's hit the fan before I read about it in the papers,' Sawyer said.

Although he had spoken softly, Harris stiffened. He gulped down his drink as though it contained something stronger than Singha beer.

'OK,' Harris began. 'As you probably know, the Vietnamese have a vital interest in Cambodia and Laos. On the one hand, it's critical to their security, but with China in the north and a crumbling economy at home they can't afford to keep their army there for ever. And they can't wipe out the various rebel factions because the Cambodian guerillas operate from sanctuaries on the Thai side of the border. That leaves Hanoi caught between a rock and a hard place, just like we were in 'Nam, which is perfectly OK with us.'

Sawyer shifted irritably in his chair, the wicker creaking as he moved. 'You know, Bob. I'm sure this stuff impresses the hell out of the Georgetown crowd, but I could have read this kind of crap in *Time* magazine.'

Harris flushed. When he looked back at Sawyer this time it was easy to read the malice in his eyes. Sawyer liked it

39

better that way. Like keeping the money on the table in a card game.

'All right, Sawyer. Let's get it out in the open,' Harris said, his hands jammed into his pockets. 'Let's not pretend we're old buddy-roos, because we aren't. You probably think I'm a headquarters bureaucrat who's ass-kissed his way to the top and who doesn't know shit about what it's really like on the front lines. What were they called in 'Nam?'

'REMFs — rear-echelon mother-fuckers,' Sawyer said. Once, he remembered, it had been Brother Rap's favourite word.

'Yeah. REMFs. Fair enough. And I know what I think of you. You're good, Sawyer. You're almost as good as you think you are. You're also a field agent who has maybe been out in the cold too long. You're undisciplined and a loner in a business that requires the utmost in teamwork. You also happen to have certain unique qualifications that your country desperately needs right now. So let's just get on with it, OK, because I really don't give a shit what you think of me.'

Touché, Sawyer thought, raising his beer in a vague kind of toast. Harris took his hands out of his pockets and tapped the guidebook map again.

'OK,' Harris said. 'Here's the part I hope to God you never get to read in *Time* magazine. We believe that the Vietnamese army is about to launch a full-scale invasion across the Thai border to root out all Cambodian resistance. That means war with Thailand. Now, you might remember that the United States never signed the '54 Geneva accord on Indo-China, nor did we ever have a single written or verbal obligation, yet we felt it was imperative to send troops to try to save South Vietnam, Laos and Cambodia.

'Well, you know what happened. Everybody knows what happened. There's a black wall in Washington, DC, with a lot of names on it in case maybe somebody's forgotten what happened,' Harris said bitterly.

'Nobody's forgotten,' Sawyer said.

Harris nodded. 'OK, remember this: unlike South Vietnam, Thailand was, and is, a fully fledged member of SEATO and has a mutual defence treaty with the US.

Diplomatically, politically, any way you slice it, we would have no choice. No choice at all.'

'A second Vietnam war,' Sawyer murmured, almost to himself.

'Worse,' Harris snapped. 'In those days we were fighting peasants in black pyjamas carrying AK-47s, and the ground fighting was mostly confined to key areas south of the DMZ. This time the Vietnamese have the fourth largest army in the world, fully equipped by the Russkies, and we can expect the theatre of war to encompass almost all of South-East Asia. A Rand report commissioned by the Joint Chiefs projects at least ten times as many American casualties as the first Vietnam war. The Company did its own independent study, of course. It found the Rand estimates too low,' Harris concluded.

'What about nukes?'

Harris shook his head. 'Apart from all the other negatives, political damage to NATO, nuclear genie out of the bottle and all that crap, there's something else. We have very firm information,' Harris said, rolling his eyes heavenward to indicate the absolute impeccability of the source, 'that if we used nukes in Asia, the Russians would use them against American installations in Europe. It seems the Politburo figures that, without Vietnam threatening China's back door, the Chinese and Americans could close the noose around Mother Russia.'

'Land war in Asia or World War Three. I take it Washington didn't like either of those options,' Sawyer ventured.

Harris leaned forward. Sweat dripped from his face down on to the table. The sound of the pi-nai on the radio grew stronger. 'There's a third option. A mission. One last chance before the balloon goes up.'

'When are the Vietnamese supposed to move? Any idea?'

'The best time for them would be under cover of the monsoon season. We figured we didn't have much time left. There's even less now,' Harris finished glumly.

'So the DCI authorized Parker's op?'

Harris shook his head and allowed himself a small smile as he showed his trump. 'Uh-huh. This one's straight from the Oval Office. You don't get to vote on this one, Sawyer,' Harris said, with a cold gleam in his eye that told Sawyer if he'd refused the mission, he'd never have made it to Don Muang airport.

Sawyer's mouth went dry. They had to be desperate to lay it out that crudely. 'Which do you want? Me to find Parker or to take his place?'

'Both. Parker obviously found a way in. We need you to find the same rabbit hole, go down it and come out the other side.'

'And if I have to choose — Parker or the mission — which is it?'

'What do you think?'

Sawyer massaged the skin near the corner of his bad eye, a habit when he was thinking. Harris had a genius for stating the obvious, but this time he couldn't fault him. The whole thing was a little like a lottery, Sawyer thought. The odds were lousy, but the stakes were too high not to play. For some reason he found it hard to breathe, and it took him a few seconds before he realized what it was. He was afraid. 'What's it called, this little op of yours?' Sawyer asked finally.

'The operation has been codenamed Dragonfire,' Harris said.

Prince Ramindhorn's entrance was announced by the banging of gongs, to frighten away evil phi bop spirits, and the band's enthusiastic, if noisy, rendition of the Thai national anthem. Everyone bowed deeply as the Thai prince, preceded by two royal guards wearing the traditional white jackets, baggy black breeches and gold caps, but carrying very untraditional loaded M-16s, came out on to the terrace. The prince, a handsome man in his thirties, tall for a Thai, wore sunglasses and the white and gold-braided uniform of a commander in the Royal Thai Air Force. He made the wai sign and beckoned them all to rise, as Lady Caroline came rushing over, smiling broadly at her social coup, for the promise of the prince's presence had been the main draw for the charity benefit.

In all the commotion no one noticed Sawyer slip behind an embroidered black-silk screen and past busy waiters to a side door that led to the main corridor. He saw no one as he went down a flight of stairs and along another corridor to the last room on the side of the hotel facing the river. He knocked twice, then once and pushed the door open. He had expected plainclothes guards, but the only person in the room was a small, elderly Thai sitting in a chair that looked too big for him. The curtains had been drawn, and at first the room was too dim for Sawyer to make out his features. Then he came closer. As the old man made the wai sign, his fingertips coming up to his chin, which is the sign made to those of indeterminately inferior status, Sawyer saw that the old man was indeed Field Marshal Bhamornprayoon.

Sawyer made the wai sign in return, his fingertips reaching his nose, which is the sign made to superiors, and the old man smiled warmly. Face had been preserved and it would go well, which was a good thing, Sawyer thought, since the whole damned party upstairs, including the arrival of the prince, had been arranged solely to get the two of them together.

Sir Geoffrey had set it up to avoid the appearance of American involvement. 'What else are the British good for?' Harris, who fancied himself a wit, had said, reflecting the persistent Langley prejudice that MI6 was populated largely by Old Boys who were KGB moles or pansies or both, even though Harris really knew better. What Harris might have given Sir Geoffrey in return – probably the keys to the executive bathroom, Barnes had conjectured – was of less interest than the fact that Harris had even involved another service in what was, for the CIA, a salvage operation. That was curious, Sawyer thought. In fact, he was beginning to think that there were a lot of curious things going on in Bangkok.

The old man gestured for Sawyer to sit facing him. His face was the colour of teak and hardly wrinkled, the eyes tranquil as a monk's, but his hands were old and gnarled.

'Sawat dee khrap. Sabai dee rue-ah, your Excellency,' Sawyer began.

The old man shook his head, a faint smile dancing in his eyes. 'Please, young sir. I am not here. This conversation is never happen.'

'Dai prod. It is understood, your Excellency.'

'Your Thai is most good for a farang,' Bhamornprayoon said approvingly.

Sawyer shook his head. 'The tones are weak. And I have difficulty with the honorifics.'

'The tones of you are much similar to the Thai Isan, which is spoken by the people of the north. That is of no matter. But you must practise. Much depends on it.'

'Of a certainty, Excellency,' Sawyer said, glancing around the hotel room.

The old man caught his drift at once, a smile cracking his face. 'Let not the khwan of you to be disturbed. My men have, how you say, "exterminated the insects from the house".'

'Swept the room for bugs.' Sawyer grinned.

'Even as you say. And they have left a device that none may hear us,' Bhamornprayoon said, pointing towards a small sonic interferometer on a table near the door, developed by the American DIA to scramble sound waves outside a given perimeter area for up to twenty metres, sufficient to disrupt most electronic eavesdropping.

'Khob khun krap. These are wise precautions in such times as these, Excellency,' Sawyer said.

'Precautions are of importance. In my country we say, "Dig the well before you are thirsty," ' the old man agreed. 'But you will take some cha. It is jasmine tea and the sahim are good,' gesturing at a coffee table set for tea and a plate of sticky Thai sweets covered with coconut-milk syrup. Although tea was the last thing on Sawyer's mind, to refuse it would have shown poor kreng chai and both men would have lost face.

'Narm cha lorn,' Sawyer said, munching a sweet.

'No milk?' the old man inquired politely. 'Odd. The British always would to take their tea with milk and sugar.'

'They also lost the Empire,' Sawyer replied.

'That is so,' the old man cackled. 'Most good, Sawyen-khrap,' he wheezed, raising his tea cup with a hand that faintly trembled with age. As he drank, he surveyed Sawyer over the rim of his cup with the careful objectivity of a doctor evaluating a patient's potential for surviving surgery. Although he held no formal post in the Thai government, it was said that in Bangkok even the swallows could not light on the telephone lines along Yawaraj Road without Bhamornprayoon's approval.

'This thing you do is most dangerous,' Bhamornprayoon said, carefully setting down his cup.

'It is of equal danger to wait and do nothing,' Sawyer said.

'That is why we agreed. You are to establish a most unofficial communication with the Cambodian rebels. Of this we of the Thai government know nothing.'

'That is so,' Sawyer nodded. 'We will trade American arms and gold for opium. The arms will give the rebels the means to launch a pre-emptive attack against the Vietnamese in Cambodia, thus forestalling the Vietnamese invasion into Thailand. Essentially it is the principle we call a "back-fire"; one sets a fire to stop a fire.'

'Still, there is much danger. Sometimes the fire one sets can engulf one.'

'Yes, Excellency. Fire is always dangerous.'

'I am most curious concerning the opium. Why does not rich America just to give the guns to the Cambodians?'

'Would you trust a farang who wished to give you something for nothing, Excellency? Also it will help the rebels gain favour with the local tribes by buying up their crops. We may be able to enlist some of the local tribes against the Vietnamese. And we also gain. By buying up much of the Golden Triangle opium harvest we can reduce the supply of heroin to the US by one half. There are many good reasons for such a transaction.'

Bhamornprayoon raised his hands as if in admiration at the deviousness of the Western mind. From upstairs they could hear the faint sounds of khon music and applause. Lady Caroline had arranged for a traditional dance troupe to entertain the prince and her guests. They listened for a moment and sipped the sweet tea. With his eyes closed, the old man looked quite dead. When he opened his eyes there was a sadness in them.

'Tum mai, young peu-un? I say peu-un, which means "friend", but is truth? I have much fear America wishes only to fight communists to the last Asian. Now, you tell, is truth?'

Sawyer shrugged. 'I cannot say, Excellency. These are political matters. But surely it is better for Viets and Kampucheans to die than Thais.'

'Thus spoke the first one, whom you call Hawken-khrap,

though his true name Pakah. A brave man and of much confidence. Yet he is no more.' Bhamornprayoon held his palm up in a Thai Buddhist gesture that suggested the evaporation of dew in the hot tropical sun.

'It is to speak of Parker that I requested this meeting, Excellency.'

The old man's face tightened. He gestured for Sawyer to proceed.

'My mission, Excellency, is the same as Parker's. Somehow to reach the Cambodian leaders, not through any official channels, to make the guns-for-opium deal and to get them to launch an offensive inside Cambodia that will prevent the Vietnamese invasion of your country. So much you know.

'We also know that Parker had found a way in. He had signalled his control that he'd made a contact and would be meeting with someone – we don't know who or where – that night. The fact that he disappeared only confirms that he was on to something. That's all we know.'

'Nor do I know more, young peu-un,' Bhamornprayoon objected and stood up. He looked around at the dim hotel room. 'And now we must to say, "Lah gorn la krup," for we two have much to do, do we not?'

Sawyer remained seated, a faint glimmer of amusement in his good eye. 'Alas, Excellency. I fear you have not spoken all the truth to me.'

Bhamornprayoon sat down stiffly. In his bearing was a lifetime of military parade grounds. His eyes were utterly opaque as they stared at Sawyer, who found himself wondering how many men this devout old Buddhist had ordered executed. Bhamornprayoon had initiated and survived at least a dozen coups and despite the Buddhist precepts against killing, his enemies had a nasty habit of being found floating face down in the Chao Phraya.

'What you mean?' Bhamornprayoon demanded.

'Something's been bothering me all along about Parker's disappearance, Excellency. On a mission of this seriousness my people have given me the "white tablet". You understand? I can call up an air strike or an entire division of US Marines if so needed. This much has been authorized by the President himself. With so much at stake I ask myself, why wasn't Parker shielded? Then, too, why didn't my case officer on this mission offer me any such protection? True, he knows I would have refused, for I prefer to work alone, but standard procedure requires that he make the offer. But he didn't. Is that not most curious, Excellency?'

Bhamornprayoon shrugged with an eloquent gesture that somehow had all of Asia in it. 'Mai pen rai. For Asian peoples, peu-un, much of what the white man do is curious. Truly, how can I to know why American do anything?'

'Unless,' Sawyer continued, 'unless Parker *was* shielded, whether he knew it or not. Just as I have been dirty since I returned to my hotel last night, Excellency.'

'Dirty? Chun mai kao chai. I do not understand. What is this "dirty", please?'

'Dirty is two tails, "watchers" they are called in the trade. One in front, one behind. Both Thais and, unless I miss my guess, both from the Thai Central Security Police. If Parker had been covered, Excellency, it would have been with Thais. A farang stands out on an Asian street like a black man at a Mormon convention. It would also explain why Washington is going crazy over this. Because an agent disappearing is serious, but a shielded agent disappearing is a total disaster.'

Bhamornprayoon poured himself another cup of tea and sipped it thoughtfully, the faint scent of jasmine tickling Sawyer's nostrils. 'This is most interesting, peu-un. But, alas, even if truth, what all such things to do with this humble servant?'

'Because, Excellency,' Sawyer said intently, 'if Thais were used, you had to know about it. So now tell me, Excellency: what happened to Parker?'

The old man sipped his tea calmly, giving nothing away. When he had finished he touched a napkin to his lips and looked up at Sawyer. It was a curious look and Sawyer wondered if he hadn't pushed the bounds of kreng chai too far. Then the old man smiled a strange half smile, the kind emulated by a million statues of the Buddha.

'Among our people it is said, "The father basks in the warmth of the good son". Do you understand, peu-un? You are wise beyond the years of you. That is most good. More better than the confidence of such as this Nai Pakah-khrap you seek. So I will speak truth, khwan to khwan. We watch

47

to Pakah-khrap, yes, but no to tell him. Two watchers, as you say. This much, yes. But so sad, peu-un. Of what happen to Pakah-khrap I know no thing,' Bhamornprayoon said, touching his head, which is the seat of the khwan soul and may not be touched except when speaking the truth.

Sawyer's mouth went dry. He'd counted on getting a lead from the Thais. It also meant that things were worse than even Harris had led him to believe. He licked his lips.

'Chun mai kao chai, Excellency. How can your watchers not have reported what happened to Parker?'

'Because there is no report, peu-un. We find body of one "watcher" in WC of cinema in Silom Road. His head broken, but that not kill him. Coroner find tiny poison flechette in leg. Most bad poison.'

'What of the other watcher, Excellency?'

The old man shrugged again. 'Alas, he too has disappeared.'

CHAPTER 4

Wind blows across the marsh.
The moon is nearly full.
One horse breaks his traces;
Only one horse remains.

For a price the boat people of Bangkok will smile for the
tourists and their cameras. But in the klongs off the Chao
Phraya questions go unanswered and the river keeps its
secrets. So Sawyer, dressed like a tourist in a gaudy yellow
shirt criss-crossed by a camera strap, munched a kow larm
from a near-by street stall and asked no questions. Now and
again he snapped a picture of a mama-san in blue pyjamas
and straw hat rowing a sampan against the backwash of a
water-taxi, or a monk in a curry-coloured robe sitting cross-
legged at a kerb, oblivious to the traffic around him, but there
was no film in the camera and his thoughts were elsewhere.

'Why we come here?' Sub-lieutenant Somsukiri had
demanded just before Sawyer had left him sweltering behind
the wheel of the car. Although the Thai's boyish face had
been calm, his fingers were tapping nervously on the burning-
hot steering wheel. He was clearly ill at ease out of uniform,
Sawyer had noted, and probably more than a little pissed
off at being yanked away from his regular duty to nursemaid
a farang who seemed to have nothing better to do than play
tourist.

'Because missing farang come here maybe,' Sawyer had
replied.

'How you know this?' Somsukiri demanded, the disbelief
plain on his face.

'In order to hunt the tiger, you must know what a tiger

49

is. One reason why I was chosen for this is because I knew the missing farang and this may help in tracking him,' Sawyer said, wondering if he sounded as fatuous as he felt. What he had carefully not mentioned was that, by the same reasoning, it was because Somsukiri had been the best friend of Sergeant Tarasang, the missing second tail, that Sawyer had requested him. Of course, all Somsukiri had been told was that a farang official investigating the case had requested an undercover officer as a driver, no doubt because the farang did not know his way about the city and, as an American, was unaccustomed to traffic on the left.

Glancing out of the corner of his eye from behind his big plastic sunglasses, Sawyer could see Somsukiri sitting rigidly in the parked car, sweat pouring down his face in the fiery morning heat. Let him simmer for a while longer, Sawyer thought, with a little inward grin, turning his mind back to the question that had been gnawing at him since the mission began.

What had happened to Parker?

'Dead reckoning' it was called in the 'trade', itself an egocentric euphemism for the spy business, just as people in Beverly Hills call the movie business the 'industry', as though there were no other. Dead reckoning – known as 'inductive surveillance analysis' in official CIA double-speak, although some Company wags persisted in calling it 'going up the yellow-brick road' – was based on the same principle as old-fashioned navigation in the days before satellites. To determine your location you took readings and then combined the data with the information in the charts and some basic mathematics. For Sawyer that meant that, by combining the few facts he had with his knowledge of Company field procedure and of Parker's 'signature' – another trade term meaning Parker's general *modus operandi* – he could somehow pick up Parker's trail. The technique was pooh-poohed by establishment types like Harris, who maintained that it was no more scientific than trying to find water with a divining rod. Sawyer himself conceded as much, yet those who were good at it were said to strike gushers regularly.

The problem was compounded by the fact that there was little point in questioning any of the locals who might have seen something. Nor would the Thai authorities fare much better. Either there would be no reply, in which case you would come away with the notion that Bangkok was a vast city inhabited only by the blind, the deaf and the dumb. Or else, if you pressed them, you would be told whatever they assumed you wanted to hear – the invariable reaction of Asians dealing with outsiders or those in authority. It used to infuriate the Americans in Vietnam, but in a way you couldn't blame the natives. Barnes had taught him that, Sawyer remembered. It was at that Chinese restaurant in the Cholon section of Saigon, all of them long since pissed on 33 beer and plum wine, the curfew past and nothing to do but drink and wait for the dawn.

'Confucius say: "When the wind blows, the fucking grass gotta bend." The auth-aaaarh-ities,' Barnes belched loudly, extending it *fortissimo* as though playing an instrument, 'are the wind. The peasants are the grass. And the grass don't get no choices. No choices at all. These new MACV hotshots think the reason the peasants just tell 'em what they want to hear is 'cause they're dumb. That's bullshit, man. That ain't dumb; it's smart. Just remember,' Barnes had said, playfully wagging an admonishing finger as he delivered one of those lines of his that embedded itself in the memory like a splinter, 'there ain't no such thing as a dumb gook.'

So that left Sawyer staring blankly at the river, trying to figure out which way Parker had gone from here, assuming he had even been here.

It had been Bhamornprayoon's remark about how and where the first tail had died that gave Sawyer the idea that dead reckoning might work in this case. Because there was a grain of truth in what he had told Sub-lieutenant Somsukiri. Although it had been a long time, Sawyer remembered Parker. Except for a dangerous tendency to shoot the works when he thought he had a chance of a coup, Parker's signature could have come right out of the Farm ops manual.

Dead reckoning.

A movie house was right out of the manual's section on how to flush a tail. It had been a front-and-back tail, Bhamornprayoon had confirmed that, and while Parker wouldn't have spotted something sophisticated like an '8-box' – for that matter, even an experienced round-eye could spend a year on any street in Asia and still miss most of what was happening right in front of his nose — Parker was certainly good enough to spot a simple front-and-back. And he hadn't been told they would be there; Harris hadn't known about it. That meant Parker didn't know whether they were friendlies or opposition, and when in doubt, the book says, assume opposition.

So Parker took the first tail out in the john. Again, SOP. Except he wouldn't have killed him unless he was sure the tail was opposition or he was under great pressure. That also went along with the coroner's report that the tail had been cold-cocked from behind before he was killed.

Sawyer was pretty sure Parker hadn't killed the tail. First, because the poison flechette wasn't standard issue. In fact, the only thing the Company had like it was something that came out of a ballpoint pen. All very James Bond and the kind of thing that impressed the hell out of young CTP trainees, but to Sawyer's knowledge the thing had never actually been used in a real mission. Besides, that wasn't Parker's job. Then, too, why kill someone if you've already taken him out of action? Especially if you're not sure who he is?

Another thing. Why didn't Parker flush the tail and then — again out of the manual — do a 'reverse' to track the tail back to his base? That went along with the question of the missing second tail. Another mystery. For if there were two tails, what would Parker have gained by taking out only one of them? And while he was taking out the first, where was the second?

The second tail wasn't calling his control because Bhamornprayoon had told him there had been no report. That meant the second tail was somewhere else. The only circumstance that Sawyer could think of to explain the missing second tail was — another trade term — a 'split'. In other words, there was someone else. Either Parker had met the 'contact' he had called in earlier that day or Parker was himself tailing someone.

Standard police procedure everywhere is that when the target splits, the watchers also split. So the second tail followed the contact. The first stayed with Parker who, still wanting to remain with the contact — that was his signature all right, to go for it, Sawyer mused – would have had to take his own tail out first.

Parker pulled it off, Sawyer decided. Otherwise there would have been no disappearance and no body in the movie house. Then, having eliminated the first tail, Parker went either after his contact again or to some pre-designated rdv. Somebody else then came along later and finished off the unconscious tail with the flechette.

That left the three of them: Parker, the second tail (now known to be the missing Sergeant Tarasang) and the contact maybe, all going somewhere. That was what had brought Sawyer to the New Road water-bus landing.

Where are you, you bastard? Sawyer asked himself, seeing Parker in his mind as he had been that night so many years ago, his handsome face twisted with fear in the dim light from the corridor. 'It's the regs!' Parker had whispered, and Sawyer remembered grabbing him by his shirtfront and hissing something.

Parker had called in a lead, a way in, earlier that day. But at the time he hadn't alerted them to an rdv, presumably because it hadn't yet been set. The contact would have let him know at the last minute, maybe playing telephone tag, leading him from one location to another. But neither Parker nor the presumed contact would have ever agreed to any kind of an rdv except in a public place. The same Parker who had said, 'It's the regs!' would have played it by the book. At that hour of the night the most likely place was any one of the hundreds of joints in the Patpong or Soi Cowboy or Phet Buri districts. Loud, noisy, the neon turning the night to reddish day and no one noticing or caring about a couple of men talking a little business over drinks.

Now if you drew a line between Patpong One and Two streets and the movie house where the dead tail was found – the Patpongs were closer to the theatre than either Soi Cowboy or Phet Buri – then Parker could have either gone up towards Rama Four Road or down towards the klong. Sawyer figured the klong was more likely because Parker knew he was under surveillance and that direction gave him more dark corners and byways to slip or flush the second tail. Also, if Sawyer was right about the sequence, Parker came to the movie house after the Patpong rdv and would then most likely have continued in the same direction, going the extra few blocks to the water.

There was another reason for assuming he had come this way. Parker had probably been snatched. It's much easier to pull a gun on someone when he comes on board a boat than to hustle him into a car with plenty of rubbernecks looking on. It's also easier to get rid of someone on the water, Sawyer noted. A muffled shot or maybe another fletchette. Weight the body with stones and dump it overboard in the middle of the night. Very private and in Bangkok, where a dozen bodies are fished out of the Chao Phraya every day, almost foolproof.

Whoever had snatched Parker had done it right under the noses of the Thai Central Security Police who were tailing Parker. That meant they knew what they were doing. They might have lured him or trapped him but, whatever had happened, it wasn't a Chicago-style street-corner snatch, Sawyer's gut told him. So Parker was on the water that night. Probably on a water-bus or water-taxi. And at that late hour, assuming he had boarded on the Sathan Nua klong, the water-buses and taxis ran only to the New Road Landing, which was where Sawyer stood at that instant, trying to figure out where to go next.

Sawyer leaned back against the kow larm stall, ripe with the scent of roast coconut, and watched the landing. A barge loaded high with sacks of rice moved slowly downstream, its wash almost tipping a sampan in which a small boy balanced nimbly as a monkey as he squatted by the stern, brushing his teeth with river water. A young Thai woman in European clothes, carrying a green-and-yellow umbrella to shade her from the sun, dropped something into a monk's begging bowl as he sat meditating near the water's edge, his close-cropped hair and eyebrows making him look both sinister and innocent all at once, like a young trainee at a military academy. A Chinese businessman in a white shirt and flaming red tie stood stiffly, staring blankly at the brown river. He was probably waiting for the water-bus to take him up-river to the Chinatown landing, Sawyer thought. Under a sagging palm tree blighted by automobile exhaust, a young street boy of about eight-going-on-thirty, wearing an over-sized UCLA tee-shirt, hawked joss sticks that filled the air with incense, a cigarette dangling from his lips.

What is it about Asia, this filthy, noisy, god-awful place, that tugs at us in the odd moments of the night like the memory of an old lover? Sawyer wondered. And where in all this did you get to, you dumb son-of-a-bitch? he thought, angrily addressing Parker in his head, as though Parker had deliberately left no tracks for no other reason than to frustrate him. Because here dead reckoning failed him. There were just too many ways to go from here.

Parker could have headed up New Road, so called despite the fact that it was one of the oldest streets in the city. There were plenty of offices, shops, restaurants up that way where he could have made contact. He could have stayed on the water, boarding another water-bus, or water-taxi, or maybe the ferry across to the Thonburi side of the river. He could have gone on foot, up-river towards the Oriental Hotel, legendary since the days of Somerset Maugham, or down towards the Krung Thep bridge. He could have gone anywhere.

Sawyer was about to give it up. He had even started to head back to the car when a thought struck him. He had been looking through the telescope from the wrong end. Parker had been either hit or snatched. No, snatched, he decided. They would have wanted to sweat him for information before they terminated him. To figure out where the snatch had been done, he had to look at it from the snatcher's point of view.

If Sawyer wanted to set up a snatch from here, he wouldn't choose to do it under the bright lights of New Road or the posher quarters near the Oriental. It would be better over on the Thonburi side, where the real slums are, or down towards the bridge, where the sampans cluster along the riverfront and the street lights are few and far between.

If the snatch had taken place on the Thonburi side, or if Parker had gone back on the river in either direction, forget it. The area was just too vast to cover and there were no tracks. No body. It would be like trying to find an invisible needle in a haystack the size of Mount Everest. Also if they had lured or forced Parker on to another boat, the timing would have been very tricky. Too many things might go wrong while waiting for a water-bus or ferry. That left only one option: if Parker had headed towards the Krung Thep bridge on foot along the riverfront.

Sawyer turned and beckoned Sub-lieutenant Somsukiri, admitting to himself as he did so that the only real reason he had chosen this direction to investigate was because it was the only one he could investigate.

Sub-lieutenant Somsukiri was seething. Keep the heart cool cool, he told himself again and again, for to show his anger would be most terrible kreng chai. That the American farang had turned out to be inconsiderate, leaving him to swelter in the parked car, was unfortunately only to be expected. The Americans were like elephants crashing through the world and trampling little peoples without even noticing.

And although his superiors had told him that this assignment was of much importance, Somsukiri secretly suspected that he was being passed over for his heart's desire, an appointment to the Lumpini district, and that First Lieutenant Chaiyamajith had thrown him to the farang as one throws a gnawed and useless bone to a dog.

All this coming just now was most unfortunate karma and, alas, Somsukiri had to acknowledge his own fault in this. For he had been late this morning and had forgotten to show his proper respect to the spirit house on the east corner of the apartment balcony. His mother had warned him against such foolishness and he had no doubt offended the protective phi poota, although his karma had been so wonderfully good of late. First, the beautiful Sumalee, who danced for the pig-faced Japanese in a club on Silom Road, had confided that her 'agent' had demanded four thousand baht to let her out of her contract. A serious but not impossible sum.

He had tried to think of whom among his regulars he could squeeze, but then his dearest peu-un, Sergeant Tarasang – whom he had thought a snake for not repaying the eight, no, nine hundred baht that he, Somsukiri, had invested, upon Tarasang's advice, in 'Fists of Iron' Meang of Songkhla, whose iron fists, alas, were no proof against a cross-kick to the mid-section in the fourth round at Ratchadamnoen – had not only appeared with new-found riches to repay the loss but had given him another eight thousand besides. And then, most conveniently, like the spirit in a hang shadow play, had disappeared again.

The eight thousand, Tarasang had confided, was to be bet on a black-and-red cock named Baby See Dum Daang, who had been bred and trained in great secrecy by his best squeeze to challenge the great champion, Prince Nung Pan Victory. At first sceptical, for odds of eight and more to one were being quoted for any challengers to the great champion cock, Somsukiri had himself seen Baby – deliberately misnamed to lengthen the odds. He was a large cock of incomparable speed and viciousness, and watching him peck the eyes out of a training bird made Somsukiri's heart soar. The beautiful Sumalee and many baht besides were almost his.

And now this. Playing amah to a farang who seemed to have nothing better to do than to wander aimlessly around the city like a pai thiaw. Today of all days. For the cockfight was to be this very afternoon. Somsukiri squirmed on the hot car seat like a child that has to go to the bathroom and vowed to burn a joss stick to the Lord Buddha at the Temple of the Dawn if only he could make the fight.

But the farang just stood at the water-bus landing snapping pictures like any tourist. No, not even a proper tourist, despite his dressing stupidly as the other farang tourists. They were a common sight on the tour boats from the big hotels, mostly fat and aged and the women with hair of a curious bluish colour. They would enthusiastically snap pictures of the floating market of Thonburi as though it were a real market instead of one that existed solely for the farang tourists, after which they would be led in platoons to whichever shop had bribed their guide the most, where they would squeal in excitement over bargain 'authentic' antique carvings mass-produced in sweatshops all over the city and marked up at twenty times their cost.

It was infuriating. He, Somsukiri, an important officer of the Security Police and one of integrity, for he took far less squeeze than was his due, playing guide to a farang who, if he wanted to be a tourist, didn't even have enough sense to go to the important sights like the Royal Palace or the Temple of the Golden Buddha. And in the evening, no doubt, he would want to be taken to a massage parlour. By rights, instead of a massage girl he should find the farang a kra toe, one of those provocatively dressed male transvestites – some of whom were beautiful enough to attract any man – who paraded nightly along Silom Road, and for a few moments Somsukiri amused himself by picturing the farang in various obscene postures with a kra toe. Alas, his reverie was suddenly ended by a signal from the farang to come down to the landing.

As Somsukiri hurried over, Sawyer could see he was upset. That was OK, Sawyer thought. Keep him emotional, not thinking.

'Most bad leave car. Bad peoples come. Steal car. Steal everything,' Somsukiri declared unhappily.

'Mai pen rai. It is of no matter. I will tell them it was the fault of this farang and no fault of yours,' Sawyer said, touching his own chest.

'Plenty bad peoples in Bangkok,' Somsukiri insisted, pushing out his lower lip like a sulky child.

'Plenty bad peoples everywhere. Please to show me this way,' Sawyer said, indicating the street along the embankment.

'What for you go this way? Go other way. See Grand Palace. Many wats most beautiful. Take many pictures,' Somsukiri said, still hanging back.

Now, Sawyer thought. Now it was time to enlist him – in the jargon, to 'turn him'. It was for this moment that he had spent half of yesterday secretly closeted with First Lieutenant Chaiyamajith, learning everything he could about the missing Sergeant Tarasang and his best friend, Somsukiri. It was a spook's most delicate yet essential task, to use someone by making him think he's using you. First he had to shock Somsukiri, then seduce him. When Sawyer replied, the harshness in his voice was like a jolt of electricity.

'There's no bloody film in the camera and I am not here for sightseeing and a little fuckee-fuckee on Patpong, Sublieutenant.' Now the bribe, Sawyer thought. 'You have been selected for a most important assignment. One of great opportunity. A man of lesser character than yourself could "touch the dragon" with such an opportunity. This requires a man of metta and of most excellent kreng chai such as you are said to be.'

Somsukiri almost visibly swelled. He had not offended the phi poota! Although, to be safe, he would still light a joss stick to Lord Buddha as he had promised. His karma was most good. The farang was not a fool tourist, but a man of power and significance. He, Somsukiri, had seen that at once. Everyone knew the Americans had money to burn, he thought, and when he smiled at the farang this time there was a genuine desire to please in his eyes.

'Where we go now?' he asked enthusiastically.

'Water-taxi,' Sawyer said, hailing a hang-yao and telling the driver to head towards the Krung Thep bridge, but slowly, so he could take pictures of the colourful Bangkok waterfront.

'What we do?' Somsukiri whispered over the asthmatic hammering of the ancient outboard engine.

'We watch,' Sawyer replied, enigmatically gesturing at the riverbank.

Somsukiri smiled and gazed intently at the riverbank, although he hadn't the foggiest idea what he was supposed to be looking for.

No one spoke. The burning sun glittered on the muddy grey surface and across the water came the faint whine of one of those endless Chinese love songs. The driver, a wizened old man, his lips and gums stained a permanent reddish-black from betel juice, hummed mindlessly along as they moved slowly down-river.

Sawyer reached into his pocket and handed Somsukiri a piece of paper. It fluttered slightly in the breeze of their passage like a living thing. When he saw it, Somsukiri's heart plummeted like a stone and he mentally cursed himself for having once again underestimated this demon farang with his one devil's eye.

Because the paper was his beloved Sumalee's contract with her agent. He recognized her childlike scribble of a signature in the margin at once and only a lifetime of jai yen yen kept the fear from showing in his face. Too late Somsukiri understood the strange look in First Lieutenant Chaiyama-jith's eyes when he told him to go with the farang. He was under suspicion! Now, as the saying went, he held his khwan in his hands like a palmful of water. He touched the Buddha amulet that hung around his neck and stiffened himself to face the devil farang who sat in judgement in the prow of the boat like the Lord of Death himself.

'What should such as I do with this thing I purchased?' Sawyer said quietly, letting the contract flutter in the breeze like a flag. 'Shall I,' he went on, 'use her as it pleases me, then throw her into the streets like a useless thing when I am done? Or perhaps sell this paper to another? And he to yet another? Or shall I,' he said intently, 'make you a gift of this thing as a gesture of my appreciation for your help in this investigation?'

Dry-mouthed, Somsukiri nodded, scarcely daring to believe his karma, yet still fearful what price the farang demon – for so he named him in his mind – might yet exact.

'Dee mark,' Sawyer murmured, not permitting himself a smile yet. Now came the tricky part. Convincing the young Thai that he knew more than he really did. 'We need only to confirm some information,' he said, tapping a folded piece of paper sticking out of his shirt pocket, which was in fact only his laundry receipt. 'Tell me, dai prod, where has Sergeant Tarasang gone, yes?'

The blood hammered in Somsukiri's temples. Sumalee was lost! 'I not to know,' he blurted out.

Sawyer's heart sank. The Thai seemed to be telling the truth. But he smiled as if he had got the answer he had expected. 'We know this, Sub-lieutenant. We know you know your duty. This is not in question,' Sawyer said, tapping an admonishing finger on the contract. 'But perhaps there is some little thing, some change in Sergeant Tarasang just before he disappeared.'

Somsukiri shook his head no. But there was a slight hesitation before he did and Sawyer looked down to conceal his interest. The Thai was holding something back.

'No word? No thing of this assignment to his most best peu-un? No see good-time girl? Chase dragon maybe? Or money maybe? Plenty baht?' Sawyer demanded.

Again the faintest hesitation before Somsukiri shook his head again. Money, Sawyer thought. Maybe somebody had Tarasang in his pocket. Bought and paid for. Because Tarasang was most likely alive. Otherwise they'd already have found him floating face down in one of the klongs. Somsukiri was protecting Tarasang. Was that friendship or something else? Sawyer wondered. He might be hiding nothing more than a lousy hundred-baht squeeze, and Sawyer had to let the Thai know that he wasn't going to be taken to the woodshed for copping a mango from the corner pushcart.

'It is said that when the prince hunts the tiger, the deer may safely pass the bowmen,' Sawyer said carefully. 'All men have a thing to hide. A squeeze. A female companion the wife does not to know. Mai pen rai. Among men of metta such things are of no consequence and need not to reach the ears of those on high,' Sawyer smiled, one man-of-the-world to another.

Somsukiri watched him as one watches a cobra. He wondered if the demon farang was setting a trap for him.

'Life in the streets is most difficult,' Sawyer said wistfully. He started to stick the contract back into his pocket with an indifferent shrug, but his thoughts were seething. Come on, he thought. Shit or get off the pot!

Suddenly, Somsukiri stretched out his hand for the contract. His eyes were dark and determined. 'Before he go that night, Tarasang pay me money he owe me. Four thousand baht,' Somsukiri said, lowering the amount to keep as much of it as possible, though the demon farang would surely demand the tiger's portion. 'He have plenty baht that night. Most excited. But he not to say of where money come or where he go.'

'Squeeze maybe?'

'Plenty squeeze maybe,' Somsukiri agreed.

'But he not to say of where he go?' Sawyer asked, tapping the contract against his knee, just out of Somsukiri's reach.

Somsukiri shook his head firmly.

They were nearing the Krong Thep bridge. Sawyer told the driver to turn around and head back. The old man took them in a wide circle around a big bridge piling where the greasy water lapped like surf in the wake of a water-bus. Land's end, dead end, Sawyer thought.

'Was maybe some place of most importance to your peu-un Sergeant Tarasang? Family maybe? No. No family. If you have plenty money, maybe win big Elephant lottery, where you go, Sub-lieutenant?'

Somsukiri shrugged. 'Ban Phattaya maybe,' he offered, naming the big seaside resort on the Gulf of Thailand.

'And Sergeant Tarasang. Where he go if he have plenty baht?'

'Ban Phattaya. He say many funs there. All time talk Ban Phattaya.' Somsukiri nodded enthusiastically as Sawyer handed him the contract.

'Khob khun khrap, peu-un,' Sawyer smiled.

'Dai prod. What we do now?' Somsukiri said, smiling happily back. His karma had been most wonderfully good and he would light nung roi, yes, one hundred joss sticks to the Lord Buddha.

'We watch,' Sawyer replied, gesturing at the riverbank slowly sliding by.

'Yes, Nai Soyah-khrap, but what we to look for?'

Sawyer made a face. 'I not to know, but I will to know when I to see it,' he said, leaving Somsukiri staring blankly at the shore and telling himself that he could never understand the white man. His thoughts were utterly incomprehensible.

As for Sawyer, if there was a clue to Parker's whereabouts along the riverfront, he couldn't see it. There were small stores, their most common advertisement a Pepsi sign, concrete landings for boats and rice barges crowded with food stalls, flies buzzing among the big open metal pots, a wharf for a big white-and-blue tour boat with a sign in English that read 'Cruising to the Siamese Gulf. Ko si-Chang. Ko Lan-Pattaya. The Biggest Bronze Buddha in the World at Supanburi and Thousand of Birds', dilapidated white apartment buildings, naked children playing on the balconies, long warehouses with corroded metal shutters and, further on, squatters' shacks perched on teakwood pilings just inches above the surface of the river. It was a pointless exercise really, Sawyer admitted to himself. He could be staring right at where they were keeping Parker – in the unlikely event he was still alive – and not know it. For instance, if you wanted to snatch someone, where they were passing at this very moment was as good a place as any.

It was a long concrete wharf for a huge two-storey warehouse that belonged, according to a faded white sign over an open loading gate, to the South-east Asia Rice and Trading Company. Big hundred-kilo sacks of rice were stacked all over the wharf, and through the open gate Sawyer could see a deep canyon between two rectangular mountains made of sacks of rice piled up to the ceiling.

It would be dark here at night. A perfect place to take someone or maybe to lure him on to one of the sampans tethered near the far end of the wharf.

Sawyer shrugged. There were a million perfect places. This was Bangkok, a city where you could walk into any waterfront bar and hire a hit man for five hundred US dollars. He was wasting his time, he told himself and started to signal the driver to head back to the New Road landing when he caught something out of the corner of his eye.

Dammit, that was the trouble with having only one eye, he cursed mechanically. After a while you learned to compensate for the depth perception, but there was no way to make up for the fractional loss of peripheral vision or the partial blinder that your nose becomes on the bad side.

What he had seen was a hand-lettered sign on a small door in a metal shutter that closed off part of the warehouse, no doubt leading to an office. It had caught his attention because it looked as though it was in French.

Turning casually as if to take a snapshot, he angled himself to get a better view, pointing the camera full into the sun like an idiot as he clicked. He turned away and told the driver to take them back to the landing. As they headed back, Sawyer hoped Somsukiri couldn't spot his excitement. Because the sign read: 'Comité National pour l'Aide aux Réfugiés Kampucheans'.

And although he couldn't pin it down, the name rang a bell. Sawyer was sure he had heard it before somewhere. More to the point, Kampuchea – Cambodia – was what this thing was all about.

Of course, it might have meant nothing at all, he thought, trying to play devil's advocate, the position he was sure Harris, who hated hunch plays, would take. So somebody rented a little extra office space to a Cambodian refugee outfit. Bangkok was full of them. So what?

So nothing. Maybe it was just a coincidence, Sawyer thought, remembering how Koenig used to lecture them in that Quonset hut on the Farm. 'There are no coincidences in this business. None,' he used to say, slapping his ruler against the side of his leg as though it were a riding crop. 'The minute you spot something that even smells like a coincidence, you've either struck paydirt, or it's about to strike you. Either way, you'd better haul ass.'

The hang-yao came into the landing with a faint bump. Sawyer paid the driver and followed Somsukiri up on to the landing. As they hurried back towards the car, Sawyer thought that it might be very interesting to find out who owned the South-East Asia Rice and Trading Company.

The contact was set for a souvenir stall in the courtyard of Wat Po, the huge Temple of the Reclining Buddha. The stall sold good-luck amulets, joss sticks, carved elephants and other such trinkets and was indistinguishable from the dozens of similar stalls clustered near the gate to the inner temple. The gate was made of stone and defended for eternity by intricately carved gold-gilt yaks, the fearsome spirit guards of the Other World. A teak elephant encrusted with bits of glass and tin hung from the left side of the woven awning over the stall, indicating that it was safe to approach, but still Sawyer hung back. There was something wrong, but he couldn't quite pin it down.

He had felt it before, this sense that somewhere just ahead was a booby-trap with his name on it. Some called it 'mission feel', but it had nothing to do with tradecraft. It's the thing that makes you jump when you're alone in the house at night and you hear a noise, and no one has to learn it. His instinct had picked up a danger signal too well hidden for his conscious mind to catch and he didn't need Harris's warnings to keep clear of all established rdvs and safe houses to tell him he was in the red zone on this one. Which was why, when he had called the Snake Farm from a public phone in the Oriental Hotel Lobby to get them working on the South-East Asia Rice and Trading Company and the Kampuchean Committee, they had set up the rdv at the temple. Standard procedure and, as a big public attraction, it went with the tourist cover he had adopted for today. He should have been able just to walk in, exchange counter-signs with the stall keeper and get the data. Everyday stuff. Except that the stall signalled that the approach was clear, while Sawyer's instinct told him it was hot.

It can't be hot, he reasoned with himself. He hadn't knocked on any doors yet. Except for Harris and friends, no one even knew he was in Bangkok, and just to be on the safe side he had changed the image, swapping his eye-patch for sunglasses and tourist garb. And although the call to the Snake Farm had been an open call, it had been routed from there on a secure scrambled line to wherever the hell Barnes was. Max had handled it himself because Sawyer had recognized his voice even through the faint distortion of the scrambler. So it was safe. All he was feeling was 'buck fever'. Sooner or later it happened to everyone, even old-timers on their hundredth mission into Indian Country, he told himself.

Except it was all horseshit because his instinct – Sawyer always called it the 'Reptile' because he had a pet theory that it was a part of the brain that had developed long before man was man or even before we were mammals – was sounding the alarm for all it was worth.

So he did what they had learned to do in 'Nam. Stop. Look. Listen. Find the invisible trip wire in the foliage, glistening with dew like a spider thread because if you miss it, half your body may say goodbye to the other half and, if you are lucky, you won't survive to see the letter your mother gets from the President of the United States.

Although the Reptile was telling him to get out now, Sawyer methodically divided the courtyard into sectors and began to quarter each sector, first at ground level, then up. Back towards Jetupon Road the halls and huge towers, called prangs, swarmed like hives with monk trainees, vendors and sightseers. From here he could see the great bell-shaped chedis that housed the ashes of the Chakri Royal House, encrusted with green and blue and white mosaic glistening in the afternoon sun. Near the paved walkway a monk and several Thais from the city, in white shirts and slacks, meditated in the shade of a holy Bodhi tree, said to be descended from a seed of the original tree in whose shade Buddha attained enlightenment. Vendors along the walls and galleries sheltering hundreds of sitting Buddhas were selling joss sticks and amulets said to be especially efficacious for gamblers –

Somsukiri had bought a handful of joss sticks there and was on his way over — and frustrated lovers.

In the centre of the courtyard stood a large black lingam, its phallic shape symbolizing the Hindu god Shiva and the Yang force that is far more ancient than Buddhism. It was said to inspire fertility and was covered with orchids and paper prayer flags placed by childless women, one of whom knelt before it even now. Beyond the lingam a guide was ushering a Japanese tour group, with their plastic badges and cameras and drip-and-dry suits wilting in the heat, past the bronze lions guarding the gold-roofed bot, from which the sound of monks' chanting could be heard.

Everything was as it should be, Sawyer thought. There was no one more interested in him than in saving a few satang on the price of a plastic Buddha, nor was any local at a noodle stall more interested in his copy of *Siam Rath* than he should be. It was clean, dammit, and yet, if anything, the Reptile's signal was getting stronger. He had to do something. Not even mad dogs and Englishmen would just stand there in the blazing afternoon sun, taking snapshots of the pigeons clustering on the carved eaves of the gateposts near the rice-seller stalls. As was the custom, Sawyer had purchased a handful of rice and dropped it in the begging bowl of a young apprentice monk sitting in the lotus position near the contact stall. As he dropped it in, the monk had murmured, 'Khob khun khrap,' and . . .

Sawyer's blood froze.

A Buddhist monk never thanks anyone. By accepting alms he allows the giver to acquire merit.

Sawyer started to turn back towards the monk, but it was too late. The monk was already pulling an air-pistol out of the folds in his robe. Sawyer cried a warning as he dived sideways, but it was like watching an accident happen, everything seeming to be in slow motion, yet no way to stop it, as Somsukiri came up to him, smiling and holding his lucky joss sticks. Somsukiri suddenly straightened at the sting of the dart in his back. He whirled and started to slap at it, as at a mosquito. Then they were both running towards the monk who, raising the skirt of his robe, scampered on bare legs towards the inner temple gate.

Somsukiri started to head him off, still trying to clutch at his back, and then Sawyer saw him slow down, still pumping hard but the legs moving heavily as if he were wading. Almost at the gate, Sawyer watched him try to draw his gun, not realizing he wasn't wearing it, the legs caving, and then he was down. As the monk leaped over him towards the gate Somsukiri was still trying to crawl. Sawyer wondered what was keeping him going. Somsukiri started drifting sideways, his movements out of synch, like a broken toy. And then he just stopped and lay down on his side.

Somsukiri's eyes were already glazing over in the second or two that it took Sawyer to reach him. They held the dark certainty that he was about to die, and Sawyer didn't try to sugar-coat it by telling him he'd be OK, which Somsukiri wouldn't have believed anyway. He owed the young Thai that much. Somsukiri's lips moved, but no sound came out. His eyes looked desperately down. He was going. Sawyer felt like an idiot for not knowing what he wanted. In desperation he tore at the Thai's shirt because that was where Somsukiri had looked. And then Sawyer saw it. Hoping he had enough time, he grabbed the little hai-huang Buddha amulet that hung around Somsukiri's neck and put it into the Thai's mouth. Somsukiri felt it and looked gratefully up at Sawyer. At least he would not go to the Lord of Death empty-handed. And then he died. Before he had stopped breathing, Sawyer was already up and sprinting through the temple gate where the monk had disappeared.

Just before he entered the Hall of the Reclining Buddha he remembered to kick off his shoes – he didn't need a Buddhist lynch mob after him for desecrating the shrine – and dropped down to a crawling position. Fortunately, because as he came through the door he heard the whispered snick of another flechette splitting the air where his chest would otherwise have been. Before the monk could reload Sawyer scuttled sideways on all fours, like a crab, then dived behind a massive stone pillar. Hidden in the shadow, he tried to catch his breath and figure something out.

That was pretty goddam stupid, he cursed himself, trying to blink the sweat out of his eye. Just because he's a punk kid doesn't mean he can't take you out. That was the mistake some of the green American troops used to make in 'Nam. Because they were big and strong and had muscles like John

Wayne, they couldn't believe that some runty teenaged gook in over-sized black pyjamas could blow them away before breakfast. He's already killed Somsukiri and probably the first tail too, so he's plenty good, and you'd better watch your ass, Sawyer thought, starting to edge his way around the pillar.

Take him alive, Sawyer told himself. He's the way in if you can sweat him – and if he doesn't get you first. Moving carefully now, head low, trying to think only of tactics and not about the question starting to nag at him: what kind of Thai, no, he couldn't be Thai, of South-East Asian wouldn't have known how a monk is supposed to behave?

Don't think about that now, Sawyer thought. He's had time to reload that thing. Peering around the pillar for a second, just long enough for his good eye to catch a glimpse of the vast, half lit hall shuttered against the afternoon heat. At the far end was one of the most awe-inspiring sights on earth, the great Reclining Buddha, half the length of a foot-ball field in size and covered in gold leaf, bathed in golden rays of light seeping through the lattices and filling the hall with its glow. Despite its massive size, the stupendous figure seemed almost to float above the ground. Although stylized, as all Buddhas were, it was strangely lifelike, every fold of its robe artfully designed to convey the reality of the exquisite moment when the Enlightened One glided into nirvana. But Sawyer's thoughts were far from enlightenment. He had picked out the monk's silhouette lurking in the shadows near the giant soles of the Buddha's sandals.

There were a few monks and other worshippers all around the hall in various postures of meditation and, along the walls, dim bas-reliefs from the Ramakien, the Thai version of the Hindu Ramayana. The rest was empty space. But getting close wasn't the problem, Sawyer figured. The effective range of the air-gun couldn't be more than twenty feet or so. The kid – no, don't think of him that way: 'We're in an inhuman business,' Koenig used to say; 'Humanize your enemy and he'll blow your brains out' – the phoney monk would let him get close. He wouldn't have time to reload for a second shot, so he'd want to be sure.

Except it didn't matter because the monk was good. He'd already proved that. He wouldn't miss the first shot. So the problem wasn't getting close. The problem was how to cross an open space and get so close that the monk couldn't get a shot off before he realized what was happening. What made it even harder, of course, was that the monk was just waiting there, like a spider, for Sawyer to come within his killing range.

The only way was to come in contrary to the monk's expectations, Sawyer decided. The monk would probably fire low to be sure of a body shot, so he would come in high. The monk would anticipate him coming straight on, so he would have to come in around the corner. And he would have to change his image. If he could make the monk hesitate over whether he was shooting the real target for even a fraction of a second, it might make all the difference. And just to make life interesting, Sawyer added, he had to do it without attracting attention to himself, both because the monk would zero in on him otherwise and because he was on holy ground in a kingdom that took religion more seriously than American football coaches take winning.

Sawyer briefly debated going back outside and buying a change of shirt from a vendor but rejected the idea. Right now he had the monk spotted. Once he left, the bastard might go anywhere. So that was out. Yet he had to change the image somehow.

He looked around the hall, but no one was paying attention to him. The Thais were meditating in the tranquil dimness, the golden light suggesting an eternal twilight. Nearby an old man in ragged clothes sat on his haunches facing the Eternal. His eyes were downcast. His hands made the wai sign to his forehead. He was motionless as a statue. Behind him he had placed a weatherbeaten straw hat. Sawyer took the hat, leaving a five-hundred-baht note in its place. Perhaps the old man would take it as a sign that his prayers had been heard, Sawyer thought.

He took off his sunglasses and removed the eye-patch. Then he took off the gaudy yellow shirt that he had worn loose, turned it inside-out and put it back on, tucking it in this time. He put on the hat. When he was ready he took a deep breath and moved from behind the pillar towards the distant head of the Buddha in an obeisant crouch, his head bowed and his hands in the wai sign over his face.

He padded forward, glancing left and right, but no one paid him any attention. In his stockinged feet he hardly made a sound. As he approached, the staggering size of the Buddha began to fill his range of vision. He was the only thing moving. He felt very exposed.

Just then he caught a movement in the dim recesses near the Buddha's feet. He'd been spotted. The Reptile was telling him to dive for cover, but he ignored it and kept going. A crouched-over figure in a straw hat was all the monk could have seen, Sawyer told himself. The monk was just popping out to check. He couldn't be sure yet.

Now he was at the great golden head, craning his neck to stare up at the caste mark on the Buddha's forehead in the place where the third eye is said to be. An iron spike-topped fence ran around the statue, preventing anyone from getting close enough to defile the great Buddha by touching it. It ran back to the rear wall of the bot, so he couldn't try to come around behind the statue. He would have to walk all the way across the front of the statue, from left to right. But how could he cover the distance without the monk seeing him?

Then he remembered something. The monk wasn't a true Buddhist. It was impossible that he would not see Sawyer, but he might not know what he was seeing. It wasn't a great idea, but Sawyer couldn't think of anything better. And he had to do something fast. Somsukiri's body was no doubt attracting attention out there, the way garbage attracts flies, and before too long he'd have to spend a week playing tic-tac-toe with the Bangkok police and never get a shot at a Company-style interrogation of the monk.

Sawyer took a deep kokyu no henko breath to calm his emotions because it was like jumping from an airplane. Once you took that first step there was no going back.

Sawyer shuffled in an obeisant crouch towards the Buddha's feet for a few yards, then sank down in a head-to-earth bow. He waited for a minute, then got up and repeated the process, working his way down the Buddha's length as if in fulfilment of some private vow. It wasn't normal Buddhist practice, but the phoney monk might not know. He'd already made one mistake about that. Sawyer fervently hoped so because he was already at a fold in the Buddha's robe some-where around the mid-section.

Head bowed in meditation, he glanced out of the corner of his eye but could see nothing near the feet. There was no way of knowing if the monk had changed position or had begun to notice him. Others had, though. He caught a glimpse of a monk staring wide-eyed at him and others were beginning to watch. But no one made a move to interfere, perhaps because of kreng chai or because the essence of Theraveda Buddhism is that each man must find his own enlightenment and perhaps this was one individual's way along the Eightfold Path. But they watched as he got up and went on.

There was still no sign of movement from the monk. By now Sawyer was near the folds draped over the Buddha's knees and there was no way he hadn't been seen. Something's wrong, he thought, getting up and moving closer to the giant soles of the Buddha's feet, each of them a good five yards long. Why hasn't he made a move? Sawyer wondered, his face beaded with sweat as though he had broken out in some horrible skin disease. Come on, you mother-fucker. Where are you?

Don't kneel – *charge*, the Reptile has hissing in his ear as he sank down near the Buddha's ankles. He was within the air-gun's range now, a sitting duck if the monk made his move. He bowed his head again, unable to keep his right side from twitching as it anticipated the prick of the poisoned dart. He waited, unmoving, counting each breath.

Still nothing. A sudden excitement began to stir in Sawyer. He's buying it, he thought, getting up and moving almost to the Buddha's toes. The next move would take him around the corner and he'd know for sure, one way or the other.

Head bowed for the last time, he rehearsed the sequence in his head: how he would use the fence and a diversion because, ready or not, it would be a matter of hundredths of a second either way. He heard a quiet sigh that might have come from anywhere in the vast hall or from the great Buddha himself. He felt a prickling at the back of his neck. The tiny hairs were standing on end.

And then it didn't matter because he was moving at a flat run around the Buddha's toes, and in a single instant he saw it all, the lone ray of light from a crack in the ceiling lattice embedded in the floor at the monk's feet like a spear, the hundred and eight symbols inlaid on the Buddha's giant soles in mother-of-pearl and the monk's death's-head grin as he stood ready, a good ten feet away, not fooled for a second by the stupid farang, his gun aimed right at Sawyer's belly.

Sawyer didn't have an instant for despair because there was no time for it or for anything except the sequence. He feinted to the right with a slight lurch, sailing the straw hat at the monk like a Frisbee, anything to distract his aim, even as he leaped up to the left, using the fence spike to lever himself up and kicking out with his right foot in a flying tiuchaki. The blood was roaring in his ears and he never heard the pop of the air-gun, only the slight tug at his pant leg as the flechette hit the fabric.

He wasn't sure whether he'd been hit or not. All he could do was finish the kick and . . .

He saw the flechette. It hadn't hit his leg. The bastard had anticipated him going down, not up, and had aimed low, Sawyer thought exultantly.

But he missed the kick and stumbled as he fell forward, the monk dancing out of the way. For a moment Sawyer teetered on one foot, almost losing it and, always conscious of the flechette embedded in the fabric, twisted sideways and plucked it out and away as he fell over and rolled towards the monk. Then they were both up, the monk backed against the iron fence, his black eyes darting back and forth like a cornered animal. He pointed the gun at Sawyer's chest. Sawyer held his hands up as if believing the threat and starting to back away, left foot behind his right, and into the feint that Koichi always used to say was Sawyer's best, pivoting on the right foot and whirling into a spinning back kick to the monk's knee.

The monk went down. Sawyer scrambled on top of him. The monk tried to club Sawyer with the gun butt but Sawyer just brushed it away with a forearm block. No clever tae kwan doe moves now, he simply jammed his thumbs into the monk's throat and pounded his head against the stone floor, the killing rage on him and only somewhere a faint voice reminding him not to waste the little bastard.

The monk's face had swollen tomato-red and Sawyer was

just about to haul the son-of-a-bitch to his feet when he was hit with a savage blow to the side of the head. The great Buddha started to topple over. An octopus wrenched him off the monk. Sawyer held up his arms to shield himself and clear his head. Then all at once the world righted itself for a second and he realized that a crowd of Thais were beating him for attacking a holy monk.

Others helped the monk to his feet. He stood shakily for a moment, gathering his robe around him. His eyes were slits. His face was an impassive mask; a mottled red necklace showed where Sawyer's fingers had been. Some in the crowd were calling for the police and there were dark mutters against the farang who had desecrated the shrine.

Sawyer tasted blood in his mouth as two husky Thais hauled him roughly to his feet. For an instant, through the crowd, his eye met those of the monk's, gleaming with triumph, and Sawyer, feeling sick to his stomach, knew the little bastard was right. He had blown the mission even before it had begun.

A Bangkok policeman came over and, puffing his chest out like a pigeon to assert his authority, began to jabber something to the monk, both of them looking suspiciously over at Sawyer and then at a teenage boy who had picked up the air-gun and was examining it with great curiosity. The policeman held out his hand for the gun, but before the boy could hand it over, the monk darted away and grabbed it out of the boy's hand. The monk ran straight for the temple gate, shoving bystanders out of the way, the gun clutched to his chest.

The crowd buzzed, confused. They stared after the monk. For the moment no one was paying attention to Sawyer, who was still held by the two Thais. Someone said something. The policeman started to come over and Sawyer knew it was the only chance he was going to get.

Sawyer sidekicked the knee of the man on his right, knocking him over like a bowling pin. His right hand freed, Sawyer hooked his fist into the man on his left's mid-section. The policeman tried to stop him, but Sawyer just barrelled over him like a running back on fourth and goal to go, and then he was running like crazy through the crowd, too quickly for them to react.

He blinked blindly in the brilliant light outside, hesitating for a second over which way to go. Then he saw people looking towards the great prang towers and chedis as if watching after someone. As he pounded across the burning-hot stone pavement in his stockinged feet, Sawyer spotted a crowd clustered around the place where Somsukiri still lay.

The little bastard was fast, Sawyer thought, weaving across the courtyard towards the corner of the great golden bot. He was starting to get winded and hoped to God the monk would trip or something because otherwise. . . . He rounded a corner fence post, intricately carved and leafed over with gold, and saw something that made him stop dead in his tracks.

A long line of young monks in identical curry-coloured robes was filing into the massive golden chedi of King Rama the Third. It reminded Sawyer of Koenig's famous 'purloined letter' lecture, the one that ended with the line about how the best place to hide a suitcase was in the luggage department. What better place for a monk to hide than a monastery? Sawyer thought. After all, he had seen the monk only twice, very briefly, and in those instants his attention had been focused on the gun. If the monk played it cool, Sawyer wasn't sure he'd be able to pick him out among all the other monks.

Except he won't play it cool, Sawyer thought. He's an impulse player – the business with the gun proved that. You don't have to identify him; he'll identify himself once he sees you. Just check near the end of the queue. Suppose he's had a chance to reload and you walk right up to him – what then? the Reptile whispered, and Sawyer didn't have any answer to that.

Nothing happened. Sawyer didn't spot the monk and the monk never broke ranks. But the crowd from the Hall of the Reclining Buddha was heading this way and he had to do something fast. Sawyer, trying to look as inconspicuous as a five-foot-ten-inch farang at the end of a line of Buddhist monks all under five foot five can look, filed past carved teak doors inlaid with pearls and into the chedi.

Hundreds of chanting monks were seated in the huge circular hall like a field of talking yellow flowers. Along the curving walls frescoes showed scenes from Buddha's life. A golden Buddha sat enthroned on an altar rising like a miniature mountain peak above the clouds of smoke from hundreds of burning joss sticks. Sawyer sensed a stirring as, one by one, the monks looked his way. He began to back away and look for a side exit because not only was he an intruder but not even Sherlock Holmes could have found one monk among so many.

But if he couldn't spot the monk, he was himself spotted. There was a slight commotion near the side door that led to the towering white-stone prang tower adjoining the chedi. And then Sawyer spotted the monk, still clutching the gun, barging through the doorway.

You couldn't hold your water, could you, you green son-of-a-bitch? Sawyer thought, leaping over a seated monk lost in meditation. He ran around the circumference of the hall. Behind him the chedi began to buzz, but Sawyer by then was through the doorway. He charged up the circular stone staircase that wound around a giant central pillar.

His breath was getting shorter as he pounded up the stairs, round and round in the dizzying heat. Watch it, he's had a chance to reload, he told himself, stopping now and again to catch his breath and to listen for footsteps above. But either he was too far behind or he couldn't hear over his own heavy breathing.

And then he caught something. A tapping sound. But coming downstairs instead of up, getting closer, as if something were rolling down the . . .

Sawyer began moving back down the stairs in great leaps. He bounced off the circular outside walls, pushing off with his hands, tripping and recovering, racing down, relentlessly pursued by that clicking just around the corner behind him and coming faster.

The explosion was almost deafening in the confined space of the stairwell. Burning-hot fragments of the grenade rattled against the stone stairs and walls like hail, one of them skipping off the step Sawyer was on. He waited only a second. His ears still ringing, Sawyer began the long climb back up. This time he did it slowly. When he started to think again, he had realized that once the monk got to the top of the tower, where could he run?

Now he paused more frequently, husbanding his strength and listening for a footfall on the stair around the corner. The one good thing was that in his stockinged feet he made virtually no sound at all. Suddenly he stopped.

He sensed something just around the next turn. It wasn't a sound. He heard nothing, not even breathing. Only the distant buzz of voices somewhere far below. And then he realized what it was. A slight bump in the shadow of the pillar against the outer wall

Sawyer's heart pounded against his chest as if it wanted to come out. The monk was waiting there with that thing cocked.

With a savage growl, Sawyer popped around the turn like a jack-in-the-box, catching a blurred glimpse of the waiting monk, the air-gun, the motes of dust floating in the light slanting through the scrollwork on the outer wall, before jumping back down. The dart clattered against the outer stonework and Sawyer was already pounding back up the stairs, taking them two and three at a time, feeling it in his thighs and hoping they wouldn't give way. The monk's feet were just ahead of him. He grabbed for the ankles, missed, fell down and got back up again. Coming around the next turn, he found the monk, his chest heaving, trapped against the wall next to an arched opening to a narrow ledge outside. The ledge led nowhere. It was a good hundred feet high. Through the sunny opening Sawyer could see the spires and carved eaves of the entire temple complex and, far below, the toylike people and grey paving stones shimmering in the appalling heat. The two men looked at each other.

Sawyer moved into a fighting stance.

The monk's eyes were black with hate. They had the look of a snake when it's pinned by a forked stick. All at once, the monk's expression changed. His eyes acquired a strange shine, as if seeing something that had been hidden from them before.

Sawyer had seen that look before. He started to move forward. The word 'Yoot' escaped his lips, but it was already too late.

The monk had dived straight through the opening. Sawyer got there just in time to see him rocket head-first on to the paving stones below. The head disintegrated with a horrible

76

splat, and even as it happened Sawyer knew that he would be hearing that sound, like a sack of wet clothes hitting the ground, in the silences of the night for a long time to come.

CHAPTER 5

Thunder within the mountain
  explodes from the volcano.
The superior man controls his
  mouth;
what comes out of it
and what he puts into it.

By the time Eddie Macbeth missed the second rdv at Mother Grace's, Sawyer knew he was in trouble. Langley rules were that if a scheduled rdv was missed, you tried again at the same place exactly one hour and ten minutes later. And if you didn't connect then, you aborted.

Except that Langley rules weren't made for someone like Eddie, who had stringy, shoulder-length hair that hadn't been washed for a year, one gold earring that he fancied made him look like a pirate but actually made him look like a vaguely psychotic homosexual, a thin, nervous face that might have been handsome if you added twenty pounds and subtracted as many years and a brain three-quarters fried by some of the purest heroin known to man.

Besides, Mother Grace's bar in the village in Ban Phattaya was the closest thing to an address Eddie had. So, instead of aborting Sawyer decided to stick around, figuring that if Eddie was still functioning, sooner or later he would show.

Sawyer signalled the Chinese bartender for another Singha beer and stared gloomily at his reflection in the mirror behind the bar. In the red neon light the eye-patch made him look sinister, which was almost normal here, he thought, using the mirror to check the room. One of the bar girls started to get up hopefully, but he shook his head and she went over to join her friends at the table of two young American sailors in civvies, their fresh red faces, peach-fuzz haircuts and service shoes making them dead giveaways. They were looking for a story to tell their shipmates and Sawyer was sure they'd have one because it was five to one that, come morning, they'd never see their wallets again.

An American flag hung behind the bar, the neon light turning the red stripes purple. The uncanny tug of *déjà vu* made him very uneasy. It was like the Vietnam days, when all the married guys on R 'n' R wanting beach went to Hawaii and all the single ones came to Ban Phattaya. Or maybe it was the young Thai with the tray of what looked like Christmas-coloured candy, saying, 'Fi' dollah, you see dragon,' that brought it all back. At the other end of the bar were a couple of American vets, deposited on the beach like wreckage after a naval battle, living off their VA cheques and still arguing about whether General Westmoreland knew about the NLF build-up before Tet in '68.

Re-runs, Sawyer thought. All they're showing are re-runs, and if there was anyone interested in him except the girls who hadn't made their quota for the night, he couldn't spot it. But he had to assume they were looking for him, despite everything Harris and Bhamornprayoon had done to smooth over the incident at Wat Po.

All the damage had been blamed on the phoney monk, and as for the mysterious farang desecrator, they had even found a fall guy in the person of a middle-aged American tourist sentenced to a year in a Bangkok jail for the inexcusably stupid act of tearing up a twenty-baht note in a fit of pique over an excessive taxi fare, thereby insulting the King of Thailand, whose sacred picture was printed on the money. In exchange for confessing to the crime at Wat Po temple – committed while he was in jail – the American tourist was sentenced to be deported to San Francisco, where presumably he would entertain his friends with the story of how it was possible to become a major criminal simply by getting into the wrong taxi.

But although Sawyer's part in the affair at Wat Po had been covered up, Harris had been furious. He stood rigidly at the window of the Pasteur Institute office at the Snake Farm watching a quick-handed attendant milk a banded krait into a glass vial, his hands clasped behind his back like Napoleon reviewing his troops.

'Irresponsible. Absolutely irresponsible. Especially in the light of the situation here,' Harris said, not looking at Sawyer.

'The stall was flying the safe sign,' Sawyer said.

That shut Harris up. It was Harris's screw-up at the Temple and they both knew it. The safe sign is supposed to be sacrosanct. Making sure it happened was how a senior case officer earned his salary. And it couldn't have happened unless communications were leaking like a sieve, also Harris's responsibility.

Sawyer got up and stood beside Harris. For a moment, the two of them stared through the glass at the cobras and kraits gliding lethargically over each other in the stifling temperature. When Harris turned to Sawyer his sweating face was beet-red, although Sawyer couldn't tell if it was embarrassment or just the heat.

'We're working on that,' Harris admitted.

'Terrific. That's like the captain of the *Titanic* saying he's going to send out a party with bailing buckets.'

Harris turned even redder. But he was smart enough not to say anything. He stared at the tangled snakes as though they formed a knot that could somehow be unravelled. His shoulders sagged and when he looked back at Sawyer his eyes were shiny with sincerity.

'We're stymied, Sawyer. Did you ever feel like a player in a chess game when an opponent says, "You can't move that piece"?'

Sawyer massaged the skin at the side of his bad eye and tried to think. They were handing it to him and he wasn't sure he wanted it. Be careful, he warned himself. With Harris honesty is just another ploy. Finally, he just threw it out.

'The whole thing is cock-eyed, Bob. We don't even know who the opposition is, or what they want. Or what kind of an Asian it is who knows how to use poison flechettes, but not how a Buddhist monk behaves,' Sawyer said.

Harris sighed heavily, like a husband whose wife has her heart set on a dress he knows he can't afford but knows he's going to have to buy anyway.

'What do you want, Sawyer?'

'I'm on my own from here on out.'

Harris looked at him curiously. 'It's what you wanted all along, isn't it? The file is right about you, Sawyer. You're just not a team player.'

'It helps to know who's on my team,' Sawyer said and was gratified to see Harris redden at that.

'What else?'

'We've got a leak. So from now on no standard communication drops or rdvs. No embassy, no Snake Farm, no more so-called intermediary lines. Just you and me. Private line.'

Harris nodded again. 'Anything else?'

'Yeah. Who owns the South-East Asia Rice and Trading Company?'

Harris's face expressed impatience. 'Look, why don't you just get on with the damn mission instead of going off on these wild-goose chases? We don't have time for this shit.'

'You mean like Parker did, huh?'

Harris recoiled, as though he had been slapped. Then he looked away, obviously not convinced.

'And you still haven't answered my question,' Sawyer added.

Harris exaggerated a sigh. 'We're working on it. It's a tangle. Holding companies owned by other holding companies. We've tracked it from Bangkok to Hong Kong to Macao back to Bangkok so far, and we have to be careful with our inquiries, you know.'

This time it was Sawyer who sighed theatrically. 'Save the bedtime stories for the kiddies, Bob. Just tell me who owns the fucking company.'

Harris smiled unwillingly, as though in spite of himself he had chosen the right bloodhound for the job. 'It looks like a wealthy businessman. Name of Vasnasong. As a matter of fact, I think you might've seen him at Lady Caroline's party. But I think you're barking up the wrong tree, Sawyer.'

'Oh?'

'Don't give me that crap, Sawyer. We checked out Vasnasong long ago. He's pro-Western, pro-Thai monarchy. Wealthy pro-Capitalist. Very well connected. Done favours for MI6 and us, I might add. Besides, what's his motive? He has nearly everything, and anything he doesn't have we'd be happy to give him.'

'You know, Bob, some people in our business might call that "deep cover",' Sawyer said mildly.

Harris looked sharply at Sawyer. He tapped his forefinger thoughtfully against his lip. All at once Sawyer could see in him the Ivy League *Wunderkind* he was supposed to have been.

'It's possible. We'll have to look into that,' Harris muttered, still tapping his lip.

'No, don't! We can't afford it,' Sawyer said.

Harris looked straight into Sawyer's good eye and nodded once. The nod meant both that he understood what Sawyer was driving at and that he had reversed his position and agreed. The advantages were obvious. Because what Sawyer was implying – which was that the local CIA station apparatus could no longer be considered reliable – not only explained everything that had happened but also got Harris off the hook for the screw-up.

'What about that Cambodian refugee outfit?' Sawyer asked.

'This is the first we've heard of them,' Harris admitted, looking troubled.

There was something wrong with that, Sawyer thought. He knew it was wrong the way you know something's changed when your lover kisses you and it's different, although you can't say what the difference is. Only he couldn't say so because he wasn't even sure at this point if Harris was a part of it or not. So he contented himself with an admission of his own.

'It's all bits and pieces. It's not a mission; it's like the wreckage of a mission. I feel like one of those palaeontologists trying to piece together a dinosaur from odds and ends. A tooth here, a bit of toe there. There's a missing piece somewhere and that's the way in,' Sawyer said.

Harris nodded slowly. 'How will you know?'

'By finding out who got to the missing second tail, Sergeant Tarasang,' Sawyer said.

The attendant suddenly slapped the snake he was milking and jerked his head back. There was something about the way he did it that made Harris smile.

'You'll need a local contact in Phattaya,' Harris said, still watching the attendant and the snake.

'Max suggested Eddie Macbeth.'

Harris's handsome face looked pained, as though he had just stepped on something left behind by a dog.

'You know him?'

'Just keep him on a tight leash. Don't let him do any thinking, if slime like that is capable of thought,' Harris said.

'How'd he get the nickname "Macbeth"?' Sawyer asked, wondering at Harris's reaction. Who the hell did Harris expect to find in a honky-tonk Asian beach town? Snow White?

Harris raised his eyebrows in surprise. 'I thought everyone in 'Nam had heard that one. It even made the papers briefly before the Marine brass could squash it.'

'Must've happened after I left,' Sawyer shrugged.

Harris nodded. 'It was a Stars and Striper in Eye Corps who came up with the nickname. You know the type. English major. Copy sprinkled with literary allusions. Anyway, the story was that when Eddie was a second looie, he fragged his captain to take over command of the company. Just like in Shakespeare.'

'How come he wasn't court-martialled?'

Harris shrugged again. 'The Corps was dying to nail him, but there wasn't a thing they could do. The whole company swore that at the time somebody dropped a grenade in the captain's hootch, Eddie was in the CP with nothing more lethal in his hand than a can of Coke.'

'Maybe he didn't do it.'

'Oh, he did it all right. Everybody knew he did it. But it was touchy. Very touchy. A lot of people felt the captain deserved it.'

'What happened?'

'The company had just suffered eighty-five per cent casualties after three days of murderous fighting to take some hill near the Rockpile. The VC had honeycombed the place with caves and tunnels like an anthill. It was a mess and by the time the Marines took it, Eddie was the only officer still walking. Then the choppers came and airlifted what was left of the company off the top of the hill. Two days later this captain ordered Eddie, in charge of the survivors and some green replacements, to retake the same fucking hill. It seems that after the Marines had been evac'd out, the VC just infiltrated back. I guess Eddie just couldn't see the point,' Harris said.

'After a while it got a little hard for anybody to see the point,' Sawyer agreed, staring through the glass at a cobra twining around another rearing cobra as though creating a medical symbol.

'Anyhow, there wasn't another officer available, so they had to give the company to Eddie. That's when the Stars and Striper coined the nickname and it stuck. It was in all the papers.'

'Are you saying not to use him?' Sawyer demanded.

'I'm saying if something happens to Macbeth, nobody's going to lose any sleep over it,' Harris said in a tone that gave Sawyer the creeps.

They watched the snakes through the glass. Finished, the attendant cautiously backed away. As he passed, the snakes stirred softly upright, swaying in the heat like silent, deadly flowers.

Sawyer wiped the beer froth from his mouth and tried to remember if there had been anything in his meeting with Macbeth at the cockfight earlier that evening, anything, to justify Eddie's failure to make the rdv at Mother Grace's. Christ knows, he had made it clear from the start that he was keeping Eddie on a very short string.

'I'll be there, Sawyer. Don't be an old lady.' Eddie had grinned, showing a gaping mouthful of discoloured teeth, stained and tilted haphazardly like tombstones in an old cemetery.

'That's a comfort, Eddie,' Sawyer replied, a roar from the crowd distracting him for a moment. In the pit the two cocks, one a pure black, the other a black speckled with green, flew at each other in a flurry of feathers. The black's spur got twisted as he landed and he tried to hop out of striking distance. The crowd buzzed as the green leaped again, bloodying the black. It was only a matter of time.

Although the fight hadn't ended, the betting for the next match had already started. Sawyer glanced at the ring as if looking for a wager, then down at the neatly slicked hair on the back of Sergeant Tarasang's head, three rows below him. Tarasang got up and turned so Sawyer could see his face.

Tarasang was smiling broadly and waving a thick wad of bahts at the Chinese bookie standing in the aisle. Tarasang seemed to have no idea they were interested in him.

All around the stands were filled with Thais and Chinese shouting bets, kids peddling cigarettes and drinks and women in warpaint peddling something else. The heat was intense enough to melt metal, and the air was thick with noise and smoke and cock crows, the endless tumult of Asia.

'I said I'll be there. I always come through, don't I?' Eddie said truculently. His pupils were needle-points. A nerve along the side of his jaw began to twitch and Sawyer wondered how soon it would be before Eddie would have to have his next fix.

'I found Tarasang, didn't I?' Eddie insisted. When Sawyer didn't reply, the nerve in Eddie's jaw began pulsing like a line on an oscilloscope.

'You've got a big mouth, Eddie. In our business that's not an asset,' Sawyer observed.

In the pit the green was pecking viciously at the black's eyes to finish him off. The crowd roared its encouragement. Eddie looked straight at Sawyer, but his mind was up a dark alley somewhere else.

'Don't threaten me, Sawyer. Everybody knows you can't threaten Macbeth,' Eddie replied, his hand going to his pocket where Sawyer knew he kept a switchblade.

Sawyer didn't even tense. In Eddie's vacant eyes he had already seen that whatever had flamed inside the young Marine lieutenant had long since burned out on Phattaya beach.

Time to jerk the string, Sawyer thought. He needed to know where Tarasang was getting his money. Who had bought him off? It wasn't complicated and it wasn't difficult. God knows, it had been easy enough to find Tarasang. Ban Phattaya was too small a town for a newcomer like Tarasang not to be noticed. And it was a town for noticing people. Even the fat Germans turning lobster-red around the palm-lined pool at the Phattaya Palace and endlessly complaining about the *verdammt* slow service were noticed.

Eddie Macbeth's job was to find out what was the crooked cop's hot button. Dope, girls, money. Odds-on money, Sawyer had coached Eddie. Tarasang would probably ask

85

around and find out that Macbeth was what used to be called a 'serviceable farang'. Then all Eddie had to do was lead him like a Judas goat – 'Tell him it's a quick couple of thousand American and have him meet you,' Sawyer had told Eddie – to some place where Sawyer could sweat him. And to show up on time, Sawyer thought irritably.

Down around the pit there were good-humoured catcalls and frenetic wagering as the disgusted owner dragged out the dead black and handlers showed the next pair of cocks to each other to get their blood up.

'What're you gonna do, Eddie? Frag me?' Sawyer said, deliberately provoking a dangerous spark in Eddie's eyes. 'Don't you get it, asshole? Somebody like you breaks the law a hundred different ways just by breathing in and out. The last time they cold-turkeyd a junkie in the farang section of the Bangkok prison, he thought he was being attacked by a million spiders and gouged his own eyes out with his bare thumbs.'

A roar went up from the crowd as the handlers swung the cocks towards each other like trapeze artists, then let them fly at each other, clawing savagely as they fluttered to the ground.

'You don't have to be such a hard guy, Sawyer. I'll be there,' Eddie Macbeth whined, defensively pulling his head down to his shoulders like a tortoise. It was hard not to feel sorry for him, Sawyer thought. He had been a good soldier once and maybe he had even thought he was being a good soldier saving what was left of his outfit from an asshole CO the day he became Macbeth. And then going home a junkie and getting it on the other side from a wife he couldn't talk to and pretty girls with long hair who wanted to know how many babies he had napalmed. But feeling sorry for Eddie was like mourning the deaths at Pompeii, Sawyer reminded himself. He had burnt away a long time ago and the only thing that mattered any more was that he do what they were paying him to do.

Except that Eddie Macbeth hadn't shown up at Mother Grace's and Sawyer was starting to get a very bad feeling even as he sat there, nursing a Singha beer and watching the girls work the Navy.

He motioned the bartender over. He was a small

Chinaman with a set of absurdly white false teeth that gave him a headwaiter's smile. Sawyer ordered another Singha and put two five-hundred-baht notes on the bar.

'Have you seen Eddie Macbeth tonight?' he asked in English, raising his voice over the din of hard-rock music from the disco next door.

'Who dis Eddie?' the bartender shrugged.

'Eddie Macbeth,' Sawyer repeated, suggestively tapping the money.

'Eddie – you flend?' The bartender squinted suspiciously at Sawyer.

'Eddie's everybody's friend.' Sawyer grinned and the bartender giggled. As they were laughing, the bartender pocketed the money slick as a gipsy.

'He good flend evelybody 'cept self him maybe.' The bartender giggled again at his own wit. His false teeth were exactly even all the way across. They gleamed in the neon light like pink piano keys.

'Have you seen him tonight?'

'Him no come tonight.'

'Maybe later?'

'Him no come tonight.' The bartender shook his head firmly. He started to move down the bar.

'In case he comes, tell him Morrison was looking for him,' Sawyer called after him. They had chosen the name Morrison because Eddie, whose brain was still lost in the Sixties, had been a big fan of Jim Morrison and the Doors.

The bartender came back. 'You Mollison?' he muttered suspiciously.

Sawyer nodded.

'Eddie say tell Mollison meet him by beach.'

An icy chill shivered through Sawyer. Eddie Macbeth was breaking every rule in the book by passing messages in the clear through a civilian. Either Macbeth had lost the few marbles he still had left, in which case Sawyer would have his balls for breakfast, or he had been desperate.

'Who brought the message?' Sawyer asked.

But at this the Chinaman's face shuttered closed and he walked on down the bar. By the time he reached it, Sawyer was already out of the door.

*

The buzzing of the flies should have warned him. He had heard them clearly as he crouched behind a palm tree near the thatched beach hut where Eddie sometimes crashed and where he was supposed to lure Tarasang. And going in, Sawyer had known that it could – almost had to be – a trap. So that, padding along the shore in his bare feet, his shoes in one hand and a ridiculously inadequate NATO-issue 7·62mm Beretta with a silencer in the other – he'd have to talk to Harris about getting him the Ingram M-10 – Sawyer had tried to find some excuse not to go in. Except that there was a slim chance that the message had been a bona fide distress signal from Macbeth, leaving him no real choice.

The beach was deserted so late at night and, despite the feeling that he was exposed, he knew he was virtually invisible in the darkness. The sand was still warm under his feet, and any noise he might have made was masked by the sound of the waves. If the opposition was there, he was counting on being able to hear them before they could hear him.

The night hung heavy with the suffocating heat that comes in the last days before the monsoon. A crescent moon was a sliver that cast almost no reflection on the sea. Along the surf line small breakers were rolling in like logs. Just beyond the reach of the water lay overturned Sunfish and wind surfboards, beached like giant shells from the mesozoic era. Dense, dark foliage and palms shielded the beach from the traffic along the shore road. In the distance he could see the lights of the Merlin shimmering in the heat, as though the world was a normal place where the worst a farang had to fear was sunburn or a case of 'Thai tummy'. But, just to be on the safe side, he crept into the foliage to approach the hut from the tree side.

That's when he heard the flies. Maybe he would have waited and figured it all out if he hadn't heard the crashing sounds of the hut being ransacked and known he had to move because there might still be a chance for Eddie.

Coming around the tree, Sawyer saw two dark figures, grotesquely elongated shadows in the smoky light of an old kerosene lantern. They were pulling things apart, obviously searching for something, and then one of them hissed and straightened up. Whatever it was, he had found it. Coming through the foliage Sawyer knew he was making too much noise. He was still hoping to surprise them. But they heard him.

In the split second as he approached the opening to the hut, he saw one of them already heading out into the darkness on the beach side as the other, the one who had found what he was looking for, was swinging around towards Sawyer, a Mark VII machine pistol in his hand. There were two other shadowy figures that Sawyer hadn't seen till now, lounging across a table from each other like cardplayers. There was no time to dodge or retreat. The Mark VII was coming up, and as the first shots were fired Sawyer sprang on to the sand under the eaves. The Mark VII's shots were loud enough to wake the dead. They shredded the thatching above Sawyer's head. He rolled into a prone position, close enough to see the briefest flicker of panic in the Asian's eyes, and fired twice.

The Asian's head jerked back. The bullet had hit him in the eye, blasting a glob of blood and matter out of the back of the skull. He crumpled backwards, twitched and was still. Once again the only sound was Sawyer's breathing, loud in his ears, and the nearby rumble of the surf.

Sawyer got slowly to his feet, wiping the sweat and sand from his good eye against his sleeve. Then he was up and could see it all and wished he couldn't.

The two seated figures were Eddie Macbeth and the missing Sergeant Tarasang. At least, that's who Sawyer thought they were from their clothes, general appearance and hair. Because there was no way to tell from the bloody masks swarming with flies that they wore instead of faces. Even if they weren't both dead, they couldn't have talked, Sawyer thought bitterly, because their tongues were among the various pieces of flesh displayed on the brass-topped table from Calcutta that had once been Eddie's pride and joy.

Sawyer felt sweat prickling all over his body. Bile rose in his throat and all he wanted to do was get out of there. Then he remembered that the dead Asian had found what he had been looking for. He knelt over the Asian and pulled a crumpled piece of paper from fingers still warm and sticky with Eddie's blood.

It was with a sense of anticlimax that he unfolded the paper and read it in the dim light, as though he had known all along what it would be. It was a sight draft for twenty-five thousand baht, made out to Sergeant Tarasang. It was drawn on a Bangkok bank and the payer was the South-East Asia Rice and Trading Company.

Perhaps if he hadn't been so engrossed in trying to spell out the spidery Thai letters, he would have heard them sooner. From the shore road came the sound of a police siren, then outside the hut he could hear the sounds of muffled orders. It had been a trap after all.

Through the gaps in the thatch he could see the dancing beams from flashlights as the police moved into position around the hut.

CHAPTER 6

The sky above, the marsh below.
He has one eye and thinks he can
   see well;
he is lame and thinks he can walk
   well.
He treads on the tail of the tiger.

The sampan stirred in the current like a restless sleeper. In the distance a temple bell tinkled once and was still. Night hung over the river, the air thick with the heat. Sawyer checked his watch one more time. The dial gave a zodiac glow in the darkness. The temple bell tinkled again, giving the illusion of wind. But it was just hot air rising, Sawyer thought. There would be no more wind till the coming of the monsoon.

He scanned the shadows along the wharf for the guard he had spotted earlier and wondered if he wasn't pushing his luck too far. It was only by the skin of his teeth that he had escaped from the burning hut and the police.

'So you managed to get away. That was very clever of you,' Vasnasong had said. He was grinning hugely as though it were all a big joke on him.

For an instant the image of the police surrounding the hut leaped into Sawyer's mind. He saw himself smashing the kerosene lamp against the wicker chair, the leaping flames, confusion and shouting in the darkness, as he slithered through the dense foliage. It didn't seem all that clever to him. Not very clever at all, he thought.

'Most excellent clever,' Vasnasong repeated, still working hard on his smile like a *maître d'* trying to entice an uncertain couple into an otherwise empty restaurant. 'You are better, I think, than the first one, this so-called Hawken-khrap.'

Vasnasong was far too smart to try to pretend he knew nothing of Parker. But then Vasnasong hadn't become one of the wealthiest men in Asia by being stupid, Sawyer reminded himself. He glanced around the teak-panelled office, almost shivering in the exquisite coolness of the air conditioning. The panelling, Danish modern leather-topped desks and brass lamps gave the office the feel of a successful East Coast lawyer's office. But few law offices could have afforded the collection of Ming vases displayed on a teak credenza from one of Vasnasong's furniture factories. A pair of planters in the centre of the room, a giant fern in the corner and fresh-cut orchids in rare green Celadon ceramic vases helped soften the masculine austerity. Dominating the room was a stone bas-relief mounted on one wall. It was an apsara, a celestial dancer. The figure was nude from the waist up, except for an intricately carved necklace and crown, and possessed of that rare combination of willowy sensuality and otherworld-liness characteristic of the best Khmer art. It was priceless, yet private. A voyeur's fantasy.

A number of framed photographs hung on the wall behind Vasnasong's desk. They were of Vasnasong and various heads of state, including one with De Gaulle, one with a former US Secretary of State and one of Vasnasong being greeted by a smiling Chou En-lai and a troop of Chinese schoolgirls waving red flags of welcome. Apart, and in a place of honour, was a large picture of Vasnasong, head bowed in an impeccable posture of correctness, standing next to King Bhumibol. As Barnes had said, Vasnasong had 'muchee squeeze'.

One entire wall of the office was a single floor-to-ceiling plate-glass window covered by a white gauzy curtain with heavy grey-silk curtains gathered at each end. Through the window Sawyer could see the incredible vista of the teeming city stretching all the way to the horizon, and some twenty storeys below the river glittering like metal in the sun.

Sawyer looked down at the toylike figures of coolies loading a rice barge, as Vasnasong no doubt did from time to time, and thought of Vasnasong's painful, inch-by-inch climb from the muck down there up to this office. 'Started as a coolie,' Barnes had remarked. It must have taken a relentless intelligence, none of which was remotely visible on the good-natured bespectacled face before him. Vasnasong seemed relaxed, his pudgy hands clasped comfortably on the mound of his belly. Sawyer was fascinated by his hands. When he talked he would gesture with the grace of a temple dancer. His lips were fleshy and sensual. They wore an easy, almost self-satisfied, smile that seemed to imply that it was a very fine thing to be a millionaire. Except that you couldn't let the modern skyscrapers fool you. This was Asia, Sawyer reminded himself. In the West we create our images in order to impress others; in Asia one creates one's image to conceal.

Or was it only the expression around Vasnasong's eyes that were lined with good humour? The eyes themselves were unblinking as a carving, Sawyer noted, trying to eliminate any sign of wariness from his own eye. He thought about what they had done to Tarasang and Eddie Macbeth. Vasnasong would no more have a qualm about killing him than a tiger would feel a tinge of regret for his prey.

The two men faced each other with deadly attention completely masked by an air of lounging relaxation. They were both carnivores.

'So-called?' Sawyer asked, his eyebrows raised.

'His real name Pakah, yes?' Vasnasong smiled blandly, as though he was merely repeating what everyone in Bangkok already knew.

Sawyer kept the surprise out of his face. He'd used the technique of implying that he knew more than he really did too many times himself to give it away free to this son-of-a-bitch.

'So you did see Parker that night?' Sawyer said.

'Ah, yes. We met at the Roxy Club. A very good fellow this Pakah-khrap, but also perhaps impetuous. I tried to warn him that the Golden Triangle was a most dangerous place, but he seemed not to mind. Mai pen rai, you understand?' Vasnasong said, tsk-tsking like a Chinese grandmother.

'Where is the superior man who lacks all faults?' Sawyer said carefully.

A hint of amusement flickered in Vasnasong's eyes. 'Let us be candid, Soyah-khrap. The man you seek was a fool,'

Vasnasong said, not bothering to complete the rest of the thought, which was the implied question, 'Are you going to be one as well?'

'Unfortunately, Parker was engaged in matters of interest to our organization,' Sawyer said, holding to the tattered shreds of his Red Cross cover.

'The Red Cross, of course,' Vasnasong smiled.

'Of course,' Sawyer smiled back. Vasnasong was good, he thought. So good he didn't bother to dispense with Sawyer's cover, though they both knew that nobody was fooling anybody.

'Tell me about Parker. What happened to him?'

Vasnasong leaned forward, sincerity shining in his eyes like faith in the eyes of a true believer. 'Of this I know nothing. Your Pakah-khrap is, as it is said when one knows nothing of another's fate, in the hands of the Lord Buddha.'

'But you set up the contact.'

'Excuse, dai prod?'

'Whom did you arrange for Parker to meet that night?'

'A most beautiful woman. One not to be forgotten easily, not even by old man like myself.' Vasnasong smiled, his fleshy lips parting for a moment, then snapping shut like a trap.

It wasn't what he said but the way he said it that jarred Sawyer. There was something obscene about it. For some reason it reminded Sawyer of that rdv in a Columbian brothel when he opened the wrong door and saw the pale faces of young children crouched in the darkness waiting to be summoned. Sawyer thought he had masked the thought, but Vasnasong picked up on it immediately.

'Ah, you disapprove, Soyah-khrap?'

Sawyer mentally cursed himself. You've got to do better, he thought, remembering Koenig's endless lectures: 'Being a spook is like being an actor. Only if the critics don't like your performance they'll kill you,' he used to say.

'Mai pen rai. It is not for me to approve or disapprove anything. Besides, it is no matter to me how any man takes his pleasure,' Sawyer shrugged.

Vasnasong's eyes glittered. 'I fear you lie, Soyah-khrap. To you if not to me. Ah yes,' he continued, holding up an admonishing finger, 'you see me and you think it is bad thing,

94

this old man and beautiful young girl, like slug crawling on lotus flower. So self-righteous! Such foolishness! How little you Europeans understand sex passion.'

'Ah, the ancient wisdom of the mysterious Orient,' Sawyer mocked, damned if he was going to let Vasnasong get to him.

'Not at all.' Vasnasong smiled. 'It is you Europeans who make mystery of man and woman. I remember coloured cards shaped like hearts I used to import for GI to send home to America. With little poems. I love you this. I love you that. What nonsense, Soyah-khrap. What is this to do with man and woman matters?'

'Come on, Vasnasong-khrap. Let's not make a religion out of something you can buy for a few hundred baht on any street in Bangkok.' Sawyer grinned impudently.

Vasnasong sighed, patiently tapping the desk with his finger like a teacher with an obstinate pupil. 'You laugh, Soyah-khrap, but I see you heart. You are not of those who can rest content with half truth, no matter how comfortable. You are of those who for truth would leave the world shattered behind you, gasping for breath like fish on the shore. Truly, Soyah-khrap,' Vasnasong said, looking sidelong at him, 'you are dangerous man.'

'And what is this great truth I feel sure you're about to impart?' Sawyer half smiled. But Vasnasong was almost solemn.

'For herself, beautiful woman is one such as you or I. But for men she is also image of all we desire, a living cinema, what our Lord Buddha calls "tanha".' Vasnasong paused. He looked sharply at Sawyer. 'One thing you must to remember, Soyah-khrap. Sex is older than mankind.'

'Chun mai kao chai.'

'You understand most very good, Soyah-khrap. There is more truth in drake who pins duck by her neck to ground as he mounts her than in all the songs of love and coloured heart-shaped cards.'

'Then if it's truth we're talking, tell me about the girl – and Parker,' Sawyer said, an edge coming into his voice.

Vasnasong splayed his pudgy fingers in a helpless gesture. 'It was arranged she come to Roxy that night after I have gone. I myself left before she come. So, you see, I am mystified as you, though why you not come to me from the first, this I do not understand.' Vasnasong shrugged.

'We had no idea whom Parker was meeting that night,' Sawyer admitted, hoping he sounded casual enough. Because the terrible implications of their not knowing about Vasnasong and Parker before were beginning to harden his suspicions into a certainty. He opened another line of questioning to allay any suspicion Vasnasong might have that he was on to the scent.

'What about the girl? Who is she?'

'Ah, the girl.' Vasnasong smiled. 'That is some girl, believe me, Soyah-khrap. Her name – Suong. This means "Springtime". Only this Springtime most special. She say she can put Pakah-khrap in touch with the warlord of the Shan, Bhun Sa, and also the Cambodian rebel leader, Mith Yon.'

'Why Bhun Sa?'

'He has an army. Also much opium passes through his hands. Some say he have mountain of morphine base, all the opium of the third and best cutting, hidden across border. Maybe Burma-side. Maybe Lao-side. No one knows for certain. Most interesting, mm-hai?'

'Most interesting,' Sawyer agreed. So Parker was going to work the deal through Bhun Sa, he thought. It made sense, given the fact that Bhun Sa was rumoured to control much of the opium trade in the Golden Triangle. He could cross borders at will, and a secret cache of morphine base of the size Vasnasong was talking about would be worth billions. It could finance the whole operation. And if he could add Bhun Sa's army to that of the Cambodian rebels, it would be a force that could keep the Vietnamese so tied up in Cambodia they wouldn't be able to even think of mounting an invasion against the Thais. No wonder Parker decided to go for broke, Sawyer thought excitedly.

'How did you find the girl?'

Vasnasong glanced at Sawyer with the kind of half pitying, half disgusted look corporate vice-presidents give a junior executive who has just, very publicly, stuck his foot in his mouth.

'I don't find people, Soyah-khrap. They find me,' Vasnasong said.

Sawyer lowered his head to make Vasnasong think he was

acknowledging having lost face. The veil had dropped a fraction. He had caught a glimpse of the real Vasnasong.

'You mean a strange female calls you up, an important man like you, spins you some fairytale about warlords in the Golden Triangle and you agree to face-to-face meetings just like that?'

'Ah, yes, Soyah-khrap. I always listen,' Vasnasong nodded agreeably.

'A female,' Sawyer said, implying that it was curious in patriarchal Asia for Vasnasong to do business with any female, especially one not of his own family.

'Ah, yes,' Vasnasong repeated, this time allowing condescension to show through his smile. 'I will tell you story, Soyah-khrap and perhaps you will understand.

'I began most poor, Soyah-khrap. Most poor. Europeans do not know of this kind of poor. But then the Lord Buddha smiled upon myself and I began, with much difficulty, to acquire money.

'One day a female who is dear to me and is later to be wife to me tells me story. She has befriended farang acquaintance' – reading between the lines, Sawyer surmised that Vasnasong's wife had probably started as a Suriwongse-style hostess – 'who is having most terrible difficulties with the Thai bureaucracy. This farang wishes to arrange for supply of Coca-Cola and other such things for United States soldiers when they come to Thailand for air bases and also for holiday time from war in Vietnam. Now, it is well known, Soyah-khrap, that peoples in strange lands hunger for the food and drink of their mother land. With help of this female, I persuade this farang for me to be agent, handle Thai bureaucrats who I know how to deal with,' Vasnasong said, rubbing his thumb against his first two fingers in the universal sign for pay-off money. 'With result that soon I earn commission on every bottle of Coke, Pepsi, et cetera, sold in Thailand. Then we expand. Pretty soon we handle hamburgers, toothpaste, all manner of things for soldiers. Vietnam was very big war. Many soldiers, Soyah-khrap. Many Cokes and Pepsis. So you see, Soyah-khrap, I make many profits from listening to female who have story to tell,' Vasnasong concluded solemnly.

'And I suppose you have no idea what happened to little Miss Springtime either?' Sawyer persisted.

Vasnasong shook his head, his eyes filled with an infinite sadness like those of Christ contemplating the sorry human spectacle.

'No, I don't, Soyah-khrap. But I fear you are not believe me.'

Sawyer lounged insolently back in his chair. 'What about the late Sergeant Tarasang? Why was he on your payroll?'

A dangerous gleam appeared in Vasnasong's eyes, and Sawyer knew he had pushed things too far. Then Vasnasong smiled and the gleam disappeared as though it had been merely a trick of the light.

'I have many people I pay money to, Soyah-khrap. For information – and other things. But someone must have purchased this Sergeant Tarasang's loyalty before I. This Tarasang make no report for me. As for the draft from my company, it was, as you know, never cashed.' Vasnasong shrugged.

He acted as if none of it had anything to do with him, but this time Sawyer wasn't having any of it.

'Forgive my scepticism, Vasnasong-khrap, but that still doesn't explain Le Comité National pour l'Aide aux Réfugiés Kampucheans.'

At this Vasnasong looked confused and that really threw Sawyer. He had said it just to rattle the tree and see what might fall out, but if he didn't know better he would have sworn that he had finally shaken the old bastard, though he wasn't sure why. Whatever the reason, his question had acted like a slamming door on the conversation.

'Perhaps you should ask your own people such questions, Soyah-khrap,' Vasnasong said, his face drawn tight as he stood and abruptly offered his hand, Western-style. 'A pity you must go now. I am so sad not to be of more help, Soyah-khrap.'

'So am I, Vasnasong-khrap,' Sawyer said, making the wai sign, his thoughts churning. 'So am I.'

Sawyer slowly pulled the sampan up to the wharf. Going in via the front door had been of no help; maybe he could find out what was going on by the back door. Whatever it was, it had to be soon because if what he suspected was true, he had very little time left. He wondered if he wasn't being used for bait. Because he *had* asked his own people about the Cambodian refugee outfit, dammit! You'd better not think about where that's leading, he told himself. You'd better get the goddam facts first. Timing it carefully, he jumped up, landing catlike on the concrete.

He crouched in the shadows, waiting for the hidden guard to move and reveal his position. He hadn't seen a rifle, so the most the guard had would be a pistol, probably holstered, and in his black shirt and pants and rubber-soled shoes Sawyer figured he could probably sit right next to the guard without being spotted.

A cigarette glowed about ten feet to the right of the stanchion where he crouched, and he started to move.

He had the sequence rehearsed in his mind. The choke-hold from behind. Forget the Hollywood movie bullshit about people getting tapped on the head and going nicely to sleep. It was very difficult to hit someone with the precise degree of force needed to cause sufficient brain haemorrhaging to render him instantly unconscious without killing him or causing permanent brain damage. And although the rules changed, depending on who was DCI that year, in general Company policy frowned on terminating civilians not clearly identified as opposition. The choke-hold was the best non-drug approach that would allow him to keep the guard alive.

Except he must have made some sound because at the last moment he saw the guard's eyes widen. Instead of the head move first, as he had planned, Sawyer spun into a sidekick to the mid-section, knocking the wind out of the guard to prevent him from crying out, followed by a smash to the face to bring his head back up. The guard gasped and tried to reach for his holster, but Sawyer was already behind him with the choke-hold, pulling him backwards to keep him off-balance.

Sawyer pinned the holster with his leg, preventing the guard's hand from reaching it. They swayed in a desperate dance of kicking feet and clawing hands, the guard tearing at the rock-hard forearm Sawyer had jammed into his windpipe. Sawyer held on grimly as the fingernails dug deeply into his arm. The guard hit him with an elbow chop to the ribs that Sawyer knew he would feel later on, followed by three enormous jerks of the guard's entire body, which almost wrenched him free. The guard's thrashing began to subside after what seemed much longer than the thirty to forty seconds it was supposed to take. All at once, the guard was dead weight and Sawyer sagged to the ground with him, still holding his death's grip even tighter, at first in case it was a ruse and then, as the seconds ticked away, because he had to bring the guard close to the edge of death to keep him out for more than a minute or so. And there was no real way to tell where the line between life and death was.

When he finally let go, Sawyer's hands were slick with sweat. It took him a minute to find the guard's pulse; fluttery, but it was there. Sawyer retrieved the man's pistol from the holster and heaved it far out over the river. In the blackness the distant splash might have been a fish breaking the surface.

The lock in the corroded metal door to the warehouse was one of those heavy, iron tumbler devices of ancient design that would have taken the balding 'flaps-and-seals' instructor in Langley less time than to tie his shoes. As it was it took Sawyer an agonizing four or five minutes with the pick until it clicked open and he stepped inside.

It was a city of rice. Tall cubed buildings made of big sacks of rice stacked like bricks and between them ran rectilinear aisles like narrow streets. The warehouse was cavernous and gloomy, the yellowish light from a few bug-spattered bulbs not penetrating down the dark aisles. You could hide an army in here, Sawyer thought, holding his breath to listen. The silence was thick as the gloom, but all around there were faint, almost imperceptible, scratching sounds. Rats, burrowing insects, Sawyer thought, turning a corner, the Beretta in his hand.

At the far end of a very long, straight aisle was a mountain of unsacked rice. It towered over the stacked cubes like Vesuvius over Naples. Something about it beckoned Sawyer closer. A signal from his Reptile, perhaps, Sawyer thought, as he tiptoed down the long corridor, pausing at each intersection to check for anything that might come at him out of the shadows. But there was nothing except the tiny chewing sounds of things that lived in the dark. And then Sawyer realized what had attracted his attention. Almost concealed by the mountain of rice was the partial outline of a ventilator panel.

Parker! The image of Parker, bound and gagged in a little room, crackled in his mind like electricity. It would be a perfect hide-out. A few shovelfuls of rice was all it would take to seal the door from view behind the rice mountain, Sawyer thought.

He took off his shoes and socks. The rice was pale as snow in the gloomy light. It felt firm and granulated under his bare feet. Moving carefully, one step at a time to make as little sound as possible, he began to climb the rice mountain. At each step a tiny avalanche of rice grains tumbled a short way down the slope. He made no more sound than a large rat as his head came up to the open ventilator panel.

Slowly Sawyer raised himself up. He held his breath and peered over the top of the panel.

He could see nothing. It was pitch-black down there. A sharp chemical smell filled his nostrils. He had smelled it before, but he couldn't remember where. Sweet Christ, what have they done to him, he thought. Then he realized that if Parker was down there, he would be unguarded. They wouldn't have left a guard without a light.

Sawyer reached into his back pocket and took out a small pencil flashlight. The narrow circle of light revealed a tiny room filled with small wooden boxes and a table on which were some iron pots, glass jars and a couple of bricks made of something that looked like white chalk. No Parker, of course.

Sawyer felt like kicking himself. He recognized the chemical smell now all right. It was acetic anhydride. The white bricks were morphine base. They'd had something to hide, but it wasn't Parker. It was a small heroin factory.

He had just started to turn around when he was blinded by powerful floodlights. He blinked desperately to clear his eye, his gun already in position, but it was pointless. They had him covered on three sides with AK-47s. He tossed his gun down the rice slope and raised his hands over his head.

The one in the middle, whom Sawyer took for the leader, barked something Sawyer didn't understand in a language that might have been Cambodian. He shouted again, this

101

time in French, for him to descend with the hands on high. So they were Cambodians all right. His throat went dry as he came down. He remembered all the stories from the war, the ones that always sounded too Hollywood chainsaw-massacre to be true. Then he thought about what they had done to Tarasang and Eddie Macbeth.

The leader kept his AK-47 trained on Sawyer's chest all the way down. When Sawyer got closer he could see the leader's face drawn tight, the eyes red-rimmed, and then everything looked red because the leader had smashed the muzzle of his rifle across Sawyer's good eye. Sawyer staggered back, his hands coming up to protect his face, and the leader screamed at him in a high, unnatural voice to make the hands come down, behind his back. His voice carried the strange, almost hysterical, note of orders shouted during a bombardment, though the warehouse was dead quiet. As they roughly tied his hands behind him, Sawyer tried to blink the red film of blood from his eye. He could see, but everything stayed red: the stacks of rice, the long aisle and the three Cambodians with the smoky-eyed look of guard dogs straining to slip the leash.

'Who are you?' demanded the leader, waving his rifle in Sawyer's face. He only had one chance, he knew: they weren't acting under orders about him specifically. Otherwise they would just kill him now and dump him in the river. It was the perfect place for it, and the only question then would be whether they would do it quickly or take their time. He tried to take a breath, but it wouldn't come. Keep authority in your voice, he told himself.

'These are affairs of interest only to myself and your commandant. Take me to him immediately or, I assure you, he will make you regret it.'

'Answer me at once or it is you who will regret,' the leader said, his voice thick with rage. One of the other two Cambodians picked up Sawyer's pistol, cocked it and put the muzzle to Sawyer's temple.

Their eyes had the vacant stare of those to whom killing was nothing. He had only an instant.

'I am called Sawyer. International Red Cross representative,' he managed to mutter.

The leader reached into Sawyer's back pocket and took

out his diplomatic passport. He squinted at the lettering and held the photograph up to Sawyer's face. When he was satisfied, he put Sawyer's passport in his own pocket and grinned at Sawyer as though what he was about to say was going to give him great pleasure. His breath stank of fish. His teeth were bad, and in the reddish haze through which Sawyer saw everything his smile was that of a demon.

'We know who you are, Monsieur Sauyair. You are not from the Red Cross International. You are an American spy and my orders are to kill you,' said the grinning demon mask.

Sawyer looked into the leader's burning eyes and saw that he meant it. The only question left was fast or slow. If it was slow, he would try to make a break for it, hopefully forcing them to shoot him, he decided, already beginning to look around and calculate angles. But they were starting to back away from him and raise their AK-47s, so they weren't going to waste any more time and it didn't matter whether he ran for it or not.

'I must speak with your commandant. I have vital information for him.'

'Please, monsieur. Let us not insult each other with these nonsenses. Only to stand there – comme ça!'

'Your commandant will punish you when he hears what – '

'No, monsieur, he will not. But in any case you will not be here to know.' The Cambodian shrugged and nodded to his men to make ready.

So this is where it ends, Sawyer thought. He looked around the gloomy warehouse as if there was some meaning to be extracted from the last thing he would ever see, but there was nothing. They'd been expecting him. Vasnasong had outsmarted him and he was paying the prescribed penalty for a mistake in this business. He had blundered into it like a fly into a spider's web, and the worst part was knowing that he deserved it for having been so stupid. All out of vanity. Because he was good at what he did and knew it. But not good enough, you prick, he cursed himself. Because it was all in front of him and he had missed it, like the way he had forgotten where he had heard of the Cambodian Refugee Committee before.

And, just like that, he remembered where he had heard of it. A desperate gift from his subconscious on the brink of death. And he saw them all clear as day, exactly as they had been at Lady Caroline's reception that day: Sir Geoffrey, Robert, Barnes, Lady Caroline, Bhamornprayoon and Vasnasong, of course. Let's not forget Vasnasong, he thought bitterly, moving them around in his mind like chess figures, all the pieces finally falling into place, now that it was too late. And all he needed was for Harris to make one call to London to confirm. Only now it would never be made.

The Cambodian shouted something and they raised their AK-47s like a firing squad. Too late, Sawyer thought. He had understood it too late. Because he had been a child all along. Because deep in his soul he had still held on to that naïve American notion that things would somehow turn out all right in the end. But now, in this last moment before dying, the leader counting, 'One . . . two . . .', Sawyer knew it was all bullshit. He had lived his whole life believing a fairytale and had never known it until this instant. There would be another Vietnam war and thousands would die because he had been a goddam fool.

He blinked his eye open to look at the last thing he would ever see: the demon face of the Cambodian sighting his AK-47 at his head.

But there was something else. Floating dreamlike in the darkness, like the image of the moon on still water, was the face of the most beautiful woman he had ever seen.

He wondered if he was hallucinating, or was he already dying? His chest tightened. The sound of his own breathing was loud as a bellows. He saw the mouth of the Cambodian cry, 'Three!' but he couldn't hear it over the roaring in his ears.

The night exploded in bursts of automatic rifle fire.

CHAPTER 7

The sun shines above the earth.
The man advances horns first.
He uses them against rebels
within his own city.

Fong Wu rolled the black ball in his palm, then held it up
between his thumb and forefinger so the man could see its
size. The man nodded and Fong Wu tamped the opium into
the pipe bowl and lit it. He waited while the man's cheeks
hollowed to make sure that the pipe was drawing well. When
the man had sucked the smoke up the long stem for the first
good puffs, Fong Wu turned to the woman.

Like the man, the woman was also European. She lay
curled on her side facing the man's bunk. She wore heavy
make-up as though she were a common Suriwongse whore
and an expensive Western-style evening dress that almost
completely exposed her sluttish bosoms. As he knelt close to
prepare the pipe for her, Fong Wu could smell the musky
scent of recent fornication on her. It mingled with the thick
perfume she had splashed on to mask the offensive body
odour of the European. Fong Wu ogled her huge bosoms,
bigger than any Chinese girl's, allowing himself a brief
fantasy of coupling with her. But the woman, foolish as all
her kind, noticed nothing. She merely murmured a polite
'Khob khun kha' in a disgusting English accent. All this with
a grateful little smile as she looked across at the man, her
eyes warm and soft.

As always, these two had come here after coupling and
even now they reached out and held each other's hand in an
unseemly display of affection.

Busying himself with final preparations before leaving them in their private teak-lined cubicle with the two cots, the tea on the low table, the lamp turned down just so to ensure an easy entry into dreams, Fong Wu still hadn't decided whether he should warn the man on the bunk or not.

The other European, the one-eyed man with the fierce expression of the hawk, had given him a five-hundred-baht note, which was most excellent good joss. In his mind Fong Wu could already see the expressions of the other players when he tossed the note on the table of the mah-jong game of his mother's brother's son, Chin. They would covet it, but he would outbid them and win back some of his losings. Thus would he silence the endless grumblings of his foolish wife.

But if he should warn the other European, perhaps he could get a second five hundred baht. And what if the one-eyed man meant to do evil to the other European. These were farangs. Who could say what a farang might do?

Fung Wu prepared to leave. If he were going to say something, now was the moment. But the man and woman ignored him as though he weren't there. The man said something in their barbarous tongue and the woman pursed her lips and made a kiss at him. The slut!

Fong Wu deliberately made a sound as he lifted the tray. The man frowned, then relaxed, his eyes already growing dreamy from the opium. The man dropped a ten-safang coin in Fong Wu's hand.

So be it, Fong Wu decided. One who tips so miserly will never part with five hundred baht, he thought, as he bowed and backed away through the beaded curtain. Let the farangs kill each other. What were the farangs to him?

As he passed the one-eyed man, lurking in the shadows of the big room where the smokers lay side by side, Fong Wu nodded.

After the Chinaman passed Sawyer stood there in the darkness, listening. He listened to the sounds of those who were sleeping and the sounds of those who were still awake. Occasionally there would be a flare in the darkness as someone relit his pipe, followed by deep sucking sounds.

Then the darkness, composed of small, restless turnings and sighs, would again settle over the room.

Time to go, Sawyer thought. He glanced over towards the side-exit door that led to the alley in the back, setting its location in his mind, just in case. He hefted the Beretta in his hand, checking to be sure the safety was off. He hoped to God he wouldn't have to use it this time. Not this time.

He moved silently down the dark corridor, stopping in front of the beaded curtain over the doorway. The beads parted with faint insect clicks and before the two smokers could look up from their pipes, he had the muzzle pressed against the man's head.

'Hello, Max,' Sawyer said.

Barnes blinked stupidly up at Sawyer. He looked confused, as though he couldn't remember where he had put something. Then his eyes narrowed as he felt the muzzle against his temple and realized what it was.

'I don't like people pointing guns at me, kiddo,' Barnes said.

'That's too bad,' Sawyer replied, running his free hand over Barnes. When he was sure Barnes was clean, he moved away. He sat near the foot of Lady Caroline's cot, but he kept the gun on Barnes.

'How'd you find us?' Barnes asked, eying the Beretta.

'It wasn't hard,' Sawyer shrugged. 'I knew you wouldn't take My Fair Lady here,' nodding at Lady Caroline, 'to any old dive. Everybody knows that Fong Wu's is the best fumerie in Chinatown.'

'Perhaps I should just leave you gentlemen to conduct your business,' Lady Caroline said carefully. She started to get up.

Sawyer motioned her back with the gun.

'Oh.' She sat back against the wall, her knees drawn up, arms around them like a young girl in a window seat. 'I'm afraid I don't understand,' she said, not looking at Sawyer and not taking her eyes off the gun.

'Not bad,' Sawyer grinned. 'In fact, you're both pretty good.'

'What's the beef, Jack? So we both like to kick the gong a little, the lady and me. So what? After all these years in the Orient you wouldn't figure me for a candidate for a

Baptist choir anyway, would you?' Barnes said, putting down the opium pipe and shaking his head to clear it as he sat up.

'Oh, Christ, Max. Save the horseshit for the Washington crowd, will you?' Sawyer said.

'Well, this is ridiculous, Mr Whatever-your-name-is. I never thought Geoffrey would stoop so low as to have us followed by some little man with a gun. Well, what do you want, little man? Money?' she snapped contemptuously, her eyes blazing. She looked older as she glared at him. Not so pretty, Sawyer thought.

'She's even better than you are,' Sawyer grinned over at Barnes.

'Well, you can put up with this tuppenny-ha'penny extortion if you want to, Max, but I'm leaving – right now,' she said, reaching for her handbag and tossing her hair like a young actress at a Beverly Hills bistro when a movie producer sits down at a nearby table.

Sawyer cocked the hammer and pointed the Beretta in her face. 'Make another move, lady, and I'll blow your fucking head off,' Sawyer said quietly.

Lady Caroline slumped back. She stared up at him with a dark expression that could not be read.

'Come on, Jack. Take it easy, huh. I mean, OK, you got us. So Caroline and me are having an affair. So what? Is that supposed to shake the Anglo-American alliance, or what? I got to tell you, amigo,' Barnes said, pursing his lips. 'She wasn't exactly a virgin when I got her. Come to think of it, neither was I,' he shrugged, screwing his face up in a slap-happy grin.

'Why'd you do it, Max?' Sawyer asked sadly.

Barnes pulled himself heavily to a sitting position at the edge of the bunk. He looked at Sawyer as if calculating something. Then he looked at the gun and obviously thought better of it. He folded his arms across his chest, his forearms with their Marine Corps tattoos bulging like a stevedore's, the massive knuckles white. His brow furrowed, bringing his eyebrows close together so they almost formed a ridge, giving him the appearance of an intelligent Neanderthal.

'Why'd I do what, Sawyer? Fall in love with the most fabulous, beautiful woman I've ever known? A classy lady like her and a monkey like me – you've got to be kidding.

Call it "attraction of opposites". Call it anything you like, but I'll tell you one damn thing, Jack, old buddy. She's the best goddam thing that ever happened to me,' Barnes said, shaking his head. 'Go ahead. Be a rat. Tell Sir Geoffrey,' Barnes shrugged. 'I don't give a shit. Maybe it's better this way, out in the open,' he said looking across at Lady Caroline, his eyes shining.

'Oh, Max,' she said, biting her lip.

For a moment the three of them just sat there. From beyond the wall came a racking smoker's cough that started a round of coughing followed by stillness and a faint echo of Chinese music on the radio.

An odd sound came from Sawyer. They both looked up and he shook his head, trying to stifle his laughter. 'Jesus, you two are really something.'

'Watch it, Jack,' Barnes warned.

'I don't mean this fucking joke of an affair, Max. Although I'm not sure whether you're lying to me, or to yourself, or both. I'm not sure anybody, not even Sir Geoffrey, really gives a damn who you or the lady smoke with, sleep with or anything else with,' Sawyer said.

He watched the hate kindle in Barnes's eyes. He saw the muscles bunch as for a rush and began the slow, imperceptible pressure on the trigger. Barnes saw it and his muscles sagged. He looked up at Sawyer, shaking his head sadly from side to side. 'You don't understand, amigo. You just don't understand.'

'No, I don't understand, Max. Explain it to me. Explain how you and Vasnasong cooked up this whole thing. Explain about Parker. What happened to him? And Sergeant Tarasang and Eddie Macbeth. Remember him? And how you tried to terminate me not once, but three fucking times, amigo. Tell me about it, old buddy-roo,' Sawyer snapped.

Barnes looked confused. 'Jeez, Jack. What makes you think I had anything . . . I swear . . . ,' Barnes said, looking at both of them.

Sawyer made a face. 'Come on, Max. You're better than that. Someone on the inside had to set Parker up for Vasnasong. Someone who knew the terrain and the op and Parker. Like you, Max. Then there was the mysterious Cambodian Refugee Committee that Lady Bountiful over here did her benefit for – that was my own dumb mistake,' Sawyer said, turning to Lady Caroline for a moment. 'The Committee name was on the invitation in English and I should have remembered it, even when I saw it in French. The Committee was tied both to Vasnasong – their office is at his warehouse and he was at the reception too – and to your lady-love, Max. And you, right in the middle. So you knew about it. Christ, everybody in Bangkok knew about the goddam Committee except Harris. And the only way that could've happened was because you didn't tell him. Not very nice, Max. Definitely not according to Hoyle.

'Then there was the attempted hit at the Temple. The booth was flying the safe sign and it was your voice I heard at the other end of the line, amigo. You set me up. Only you ran into some tough luck and Sub-lieutenant Somsukiri bought it instead of me.

'I should have suspected you then, Max. You were the logical candidate. But I didn't. You know why? Because I liked you, dammit. I didn't even want to think of you as a double. But it was you, all right.

'You knew about the rdv at the Temple. You also tried to warn me off the op right from the beginning. And then the Good Housekeeping Seal of Approval for Vasnasong. Harris got that from you. Christ, you'd have thought Harris was going to nominate Vasnasong for Man of the Year. All to try and lead me off the scent. And then no data available on the South-East Asia Rice and Trading Company or anything about its connection with Vasnasong. The only way Harris could have got it so wrong was because of an inexcusable failure on the part of the local station watchdog. Or because maybe someone was deliberately trying to mislead him, eh, Max?'

'You've no proof . . .' Barnes began.

Sawyer looked at him ironically. 'Don't you get it, Max? You're like the hound in Sherlock Holmes. The one that should have barked and didn't.'

'Listen Jack . . .' Barnes tried again, running his tongue along his lips as though sealing an envelope.

Sawyer waved the interruption away with the gun. 'But now I was getting too close, wasn't I? So you tried again at the beach in Ban Phattaya. Vasnasong had bought off

Sergeant Tarasang so they could set up Parker. The bank draft proved that. But I showed up, so Vasnasong had to get rid of Tarasang. Poor Eddie Macbeth got in the way. So you and Vasnasong set a trap to frame me for what those goons left of Tarasang and Eddie. Only I arrived a little too early, before the police, alerted by an anonymous phone call, just happened to show. Third time was the charm. You almost got me in the warehouse, Max.' Sawyer winked.

'How'd you get away?' Barnes asked, looking strangely up at Sawyer.

'Girl saved me. She came charging in like Annie Oakley with a squad of Cambodians packing M-16s. Killed the guards. Bing. Bing. Bing. Just like that. Like Vasnasong said, that's some girl.'

'What do you want, Sawyer?' Barnes said in a strangled voice. It didn't sound like Barnes's voice. A change had come over his face too. His eyes were shadows in his skull. He was watching Barnes die inside, Sawyer thought.

Lady Caroline gazed at them both with a kind of horrified fascination, as though she were watching a very beautiful, very deadly snake stalk a mouse.

'Where's Parker, Max?'

'They've got him. I don't know where,' Max said, a deadness in his voice.

'Who's got him?'

'The Khmer Rouge. Pranh. Pranh's got him.'

Sawyer went very quiet. So quiet they thought he might have gone away and left his body behind. So quiet Barnes thought Sawyer was going to kill him then and there.

'What a shit you are, Max. They'll think he knows something. They're probably killing him by inches. Inches,' Sawyer said, his voice so soft Barnes had to strain to hear him.

'It wasn't me. It was Vasnasong,' Barnes said.

'Sure, it was Vasnasong. Him and his goddam Cambodian sculptures hanging on the wall right in front of my eyes. You were just along for the ride, weren't you? Parker was bait. Vasnasong was using him to get to the Khmer Rouge. To let Pranh know about the arms-for-opium trade. Vasnasong wanted to let Pranh know that he had something to deal and

111

that Pranh should deal through him and not the Americans. Only how did the Khmer Rouge come into the picture?'

'Grow up, Jack,' Barnes said, a trace of the old annoyance showing in his voice. 'There's a rumour up in the hill country that Bhun Sa and Pranh are working together. Between them they control most of the opium in the Golden Triangle, and together they're the only fighting force with a real chance of keeping the Vietnamese out of Thailand.'

'Shake hands with the Devil,' Sawyer murmured, almost to himself.

'Grow up, kiddo,' Barnes repeated. 'This is business. We're talking three, maybe four metric tonnes of one hundred per cent pure heroin, worth over two billion dollars – *wholesale*!'

'Why'd you need the money, Max? Her?' Sawyer asked, looking at Lady Caroline.

Barnes's face worked.

'How can I make you understand, amigo? Her husband treats her like shit. He's . . . well, sexual abuse. All kinds of stuff I don't even want to get into. But what can a mug like me offer her? The few bucks I can get out of Houlihan's and a Marine Corps pension? Are you kidding? One of her goddam Hermès handbags costs as much as I make in a couple of months. We're too old to start over with nothing, her and me. Sure, the money. You're goddam right, the money,' Barnes said bitterly.

'Love. The holy grail. Is that it, Max?'

'A new start, kiddo. For her and me,' Barnes said, his eyes shining in the lamplight.

'Maybe you should grow up, Max. Do you really think the local head of MI6 doesn't know where his wife spends her nights? Take a good look at her, you pathetic bastard. Do you really think she's going to wait around for the next twenty years till you get out of the Federal penitentiary?'

'You don't understand. We love each other,' Barnes insisted stubbornly.

'Look at her, Max! I can't believe you didn't see through that phoney dog-and-pony show she and her husband put on at the reception. For the Cambodian Committee, you jerk! Suong, the girl who saved me – she's with a splinter group of Mith Yon's KPNLF. They're trying to make the connection between the Americans and Bhun Sa. Don't you get it? Lady Caroline's the one who put the girl and Vasna-song together!' Sawyer said, shaking his head as if he couldn't believe Barnes didn't see it. 'They led you up the garden trail, Max. Harris finally admitted that London was the source on the Vietnamese, for Chrissakes. It originally came from their Bangkok station. God save the Empire! And what a coup for Sir Geoffrey! The cap on a brilliant career and home to England and the society where she belongs, where everyone has goddam Hermès handbags or whatever the hell it is Sloane Rangers are wearing these days.'

'You're wrong,' Barnes said, not looking up.

Sawyer stood up. 'I'm not going to shoot you, Max. Call it auld lang syne. You have a few minutes, till I get to a phone, to go to ground. It's either that or go back to Wash-ington, where they still think treason is a dirty word.'

Barnes just sat there as though he hadn't been listening. His face was grey and wasted.

'As for the lady, I think she's coming with me. It's her only way out,' Sawyer said, offering her his arm.

'She won't go, Jack. She loves me,' Barnes said, his voice so hollow it seemed to carry its own echo.

Lady Caroline got up with a silken swish of her dress and took Sawyer's arm. She wouldn't look at Barnes.

'Go away, Max. Hide. Don't let them find you,' Sawyer said.

They walked out and down the dark corridor together. When they got outside Sawyer detached himself from her. The street was deserted and silent in the night. He watched her face, looking for something, but he wasn't sure what. In the red glow from a neon sign her face looked enamelled, like her nails.

'Where can I find the girl, Suong?' Sawyer asked.

She looked amused. 'Don't tell me you've misplaced her?'

'They had a hang-yao waiting. Left me standing on the wharf. She was afraid. Didn't know who to trust.'

'Oh, that's bloody funny. The Great American who's got us all figured out – outsmarted by a woman!' She gave a forced laugh. It pealed in the dark street like a cry for help.

Sawyer stuck his hands in his pockets. How do they get that way? he wondered. These brittle upper-class women who can be as tireless a predator on one man as the vulture that daily fed on Prometheus's liver. He felt grateful that it was Max and not him who subscribed to the fantasy of Rich and Beautiful. He waited for the mockery to fade from her expression before he spoke.

'An American agent is being tortured right this minute by people who have so few qualms that they put three million of their own countrymen to death, lady. And Max isn't here to cover for you any more. So if you want to walk away from this in one piece, just answer the question.'

She bit her lip. He could see the awareness of her position starting to dawn on her. In Whitehall they used to say that when Washington sneezes, London catches cold.

'Aranyaprathet. The refugee camp,' she said in a low voice.

Sawyer nodded and started to walk away.

'Wait a minute,' she said, grabbing his arm. She squeezed close, her breasts pressed against him. 'Where are you going?'

Her eyes had a desperate, bruised look and it suddenly occurred to Sawyer that she was one of those women who know how to use men superbly but not how to function without them.

'As far away from you as I can,' he said, shaking her off. He began to walk down the street.

'Sawyer! Your turn will come, you bloody bastard!' she cried after him, her voice echoing in the night.

'Why not? Everyone else's has,' he tossed back over his shoulder.

'Sawyer!' he could hear her shriek as he turned the corner into Yawaraj Road. Streamers of swallows were perched on sagging telephone lines. It should have told him something, but he wasn't paying attention. Up ahead he could see the lights of an all-night market. The proprietor would have a phone he could use, he thought.

Just then something hit his forehead. It felt warm and wet and he had automatically started to brush it away like an insect before he realized what it was. He looked up. Bloated drops of rain were starting to fall through the light of a streetlamp.

A solid curtain of rain swept down the street as it does only in the tropics, instantly soaking him to the skin. He had left it too late.

The monsoon had begun.

PART TWO

The dragon rises from the deep.

CHAPTER 8

The earth covers the deep.
The superior man educates the
  people
making soldiers of the multitude.
The soldiers set forth under
  orders.

The village lay hidden in a fold in the hills. It was a Meo village by the look of it and a big one. Sawyer counted almost a hundred wooden huts on stilts, their roofs slanting steeply to turn the rain. It was well situated on an incline so the water would run down to a narrow gorge where, hundreds of feet below, the river, muddy and swollen with rain, wound through the bottom of the gorge. A snaking trail led down one side of the gorge to the only road, which ran alongside the river.

Sawyer studied the village with his binoculars through a gap in the pines. They had done it well, he thought. Leaving trees interspersed among the huts so the only way you could see it from the air was if you already knew it was there. Below the village enclosure were stepped fields cut into the slopes. The poppies were green and yellow; the time of the fourth cutting. The white petals that in the spring turned the fields into carpets of snow had long since fallen away. Now the hills were deep green and a heavy sky, the colour of pewter without the shine, lay over the village like a roof.

A black-clad sentry, who had foolishly given away his position by lighting a cheroot, sat behind a tree on a rise near the bamboo fence that enclosed the village.

'See, there,' the girl said, pointing at the sentry. From up here they could smell the rising smoke of his cheroot. Among the hill tribes it was said that a man with a good nose could smell cheroot smoke from across the Salween and name the village where the tobacco was grown.

'Meo. Two of them,' Sawyer whispered back and pointed his M-16 at a well camouflaged tree platform up the slope from the first sentry.

The girl nodded. 'Always two,' she agreed. 'But do not call them "Meo",' she corrected him, her eyes serious. 'This means "barbarian" and is a name given to them by the Chinese long ago. Ce n'est pas gentil, tu comprends? They call themselves "Hmong". This means "free men". You must make attention. Since the Thai Border Patrol came last year and burned the poppy fields to stop the opium trade, they do not like strangers.'

That was true enough, Sawyer thought. Even though the rains had already made the roads newly impassable, the villagers had blocked the road with giant logs in half a dozen places. And they had found traps of sharpened pungi sticks and vines strung neck-high along the hill trail.

'Is that your opium trader?' Sawyer asked, indicating the bamboo corral, where perhaps twenty mules and half as many plump Karen ponies were grazing.

She reached for the binoculars and adjusted the focus. 'Yes. Those are Burma-side ponies. And see there – the smoke from the hut of the headman. That means they are finished bargaining and are ready for rice and cha, green tea.'

She stood up and brushed the brown pine needles from the red-and-white checkered krama that she wore over her shoulders like a shawl.

'Wait here. I go ahead to tell them of your coming. A woman is less likely to be shot at than a farang with an M-16.'

Sawyer nodded. And from here, with the telescopic sight, he could cover her if she got into trouble.

She started towards the trail when he called softly after her. She looked back at him with those strange eyes, deep blue at the centre surrounded by black, and he tried to remember his excuse for calling. The real reason was to see her face again.

'This Thai opium smuggler. Can he be trusted?'

'Who can be trusted?' she replied softly and was gone.

He watched her climb gracefully down the steep slope, now and then raising the hem of her black phasin to step over a root or a pungi trap. She moved with confidence, finding her way as though she had been raised in this village. Watching her lithe figure through the binoculars, it was hard to believe that she was the same glamorous woman who'd sat across from him at dinner the night before last at the hotel in Chiang Mai.

'I knew you would find me,' she had said, the reflection of the table candles in the restaurant window shining around her hair like stars against the misty lights of the city below. She wore blue silk that matched her eyes, and Sawyer felt that curious mixture of self-satisfaction and unease a man feels when he's with not merely the most beautiful woman in the room but one who will not soon be forgotten by any man who sees her that night.

'How did you know?'

'I knew. Haven't you ever just known something without knowing how?'

'Yes,' he admitted. 'But it wasn't knowing. It was wanting.'

'Do you have to hear the words? Is that it? That I wanted you? Ah, les hommes.' She smiled, showing sharp, perfect little teeth.

And later that night in the dark hotel room, the sound of the rain against the window barely audible over the hum of the air conditioning, the whisper of silk as she came to him, putting her finger to his lips to keep him from speaking. She pressed her soft white breasts against his chest and stretched her legs against his. They swayed together, watching themselves and each other in the full-length mirror, enjoying the contrast of her ivory skin against his sun-darkened body. His lips glided over every part of her, thinking he had never touched anything so silky in his life. And then she was over him, her sleek black hair enclosing them like a tent, moving and then moving faster, crying out, 'Vite, ah, vite,' and later there were sounds and no words at all.

Afterwards, her head on his shoulder, her throaty voice murmuring in his ear like a conscience, 'C'est vrai, tu sais. When I saw you again at the camp, I knew.'

'Why me?'

She looked amused. 'Do you not understand women, my So-yah? We are drawn to power like iron filings to the magnet. You should have seen yourself when you entered the hut in the camp, dripping with rain, black patch for one eye, the other eye like fire and gun ready for killing, like a hawk among squabs. What woman could resist?'

'Some have managed,' he admitted.

'Pah! Scaredy women!' She snorted. 'A woman in a fire wants safety of the nest. A woman safe in the nest wants to play with fire. True man, who can offer both nest and fire, can have any woman in the world.'

'Is that what your look meant?' he asked, remembering how she had looked up at him when he had entered the hut after searching the muddy refugee camps till a small boy in the Khao-I-Dang camp who had lost a foot to a mine led him to the right hut for ten baht and a cigarette, the light from the lamp shining like candles in her eyes.

'My look mean I see you and I see my karma,' she said.

Sawyer held her close, thinking how lucky it was that she had felt something because when he had entered the hut there were about a dozen of them already putting down their rice bowls and reaching for their weapons, when she had said, 'No!' sharply in Khmer, all the while looking at him with that strange, wild look of hers that was like no one else's. And yet strangely familiar. He knew he had never seen her before, no way to forget that face, but there was something about it that rang a bell somewhere. An earlier life, the Buddhists would say.

A young man with hard eyes, whom Sawyer later learned was the rebel leader, Mith Yon, pointed an AKM, which he must have got from a dead enemy because it still had the symbol of the RPK painted on the stock, straight at Sawyer's belly. For a moment no one moved. They listened to the rain clattering on the tin roof like pebbles.

'Vous vous êtes trompés . . .' the young man began, when the girl interrupted with a torrent of Khmer that Sawyer couldn't understand except for the odd phrase. Something about 'the one' and 'the warehouse' maybe.

Sawyer saw recognition come into the young man's eyes. But the rifle was still pointed at him.

'I owe you a life. If I owe you more than one, you will have to wait till the next life for repayment,' Sawyer said, going from French to Thai.

'That is truth,' someone said.

'With joss that is too long to wait,' another cackled and the others began to smile.

The young man shook his head obstinately. 'If my brother wishes to become old, he will learn not to give trust so easily,' the young man snapped over his shoulder.

But he wasn't going to shoot any more. They could all feel it, and one of them even picked up his rice bowl again.

'Why did you run away at the warehouse?' Sawyer asked the girl.

'To be certain you were the one,' she said, coming between the AKM and Sawyer. She touched the young man's arm and he lowered the weapon. There was something proprietary in the touch that made Sawyer wonder if they were sleeping together and if maybe part of what was happening was jealousy. Sawyer deliberately resisted looking at her so as not to provoke him. A jealous twenty-five-year-old with a gun was no joke. 'How else could we know that you were the one we had been told to expect? That Vasnasong-kha had already lied about the first American farang. And look what happened to him! Il est tombé entre les mains des Khmers Rouges,' she said, and despite the danger he couldn't help looking at her. 'We knew only a true CIA man could find me,' she added as though it were not only a test to confirm his bona fides but an article of faith, just as only the true prince can pull the sword from the stone, and he knew then that they would be lovers. But he had to defuse the young man's jealousy, if that's what it was.

'We have a common enemy in the Vietnamese. That is a good basis for friendship,' Sawyer said to Mith Yon.

'That is truth,' the same voice as before called out.

Mith Yon lowered his rifle, all at once looking very young. But his eyes were still suspicious. 'You will to sii bay with us.' Gesturing for Sawyer to come and sit.

The girl scooped a bowl of rice from the pot and they made a place for him. 'I will take you to Bhun Sa,' she said, her strange eyes unreadable as she handed him the rice.

That night Sawyer had a final rdv with Harris before going

back to the camp in a rented Isuzu to pick up Suong. The meeting had to be hastily arranged, and the best they could do was the back room of a Honda motor-scooter shop in Aranyaprathet, whose Cambodian owner, a swarthy former army officer who had managed to get away before the débâcle, accepted payment only in gold, rubies, opium, chickens and sexual favours – the currencies of life here.

Harris gave him the pack and the equipment he had requested. As Sawyer went over the equipment, the concealed transmitter, the gold links and dust, the stubby Ingram M-10 – he had dumped the Beretta in the Chao Phraya river at the first chance – and sound suppressor, the M-16, Harris briefed him on the latest updates in the 'Three Cs': Communications, Codes and Cut-outs. He told Harris about the girl. Harris told him about the SR-71 Blackbird they now had flying unseen, unheard, twenty miles straight up, almost directly overhead. The Blackbird's infra-red cameras and sophisticated radio equipment had reported a sharp increase in Vietnamese military activity across the border.

The rain drummed against a small window they had covered with a black rag. Harris told him they would keep a Blackbird up on a round-the-clock basis to monitor the situation and to pick up any message Sawyer could get out in case of emergency. For back-up they had secretly moved the Delta Force to an out-of-bounds area of Clark Field in the Philippines. They were now on stand-by alert.

They're scared, Sawyer thought. They're really scared. 'What about the Limeys? Sir Whatsis and Countess Dracula?' he asked.

'Don't worry. They won't get near the "coconuts".' Harris mulishly insisted on this term for heroin, as though that kind of crap would fool a CTP trainee.

'And Vasnasong?' Sawyer looked curiously at Harris.

'We're leaving him in place for the time being. There are reasons . . . ,' Harris said, a little too casually, Sawyer thought, and he started to get a bad feeling. But he pushed it away. Harris was within his rights as the senior case officer for the op. They never did tell you everything. Less baggage to carry.

'What about Barnes?'

Harris made a face. 'You think we're all a bunch of wimps back in Washington, don't you?' he said quietly.

It sent chills down Sawyer's spine. He didn't say anything.

'Houlihan's won't be the same without him,' Harris sighed. 'Everyone was shocked. But they gave him quite a send-off. Like the old days. Asian go-go girls. The works. Shame you had to miss it.'

That was how he learned that Barnes was dead.

The next day, after using every switch in the book through the murderous Bangkok traffic to flush any tails just to be safe, though Sawyer knew that where they were going no tail could follow unnoticed, they sat by the window of the first-class couchettes express to Chiang Mai, watching the jade-green hills and rice paddies racketing by. He waited until he had checked out their compartment and the rest of the car before he finally asked what he couldn't delay asking any longer.

'You led Parker to the sampan, didn't you?'

'To meet someone who would take him to Bhun Sa,' she nodded. 'But when I saw no one aboard I feared betrayal and hid myself.'

'Where?'

'In a space behind un faux side of boat. It is common in sampan for smuggling.'

'A false bulkhead.'

'Oui, c'est ça.'

'How did you find it?'

A smile dimpled her cheeks. 'I was born on sampan, elder brother. My father was French rice merchant, my mother sampan girl, but so pretty he keep her like wife in big apartment in Phnom Penh.'

'And Parker?'

'I heard him come on sampan. Then others came and took him away. They were Khmers Rouges.'

'How do you know they were KR?'

She turned towards the window. The train rattled past a village. Bamboo huts, a rustic pagoda, a peasant boy riding a water buffalo flashed by the window and were gone. She didn't look at him when she finally spoke. 'Once you have heard the voice of angkar, elder brother, you do not forget.'

That night, drowsy from the rhythm of the train, he fell

asleep on his sleeper bunk beneath hers. Some sound, something woke him. Instantly the Ingram was in his hand. He found himself pointing it in her face.

'I am unarmed. See for yourself,' she said, dropping her slip to the floor and standing naked before him, swaying to the movement of the train. She was tall for an Asian, perhaps five foot six and perfectly made. Unbound, her hair was long and sleek and very black against the whiteness of her skin. White and black. Ivory and onyx, he thought as she came to him for the first time, and even then he knew it was how he would always think of her. Ivory and onyx. She stepped into the circle of his arms, soft, pliant, her eyes shining and he knew he could do anything he wanted with her. Then, telling himself he was a fool but knowing he couldn't afford to make a mistake, he forced himself to push her away.

'What of Mith Yon?'

She raised her head and looked at him curiously. 'What is that to us?'

'He acted jealous. I thought you . . . and he . . . ,' he finished lamely.

She made a face. 'I love Mith Yon like elder brother. If he wanted me for pleasure, I would give him. Gladly. This he knows, but it makes nothing. Mith Yon is a man, but he cannot be a man with a woman. The angkar, they did things to him, tu comprends?'

'What things?'

'You do not want to know,' she said, not looking at him.

She shivered. He held her tightly against him until the shivering subsided. They stood naked, moving with the motion of the train. Raindrops skidded, slanting across the window. The train rocked them against each other, the touch of flesh making warmth and then it began. The old tickle and she made an awkward move and then the exquisite sliding, locking them together. The rhythm of the train became their rhythm and both of them conscious of every sensation, the air moist and warm as a kiss, the sound of the rain and the wheels moving under them, the jasmine smell of her skin, and then the moving growing wilder, more intense and they tumbled on to the bunk, hard now, pounding against her, no more tenderness, only the ache to be deeper and deeper inside her. She pulled him to her, tearing at his skin with her nails, and he felt the scorching heat of her. The tempo rose rhythmic and harder and she moved desperately against him as if she could never have enough of him, both of them moving faster, wilder, the tingle at the peak and she cried out as they slid down the far side, still grinding away at each other, as if to drain the very last drop, until they were still at last.

'I have to know,' he said later, and when she asked why, he just shrugged.

She smiled ruefully. 'Thoughts spoken are like wine corks, my So-yah. Once aired, they will no longer fit back in the bottle,' she said, and finally told him of Mith Yon and Tuol Sleng prison. How they attached electrodes to that which made him a man but left his hand free to work a switch that controlled electric wires attached to his mother, stripped naked and spreadeagled like a whore. They forced him to stare at her sagging breasts and her face dark with shame. They told him the only way to avoid the pain was to give it to her. And why should he not? the cadre demanded. Familial ties have no place in the new Kampuchea.

To this Mith Yon said nothing, but in his heart, he later told Suong, he could only stare at the cadre, a boy of eighteen perhaps, and wonder how the boy had so quickly managed to forget what it is to be human. 'I am the imperialist agent. Not this old woman, who knows nothing,' Mith Yon told them with quiet dignity.

Suong frowned. This because Mith Yon's words, she said, had the ring not of words spoken but of words he wished he had said. But no matter what he really said, the cadre merely smiled, as though at a child's meaningless babble. Mith Yon remembered the smile.

Everyone in Tuol Sleng knew of Mith Yon. How he had withstood hours of it, till he was screaming if the cadre so much as smiled, until at last his twitching hand, almost by itself, gave her the first small shock and how it ended by him electrocuting his own mother.

For a long time neither of them said anything. They listened to the wheels on the tracks, and when they kissed it was because they had to, like climbers on a ledge desperately clutching each other because there is nothing else to grab. They might have slept. Sawyer wasn't sure.

'Why have you come, my So-yah?' she asked finally, her head on his chest, listening to the strong beat of his heart.

'My job. To help freedom fighters.'

'Ah, freedom fighters. What is that?' she teased.

'Anyone who kills Communists is a freedom fighter. Anyone who kills non-Communists is a terrorist,' he teased back.

'Why not say the truth? You job is to make one group of, how you say, "gook" kill other "gook" for benefit of American. No?'

'Yes, but it's never difficult to get people to kill each other. We just add technology to make it more efficient. For the benefit of America, as you say,' he agreed, letting his fingers trace the outline of her breasts, feeling the nipples grow taut and erect.

'No, wait,' she said, stopping his hand for a moment. 'You do not answer my question. I do not ask why America help us. I ask why *you* do this job.'

Sawyer paused. He wasn't given to introspection and he didn't have an answer ready. Finally he began haltingly, as if groping his way in the dark.

'It sounds . . . I don't know . . . naïve. But then, one person's politics always sound ridiculous to someone who doesn't share his point of view. America may be civilization's last hope . . . but, like all democracies, America has a fatal flaw. We don't solve problems, we debate them. Like Hamlet, we never act until it's too late. Sometimes, someone just has to do something.'

'You lie to yourself if you think that,' she said.

He reddened and was glad it was too dark for her to see it.

'Oh,' she said, clapping her hand to her mouth. 'That is most terrible kreng chai. Your little sister is silly fool and begs forgiveness.' She bowed her head.

He took her chin in his hand and raised her head. 'You can drop the little Asian girl crap, Suong. It isn't what you want of me. It isn't what I want of you. And besides, neither of us believes it, do we?'

She shook her head, not looking at him.

'Now, why don't you tell me what you really think?' he

said, turning her chin to force her to look at him. A passing signal light lit her face like a flare.

'You are most vain, my So-yah. The world makes you sad. So you seek to prove to God that you could make the world better than he. That is why you have come,' she said, her words striking home with enough force for him to feel truth in them.

'A fool's errand, then?'

'No, not a fool. You see most clearly, my one-eyed lord,' she said fiercely, her mouth upon his.

Now, watching her as she scampered into the open and made the wai sign to the Hmong sentry with the cheroot, he could still taste her on his lips. She spoke to the sentry, and after a time he stood up and elaborately scratched his crotch before gesturing for her to enter the village enclosure. He followed behind her, his eyes never straying from the sway of her hips till they disappeared into the headman's hut.

It began to drizzle. Sawyer made an instant lean-to out of two sticks covered by a giant alocassia leaf. He lay prone on the pine needles and zeroed in on the headman's hut with his sight. After a while she came out again. With her was a man in black peasant's pants and a dark shirt over a white tee-shirt, wearing a curious knitted cap with an upturned brim that reminded Sawyer of a pork-pie hat. He wore an American-made M-79 grenade launcher slung across his back. Sawyer assumed he was the Thai smuggler.

He could see him clearly through the sight; no need to switch to the binoculars. The Thai was squat and bandy-legged. He had a round face with thick eyebrows that pointed out and up from the centre like those of the Devil. He had a round head set close on broad, round shoulders, and his hands were black with dirt or opium paste and looked very strong. His eyes were protruding, and although his thick sensual lips were smiling broadly at the girl, the eyes were not smiling at all.

Then she turned and made a beckoning gesture to Sawyer. The man looked up in his direction and Sawyer got reluctantly to his feet, wishing she hadn't done it and knowing that once she had he could no longer stay where he was. He slung both their packs over one shoulder and carrying the

127

M-16 with the safety off in his free hand, made his way down to the corral where they stood waiting.

'This is the trader we speak of. His name Toonsang. He is much known in these parts. Most good trader. He says he goes to trade with Bhun Sa now. He takes us with him for eight chi of gold plus four chi for use of ponies. Half now, half when we see Bhun Sa,' she said.

Hearing this, the trader nodded his head in agreement, displaying his betel-stained teeth in a broad smile that made Sawyer want to check his pocket to see if his wallet was still there.

'Why you want go see Bhun Sa, hey?' Toonsang asked, still grinning. He spoke the Northern Thai, called Thai Isan.

'To trade, what else?' Sawyer grinned back.

Toonsang thought this a huge joke and slapped the corral rail in appreciation.

Well, this is a jolly one, Sawyer thought, his uneasiness growing. Toonsang's laugh subsided and his eyes narrowed.

'The price is agreed?' he demanded.

Sawyer calculated mentally. A chi was 3.75 grams of gold, so twelve chi was about five hundred dollars' worth, but if he didn't object they would be suspicious.

'The price is outrageous and this one will not pay,' Sawyer said, slapping his chest in mock outrage.

'Not pay! Not pay!' cried the aggrieved trader in a high-pitched tone, looking wildly around as if unable to believe his ears. 'By the phi you will pay what is agreed!'

'By the chao, I will not,' Sawyer said, letting the M-16 hang loosely down, not to threaten, simply to remind Toonsang that it was there.

Toonsang's eyes blinked once like a camera shutter. 'Your woman agreed to the price,' he muttered sullenly, not taking his eyes off the M-16.

'Did you?' Sawyer turned angrily on Suong.

She hung her head. 'Yes, my lord. Forgive this worthless one.'

'Your word will make a pauper of me,' Sawyer growled. Then to Toonsang: 'I will honour this worthless female's word though, by the phi, it goes hard. But only half now, as was said. Have you scales?' He pulled a small leather sack of gold links and dust from around his neck.

'Inside. All is inside, younger brother. Also kow and cha for guest,' Toonsang said, grinning widely as before and bowing them ahead of him. Not 'honoured guest', Sawyer noted, which a Thai used even if he were just lighting a stranger's cigarette, and 'younger brother', which was always used for an inferior.

'I am more elder than you,' Sawyer said in a joking way, not to force the issue but to let Toonsang know that he understood the insult.

'Nay, nay. Only a young stallion can service such a mare,' Toonsang cackled, roguishly rolling his eyes at Suong as he urged them up the bamboo ladder to the headman's hut.

The headman's hut, which also doubled as a guest house and tavern, was a single long room, of bamboo and teak, with a high, steeply sloping thatched roof. The hut had one side open to a porch on the east side, to permit light yet provide shade from the afternoon heat. A large iron pot, containing the sticky Lao-style rice of the northern hills, sat on a hearth near the centre, and around it half a dozen of Toonsang's ruffians were eating rice and washing it down with rice beer. These were of different races – Thai, Karen, Akha, one with a Kachin turban, a tattooed Shan – but of one type. They were all heavily armed with automatic weapons and bandoliers of ammunition criss-crossed on their chests.

The headman himself was seated at a low bamboo table near the west wall. The headman had an amiable face that, like those of many of the Hmong, could have been pure Chinese. He wore a black robe and skullcap and, around his waist, his 'trading-day' white sash. He was drinking cha served by a female dressed in the black turban and red sash of the Hmong women. Also on the table were an abacus and a balance scale for weighing gold.

Another female served rice beer to four young Hmong men in black squatting by the western wall, not seeming to be doing anything, though their rifles were close at hand, making Sawyer feel a touch less conspicuous with his M-16. He laid the packs on the ground near the table, slung the carbine across his shoulder and made the wai sign to the headman.

'Sawat dee khrap,' Sawyer said.

'And to you, honoured guest,' the headman said, gesturing for Sawyer to sit and take cha.

Sawyer sat facing Toonsang's men, implicitly placing himself under the headman's protection. The Hmong would never attack while he was under their roof. He wasn't so sure about Toonsang. He laid the M-16 across the packs, within easy reach. Suong scuttled to a corner to wait. As a female she had no place at the table. Toonsang, an impudent grin on his face, came over and sat at the table with his back to the open porch, as if to show that he hadn't an enemy in the world. A Hmong woman brought them bowls of rice, but Sawyer motioned her to wait.

'Later, with your permission, uncle,' to the headman. 'I owe this man,' indicating Toonsang, 'six chi of gold and would first pay my debts.'

The headman nodded as though appreciative of such prudence. He had a good face, lined with age but alight with curiosity at the unexpected appearance of a European in his village. They weighed out the gold and afterwards Sawyer added an extra chi for the headman. Toonsang's eyes narrowed as he watched the headman take his gold.

'For rice beer for all, and also rice cakes to take,' Sawyer explained.

'Younger brother is most generous,' Toonsang growled.

'I like to make friends,' Sawyer smiled.

'Any man who seeks Bhun Sa needs all the friends he can find,' Toonsang said loudly and Sawyer couldn't tell if he were bragging or simply announcing Sawyer's obituary. At the mention of Bhun Sa's name, the hut grew very quiet.

'Has the honourable stranger met Bhun Sa?' the headman asked.

Sawyer shook his head.

'Ah!' the headman clicked his tongue and said no more. It reminded Sawyer of when Brother Rap had asked a gung-ho captain straight from Fort Benning if he'd been in 'Nam before. When the captain had said no and he didn't see that it made a goddam bit of difference, Brother Rap had said, 'Yeah!' in exactly the same tone, meaning this one won't be around long enough to worry about. And, sure enough, on the captain's first patrol his back-pack caught on a twig. The captain twisted around to free it and the grenade it was attached to blew his head off.

The Hmong women brought them bowls brimming with rice beer and, as the other men were served, the silence that had been there since Bhun Sa's name had been mentioned was broken by the low hum of conversation.

'Wealth and long life,' the headman toasted and they drank.

'Bhun Sa, eh?' Toonsang grinned. He wiped his mouth on the back of his sleeve and watched them both, an amused glint in his eyes.

'What manner of man is he?' Sawyer asked.

'A friendly man. He has only friends, hey?' Toonsang called out, looking over at his men, and was answered by coarse laughter. 'Know why he has only friends, younger brother?' Toonsang's eyes were dancing. 'Because,' not waiting for Sawyer to respond, 'he kills all his enemies!'

Toonsang guffawed so hard at his own joke he almost fell down. Sawyer and the headman looked at each other.

'Have you met Bhun Sa?' he asked the headman.

'To know the servant of the prince is to know the prince,' the headman said, glancing over towards Toonsang, who finished his beer and clapped his hands for another bowl.

The women brought beer and rice with chicken, the head going to Toonsang and the comb to Sawyer, as honoured guests. As custom dictated, Toonsang loudly crunched the head as a sign for them to proceed. Toonsang drank the strong beer steadily and by the time they finished, his small round eyes were swimming. Sawyer gave a long polite belch and the headman smiled.

'Perhaps a pipe later?' the headman offered.

'A ten thousand of thanks, no, uncle.'

'A vow?' the headman inquired delicately.

'Not even, uncle. Only prudence. A trader who is his own customer will see his profit go up in smoke.'

'By the phi, there is truth,' Toonsang said thickly, slapping his thigh with a blow that cracked like a whip.

'You trade the opium, then?' the headman asked.

Sawyer shook his head. 'I buy the bricks of white powder that comes from the opium, uncle. Only bricks and only

131

large quantities from such as Bhun Sa,' Sawyer said hurriedly to forestall their own interest in doing business.

The headman looked at Sawyer with sharp curiosity. 'There are whispers in the hills that Bhun Sa has amassed a mountain of opium. Much of the second and the third cuttings of the Three Lands. It is said he has melted these into the white bricks of which our honoured guest speaks and has hidden them away. Though there are those who do not believe of the tale,' he cautioned.

'Do the whispers tell where the white bricks are hidden?' Sawyer asked.

The headman sat still, the only movement the blinking of his eyes. 'This no living man can say.'

Toonsang rubbed his hand across his mouth. 'This of a mountain of white bricks is women's chatter. It would take more gold than our younger brother's twelve of chi to buy so much,' he growled, glancing over at Sawyer's pack.

Sawyer's smile was deliberate. 'Gold can be stolen. Prudent men can find other things of value to trade.'

'What things? Your woman?' Toonsang demanded, a snigger in his voice.

For an instant all eyes turned towards the corner where Suong squatted, motionless as a statue. The headman frowned, but said nothing. This was a place of business and anyone may make an offer for goods on display.

'What say, younger brother? I make you fair trade for the woman. I give you back the six chi plus ten joi of opium and a good Kachin pony. All this and you are saved the expense of the trip to Bhun Sa,' Toonsang offered, a lopsided grin splitting his face like an overripe fruit.

'The woman is not for sale,' Sawyer replied, a sickly feeling in the pit of his stomach.

The room was very still. Sawyer could hear the creak of wood as someone shifted their weight, but he couldn't see who it was because he couldn't afford to take his eyes off Toonsang. He could hear the sound of breathing and the whisper of wind in the pines outside. His hand edged down towards the M-16. He was thankful he had kept the safety off.

'Yah, and friends should not haggle. Say twenty joi and

132

be damned.' Toonsang smiled, staring at Sawyer with eyes that had no drunkenness in them.

Sawyer's hand closed on the grip of the carbine. 'To the ghoul spirits with your twenty joi. The woman is not for sale,' Sawyer said, his voice tight. All around him he could sense men reaching for their weapons.

As if only just now realizing what was happening, Toonsang shook his head as though to clear it. 'Nay, nay, younger brother. I meant no dishonour, only a fair offer,' he whined, raising both hands, the fingers splayed apart, to show he held no weapon.

'Take your offer to the clapped-up night chickens of Mae Lai,' Sawyer snapped, naming the border town whose ramshackle brothels were frequented by smugglers and soldiers from all over the Golden Triangle.

'We will, we will! Clap and all!' Toonsang cackled, and a burst of coarse laughter eased the tension. The room once more sounded to conversation.

As a peace offering, Toonsang held out a chew of betel mixed with ground lime and wrapped in a leaf and, when Sawyer declined, shrugged and took a bite.

'Women on a trip are a cause of much difficulty,' the headman observed, accepting a chew from Toonsang now that it was over.

'Women are a cause of difficulty anywhere.' Toonsang turned and spat. The headman nodded sagely.

'How long will it take us to reach Bhun Sa?' Sawyer asked, wanting to get off the subject of women. The effect Suong had on men was scary and it was throwing a monkey wrench into the mission like nothing he had ever seen.

'Who can say? He is maybe Burma-side? Maybe Lao-side? Where does the tiger sleep?' Toonsang grinned oafishly and this time Sawyer was sure he wasn't the fool he pretended to be. Knowing how long it would take to reach Bhun Sa might be an indication of where he was.

'Wherever he likes,' Sawyer replied.

Toonsang guffawed and the Hmong tittered among themselves. At least that was better than the first time he had heard the joke, Sawyer remembered. Brother Rap had told it at the Continental Shelf terrace-bar in Saigon, only then the question had been, 'Where does a six-hundred-pound gorilla sit?' They had all laughed until a REMF captain at the next table had said, with a drawl that stretched all the way back to Alabama, 'If Ah was a nigger, Ah wouldn't be telling no jokes about no big black gorillas, boy,' and Sawyer had to grab Rap to keep him from taking the captain out then and there. 'He's an officer, man. That's just what he wants you to do,' Sawyer had breathed in Rap's ear. Later they stalked the captain through the streets back to his apartment, Rap getting close enough to drop a 'frag' in the captain's bedroom before Sawyer managed to talk him out of it.

'Make it count,' he had told Rap, who wound up spending the remainder of his R 'n' R in Soul Alley, a tawdry neon ghetto near the Tan Son Nhut airbase, eating fried chicken, flying high on Buddha grass and taking trips behind with the disease-ravaged Vietnamese girls who weren't pretty enough to make it on Tu Do Street. Sawyer finally came to collect him at Mama Jo's, where they used to hang the red, black and green striped flag of the Black Liberation Front behind the bar and where the MPs never came because the last time they had tried to move in, Mama Jo, a six-foot-four former linebacker, now a permanent AWOL, had greeted them with a blast from a twelve-gauge shotgun.

'Ain't going back, man. It's a fucking white man's war,' Rap had said.

'I'm a white man,' Sawyer had said.

'Then fuck you too.'

'OK,' Sawyer had said and started to go, and then Rap had sighed and slid off the bar stool.

'Fuck it, I'm coming.'

And Mama Jo, light gleaming through the bluish haze of marijuana smoke from the gold ring in his nostril, had simply shrugged and muttered, 'Dumb nigger.'

Sawyer remembered how even when they were back in Indian country Brother Rap always talked about looking the captain up when they got back to the world. He concocted all sorts of ingenious revenges, but they came to nothing because Rap never did make it back.

The headman smiled at the success of Sawyer's joke. 'Even so, honoured guest. Only enter the land of Bhun Sa and if you do not find him, he will find you.'

'And pay him with what, younger brother?' Toonsang wanted to know. 'By the phi, I will bring you safely to Bhun Sa, but be warned against playing these European tricks as the reaching for your rifle with Bhun Sa. You have already lost the one eye.'

So he had caught that, Sawyer thought. Well, perhaps it was for the best that they knew he didn't trust them.

'I still have two of something else,' Sawyer said quietly.

'So speaks a man!' exclaimed the headman and there was a murmur of approval from the Hmong.

'Even so. It will be good to have our younger brother's rifle with us on our journey,' Toonsang agreed. 'But it is more than idle curiosity that prompts my question. If what you bring to Bhun Sa arouses his displeasure, all our lives may be forfeit,' he argued.

'This is truth,' the headman agreed, unable to suppress the curiosity in his own eyes.

Sawyer sighed as if conceding the justice of their request. If he couldn't convince Toonsang that what he had in his pack wasn't worth stealing, the mission was over.

'I have arms to trade for the bricks of the morphine. In these packs is not gold but books with pictures of different kinds of weapons and papers for the trading.'

'Pah, only pictures!' Toonsang turned and spat a stream of juice red as blood.

'Have you no guns with you? This would be of interest to us,' the headman said. The young Hmong began to speak among themselves.

'Only a few piddling things for personal use. Of little value,' Sawyer shrugged.

'And if we wanted to buy?' the headman persisted, sensing the restlessness of his young men.

'And I too, by the phi!' Toonsang objected.

Sawyer smiled. It was what he had been waiting for. 'It would be my honour and pleasure to trade with you – upon my safe return,' he said.

'Then it is as a thing that is well and done,' Toonsang declared heartily, slapping the table like a judge with a gavel.

There was a stir as everyone got up to leave. Although the clouds were low and threatening, there were still at least three hours of daylight left for travel. Sawyer grabbed his M-16 and one of the packs and gave the other to the woman.

'Tu comprends ce qu'il faut faire,' she whispered as he handed her the pack, her disconcerting eyes looking through him. And as if he could read her mind, no, as if they were one mind, he knew not only what she meant but that he thought the same.

As they loaded the mules, Toonsang cast a rueful eye at the pack Sawyer was tying on to his pony and said, 'Only pictures after all, eh, younger brother?' as if the joke was on him.

'See for yourself,' Sawyer shrugged, knowing they didn't believe him. Anyone seeking to buy a mountain of morphine, if such a thing was possible, would have to be carrying something of great value in his pack. Without saying it, the woman had told him quite explicitly what had to be done.

At the first opportunity, he would have to kill Toonsang.

CHAPTER 9

Fire above heaven.
The wealthy man represses evil
    and honours good.
The large wagon
has a full load.

The moon wore a ghostly halo as it broke through the haze. The silvery light revealed the giant carved head atop the stone gateway, the face of the god a hazy white as if it were on a negative. A tendril of vegetation made a diagonal scar from the forehead to the chin, dividing the face into two unequal parts. Without a word, the soldiers took up positions by the gateway, joining the long columns of stone gods on either side of the road guarding the way into the ancient city.

Only then, when the soldiers had disappeared into the shadows, did a single dark figure emerge to stand alone in the centre of the road that was white as snow in the pale light. By some trick of the light the figure's face was almost a mirror image of the god's face, though few saw it. For rarely, even among his own soldiers, did any dare look directly upon the face of Son Lot.

Yet, conscious of their eyes, he strode like a conqueror through the deep shadows of the vaulting gateway into the empty city. He walked down the great roadway, the paving stones long since crumpled and broken. Once he heard something and turned, but it was only the flutter of the bats coming out to hunt. No one had followed him into the city. He was alone.

He walked through the empty streets, intricately carved galleries and towers looming on all sides. He found a high place and looked around at the shadowy ruins. A thousand years ago this place had been the centre of the universe. 'And will be again,' the voice of his other self whispered to him, and he shivered.

'But there are so many imponderables,' he told the voice.

'You have a prisoner,' the voice insinuated.

'Parker has told us all he knows. We have opened his head like a can of sardines.' He thought of Parker's screams. *Pranh! We were friends, for God's sake!* Parker had begged. *What children you white men are. Is the fact that we knew each other once supposed to make me betray the Revolution?* he had said.

'Parker has not told you all he knows, merely all he thinks he knows. Surely you can persuade him,' the voice mocked. It held an echo, like the lonely sound of his footsteps in the darkness.

He went down an old stone stairway and walked on until he came to the place he sought. A temple ruin, among a thousand other temples in the city, overgrown with vegetation. The temple was smaller than most and very old. He climbed the broken steps, the centres worn smooth and concave from centuries of bare feet, and came to where an ancient altar had once stood under a soaring dome, the roof now broken and open to the sky.

The wind whistled through the chinks and around the corners. It spoke in voices a thousand years old. The intricately carved stone walls were hidden by the darkness, and statues of gods far older than the Buddha stood in the silent dust of centuries like an army of shadows.

Then one of the shadows moved.

'Where is it?' Son Lot demanded, his voice sounding harsh even in his own ears.

'This way,' the figure said and led Son Lot down a passageway behind the altar. It was narrow and dark and they had to feel their way. The air was stale, lifeless. It smelled like a tomb. There were a number of turnings down side passages, and if Son Lot had not been following, he would have lost his way. Then he saw the light of a single candle gleaming from a subterranean passage at the bottom of a stone staircase.

They went down the stairs and into a large stone storeroom, packed floor to ceiling with thousands of wooden cases. Now the air had a medicinal smell. A squad of heavily armed soldiers lounged around the room, their eyes on the two who had just come in. Son Lot's companion grabbed a wooden case at random, took out a knife and prised it open. Inside was a single, large, white brick imprinted with the number '999', the raised numbers obviously done in a hand press. The man broke off a corner of the brick with his knife. He crumpled it to white powder with his fingers and held it out to Son Lot.

'This is the morphine base. It makes the heroin of an unbelievable purity. In this room are three thousands and nine hundreds of boxes, each of which contains one kilo. In this room is wealth enough to defeat our enemies a ten of times over,' Bhun Sa said.

Son Lot took a pinch of powder in his hand, looking curiously at it for a moment. 'A curious weapon,' he smiled. 'Lenin was right. The imperialists themselves will sell us the rope with which we will hang them,' he said and blew the powder on his fingers away like a dandelion.

'My men will guard here; yours outside the city walls.'

'It is as agreed.'

Bhun Sa looked at Son Lot, his eyes hiding in ambush under his long, dark eyebrows. 'Only a most foolish man would think to take the morphine for himself, comrade general. For such a one would have no one to trade with and, worse, he would be caught between my displeasure and the fury of the dog-eaters.'

'That would be most foolish,' Son Lot agreed smoothly. 'It is too dangerous for you to keep the morphine powder on your side of the border, too dangerous for me to take the arms we need on my side, where they might fall into the dog-eaters' accursed hands. Like all good agreements, ours is based upon a mutual dislike of the alternatives.'

Bhun Sa smiled, a crease deepening along the lines of an old scar on his cheek. 'As it is said, the superior man sees where his own interest lies. But we have lived long enough to see the wheel of karma turn strangely many a time, and men are not always wise. While we know that the comrade general is far-seeing, yet it may happen that some foolish subordinate who lacks the comrade general's great wisdom may try to take by force what is not his to take.'

'A rash and dangerous act,' Son Lot said.

'Most rash,' Bhun Sa agreed. 'To prevent just such a foolishness we have planted plastique of a sufficiency to destroy not only the morphine but the very temple around it. An attack would be both suicidal and pointless.'

'A prudent measure. The Lord of the Shan is most wise. But could ordinary men be trusted to carry out such an order? For it would mean their own deaths, would it not? Perhaps such men could be corrupted?' Son Lot smiled as he glanced around the room at Bhun Sa's men.

'These are of proven loyalty,' Bhun Sa replied airily, 'and hardly likely to sell their three khwan upon the word of an armed stranger. Yet the world is a cruel place and even the strongest may falter. Knowing this, I have taken hostages of each of these as an added precaution. These hostages would be the first to feel my displeasure.' Bhun Sa smiled.

Son Lot could sense a shudder passing through the room like a cold draught. Bhun Sa's cruelty was legendary.

'Then it is settled,' Son Lot said heartily. 'Do you go back shortly?'

'There are matters to which I must attend. Fuk Wa of the Kuomintang has had the impertinence to nibble like a mouse at our opium trade. This has aroused my displeasure.'

'Then hurry, for the time is short. Each day the strength of the dog-eaters grows in the hills and along the Mekong,' Son Lot said, then slyly, 'Where comes a buyer for such a quantity of the white powder?'

Bhun Sa smiled. 'Where there is honey, the flies are sure to gather,' he said.

CHAPTER 10

Fire over the marsh.
The superior man allows
    variations within the norm.
If he meets bad men
he can speak with them.

They could hear the crashing of gears from around the bend as the trucks downshifted to take the hill. For an instant Sawyer's and Toonsang's eyes found each other and then once again they sighted their weapons down at the road. Through the trees Sawyer could see a good stretch of the muddy road as it wound its way through the narrow defile below them.

Toonsang held his M-79 grenade launcher ready. From across the road the Kachin had signalled four vehicles coming, two jeeps and two trucks with soldiers. With the vehicles having to crawl slowly up the incline and men with automatic weapons on both sides of the defile, it should be like shooting fish in a barrel, Sawyer reasoned, still hoping the soldiers would pass them by. Even with a good ambush, there would be a lot of shooting and an unlucky bullet could do a lot of damage to the mission. Worse, they would have announced their presence here to the world.

The growl of the engines grew louder and Sawyer held his finger, light as breath, on the trigger as the first jeep crawled into view. It carried an officer and two men, one a driver and one manning a mounted M-60 machine-gun. They wore the dark-green camouflage uniforms and black berets of the Thai Rangers. They were anxiously scanning from side to side as the jeep lurched drunkenly through the slimy ruts deep as furrows. The officer looked straight up at where Sawyer was and he resisted the panicky impulse to duck. The hills were heavily forested with teak and bush and the officer would have to be Daniel Boone himself to spot anything, Sawyer reassured himself, holding his breath.

As the first jeep went by, the second came into their field of fire. They watched it slipping sideways, wheels spinning in the mud, and the soldiers getting ready to jump out. The whine of the transmission grew louder. Sawyer's grip tightened and then it was all right as the four-wheel-drive caught and the jeep spurted ahead. Sawyer could see a smile break out on the soldier's sweaty faces and shared a quick breath of relief with them as the trucks began to rumble by. Wide-eyed Rangers, their automatic rifles pointed at all angles, peered out from the back of the trucks like frightened monkeys. As they disappeared around the next bend, Sawyer nodded at Toonsang, who grinned back, his betel-stained teeth and upturned eyebrows making him look more devilish than ever.

One for you, you son-of-a-bitch, Sawyer thought irritably, knowing it was going to be a lot harder than he had thought. It was Toonsang who had halted their ponies about half an hour earlier and then, listening intently for a moment, had issued sharp orders in Shan and Isan Thai to set up the ambush. When Sawyer had looked at him questioningly, Toonsang had pointed up the road.

'Soldiers coming. Thai patrol, maybe.'

'How do you know?' Sawyer asked. He had heard nothing.

'Petrol,' Toonsang grinned, tapping his nose.

And now that he had mentioned it, Sawyer too was suddenly conscious of the faint whiff of gasoline fumes. He cursed himself for an idiot, all at once remembering how the VC used to spot the coming of American patrols in the dense jungle by the smell of the Americans' aftershave lotion. He would have to do better, he warned himself. It had been a long time since 'Nam and he was older and rusty. If he wanted to survive the next twenty-four hours, he was going to have to do a lot better.

As the sound of the trucks faded in the distance Toonsang's head popped from behind a mound of earth like a groundhog. He looked and listened and then got to his feet.

'We go now, yes,' Toonsang said, slinging the M-79 across his back and politely motioning Sawyer ahead of him. Sawyer complied, scrambling up the steep hill. Not to have done so would have been bad kreng chai, but he could feel Toonsang behind him at every step as he climbed up to where the ponies were tethered.

Suong was waiting with the animals. They began loading up with the relieved, yet vaguely disappointed, cursing of men who have avoided an expected combat. Toonsang insisted on helping Suong mount her pony. She told him she needed no help, but he managed to slide his hand between her legs as he pushed her up. She angrily kicked the pony away, her dark eyes flashing. Toonsang laughed.

It wasn't normal behaviour for an Asian, for whom public touching is offensive. Toonsang was doing it only to provoke him and maybe now was as good a time as any, Sawyer thought, anger rising. He already had the safety clicked off when he realized that the Thai patrol was still close enough to hear a shot. As he slung his M-16 over his shoulder, he felt a prickling along his spine, a warning from the Reptile. Turning, he caught a nasty grin from the Kachin coming up from below and lowering his weapon, as though he too had remembered the Thai patrol just in time.

Tough luck, you son-of-a-bitch, Sawyer thought, as he checked his pony. Another second and both Toonsang and he would have been dead and the Kachin would have had Toonsang's opium and the girl. Sawyer tightened the bed roll and saddle bags carried mountain-style, in front of the rider, and mounted.

That was the problem, Sawyer thought. There was always at least one of them behind him and they were too spread out. He couldn't hope to get them all at once. Especially now, going single-file along the narrow trail that roughly paralleled the road but was about half-way up the hill.

It wasn't going to be easy, he thought, looking back over his shoulder at the Kachin, who grinned as though they both shared the same joke. Ahead the trail was a tunnel of hanging vines and leaves in a thousand different shades of green. Wind hissed in the tree tops high above. A twig fluttered and at the same instant both Sawyer and the Kachin started to swing their weapons around, then relaxed as a parakeet flitted, a blue spark between the branches.

The hooves of the ponies and the mules made soft padding sounds on the trail, sodden with wet leaves. All around the teak trees towered straight and brown or slanted one against another till, higher up, the branches intertwined to form latticework through which the colourless light filtered, casting intricate shadows. Always there was the sound of water dripping from above and the smell of wet vegetation. Now and then they would come across a grove of dark Yang trees, the kind that are tapped for the lacquer, and across a fallen trunk a profusion of wildly coloured orchids, startling as a neon sign.

Ahead Sawyer could hear the sound of rushing water. It grew louder and they came to a tiny stream splashing down the rocks and across the trail. A brightly coloured kingfisher flew up the stream. As he guided his pony through the tumbling water, Sawyer noticed the tracks and leavings of a Lyre deer on the muddy bank.

The wind came up. The tall trees began to creak. Sawyer felt a sense of foreboding. The forest seemed very ancient, and he remembered Vasnasong's curious remark that sex was older than mankind. Well, there were a lot of things older than mankind, dark things buried deep in the make-up of men from the time before we were human, and it was as if the forest was calling them up. He didn't want to go any further. He couldn't shake the feeling that going up the trail was like going back in time. To a dark time when only force ruled and anything was permitted. But anything *is* permitted if you only allow yourself, came a secret voice from his subconscious. *Anything.*

The voice had the sound of the branches swaying in the wind. The skin at the back of his neck tightened and he let it. Remembering the quick whispers with Suong by the ponies before they set up the ambush, he would need all of the Reptile's cunning if he were to survive.

'I can't get at him. He is cunning,' he had whispered.

'Yes, but only cunning. You will need cleverness,' she had whispered back.

'But how. . . .?' he began, but it was too late. Toonsang had come up and was grinning at them both. His yellowish

144

skin, the gaps between his teeth and the crushed pork-pie hat combined to give him the appearance of a vaguely demented jack-o'-lantern.

He could see Toonsang's broad back up at the head of the column. Even from behind there was something brutish about him. Sawyer's fingers itched for the gun. Not yet, he told himself. She's right. It needs more than brute cunning. The son-of-a-bitch won't give you a shot at him unless he's already got you covered.

The trail began to dip down towards the road. The pony started to move too quickly and Sawyer had to rein him back. The mules perked up their ears and Toonsang halted. They listened to the wind in the leaves, the breathing and stamping of the mules and, always, the drip of water. Sawyer could see Toonsang's nostrils widening and shrinking as he sniffed the forest air deeply. Then he dismounted and began to probe the trail for booby-traps and mines, his pony following slowly behind.

Suddenly Toonsang stopped. He looked up and sniffed again and then Sawyer smelt it too. Smoke from a campfire. Either a very big party or fools, Sawyer thought.

They were fools. Two of them were roasting chunks of meat over a small fire, while a third soldier bent a village girl face-down over a log. Sawyer could see her white buttocks gleaming as he plunged in and out of her anus. The two reached for their rifles, but Toonsang, the Karen, the Shan and Sawyer had them covered. The two looked white in the face, but the third turned from the girl and faced them boldly, a Colt ·45 in his hand, his penis still red and impudently pointed up at the sky.

'A thousand of greetings,' the soldier called loudly in Isan Thai. He had a broad Chinese face with ears that stuck out like jug handles.

'I fear we interfere with your pleasure,' Toonsang replied, grinning hugely.

'Pah! Little enough pleasure from a Lisu bitch! Take her yourself and good riddance,' Jug-ears said, grabbing his penis and shaking himself elaborately. But he kept the pistol pointed at Toonsang.

'We will, we will — and everything else, even your pants!' Toonsang declared, and even Jug-ears joined in the harsh

145

laughter. But the two soldiers could only manage sickly grins. The Lisu girl grabbed her clothes and squatted on the ground, not daring to look at any of them.

'Enough talk! Let us kill them and go,' the Kachin said, coming up. He swung his Chinese SKS carbine into position. Jug-ears's eyes narrowed as he took in the new factor of the Kachin. The other two were frozen like rabbits caught by headlights at the side of a road.

'So be it! This one is ready for the Long Night. I take you,' Jug-ears gestured with the pistol at Toonsang, 'and, with joss, maybe one other with me,' scanning them. Then his eyes widened.

'By the phi, a white man!'

'A trader, he says,' Toonsang said, elaborately picking his nose with one hand to cover his other dropping down to a Tokorev pistol he had got from God knows where.

'What you trade?' Jug-ears wanted to know, his forehead furrowed as if debating Sawyer as a potential target. Sawyer felt all their eyes burning on him and wondered whether he had more to fear from a shot from the front or the back.

'Life and death,' Sawyer replied.

Jug-ears's face brightened. 'Then we are all in same business, neh?'

'What is this stupidity? It is a dead man who speaks,' complained the Kachin, urging his pony a few steps forward.

'But still more of a man than you,' Jug-ears retorted, grabbing his penis. But this time it didn't co-operate and as it shrivelled so too they could see Jug-ears visibly deflate.

They could kill him now, Sawyer thought, and decided to take a chance because, once they started shooting, they might decide to take care of him at the same time.

'What is the Kuomintang doing so far Thai-side?'

'Retreating,' Toonsang sneered and their guffaws echoed in the woods. Only the two soldiers and Jug-ears didn't laugh.

'They've been doing that since Yunnan,' Sawyer smiled. 'Who's chasing you this time?'

Jug-ears looked suspiciously up at Sawyer. 'How you know we are KMT?'

'Who else would stoop so low as to raid a Lisu village?'

146

Sawyer shrugged, and this time Toonsang laughed so hard he had to wipe the tears from his eyes.

Jug-ears flushed. He looked up at Sawyer with hatred. Sawyer tensed to start shooting. Then the look faded. Jug-ears had found the opening Sawyer had left him.

'We took the village to remind Bhun Sa we can come Thai-side too. Now we leave,' he shrugged. 'If this one is permitted, better to die with pants on.' When Toonsang nodded he began to pull on his clothes.

'Stupid! These not KMT. These are deserters!' the Kachin insisted.

Toonsang shrugged.

'Where there are three of the KMT, there may be more,' the Karen said, reining his pony tighter. It was a Yunnan pony, sandier in colour and less shaggy than the Kachin ponies.

At this Jug-ears looked up sharply. 'Truth,' he growled.

'Lie! He makes the pretend only to stay alive,' the Kachin spat disgustedly.

'Truth,' Jug-ears repeated.

'Truth, lie. What we do now? Shoot or eat? You say,' the Shan declared to Toonsang, speaking for the first time. He aimed his rifle at Jug-ears with his elbow out to the side, as though he were holding a cross-bow.

'We have no quarrel with KMT . . . ,' Toonsang began.

'Stupid! You not see what he trying . . .?' the Kachin hissed. The two soldiers blanched at the sound. The girl covered her head with the colourful blue-and-red scarf of the Lisu and rocked silently back and forth on her heels.

'Be still!' Toonsang snapped.

'But is lie . . .'

'I command here. Does any dispute this?' Toonsang roared, aiming the pistol at the Kachin. There was a murderous look in Toonsang's wide-set eyes and the Kachin looked away disgustedly.

'Better not to kill us,' Jug-ears said carefully, looking from the Kachin to Toonsang, who was pursing his lips with the effort of judging such a weighty matter. Finally, he leaned forward over the pony's neck and pointed the Tokorev at Jug-ears.

'You may leave with your lives. But your ponies and goods we take. Also the female,' Toonsang pronounced.

At this the two soldiers looked up in disbelief, not daring to believe their good joss.

Jug-ears eyed Toonsang warily. 'What of our weapons?' he asked.

'We take.'

Jug-ears shrugged and pointed the Colt back at Toonsang in a kind of Mexican stand-off. 'Then shoot us now. Without guns we are dead men.'

Toonsang considered this for a moment. No one breathed. A bird chirped somewhere and it seemed to Sawyer that time had stood still and that a scene such as this had been played and replayed for eternity.

'By the phi, you have a prick and balls. Take your guns and go, but quickly,' Toonsang declared magnanimously, waving them away with the pistol.

'Bad business,' the Kachin growled, but Toonsang was enjoying his moment too much to bother squashing him.

Still, Jug-ears looked suspiciously up at them. 'Truth?' he murmured.

'You have a distrustful nature,' Toonsang laughed, ostentatiously clicked on the safety and stuck the pistol into his waist sash.

At this Jug-ears growled something to the other two and they hurriedly grabbed their rifles by the slings and made ready to go. Jug-ears smiled up at Sawyer. 'May fortune follow you, One-Round-Eye.'

'And you,' Sawyer smiled.

With a last wary look at Toonsang, Jug-ears turned to join the two soldiers, who began to walk hurriedly towards the far side of the clearing. Jug-ears muttered something and they tried to make a show of it, but their movements were stiff and unnatural as marionettes'.

They hadn't gone ten yards before a burst of automatic fire cut them down like toy soldiers at the hand of a bored child. Toonsang had pulled an AK-47 from a sheath hidden under his saddle blanket. The Kachin was firing too. Jug-ears almost succeeded in turning around, rifle coming into line, before a piece of his head flew off and he toppled forward spilling blood out of his head. The others joined in firing long bursts at the bodies. The Lisu girl began to run in circles, screaming all the while, until a single shot from the Kachin knocked her off her feet. The Kachin turned towards Sawyer only to find the M-16 covering him and Toonsang, who shrugged and sheathed the AK-47.

The Shan and the Karen slid off their ponies and ran to strip the bodies and gather the ponies and booty as the Akha and the Thai came up with the mules. Suong was with them. Toonsang kneed his pony and came between Sawyer and the Kachin.

'Better this way, younger brother. More easy. If we let them live, they maybe sell us to KMT, maybe Birman army. That one have big prick and balls. If we shoot face to face, he make somebody die. Maybe you. Maybe me.' He grinned.

'Better to shoot him in the back.'

'Ah, yes, much,' Toonsang agreed cheerfully. He glanced back at the Kachin and they both began to laugh, their betel-blackened teeth giving them the appearance of demons.

Sawyer looked over at Suong. Her face was calm, but there was a faint moustache of perspiration on her upper lip. He wanted to talk to her, but it was too dangerous. Toonsang drew his pony alongside Sawyer and they rode across the clearing side by side.

'Then the feud with the Kachin was a thing of shadows, like the playacting of the nang?' Sawyer asked.

'Of a certainty. That one with prick in air was a fool to believe.'

'Brave, though.'

'Ah, yes. Big prick and no wits.' Toonsang sniggered.

'A fool, you say?'

Toonsang looked at him blankly. 'Who else would trust his life to a stranger?'

By the time they reached the pass the shadows were long across the road. It had rained earlier and grey clouds still shrouded the holy mountain Doi Tung; the pagoda near the peak could not be seen. Although they remained watchful, they had relaxed enough to come down to the road. Ambushes were unlikely here, for this was sacred ground, and it was said that a band of Communist insurgents had once passed a column of Thai Rangers on the opposite side of the road with nothing more deadly exchanged between them than wary looks.

The road was a brown gash between the hills. It wound upwards through the pass, tiny rivulets of run-off water snaking down from the muddy slope. Somewhere between here and the Salween — though no one, not even the mapmakers in Bangkok and Rangoon could say where — was the Burmese border.

The green of the hills was very deep, mostly from pine because of the altitude, with an occasional oak, and the road was bordered by a fringe of brown pine needles. The mules were strung in a long line and they moved with shortened steps to take the incline, the sound of their hooves muffled by the pine needles. Toonsang's men, mounted on ponies, were spaced at intervals, each man leading a string of four mules, so that if they came under attack, they could disperse quickly without losing all the mules. Birds chattered in the trees, a comforting sound. If they grew silent, it would be a warning of an ambush.

Sawyer and Suong rode side by side, not far behind Toonsang. Since the shooting, Suong had said little. Not far behind them rode the Kachin, the SKS held across his thighs for quick access. From the way she held herself Sawyer knew she could feel the Kachin behind her.

'He means to kill you,' she said. Her voice was soft, so soft he might not have heard and, despite the words, so sensual it was as if she had stroked him with soft fur. She couldn't help it if she wanted to, Sawyer thought. It's how she is. There was no part of her that didn't set a man to thinking dangerous thoughts.

'I know.'

'That one wants me.' A jerk of her chin indicated Toonsang's broad back, the pork-pie hat perched absurdly on the top of his round head as on a snowman. 'Always I feel his eyes on me. He will come tonight.'

'Let him come,' Sawyer said.

She looked at him, only darkness in her eyes. 'You wish this?'

'Let him come,' Sawyer said. 'I'll be waiting.'

She didn't say any more and he was grateful for that. Because he was starting not to trust himself where she was concerned. His feelings were all tangled up. He let her move ahead a bit so he could watch her tight little behind sway with the pony's stride. He felt himself harden and at that moment he wanted her so badly he could barely keep from throwing himself upon her right then and there in front of all of them. Why lie to himself? he thought. Seeing the rape of the Lisu girl and its deadly aftermath had in some dark way fired his blood. But what he felt for Suong wasn't just sex. It was more than that. Yet it wasn't love either because they were using each other. Tonight he would use her in the vilest way a man can use a woman, he thought. As a pimp for his own purposes, so he could get at Toonsang. That wasn't any kind of love, unless Vasnasong was right and love wasn't the selfless bullshit we're always taught but something far more ancient, selfishness and using as much a part of it as anything else.

Because he was so absorbed in his thoughts he was slower than the others to react and, when he did, at first he missed it. The figure up ahead was so utterly motionless he assumed it was just a roadside Buddha, one of the crude little shrines one would come across now and again in these hills.

As first Toonsang and then Suong came abreast of the figure each in turn made the wai sign to the forehead, which is reserved for holy monks and the Lord Buddha himself. The figure was draped in a ragged monk's robe, the orange colour sun-faded pale yellow, the right shoulder left bare, as is the custom. It was seated in the lotus position and, like a statue, was utterly oblivious of them. As Sawyer rode up he could see that it was an old monk, though how old it was impossible to say. The face was gaunt, yet barely creased by time and burnt the colour of teak by the sun. The head was utterly bald, so that it was easy to see the death skull it would some day become. But its appearance was not forbidding. The face wore the half lidded smile of the Buddha and the dark eyes were fixed upon eternity. So as Sawyer too wai'd, he was startled when the statue suddenly came to life and wai'd back at him.

The pony shied at the sudden movement and, with a curse, Sawyer yanked at the rein and stopped it, facing the monk.

'Blessings and greetings, holy one.'

'Greetings and blessings, brother. This humble one fears

151

he has startled your pony,' the old monk said. His eyes were younger than his face. They sparkled with intelligence.

'And not only my pony, by the phi. I nearly shot you — or, worse, this fornication of a pony,' Sawyer said, yanking the pony's head around.

The monk smiled. 'Like most shootings, that would have been of benefit to no one. As for your pony, the sight in his right eye is imperfect, hence he has fear on that side. Only let him turn his head to smell the man smell and see that this humble one poses no danger and he will stand easily.'

Sawyer turned the pony's head. The pony quieted. He leaned over and patted the pony's neck. As he did so he checked the positions of Toonsang and the Kachin. And Suong. They had all stopped to watch.

'You know ponies, then?' Sawyer asked.

'Animals are simple. Men less so,' the monk said in a way that indicated he had seen Sawyer's action.

Sawyer squinted up the empty road. Except for the hoof-prints of Toonsang's ponies and mules there were no recent tracks. The sky was a slate-grey ceiling over the hills, and when he looked back down at the old monk he smelled the wet pine needles and earth, as though the monk was indeed a crude village ikon of mud and straw.

'A lonely road to beg rice,' Sawyer observed.

'And yet you have come,' the monk replied, his eyes twinkling. Then Sawyer noticed that his begging bowl was turned face down on the ground: a sign that he sought no alms.

'That cannot be denied, holy one,' Sawyer smiled. 'But this one meant only that this is a most dangerous place. Have you no fear of bandits?'

'A monk's poverty is his safety. Is this not true?'

'Here, perhaps. In my land even poverty is no protection against bandits.'

'That is a hard land that breeds such desperate men. And are the rich safe then?'

'Not even,' Sawyer shook his head.

'Then you too live in a most dangerous place, brother.'

'Every place is dangerous, holy one.'

'That is truth — for we carry the most dangerous place of all with us always,' the monk replied, glancing down at his own chest as a way of avoiding pointing at his head, which would have been bad kreng chai.

'I have more danger than that with me, holy one,' Sawyer said, glancing back at Toonsang out of the corner of his eye.

'Yes, that is plain,' the monk said, following his glance. 'The men of the opium trade are desperate men. But perhaps,' eyeing Sawyer's M-16, 'you are such a one yourself, brother?'

'I must do business with these men. But I am not of these men, holy one,' Sawyer said, unable to keep the disgust out of his voice.

The old man got stiffly to his feet and peered intently into Sawyer's good eye as if to read his thoughts. 'Truly, you believe this, brother. But if you do business with them, are you not one of them?'

Sawyer felt as though he had walked into a wall. The old man's eyes seemed to see into his very soul. For some reason, he knew his answer mattered. He didn't know why, but it mattered. 'I don't know,' he said.

The old monk smiled. His face creased deeply along ancient laugh lines. 'That is good. Not to know is a much higher state than knowing for a certainty that which is not so,' he said, gathering up his bowl. 'I will come with you as far as the road to Doi Tung,' he said loudly so that all might hear. Then softly to Sawyer, 'There will be no killing while I am with you. Even for desperate men, to kill before a monk's eyes is most terrible bad karma that a hundred lifetimes could not redeem.'

Under Toonsang's watchful eyes Sawyer readied a mule for the monk to ride. Toonsang made no effort to stop him, and Sawyer wondered at that until he realized that the monk's presence was a safe conduct for all of them in these hills. Despite his years the monk scrambled up on the mule as agilely as a monkey.

Once more Toonsang led them up the road, now completely in shadow. The monk and Sawyer rode side by side.

'Is Doi Tung your home?' Sawyer asked.

'A monk is always at home everywhere. The bot atop Doi Tung is a place I sometimes stay. And you, brother,' glancing sideways at Sawyer, 'where is your home?'

'The village of the Angels in the land of America.'

'The Angels, as in Krung Thep?' He gave the Thai name for Bangkok.

'The very same.'

'A big village?'

'Ah, yes. A thousand of huts and more.'

'What a terrible liar you are, brother! Worse than any "guest",' the old man cackled, referring to the common belief that all Indians were unscrupulous liars who, even if born in Thailand, were always contemptuously referred to as 'guests', 'for I have seen a photograph of your village of the Angels in the newspaper. It is a great city, like Krung Thep. Only the people must hide in automobiles, for there were thousands in the picture on big roads intertwined like vines on the teakwood. But no people. Truly, the American is most strange.'

'Why strange, holy one?'

The monk looked curiously at Sawyer. 'Do you not think that to build a city for machines and not people is most strange?'

'That is truth,' Sawyer smiled, but his mind was elsewhere. He had caught a whiff of smoke on the wind. He could sense the nervousness in the ponies and mules and, up ahead, Toonsang was anxiously scanning the darkening hills.

'Soon now,' the monk said.

Sawyer turned sharply, hand moving to the M-16. 'Soon for what?'

But the monk's smile was the imperturbable calm of the Buddha. Although his lips moved, his words seemed to come from somewhere else, like a ventriloquist's trick.

'That which you seek, brother. The war without only mirrors the war within.'

Suong looked anxiously over her shoulder at Sawyer. Tightening the grip on his M-16, he spurred his pony forward, flicking off the safety as he came abreast of her. Toonsang had already gone around the far bend in the road to scout ahead.

Suong and Sawyer looked at each other. Her hands were clenched tight in her lap and then he saw that she was clutching a hand grenade.

The sky had turned a deep violet. Soon it would be night. Sawyer looked back and the Kachin grinned at him. He was cradling the SKS in his arms, but as long as the monk was there, Sawyer thought, he wouldn't shoot.

They saw it as soon as they came round the bend. The entrance to the Lisu village was a gap in a split-rail and bamboo fence about a hundred yards off the road. The entrance was lit by a towering bonfire, deliberately set to illuminate the scene before them. The flickering yellow light brought the shadows to life. The roar and crackle of the fire was all they could hear. Beyond the entrance Sawyer could see a body lying in the mud. From here he couldn't tell if it was male or female. But there was no mistaking the things lined up like telephone poles along the trail to the village entrance.

There were six of them. They looked very young. Mostly recruits, no doubt. All in the uniform of the Kuomintang. Each of them had been impaled on a sharpened bamboo stake between their legs. Their hands were tied by a cord looped over the long crossbeam of a crude scaffold. They hung from the crossbeam like chickens, the height carefully set so that they would have had to strain up on their toes to keep the point from penetrating deeper, but just high enough so they couldn't sink down and end their appalling agony too quickly. Their pants were wet with dark stains and at their feet were black pools swarming with crawling things. From the expression on their faces, they must have taken many hours to die.

Toonsang sat on his pony, a cheroot glowing in his mouth. As Sawyer came up, he spat.

'Welcome, younger brother,' Toonsang called out. He was smiling. In the flickering light his betel-stained teeth seemed to drip with blood. 'Welcome to the land of Bhun Sa.'

CHAPTER 11

The marsh drains into the deep.
Confined by a rock,
the man grasps at briars.
In his palace,
he does not see his wife.

Parker sat in the darkness of the pit, his hands tied behind him, and prayed to die. Not that he believed in God. Or in anything any more, except the pain in his feet that was more terrible than he had ever conceived pain could be. Christ, let me die. Please, sweet Jesus. Please, please, please, let me die, he prayed.

He would do anything. Sell his soul. Betray his country. Anything. He had begged them to let him confess. They could name the crime and he would swear to it. Did they want CIA secrets? He'd give them the whole ball of wax. But they didn't care. They just smiled and kept asking him the same questions over and over again.

Would the CIA deal with them directly? Would they betray Bhun Sa? Did they have secret contacts with the dog-eaters? Would they send another? One who was empowered to negotiate? He had told them everything he knew over and over. Why wouldn't they believe him? Or just kill him, please God?

He had been one of the proud ones, he remembered. One who had always refused the standard cyanide-pill issue and had looked a little contemptuously on those who took them. The pill just tells the opposition that you know something that makes your head worth opening, he used to say. Without it you might bluff your way out, or disinform them, snatching a kind of victory from the pain. There's a limit to the pain and, besides, you're worth more alive than dead to them, maybe as part of a swap, and once you know that they won't kill you and that there's an end to it somewhere, you can stand any pain, he would argue. If you want to run with the big dogs, you've got to be willing to piss up tall trees, he'd say, implying that those who took the cyanide pills with them didn't really have what it took.

Except he was a fraud. His whole life was a fraud because he didn't have what it took at all. Only now he couldn't lie about it any more. Not to himself. Not to those grinning fucking monkeys who would do things to his feet. Not to anybody.

He'd lied about it all the time. Bullshit. That's all he was, bullshit, like the time he'd sworn on his mother's life that he had taken out a VC with a bicycle chain only inches from a whole fucking NVA squad on his first time out as a LRRP. He had originally heard it from some Aussie Ranger, who used to carry VC ears in a tobacco pouch and trade them as though they were stamps, and took the story for his own. The Aussie had said that he had cut fourteen ears off VC he had personally killed, but Parker didn't believe him, any more than he believed himself the first time he told the bicycle-chain story. The truth was that he had spent the whole night cowering in the bush, jumping at every sound. In the morning, on his way in, he had found a dead VC near the trail and those were the ears he took, trying not to look at the bottom half of the body, mangled from a B-52 strike and swarming with insects, as he did it. Then he threw up.

And yet, incredibly, everyone believed him. Parker was a tough mother-fucker, they said. When he transferred from Special Forces to the Company, the stories followed him. The Company execs loved that shit as much as the guys in 'Nam did. They gave him a promotion. They used to point him out to CTP trainees who wouldn't dare approach him. After a while he almost believed it himself. In his mind's eye the image of himself wielding the black-taped bicycle chain, the VC's face as he went down, was as real as any memory.

Only once had he ever let the mask slip. The night Brother Rap died. The night they had sworn never to speak about. But he'd tell them now, all right. He'd tell anybody anything if they'd only make the pain in his feet go away. Christ, give him an axe and he'd chop his own feet off himself. Anything, please, he moaned, staring up into the blackness, not knowing if it was day or night.

The pit was dark as a grave. Then he saw a star through the bamboo lattice above and realized it was night. He began to struggle against the ropes tying him down, but all his movements did was send the pain shooting up his legs. He screamed. And screamed.

He must have passed out because he awakened to a scraping sound. They were opening the lattice on the top of the pit. 'Oh God,' he mumbled. They had been right. Brother Rap had been right. Sometimes death is better. He wondered if they had sent someone after him. They must have, except he no longer wanted to be found. He wanted to die before they ever found him. Where were they? Who was coming after him? That's what they wanted to know, only he didn't know who was coming. Except . . .

Oh, Jesus! They wouldn't send that one-eyed son-of-a . . .

The pit flooded with light from a flashlight. It hurt his eyes and he turned his head away like a thing that prefers to cower in the dark. A high-pitched voice barked a command and he obediently raised his head and tried to force his eyes open. He squinted up at the opening. It was a rectangle of grey dawn light. A teenage face wearing a KR cap peered down at him.

'Please, don't,' Parker whimpered.

'To dah dei oun. It is time to wake the earth.' The boy grinned.

CHAPTER 12

The marsh above the trees.
The beam is weak;
it will collapse.
The man places mats of white grass
beneath objects set on the ground.

'Some say the gods made the world to give them a place to fight,' said Chaw Wah, the phu yai ban of the village. He was a thin man, not old, with a narrow, triangular face and a long nose with a sideways bend that made him at once ugly and interesting to look at. At his words there were murmurs of agreement.

'The Chinamen say the gods created the world to give the bureaucrats something to do,' Sawyer remarked. It was an old joke but still successful, and the others laughed over their cups.

'That is truth,' Chaw Wah agreed sagely. 'It is said that the neak ta spirits complain that even in the Other World there is too much bureaucracy.' And the betel-chewers among them turned and spat in delight at the saying.

They had finished eating and were seated around the fire in a crude hut made to shelter villagers during the long nights in the fields during the time of planting. The hut was of pine and stood on stilts in a terraced poppy field several hundred yards from the village. The forest pressed close around. As they ate they held their weapons as unselfconsciously in their laps as Westerners might wear napkins.

It had been a poor meal. A single grilled plat taw fish. A dab of fish paste. Rice. The only fruit a few papayas and rambutans. But after the fighting the village could offer no better and, as a consolation, they warmed their bellies with potent corn liquor brewed by the local spirit doctor. Night had fallen. Rain dripped steady as time from the thatched eaves of the hut.

Only the old monk sat apart. He had eaten of the rice alone, for the monsoon season was also vossa, the time of purification. And the woman, of course. Earlier she had taken a portion of food to the Akha, who was keeping the first watch over their animals and goods. When she came back they all turned. The rain had soaked her peasant clothes, moulding them wetly to her body. Their eyes were on the smooth swell of her breasts and belly, the dark depression between her thighs. Only the monk looked away; the sight of such as her was a detour on the Eightfold Path. Toonsang had stared at her like a man in a fever. His fingers curled into claws. As she passed, her thigh brushed Toonsang's hand and Sawyer, who suspected that she had done it deliberately, curtly motioned her away. That was his part and he played it, feeling like the cuckold in a French farce. Since then she had sat in a corner, keeping tight-lipped guard over Sawyer's pack and hers like a bitch over a new litter. In the shadows only her eyes could be seen.

But though none looked at her, they could all feel her presence. Toonsang busied himself lighting a black cheroot. He avoided Sawyer's gaze because the sickness for her was burning in his own, and if their eyes were to meet, it would end with killing then and there. The Kachin smiled. But Toonsang, ever wary, found his voice as he passed the lit cheroot to Chaw Wah.

'May the phi bop take this talk of bureaucrats. What of Bhun Sa and this pestilential Fuk Wa of the Kuomintang?' Toonsang growled.

'With those two is battle unending, as that between the noble Rama and Thosakanth,' Chaw Wah replied. Rama was the hero and Thosakanth the villainous monkey general of the Ramakien tales. Chaw Wah's cheeks hollowed as he drew deeply on the cheroot.

'Ah, but which is Rama and which Thosakanth?' the Kachin said, holding up his hand, the thumb and forefinger outstretched. Everyone laughed. The sound was harsh and male. The Kachin turned his hand so the two fingers switched positions and they laughed again.

'That depends on who occupies the village!' Toonsang called out and there were more guffaws and the slapping of thighs. The Kachin, grinning like a street urchin with a new trick, turned his hand back again to still more laughter. Toonsang crumpled his pork-pie hat in his hand and dabbed at his eyes with it, as the laughing subsided. The tension had eased and when Chaw Wah, himself smiling broadly, grunted a girl in the red-sleeved blouse, coloured phanung and apron, striped shawl and multi-coloured turban of the Lisu women, poured them another round of the dark-brown liquor. It burned like acid going down and there was much lip-smacking and belching as they drank.

'That is truth,' Chaw Wah agreed. 'Always before we sold the opium to any who would pay. There were raids and stealings, but with prudence the water did not overflow the banks of the river, as it is said. The road itself was safe for those of prudence and the village also, for it lies in the holy shadow of Doi Tung. But for Fuk Wa and Bhun Sa, not Mount Meru and the world itself is of a sufficient bigness. Each will have the opium trade for his own. Thus when the Kuomintang came this time it was not to trade but to stay. They left those you see now hanging at the village gate to hold the village for them.

'At first we gave them of food and some few baht and kyat as we had, hoping they would go away. For we are a poor village,' Chaw Wah added, glancing sideways at Toonsang's men and their guns.

Toonsang grunted. Message delivered.

Chaw Wah went on. 'But they wanted all, even the scrapings of the fourth cutting of the opium. They drank and ate, and when there was no more of the corn liquor they slapped the face of Ah Chaw, the spirit doctor, and threatened to cut off his manhood if he did not find another jug. And they took the women as they pleased, anywhere, even in the middle of the village, like dogs. Any woman. Even those who were married and those at the time of their bleeding. And when finished would leave them with their skirts over their heads, though from the women's pleadings they knew that the husbands would have no choice but to put them aside.'

'Barbarians!' Toonsang said and spat into the fire. That was what you said when it was the other side that did it, Sawyer thought. But words meant little. Brother Rap had taught him that.

'What is to become of the women?' Sawyer asked.

Chaw Wah made a vague gesture that might have meant anything. 'What becomes of any woman taken in adultery? Among the American tribe does not the husband also put her aside?'

'That is not the custom, but some do all the same,' Sawyer said.

'Ah,' Chaw Wah said, meaning he understood but, with exquisite kreng chai, did not wish to comment further because, at a deeper level, Sawyer's reply had merely confirmed what they already knew. The ways of the European were beyond rational comprehension.

More liquor was passed around and, as an offering to the protective chao spirits, Chaw Wah spilled a few drops from his cup into the fire. They flared up, briefly burning with a bright blue flame.

'Pah! The most severe punishment for adultery is among the Paduang, they of the long-necked women,' Toonsang broke in. His small eyes had begun to blear from the liquor. It made him look more dangerous than ever.

'It is said the women of the Paduang wear so many neck rings that their necks are stretched to three times longer than a normal woman's,' Chaw Wah observed.

'That is truth. The rings are of heavy brass and the wearing of them makes the neck long and slender and the head seem small, which is a mark of beauty among the Paduang. And the punishment for adultery is the removal of these very neck rings. The husband must himself cut them off,' Toonsang said.

'Why is that so terrible?' Sawyer asked.

'Most terrible.' Toonsang grinned. 'After years of rings, the neck is not strong enough to hold up the head. Unless the woman carries her own head in her two hands like a basket, it just flops over.'

'A terrible punishment,' Sawyer agreed and they drank.

Chaw Wah shook his head. 'Not only punishment. Warning, like those the men of Bhun Sa left hanging at our gate when they retook the village. They warned us not to take the bodies down. They said from now on we are to sell only to Bhun Sa.'

'Have you no fear of reprisals from Fuk Wa?' Sawyer asked.

The headman made a gesture that somehow suggested all of Asia. 'What is one to do? We are a little village. As it is said, "When the elephants fight, the grass is trampled." '

'Some might flee a land of tigers.'

Chaw Wah smiled in approval at Sawyer's reference to a famous story of Confucius, who once asked a woman whose family had been devoured by tigers why she stayed in such a terrible place. She had replied: 'Because there is no repressive government here.'

'Your words have wisdom, honoured sir. There are some among us, some of the young, who say this. For we have heard stories. Always there has been fighting, but now the dog-eaters grow very numerous in Laos and in the land of the Khmers, which is already a graveyard. The air smells of thunder, and storm clouds gather in the east. Perhaps you are yourself a cloud-bringer, honoured sir, for you have the look of a warrior,' Chaw Wah said, looking boldly at Sawyer's eye-patch.

To this Sawyer said nothing. Chaw Wah took it for an answer.

'You see how it is. We must stay here and endure where our ancestors are buried. As it is said, "The boat moves off, the riverbanks remain." What else can your humble servants do?'

'Pray. We bring you a monk,' Toonsang declared rudely. All turned to the monk, still seated in the lotus position. His face was shadowed. His eyes were two flames in the firelight.

'What says the holy one?' Chaw Wah asked.

The old monk picked up his bowl and got stiffly to his feet. 'Only what you already know. Life is dukkha. No prayer will end suffering,' the old man said.

'Even as those poor wretches by the gate.' Chaw Wah nodded. 'Though we wished them ill, their screams were most barbarous to hear.'

163

'Then it was a good warning. What say, younger brother? Still wish to meet Bhun Sa? Maybe he will welcome you as he does the Kuomintang, neh?' Toonsang said, leering at Sawyer.

'More than ever,' Sawyer said.

Toonsang glanced over at the Kachin and Sawyer saw how it was then. He let his hand fall on his M-16.

'Too dangerous now. Finish trip here,' Toonsang declared. 'This one will buy the woman so you not lose profit. Better this one than Bhun Sa. For that one will take the woman and give you nothing for your trouble but a sharpened bamboo to sit on.'

'Maybe this one take her,' said the Kachin, his SKS carbine suddenly pointed at Sawyer.

It was a bad place. They were all too close and there were too many of them. Sawyer had made the classic mistake of letting his enemy pick the time and place of battle because he had thought they would hold off in the presence of the monk and wait till they could get a clean shot at him, without his being able to get any of them. But this was the place and his finger tightened on the trigger, knowing he was about to die. They couldn't miss. All he could hope for was to take one or two of them with him.

The old monk stepped between the Kachin's rifle and Sawyer. The Kachin kept the SKS aimed at the monk. His eyes had the killing look. The monk made no move.

Suddenly Toonsang turned towards the Kachin and spoke furiously in a dialect Sawyer could barely follow. It sounded like a Thai variant of North Shan.

'What manner of foolishness is this? Can you not see the farang's pestilential hand on his pestilential gun. Or the phu yai ban? Or the holy one? And if a bullet should send one of these to the Long Night, who will save us from the wrath of the Lisu? Or Bhun Sa and the SUA? Or the KMT? Or the gods themselves? May the phi bop devour your balls if I do not cut them off with my own hand, for who would not put his hand against us? There will be time enough for the woman and more than the woman, but not for one with the manure of the bullock for wits. Now go to the mules and replace the worthless Akha on guard. Perhaps you can

164

do a thing that does not require more wits than that of the bullock and leave this of the farang to me.'

The Kachin didn't move. He glared at Toonsang. But his knuckles were white on the SKS and Sawyer knew then that he would go stand guard.

The Kachin sneered. 'There is too much of talking with such as these. And of drinking, too much. When the head is dizzy, the man is weak like a woman.'

'Is this one a drunkard?' Toonsang demanded dangerously. 'Yet, even drunk, this one can lead better than one with the wits of the bullock.'

The two men glared at each other, Sawyer quite forgotten. The Kachin looked down. He spat into the fire and it hissed back. 'I go. But even the bullock does not forget an injury,' he declared, hefting his rifle.

'More better,' Toonsang retorted. 'The man wants the bullock to remember the stick.'

The Kachin went out into the darkness, his footsteps swallowed by the sound of the rain. Only then was Sawyer able to take his eye from Toonsang. The hut seemed darker, emptier somehow. Suong had gone.

She must have slipped away during the argument, he realized. Her pack was still there but open, as though she had taken something out of it. Part of him wanted to go after her at once, but he resisted the impulse. There was unfinished business here.

Toonsang plucked a burning ember from the fire and relit his cheroot. A layer of tobacco smoke hung over their heads like a raincloud.

'Bad kreng chai, that one,' Toonsang said in a friendly manner, once more speaking Isan Thai. 'It was the drink. Pay no heed. All know the Kachin people have no head for the good corn liquor.'

'I have heard this too,' Chaw Wah said, anxious to make peace.

'And you, younger brother. Forgive this miserable jesting upon the woman. Such talk is foolishness. Drink talk, no more. This one will take you to Bhun Sa, as agreed. That is of a certainty,' Toonsang said.

Watch it, Sawyer told himself. It's when he's at his friendliest that he's most dangerous. Remember what happened at the clearing.

'Mai pen rai. This one never doubted you would,' Sawyer replied, raising his cup to his lips.

At this the old monk made unmistakable signs of leaving. He made the wai to Chaw Wah and then the others, not excluding the little spirit house in the eastern corner.

'Blessings and peace,' the monk said.

'Are you leaving, holy one?' Sawyer asked stupidly. He had counted on the monk being there. So long as the monk stayed, there was a chance Toonsang might hold off.

'May you walk the Eightfold Path, brother. This humble one goes now.'

'Your humble servant wishes you to stay the night that he might earn merit, holy one,' Sawyer said, trying to keep the desperation out of his voice.

The old monk peered nearsightedly into Sawyer's good eye. 'It is better thus, brother. Bad karma if these eyes should see what is to come in this place,' he whispered.

Sawyer understood. The monk foresaw more killing. For him to witness any of it would be bad for his inner calm and bad karma for Sawyer too, whether in this life or the next.

'But it is dark outside,' Sawyer objected.

'The Enlightened One will guide my steps.' Then, seeing the look on Sawyer's face, the monk added, 'Fear not. There is that which tells this one we shall meet again.'

Small consolation, Sawyer thought. He might mean a hundred lifetimes from now. He tried one last time.

'But it is raining, holy one.'

'Then this one will get wet.'

Gathering his robe around him, the monk stepped outside. Just before he disappeared in the darkness, Sawyer called after him.

'How are you called, holy one?'

The monk stopped and turned. Rain streamed down the creases in his face, gleaming like veins of gold in the flickering light of the fire.

'Utama.'

'A fortunate name,' Sawyer joked. The monk's name meant 'good fortune'.

The monk smiled back., 'This humble one's parents were most prudent. And how is my brother called?'

'Sawyer.'

'What means this So-yah?'

'A name from a story.' Sawyer reflected that that was closer to the truth than anyone would ever know.

'May you find peace, So-yah. Though this one does not think you will,' the monk added.

'One question more, holy one,' Sawyer said, himself stepping out into the rain. 'Why were you on that road when there were no begging prospects?'

'Waiting for you, it seems.'

The monk smiled and turned away. Sawyer watched him go. He went back to the hut and got his pack, conscious of the eyes of Toonsang and the others on his back.

'This one will find the woman and bring her back,' Sawyer said.

'We will wait for you, younger brother,' Toonsang said. His eyes showed nothing.

Sawyer stepped out, keeping his back straight despite the desire to run. He thought Toonsang would wait till later, but if he was wrong. . . . As he walked away he could hear Toonsang questioning Chaw Wah about which way Bhun Sa's men were heading, Burma-side, Thai-side or Lao-side.

His thoughts were in a turmoil as he moved down the muddy path, going into the silent, groping glide they had used in the jungle trails in 'Nam. It was too dark to see and it was too dangerous to use a light, so he felt his way, hoping that there were no booby-traps so close to the village. The rain soaked his peasant shirt and phanung, worn tucked into his belt hill-style to make them like breeches. The foliage was wet, and he held the branches as he slipped through to keep them from springing back and making a noise. Looking back, he could no longer see the light from the hut. He listened to the rain on the leaves. He held his breath, but he could hear no one coming down the trail behind him.

Where was Suong? he wondered. What was she hiding? And if he could survive Toonsang's treachery, what of Bhun Sa? And Pranh? And somewhere in the back of his mind Vasnasong still in the game, despite Harris's assurances that he was handling it. And all the while the Vietnamese, with the patience of ants, were carefully moving their men into place. How much time would they give him? If he didn't get it together soon, they could start quarrying the marble for another damn black wall in Washington and . . .

He had been thinking so furiously, he almost stumbled over the body lying across the trail. His heart leaped into his throat, but from the bulk of it he knew at once it wasn't Suong. He groped for the head, hoping to feel the turban of the Kachin and, not finding it, risked turning the body over.

It was the Akha.

He had to have been killed on his way back from guard duty only a few minutes earlier. They had heard nothing in the hut, so it must have been quick and by surprise. Sawyer's pulse began to race. He had to find Suong.

He opened his pack and felt for the stubby Ingram M-10 submachine-gun. He snapped in a full clip and stuck an extra in his pocket, though if he ever needed to use more than the first clip, the most likely target would be himself. He screwed on the sound suppressor and switched to full automatic. It would be good only for close work, but at night and in dense terrain that was the way it would happen. When the time came he would leave the M-16 with the pack.

Now he had to go carefully. And it all came back, just like that. The imagining of noises and phantom black-clad snipers behind every bush. The sweats at the movement of every leaf. The foliage was dark and damp. It had a slimy feel. Something moved under his hand and he struck at it, hitting nothing but leaves. He cursed himself for making a noise and held his breath to listen. His face was wet. He wiped his eyes with the back of his sleeve, not sure if it was rain or sweat. He wondered if he were a coward because he didn't want to take another step. Something was waiting for him in the darkness. He had seen it happen to others. Sometimes it was buck fever the first time out. Sometimes later. And maybe with him it had come on slowly, the loss of nerve. Maybe people were like machines and courage was a critical part that could wear out like anything else. What did they call it with planes? Metal fatigue. That was it. Metal fatigue. And then he thought of Suong and the Kachin and began moving again.

He heard something. It wasn't imagination. He had heard

it moving somewhere up ahead. He let the pack slide silently to the ground and laid the M-16 against it. He smeared mud on his face, wiping his hands clean on his phanung. He crept forward, holding the Ingram in front of him with both hands.

At first he thought his eye was playing tricks on him because there was a tiny light shining in a small clearing. He moved to the edge of the clearing. It was a small candle inside a black box set on a tree stump, like a wayside shrine. There were things in the box, but they were deep in shadow and he couldn't make out what they were. Suong was on her knees, head bowed in prayer. He could hear the murmur of her voice but not the words. He could not see her face from here, but from the way she held her body he could sense the tension. It was an intensely personal moment and he felt like an interloper.

Then he saw the Kachin.

He was a humped shadow moving up behind Suong and whatever he had in mind, it wasn't religious. From where Sawyer was it was a bad angle. He would have to move forward into the clearing a few steps to be sure of a shot. He hesitated, wondering whether to risk the whole mission right now. Then he thought of the dead Akha and knew he had no choice. The best thing he could do was to cut down the odds. He had already stepped into the clearing when the Kachin suddenly whirled. Sawyer must have made a sound because Suong too had started to turn, her startled face white as the moon in the candlelight. For an instant they were frozen, like an image in a strobe light, the Kachin's face a ghostly mask, his SKS carbine already aimed with catlike speed at Sawyer's chest.

Mexican stand-off.

The thought flashed into Sawyer's head. No way for either of them to shoot without getting shot themselves. The look in the Kachin's eyes showed that he knew it too and didn't care.

And then it didn't matter because he was into the sequence they had drilled into them at the Fifth Recondo in Nha Trang, the sudden drop on to his back as he fired. The Ingram jumped in his hands and the Kachin, unable to react fast enough, looked down in astonishment at the spurting holes in his chest as he toppled backwards.

Sawyer got up and went to check the Kachin, though from the way he lay there was no way he wasn't dead. He started to pick up the SKS and then with a rush Suong was trembling in his arms. She wrapped herself around him, clinging like a child.

'I thought it was you. . . ,' she began.

'I know.'

He held her till the trembling eased, feeling very exposed in the candlelight. The wind stirred the tops of the trees and it came as a surprise to realize that it wasn't raining. Sawyer tried to peek over her shoulder into the black box but still couldn't make it out.

'We have to go back to the hut.'

'Yes,' she replied. Her voice was matter-of-fact. She turned, and from the way she stood he could have sworn she was trying to block him from seeing into the box. But he caught a glimpse of something just before she blew out the candle and closed the box. Except he couldn't understand it.

She stooped to pick up the Kachin's SKS and he told her to leave it in a tone that was sharper than he had intended.

'You have reason. Je comprends tout,' she said, not looking at him.

'Do you?'

'Your pistolet-mitrailleur is most quiet. You think perhaps they have not heard and will believe the Kachin is still on guard with the Akha. You desire that I make the pig-eyed one, Toonsang, to coucher with me.'

'Yes.' His voice was strangled.

She looked searchingly into his eyes. The look on her face made him want to crush her in his arms, but he couldn't.

'If you wish it, I will do this.'

Sawyer thought of Toonsang, his mouth foul with liquor and betel juice, his slimy hands all over her, kissing her, thrusting inside her, and he wanted to tell her not to do it. Give me an out, he thought. Don't do it for me.

'I wish it,' he said.

He walked ahead of her till they got back to where he had left his pack and the M-16. He took the clip out and worked the action to make sure it was empty.

'You killed the Akha?' he asked.

170

'Yes.'

'How?'

She showed him the knife. It was a tanto-style blade and he imagined how she must have smiled at the Akha and how he must have been smiling back as she put her arms around him and struck. He held out his hand and she gave it to him. He put the knife in its sheath and stuck it into his belt.

'Why?'

'You know why,' she said.

It was a way of forcing him to act and, despite himself, he knew she had been right. The feeling for her was very strong. He pulled her to him and they kissed so hard they bruised each other's lips and the taste mingled with the salt taste of blood.

'Why did you leave the hut? For the Akha?'

She shook her head. 'The Akha was chance. I met him on the path. From the way he smiled at me, I knew what he wanted. Tant mieux, I thought. One less for us to fight.'

'Then why did you leave?'

She pressed her face into his shoulder. Her voice was muffled. 'I thought it would be better if I am not there to fight over like a bone pulled between dogs. And the talking of suffering. I could not sit any more. Men-talk. If you want to know what is suffering, you must to ask a woman.'

Sawyer caught his breath. He had to ask. 'What is in the black box?'

She shook her head against his shoulder. He pushed her away, forcing her to look at him. She tried to pull away, her eyes shiny. 'I cannot tell. Je t'en prie, So-yah,' she cried.

'I'm sorry. I have to know.'

'That makes nothing. It is nothing for you and for the mission nothing. It is for me only. My khwan, tu comprends? This I will not speak of. If you demand again, it is finished with us. It is all finished,' she said, her voice surprising him by its firmness.

It must be a religious thing, he thought. He had asked because he was an agent and because you never knew what might ultimately be critical to a mission. And it was astonishing the things people would sometimes tell you in response to a straightforward question. But he couldn't risk pushing her on it. She was vital to the mission and maybe to more

171

than the mission. And if she had a secret, he asked himself, well, what woman didn't?

He handed her the empty M-16 and the pack to take back to the hut. If Toonsang asked, she was to tell him that she had found it on the trail and that she had seen no one. He hoped that Toonsang would think he was either dead or disarmed. She nodded and started to turn away. Then she came back and gently put her hand to his cheek.

'You are not a believer, So-yah?'

'No. Not in your way.'

'The angkar told us that to believe is imperialist treason. But karma requires no belief, my So-yah. Karma is what is.'

'Were you praying? Is that. . .?'

She put her fingers to his lips. 'Only do not wait too long,' she said and was gone.

He paused till he could no longer hear her moving through the foliage before he struck off the trail. He moved carefully, one limb at a time, so as not to disturb a leaf, remembering how Charley could do it and how they had learned from him to let the Reptile, the part of them that was millions of years old, take over till they could move through the night like stalking cats. And how, to prove it, Parker had once taken out a VC on a night LRRP patrol with a bicycle chain wrapped in black tape and then got away without the rest of the VC squad, only inches away, ever knowing that he was there.

He moved away from the path in a wide circle to approach the hut from the opposite side. From the shadow of the bamboo fence he could just see the fire and Suong from the side. She was leaning over Toonsang, putting something on the table. She had unhooked the top two eyelets of her shirt and her breasts swung tantalizingly close to his face. He had only to raise his hands to cup them. The Shan and the Karen stared, transfixed. Suong smiled. Toonsang licked his lips like a beast.

They were talking, but Sawyer couldn't hear what they were saying. Probably discussing him, he thought. Whatever it was, Toonsang seemed to be buying it because he was smiling like the cat with the cream. Chaw Wah and the Lisu woman had gone.

Sawyer wanted to watch it all, but he had to go around

to get into position. He started moving again. The side of the hut blocked his view as he came around. He moved from shadow to shadow, his ears straining for any sound. Whatever else happened, if he was spotted now it was all over.

A village dog started barking. He froze. The dog wouldn't stop barking. It was coming closer. Shut up, shut up, he thought. The barking got louder. The dog was moving fast. It had almost reached the last huts on the outskirts of the village nearest the field. Sawyer pulled the knife. Suddenly there was a muffled curse and a sharp yelp. The dog barked again, only now the sound was receding. Another curse and he could hear the dog growl as it slunk away.

The village was quiet. Sawyer crouched in the shadows under the hut by the outer stilts. The ground was dank and muddy enough to make him worry about his footing. He peeked cautiously over the edge. His heart almost stopped.

He was only a foot or two from Toonsang. Luckily, Toonsang was looking the other way, watching Suong prepare the bed matting. Sawyer ducked his head back down.

Now there was only the waiting. 'Only do not wait too long,' she had said. He readied the knife. The Ingram hung from a strap around his neck. He had to keep blinking the sweat from his good eye. He could hear Suong lay down on the matting and the swish of clothing. He tried not to think of what was happening, but it was impossible. Think of something else, he told himself. Why wouldn't she tell him about the box? Was it some kind of portable shrine that she took everywhere? But it made no sense. Because, unless his eye had deceived him, the only thing in the box was a pair of shoes.

He heard muttered talk and sounds of movement on the wooden floor of the hut. He tightened his grip on the knife. He tried to swallow and couldn't. Heart pounding, he waited in the dark for Toonsang to mount his woman.

CHAPTER 13

The pond is cradled by the
  mountain.
The superior man feels calm and
  chivalrous.
The man wiggles the big toe.

It was crowded on the train to Sheng Shui. That was because it was race day at the Shatin track. This showed good planning, in Lan Fong's opinion, and he approved. Luckily, he had boarded in Hung Hom and was able to find a seat. He looked at the crowd packed around him, swaying to the movement of the train, but his instructions were not to make a study of it. At this point he could be watched by a ten of ten men and not know it.

He pulled a popular racing sheet from the bag on his knee. Only two weeks ago the paper's tout had, with great joss, predicted three winners in one day, and Lan Fong noticed that there were more than a few in the crowd going over the same paper. The bag was from the Yue Hwa department store and contained only underwear and a new shirt he would not be keeping. He pretended to concentrate on the paper, glancing up only when the train slowed for a station.

As the train drew out of Tai Wai station, Lan Fong could sense a growing tension in the crowd. The race track was the next stop. Even before the train pulled into Shatin station, the crowd was already surging for the door. Lan Fong got up and pushed his way into the crowd, shoving the paper back into the bag.

The doors opened and the crowd spilled on to the platform. Lan Fong was jostled as he hurried towards the gate

174

and felt a slight tug as something was stuffed into the bag. He didn't turn around to see who had done it. He didn't want to know.

He followed the crowd into the street and all the way to the race track. There was a log jam at the general admission gate and he held on tightly to the bag. Once inside, he waited for the incoming rush to ease then darted out of one of the exit gates and headed for the taxi stand.

If there was a watcher on him, this is where he would reveal himself, Lan Fong thought. Because he would have to commit himself in order to follow.

There was one. A tall Chinese in a dark-blue short-sleeved shirt and sunglasses. Whoever he was, he hadn't been at it long, because he had made the novice's mistake of standing in front of a billboard with a white background. As soon as he saw Lan Fong move towards the first taxi, Sunglasses broke for a rank of parked motor-scooters.

'MTR. Fie dee!' Lan Fong told the driver. As they swung out into traffic, he looked over his shoulder through the rear window. Sunglasses was jumping on the scooter's starter.

As the driver manoeuvred through the traffic, Lan Fong glanced down at the bag. There were now two identical newspapers jammed into it. Lan Fong took out his original paper, marked by a small tear near the corner of the front page, and carefully dropped it in the corner of the back seat, out of the driver's line of sight, as though it had been left by a careless passenger. He left the second paper in the bag. Glancing out of the back window, he saw that Sunglasses had almost caught up.

Lan Fong's heart pounded. He wondered who Sunglasses was working for and how he had learned of Lan Fong. Many times he had been a courier and this was the first time he had ever been followed. Either he had been betrayed, an unthinkable notion, for he was known only to Wong, his father's sister's son, who had told him that all the couriers were Hakka like himself, or the message he was carrying was of indescribable importance.

Lan Fong's chest swelled with pride that he was thought worthy to carry a message of such importance. And had not his estimable cousin Wong hinted that the payment might be greater this time? Lan Fong was overcome with curiosity.

What could the message be? Always before he had obeyed Wong's injunction never to examine what he was carrying. 'That is the courier's duty. Also less baggage to carry if captured by those who wish us ill,' Wong had said. But this time, Lan Fong couldn't resist a peek. There was time, he knew. Sunglasses would stay in their rear window and nothing would happen till they got to the Metro station.

He found the little pencil notations on the fourth page of the paper, next to the line-ups. Numbers. Gau, chut, ng, baht and so on. Obviously, selections to bet on for each race. Mm gon yo, Lan Fong told himself as he refolded the paper and put it back into the bag. If there was a code there, he had no way of understanding what it was.

In fact, the numbers had nothing to do with the numbers assigned to the horses but, after a complex series of calculations were used to count backwards the letters of the horses' English names to arrive at a meaningless sequence of letters. The letters referred to a one-time pad, where each letter indicated a specific word or phrase on a single page. The only copies of the pad were held by the sender and the receiver, each of whom would destroy that page after this one-time use.

The taxi was caught in a traffic jam near the station. Slapping the fare and a twenty-Hong-Kong-dollar tip – thinking he would tell his cousin Wong he had given fifty – into the driver's hand, Lan Fong suddenly jumped out of the taxi and began weaving through the stalled traffic. Only when he reached the safety of the sidewalk did he glance back, out of the corner of his eye, at Sunglasses, who had abandoned his motor-scooter to loud honks and curses and was desperately trying to follow.

Lan Fong raced into the station and headed for the Kowloon-bound platform. He joined a number of Chinese men, most of whom were wearing white shirts similar to his, and stood next to a grey-haired grandfather in wire-rimmed glasses, tall for a Chinese, so he could observe new arrivals while staying partially obscured. He could hear the rumble of the approaching train. Fie dee, fie dee, oh pestilential train, he thought. He felt the rush of air pushed ahead by the train just as Sunglasses ran on to the platform.

The train whizzed by, the faces a blur. It came to a halt

176

with a loud screech and Lan Fong felt himself being pulled by the crowd on to the train. But he resisted, standing by the open door until he saw Sunglasses hesitating by the door of the next car down. He heard the sound of air as the doors started to close, then leaped aboard. Sunglasses dived for the doors. Just as they closed, Lan Fong jumped back out on to the platform.

He was alone on the platform. The train began to roll. He watched the windows as an agonized Sunglasses was swept by. Allowing himself a small smile, Lan Fong crossed over and took the next New Territories train to Taipo Market, where he boarded a Kowloon–Canton-line train back to Mongkuk station in Kowloon. During the trip he changed cars back and forth but could spot no one. In Kowloon he caught another taxi to the Star Ferry landing and waited until after they had docked on the Hong Kong side and were on their way back to Kowloon before he went to the lavatory, having made sure no one else in the big passenger cabin was also making the trip back, except for the dreamy-eyed girl student in braids, who had looked around in confusion when the ferry had pulled in at the Queen's Pier Landing, and the tourist couple, obviously American, the wife wearing heavier make-up than a Tsimshatsui girl, chattering without pausing for breath at the husband, belly sagging over his belt, wearing a curious shapeless hat and a camera strap diagonally across his chest like a Sam Browne belt.

The lavatory stank of years of urine and disinfectant. The third cubicle had an 'Out of Order' sign crudely lettered in Cantonese and English taped on the post. That was the one Lan Fong chose, tearing off the sign as he entered. Propped next to the toilet was a Yue Hwa bag identical to the one he was carrying. As he bent down, he could see the shoes and Western trousers of someone in the next cubicle. In a moment he had made the switch, flushed the toilet and left, feeling very pleased with himself. The sound of flushing covered the retrieval of the bag by a hand under the partition between the two cubicles.

Within the hour the coded racing paper was on the desk of the local MI6 station chief. Next to it was the page of the one-time pad. Working slowly, methodically, because he was a careful man, he translated the code. After checking it for any possibility of mistake, he destroyed the pad page.

He whistled to himself as he studied the message. London would have to be told at once, he thought. Because the message confirmed that the Vietnamese had just sent another fifty-five thousand troops into Cambodia. Before the monsoon season ended they would be completely mobilized for war.

CHAPTER 14

The stranger kindles his fire with
  a bird's nest.
This gives joy to the fire
but undermines the man.
Ominous.

The flare floated down over the village, opening a seam of
white light in the night. A machine-gun started up near the
village gate and small-arms fire flickered along the tree line.
Sawyer watched the aquamarine trails of tracer bullets spin
towards the village with dreamlike slowness. Suong, he
thought, his stomach giving a sickening lurch. He ducked
out from under the flooring of the hut and smashed through
the bamboo side-screen just in time to see the shadows of
Toonsang and his men leaping from the hut, packs and
weapons in hand.

Suong was sitting bolt-upright, her face white and strange
in the harsh flare light. It didn't look like her, and for an
instant he recoiled. It was as if he could see the skull, hollow-
eyed beneath the skin. A memory stirred. Something Pranh
had told him once, some Cambodian superstition about how
death is a pale woman in white. Through the open side of the
hut he could see the villagers firing back, red and aquamarine
tracers criss-crossing in a spider web of colour. For a moment
the scene was so like his memories of 'Nam that he just
watched, spellbound.

Then the fear hit him. It was like waking up. Suong's face
was hers. It was just that her eyes were round with terror
and he shoved her down, hissing in her ear to be still. He
leaned over her, the Ingram ready, but they were alone in

the hut. The flare went down somewhere beyond the trees and the night returned, darker than ever. He had seen no further sign of Toonsang and the others.

He could feel Suong breathing under him. She was struggling to catch her breath. He squinted, trying to clear the imprint of the flare from his eye and make his night vision return faster.

'So-yah?' She raised her voice to be heard over the sound of firing.

From somewhere off to the right came the unmistakable stutter of an RPD machine-gun opening up. It was a sound you could never forget.

'We have to go,' he said, pressing his lips to her ear.

'What is happening?'

Who was attacking the village? Sawyer wondered. Bhun Sa? The KMT? The Thai Rangers? Not that it mattered at that instant. As Brother Rap once said, on that patrol when the ARVN dug up some buried VC bodies so they could up the body count for an extra beer ration, 'It don't matter who pulls the trigger and it don't matter when. You is dead just the same, Bro.'

'They're attacking the village.'

He felt her squirming, trying to get up. Suddenly he was enjoying the feel of her moving under him. Of all times! You crazy son-of-a-bitch, he thought, feeling himself harden against her belly. He began to move, pressing himself into her.

'Please, So-yah. This is bad time. We must go now.'

'Yes,' he said, not stopping.

Suddenly there was a sound of firing from farther away and the shooting began to intensify. But their hut was well away from the village; the firing was not directed at them. They could see lights flashing like a *son ét lumière*. They had ring-side seats. Aquamarine tracers were now firing in two directions, towards the village and away from it. It made no sense. If someone was attacking the village from the trees, why would they also be firing away from the village? Unless. . .

All at once, his excitement growing, Sawyer realized what was happening.

That sly son-of-a-bitch, Bhun Sa. He had left the bodies

by the gate as bait, knowing the KMT would attack the village in retribution. Only he must have left the Lisu some arms and a spy among them to let him know when the KMT came back. That's why the phu yai ban had insisted on their staying in the field hut instead of the village guest house. At the time Sawyer had thought it was because Chaw Wah didn't trust Toonsang, but it wasn't that at all. Chaw Wah had been in on it all along. It was a trap for the KMT, who were now caught between the village and Bhun Sa.

Although he didn't think it was deliberate, Suong was moving wonderfully under him. His breathing grew short. He forced his leg between her thighs. But he kept one hand on the Ingram.

'Not now, So-yah. We go now, yes?'

'Better later, when the shooting dies down,' he said. He felt her tense under him, her thighs pressing tight against his between them.

'Please, So-yah,' she whispered, biting her lip.

Then he knew. She felt it too. With a tug, he opened her phasin, her thighs creamy-white in the flickering light. He glanced down at her naked body, at the long legs, firm young breasts, strong hips and thighs, long hair black as ink spread beneath her head and shoulders like a shawl, the haunting Eurasian beauty of her face, the sheer perfection of her, and he felt the tingle growing, knowing that she was his and he could do anything with her. Anything. He bent over her, pinning her down.

The rattle of gunfire grew louder, more deadly.

And then she was no longer fighting him but moving with him, the danger taking them quickly to the edge, making it all the more intense.

He had never felt anything like it. He was like a god, inviolable, floating, the sensation exquisite and the nearby battle merely a play of shadows like the nang. He could feel himself being pulled to her like iron to a magnet as he watched shadows break desperately from the trees towards the village gate. A hidden M-60 suddenly opened up, cutting them down, and then he couldn't watch any more because there was only her mouth, urgent, hungry, and they were like beings possessed, making love as if fighting for their lives against the surrounding shadow of death. And then they

181

were together, man and woman, each of them invading the other, completely filling the universe, obliterating everything else.

A mortar explosion in the trees lit the sky with a red glare. They could see the trees burning. The thick perfume of cordite washed over them and they were still. They lay in each other's arms, still locked together, and listened to the sound of fighting.

She rubbed her cheek, catlike, on the stubble along his jaw, sniffing at him like an animal. Her long hair brushed his face, silky, black, smelling of sex mingled with the scents of cordite and dank earth. Something stirred in the dark recesses of his mind, something very ancient.

He didn't say anything. He didn't understand what had come over him. Somehow the lovemaking had gotten all twisted up with the killing and the danger. And yet it was as exciting as anything he had ever experienced. It was crazy, yet he knew he had touched something at the very core. Something utterly primitive. And he could almost hear Vasnasong's voice whispering in his mind: 'One thing you must to remember, So-yah-khrap. Sex is older than mankind.'

The sound of the firing began to die down. He listened, hardly breathing. Short bursts of submachine fire came from the direction of the trees. It sounded like Bhun Sa's men were mopping up. Now might be their only chance.

'We have to go,' he whispered.

'I know,' she sighed, but made no move to leave.

He understood her reluctance. Somehow their passion had made the hut a kind of refuge.

The renewed rattle of gunfire came like a splash of cold water. A stray tracer seemed to fall from the sky like a shooting star. It plunked into the mud within a few feet of the hut. Someone in the trees was screaming. Sawyer couldn't make out the words, but they didn't need translation. All at once they heard a short burst from a submachine-gun and the screaming was cut short. But the scream seemed to leave a space in the sudden silence.

The firing had stopped.

They had to go. To stay in the village any longer might be suicidal. Keeping low and moving quietly, he pulled on

182

his clothes and reached for his pack. She started to say something and he put his finger to her lips. She froze.

They could hear the cautious tread and faint jingle of soldiers coming down the path towards the hut.

Still naked from the waist down, she grabbed her things. They slid silently through the gap in the bamboo screen down to the murky darkness beneath the hut. Sawyer, followed by Suong, crawled on all fours into the poppy field on the side away from the soldiers. Suddenly there were lights behind them and the sound of soldiers ransacking the hut. They scampered into the woods. In the mossy darkness behind a large fallen tree, Suong stopped and fastened her phasin around her waist once more. She hurried to catch up with Sawyer, already moving soundlessly through the dense forest as if he knew the way.

Later that night she prayed again at the little wooden shrine, despite his misgivings about her lighting the candle so near to the road. But the look on her face had told him there was no point in arguing.

They were in the small clearing near the dead sentry. It was hard to say on whose side he had been. At first Sawyer thought the sentry had them dead to rights. He had already started to raise his hands and think of ploys when he noticed the unnatural stillness of the man's head. He was holding what looked like a brand new M-16 in his lap. Suong had already begun to reach for it when Sawyer grabbed her arm and pointed at the almost invisible black wire attached to the trigger guard. By this time they were both punchy from fatigue, and as soon as they came upon the clearing they dropped their packs. She told him she would take the first watch, but he fought off his desperate need to sleep. There were still too many unanswered questions he had to sort out.

'Why didn't Toonsang try to rape you?' he asked, colouring slightly. What he himself had done wasn't that far from rape either, he thought.

She wiped her face on her skirt. 'He is crafty, that one. Perhaps he know you lie in waiting. I think he comes, but still he waits. In the darkness I felt him watching, always watching, and I thought, now he will come. Then came the brightness in the sky and they are gone like thieves.'

'It's curious he didn't try to steal my pack.'

'Maybe they fear Bhun Sa. They ran as if the phi bop chases them. Sauve qui peut. Maybe they still running.' Her voice was contemptuous.

'Maybe,' he muttered.

He felt her hand, cool on his forehead.

'You sleep now, So-yah. I pray and watch.'

He tried to talk her out of it, but the more he talked, the stupider he felt. If he could just close his good eye for a minute, maybe he could think it all out. Just one lousy minute, then he would go down near the road and stand watch.

A sudden sharp pain in his ribs woke him up. The boot kicked him again. He reached out to grab the foot and became aware of the rifle muzzle pressed between his eyes. He looked over and saw Suong, already captive, her hands tied behind her. Her eyes were frightened and there was a look of pleading in them. Or maybe it was guilt. That fucking candle, he swore to himself. It must have drawn them like moths. One of them kicked him again and Sawyer stumbled to his feet.

There were eight of them. Shan, by their tattoos, and heavily armed. They were thin and savage-looking, their hill clothes ragged. VC dragged out of tunnels after weeks underground never looked that scruffy. Their eyes had the blank stare that in Asia means a captive's life is hanging by the barest thread.

Take the initiative, went Langley doctrine. Sure, Sawyer thought, wishing the skinny prick in Langley who had thought that one up were here to do it instead of him. But he had nothing else.

He started to say something and one of them, tall, with long, greasy hair down to his shoulders and the look of a starving timber wolf, slammed him in the mouth with the butt of what looked like a World War Two vintage M-1. Sawyer staggered to his knees. Blood dripped down his chin. He felt gingerly with the tip of his tongue. His two bottom front teeth were loose and his lip was split. It hurt like hell.

A sharp pain from a hard poke to his kidneys brought him back up to his feet. Someone grabbed his wrists and roughly tied his hands behind him. Another whack in the kidneys got him moving.

An M-1, Sawyer thought stupidly, as they prodded him along the trail. An M-1, for Chrissakes. Up ahead he could see Suong look back despairingly at him over her shoulder. Timber Wolf shouted something and another blow slammed into his kidney. Sawyer stumbled forward.

By the time they reached the road a misty rain was falling from a leaden sky. A mud-splattered Land Rover was waiting in the middle of the road, its engine running. At the sight of it the Shan went rigid and even Timber Wolf stiffened and made something resembling a salute. Timber Wolf proudly pointed out their booty and captives to a large, swarthy Asian in the back seat.

The Asian wore a dark-green officer's uniform, though Sawyer could not identify the insignia as those of any army he had ever heard of. An old scar ran down into the corner of the Asian's mouth. It gave him the mean look of a veteran brawler. His eyes were dark brown and deep-set under long, dark brows. There was a ruthless intelligence in them – and something else. Something Sawyer had seen only once before, on the face of General Easterbrook when he had visited them in the hospital in Zama. It was the glint of raw power. Looking at him, Sawyer had no doubt whatever that he was Bhun Sa.

Ordinarily he would have studied Bhun Sa's face with great interest, except that he couldn't help staring at the other apparition in the Land Rover. Seated next to Bhun Sa and grinning like a banshee was Toonsang.

CHAPTER 15

The deep has been contained with
wood and made into a well.
The plan of a town may change
but the location of its wells
    remains.
There is a leak in the well.
The insects and worms are refreshed.

The two men, one bulky in the uniform of a Vietnamese
officer, the other a short civilian wearing the gold sunburst
badge of the RPK on his shirt pocket, watched the interrogation through the one-way glass. In the room beyond the
glass they saw the prisoner try to say something and the
interrogator scream and slap him viciously across the face
three or four times. The interrogator pointed at the primitive
electrical apparatus on the wooden table and then at the
prisoner's penis, then grabbed the black cables, their
serrated metal clamps making them look almost exactly like
snakes, and shook them in the prisoner's face to emphasize
his point.

The prisoner looked desperately around the room as
though there might be an escape somewhere but, except for
the table and the chair he was bound to with heavy leather
straps, the room was utterly empty. The walls were white-
washed and the concrete floor dipped to a drain in the
centre of the floor, but all the hosing in the world could not
eradicate the dark stains that spotted the floor and walls,
almost to the ceiling. A set of security regulations were taped
to the locked door.

In addition to the interrogator, two guards stood on either

side of the prisoner, their faces blank with boredom. They toyed with their heavy rubber truncheons in the monotonous manner of men anxious to use them.

Watching the interrogation in silence through the glass gave it an air of make-believe. It was like watching a movie on TV with the sound turned off. There was a speaker on the wall that could be turned on at any time, but the two men preferred to keep it off. There was nothing that either the interrogator or the prisoner had to say that was of any interest to them.

There was a knock at the door and a young RPK lieutenant came in. He saluted the general, who merely nodded and turned back to the glass, and then, after a moment's hesitation, the civilian, who beckoned him forward. The lieutenant whispered something in Khmer to the civilian.

'They want to know whether to use the electrics,' Heng Ry said in perfect Vietnamese.

'Of course they do, the idiots.' General Lu made a face. 'Mon Dieu, the stench of this place,' he added, as though the thoughts were somehow connected.

Heng Ry nodded. The very walls reeked of urine and carbolic acid and something that in an open field would have drawn vultures from a hundred miles around.

'No electrics,' Heng Ry told the lieutenant in Vietnamese, as a signal for him to speak in that language in the general's presence.

'But, Comrade General, the prisoner tells us nothing,' the lieutenant protested.

'A good thing too. Otherwise we might have to do something about it,' General Lu observed.

The lieutenant stood there, gaping. 'A thousand pardons, Comrade General. This foolish one does not understand,' he said.

'That too is a good thing. If mere lieutenants can understand a general's plan, so can the enemy.' General Lu smiled, obviously enjoying himself.

'The Comrade General already knows the prisoner's secrets!' the lieutenant exclaimed, then clapped his hand over his mouth in embarrassment.

General Lu roared and even the normally stone-faced Heng Ry had to smile.

'By the Lord Buddha! A thinker, this one. Your RPK begins to show progress, Comrade Heng,' General Lu remarked.

Emboldened by the general's good humour, the lieutenant dared to speak again. 'Our superiors have told us that an officer must learn to use his wits,' he declared proudly.

'Not really.' General Lu shrugged. 'Officers who think for themselves will enjoy very short careers. Only when one has learned not to think at all can one become a general.'

Heng Ry smiled at this. 'Surely one of the Comrade General's reputation does not truly believe such a statement.'

General Lu's eyebrows rose like crescent moons. 'You would be surprised what the Comrade General believes after thirty years of war. Une guerre sans fin. But you are right, Comrade Secretary.' He turned to the lieutenant. 'Incredible as it may seem, Comrade lieutenant, the general does indeed have a plan for the prisoner. Or rather, the Politburo itself does.'

The lieutenant snapped to attention.

'Much better.' General Lu smiled. He glanced back at the one-way glass. The guards were beating the prisoner's stomach with the truncheons. The prisoner was screaming. Bile trickled down his chin. General Lu frowned. He motioned the lieutenant closer.

'About the prisoner,' he began.

'Yes, Comrade General.'

'I want him intimidated, not damaged. He must be made to understand that he is suspected of crimes against the people. Then you are to go in there and have him released for insufficient proof.'

'Released, Comrade General?' the lieutenant asked, blinking stupidly as a bird.

'Comrade Lieutenant, do you know what a captain is? A captain is one who when he was a lieutenant did not make his superiors repeat their orders,' General Lu snapped.

'Yes, Comrade General.' The lieutenant stiffened.

'It is essential that the prisoner understand that he is still under suspicion and his every action watched. I want him to believe that his re-arrest is only a matter of days.'

'Yes, Comrade General.' The lieutenant saluted smartly and turned to go. Then he turned back and saluted again.

'Begging the Comrade General's pardon, but what is the prisoner suspected of?'

'He is a spy for the Chinese,' General Lu remarked offhandedly.

'Is he really?' The lieutenant gaped at the prisoner through the glass. It was the first real spy he had ever seen.

'Of course. The fact that we arrest someone is clear evidence of his guilt. You really must have more faith in our system of revolutionary justice, Comrade Lieutenant,' General Lu smiled.

'But if he is an enemy agent, why are you letting him go, Comrade General?'

'Because if one eliminates a spy one knows, the enemy may send another one does not know. It is often more useful to keep the spy where he is.'

'If he knows he is under suspicion, he may escape,' the lieutenant objected.

'That would be most unfortunate for the men assigned to watch him. Most unfortunate,' General Lu said in an abruptly icy tone. It was clearly a dismissal. The lieutenant blanched. His arm shot up in a jerky salute and he scuttled out of the room.

Heng Ry came over. 'Was that wise, telling such a one about the Chinese?' he wanted to know.

General Lu made a resigned Asian gesture as he turned back to watch the one-way glass. 'That imbecile will certainly let it slip out. Better to let the prisoner learn about it accidently in such a manner. Then he will be certain to believe it.'

General Lu watched the lieutenant enter the interrogation room and bark an order. The guards put down their truncheons, with some reluctance he thought, and began to unstrap the prisoner. His body sagged and they had to hold him up. They splashed water in his face to revive him.

As they worked on him, General Lu glanced around the tiny cell-like room with an air of distaste. This was an evil place, he thought. He had been in many bad places, and after nearly thirty years of war he had seen the worst that people can do to each other. But this was an evil place.

189

He turned his attention to the security regulations taped next to the one-way glass. The crudely typed sheet dated from the time when Tuol Sleng was a Khmer Rouge prison and was identical to the copy in the interrogation room. He put on a pair of wire-rimmed glasses to read it.

The Security Regulations

1. You must answer according to my questions. Don't turn them away.

2. Don't try to hide the facts by making pretexts this and that. You are strictly prohibited to contest me.

3. Don't be a fool for you are a chap who dares to thwart the Revolution.

4. You must immediately answer my questions without wasting time to reflect.

5. Don't tell me either about your immoralities or the essence of the Revolution.

6 While getting lashes or electrification you must not cry at all.

7. Do nothing. Sit still and wait for my orders. If there is no order, be quiet. When I ask you to do something, you must do it right away without protesting.

8. Don't make pretexts about Kampuchea Krom in order to hide your jaw of traitor.

9. If you don't follow all of the above rules, you will get many lashes of electric wire.

10. If you disobey any point of my regulations you will get either ten lashes or five shocks of electric discharge.

'Barbarians,' General Lu muttered, folding his glasses and putting them away. He glanced back at the glass. They were taking the prisoner away. He stumbled between them but was apparently able to walk. 'Barbarians,' General Lu repeated.

'They were merely following orders,' Heng Ry said, having

come up behind him. 'Besides, we Khmers have no monopoly on cruelty. It was the French who taught us the electric wire. And what of the Americans, preaching of the démocratie while they dropped napalm on babies and took prisoners up in helicopters and forced them to jump without parachutes? Or even our Vietnamese comrades, with your "tiger cages" and "Hanoi Hilton",' he added defensively.

'Ah, yes. Barbarism is a matter of class and circumstance, not race. We all need someone to do our dirty work,' General Lu agreed smoothly. 'Now let us exit by another way. I do not want the prisoner to see us.'

The two men left the room and were escorted by a pair of guards down long, twisting corridors, narrow and dank as a grave, to a side door where a white Mercedes was waiting, its windows tinted so it was impossible to see inside. It was parked in an alley that gave them a view of the prison's grim main entrance.

'Wait here. I want to see where he goes,' General Lu instructed the driver, separated from them by a glass partition, through an intercom phone.

'What makes you so certain he will escape to Bangkok?' Heng Ry wanted to know as the general replaced the phone.

'He knows he's blown. He can't stay in Kampuchea. Where else can he go? It's too risky for him to fade into the mountains and try to find the Khmer Rouge. If we don't kill him, they will. And he certainly won't head for Vietnam or Laos, where he knows no one and which we control. No,' General Lu shook his head. 'Thailand is the only direction open to him. When he stops panicking he will rendezvous with his Chinese contact, who has been our man all along. His contact will arrange his escape route down Highway Four. Your RPK officers at the checkpoints are to make it look convincing, but no matter how he blunders, we will make sure he gets safely to Kompong Som. From there Khmer Rouge sympathizers will smuggle him aboard a fishing boat up the coast, probably to Trat, across the Thai border. With joss – as a good Marxist–Leninist I am certain joss does not exist but as an Asian I know better – he will be in touch with Chinese agents in Bangkok within two days.'

Heng Ry nodded nervously. He began to say something

when General Lu leaned forward and tapped the glass partition. The prisoner had emerged into the street. He was blinking as though blinded by the light, despite the gloomy monsoon clouds. They watched him hesitate for a moment, trying to decide which way to go. Then he looked around suspiciously.

'If he heads east, he will be going towards his apartment. West towards Norodom Boulevard will take him towards his contact,' General Lu murmured.

All at once the prisoner seemed to make up his mind. Throwing a last furtive backward glance over his shoulder, he began to walk briskly west.

Heng Ry and the general shared a smile. The driver looked over his shoulder questioningly at General Lu, who picked up the intercom phone.

'Shall I follow him, Comrade General?'

'No.' General Lu shook his head. 'Take us by way of Monivong Boulevard to the Ministry.'

The Mercedes pulled smoothly into the empty street, heading in the opposite direction to that taken by the prisoner.

'When do you leave for the north?' Heng Ry asked.

General Lu stared out of his window. Along the side streets were piles of rusting automobiles, stacked like children's blocks for removal to tiny hand forges outside the city. He remembered how the abandoned vehicles had cluttered the streets when they had first conquered Phnom Penh back in '79. He remembered the smell, the corpses in the street half devoured by dogs that had reverted to the wild and had to be machine-gunned, the helicopters hovering just above the level of the roofs to spray disinfectant, the weeds sprouting from the cracks in the sidewalk. Now on the main boulevards the palm trees were beginning to flourish again and the intersections were crowded with bicycles and kong dups. Now and then you even came across the occasional kerb-side stall selling nems or Cha Gio. But most of the stores were still smashed and abandoned. Apartment windows above them were shuttered and in side streets he could still see broken glass and rats squashed by the motor-cycle carts.

The driver touched his horn, and a little girl in the red scarf and hat of the Revolutionary Youth who was directing traffic waved them through the intersection. The Mercedes was the only moving automobile they had seen.

'At dawn,' General Lu replied.

He watched the faces turn away as they drove by. There was none of the normal bedlam of an Asian city, the music blasting, the squawling of infants, the shrill voices.

'You can still see it,' he remarked.

'What?'

'The fear in their eyes. It's still there, after all these years. They hate us, you know,' the general said, gesturing at the pedestrians starting to run as the rain began to fall. Fat, wet drops splattered on the Mercedes windshield like translucent insects. 'Us, the Russians, all of us. They'd love to see us go.'

'And yet we are all that stands between them and the return of Pol Pot and his killing fields, the peal chur chat,' Heng Ry objected.

'But we are foreigners all the same. "Dog-eaters", n'est-ce pas? Hatred of foreigners is a force that should never be underestimated. It enabled us to drive the Americans out of Vietnam,' General Lu said.

'Not "historical inevitability"?' Heng Ry smiled wryly.

'That too.' General Lu smiled back. 'Though there were dark times, Comrade Minister, when the Marxist-Leninist "dialectic of history" did not seem so inevitable at all. The Americans were far more powerful than we. At times their weight was crushing on us, like an anthill upon which an elephant has sat. They were a good enemy.'

'A *good* enemy?' Heng Ry inquired, eyebrows raised.

'Most good.' General Lu nodded. 'Choose your enemy well, Comrade Minister, for he will be your teacher. In this matter, like you Kampucheans, we Vietnamese were most fortunate in having first the French and then the Americans. They were both good. And strong, especially the Americans.'

'Yet they lost.'

General Lu stared out at the rain. The driver turned on his lights. The afternoon was dark as night and the rain fell in ropes, as the saying went. Drops danced on the pavement like water flowers. Pedestrians huddled under awnings and overhangs. A motor-cycle cart raced by, the driver trying to hold a sheet of clear plastic over his head with one hand as he drove.

'As in jiu jitsu, it was their own strength that defeated them. They lost because they thought the war was a military matter, that the political solution would come after victory. They never understood that the political issues were all that mattered and the fighting was incidental. A Coca-Cola can filled with explosive would have been enough for us to make an incident and keep the war going for ever,' General Lu said at last.

'Yet they tried to win the peasants over.'

'With words only. "But if language is not in accord with the truth of things. . ." ' General Lu shrugged, quoting Confucius. 'They lost because they never saw us. We were invisible. Eh bien, they saw us, we were right in front of them, but they did not truly see us. They thought they were fighting for big things, for la démocratie and against le communisme, when the war really had to do with who owned the pigs in a village. And because they could not see the world this small, they could not see us. And not seeing us, the only way they could have beaten us was to kill every last Vietnamese. Of this they were physically but not morally capable. As I said, "a good enemy".' General Lu grinned.

Heng Ry nodded. Whether he agreed or not, he kept his thoughts to himself. He watched the monotonous slap of the windshield wipers. The Mercedes slowed to go through a deep puddle. The rain was already beginning to turn some of the intersections into muddy lakes. The water was dark as soup. Palm fronds floated on the surface. In the low-lying areas the Tonle Sap had already begun to overflow its banks. Along the waterfront the city resembled a Venice of squatters' shacks.

'And now it is we who take the part of the Americans against the Khmer Rouge. This time it is we who are the elephant and they the ants,' Heng Ry observed glumly.

'Yes, but we can profit by the example of the Americans. That is why the matter of this agent, Pich,' naming the prisoner, 'and the opium of Bhun Sa is of such importance,' General Lu said.

'But whose is the opium? Bhun Sa's or Son Lot's?'

General Lu made an open-palm gesture as though weighing something in his hand, which in Asia means the answer does not matter. 'Two dogs, one bone. They will not share. The bone belongs to the stronger.'

'But will we find it in time? That is the key,' Heng Ry said, his mouth pursed with worry.

There was a creaking of leather as General Lu settled back in his seat. He smiled enigmatically. At that moment, Heng Ry thought, he really did look like the Buddha.

'You should have more confidence in the skill of the Americans, Comrade Minister. Have I not said they are a good enemy?' General Lu said.

CHAPTER 16

The deep within the deep.
The depths confront him on every
    hand.
Everything is dangerous; he is
    never at rest.
His struggles will plunge him
into the chasm within the deep.

'You owe me six chi of gold, younger brother. Did I not say I would deliver you to Bhun Sa, neh?' Toonsang declared boisterously.

Sawyer forced a smile. 'For your payment you must ask of Bhun Sa. For all that was mine is now his.'

Toonsang's eyes narrowed. 'Younger brother's generosity to the Lord of the Shan shows wisdom. Did I not say Bhun Sa would have all when we were yet in the village of the Hmong? Better to have accepted my offer then,' he said, glancing out of the corner of his eye at the woman.

'Ah, but then you would have been richer and the Lord of the Shan poorer,' Sawyer offered slyly.

'By the phi, the farang speaks truth. Better with me than in this old thief's hands.' Bhun Sa's laugh boomed and the others echoed it nervously. 'But among friends there should be no talk of mine and yours. Your pack has been returned and none will dare touch of it,' Bhun Sa assured Sawyer, looking keenly into his face. Up close, Sawyer saw that Bhun Sa's eyes were dark and flat as a reptile's. His face was yellow and very Chinese, but Shan tattoos decorated his chest and back and the belly overhanging his waist sash.

'All good friends,' Bhun Sa repeated, like a car salesman

wrapping up a deal. 'What you want to drink? Whisky?' he asked Sawyer, pronouncing it 'witsake'.

'Mountain whisky or Mae khong?'

'No Mae khong piss. Real Ingrish witsake from Yuessay. See daeng Johnny Warker.' Bhun Sa grinned.

He clapped his hands and a Shan woman came out of the cave with a bottle of Johnny Walker Red and clay cups. She handed it to Bhun Sa who held the bottles up to view like a sommelier.

Sawyer squinted to see the label. 'Dee mark,' he said admiringly. 'That is the real English whisky. Where did you get it?'

'We took it from Birman officers near Kengtung. Where they go they are not needing witsake.' Bhun Sa laughed in a way that gave Sawyer the creeps.

'Pah, Ingrish witsake!' Toonsang scoffed. 'I see Ingrish cinema one time in Chiang Mai. They walk with noses held so, as if there is bad smell in room, and are all the time saying, "You give me witsake-soda preez, ho boy",' Toonsang said, screwing up his face in a striking imitation of monocled aristocratic idiocy.

Even Sawyer had to smile.

'Is truth?'

'I have been in England a ten of times and never have I seen any such as these. Besides, the whisky comes not from the Yuessay or England but from the land of the Scotsman.'

'Neh! The Ingrish drink the witsake-soda all day and night and the women wear longyi that show their bosoms, which are of a monstrous bigness,' Toonsang insisted, clownishly holding his hands at arm's length from his chest to demonstrate.

'Who are these of the Scotsman? I have never heard of these,' Bhun Sa asked Sawyer.

'They are a hill people. Their land is a part of England, yet they are not English. Once there were wars between them and the English.'

'Like the Shan and the Birmans!' Bhun Sa exclaimed delightedly. 'Now I know why they make the good witsake!'

Bhun Sha poured the whisky like water and they drank. It burned like acid on Sawyer's lip and he tried to hide it.

His mouth still hurt from the rifle butt and, when he moved, one kidney reminded him it was there.

'Are the hills of the Scotsman like our hills?' Bhun Sa inquired.

Sawyer looked around the camp in the pines. The area was honeycombed with caves and so densely wooded that not many of the Shan could be seen, although Bhun Sa claimed to have over five thousand men in this camp alone.

They were high up in the hills. The air was cooler and wet with mist and they could hear the rumble of a waterfall less than half a mile down the trail. From the air they were invisible. Sawyer knew this because a few hours earlier a pair of jets, fighters by the sound of them, had flown over, yet there had been no panic.

'Who are they, Thai or Birman?' Suong had asked.

'Neither. Lao Air Force,' Bhun Sa had shrugged.

'What do the Lao want here?'

'They search for me. The Lao government wishes the opium trade for themselves, but we do not allow them.' Bhun Sa grinned.

Toonsang spat. 'The Lao are pigs! Food for the dog-eaters!'

'A backward people,' one of Bhun Sa's savage-looking Shan chimed in.

Suong's eyes flashed. 'Fool! That is what the Europeans say of us all. I remember when I went to school in Paris I had a friend from Laos. Her father was a wealthy rice merchant in Vientiane. She was most pretty, with soft eyes like the kyi deer and when we walk in the streets together we make the heads to turn.

'One time we were invited to a party. Very très chi-chi. We were excited to wear our new French dresses but, no, they wanted us to wear our native phasin. We were a nouvelle sensation, you see. Then someone is asking her where she is coming from and she tells them, "Laos," and they don't know where it is.

' "Laos is called the Land of a Million Elephants," she tell them, and someone say, "You mean Land of a Million Irrelevants," and because we are good Asian girls our faces show nothing, but back in our room that night she is crying very much.'

'What happened to her?'

Suong made an odd gesture of dismissal. 'She fell in love with a French boy and they want to run away. They are making many plans, all very fou, but her father hear of it and make her come back to Laos, where he marry her to merchant friend, old man of sixty whose wife has died. But, of course, that was long ago, before the coming of the Pathet Lao,' Suong told them.

That had been earlier, when they were first brought to the camp. Now the light was fading and the shadows were growing longer. Because of the caves and the trees, it was impossible to guess the extent of the camp but, despite the presence of women, it had the ceaseless activity and air of purpose characteristic of a military base.

Sawyer looked around, admiring Bhun Sa's strategy. There were only two trails in, both well guarded. He could hold off an army, or he could go out the back way and be across any of three borders in a few hours.

'No, the hills of the Scotsmen are colder and there are not so many trees. Instead of wood they burn old dead plants buried in the ground, which they dry, and it is this smoke that gives the Johnny Walker its taste,' Sawyer replied.

'And do they kill the Ingrish as we Shan do the Birmans?'

Sawyer shook his head.

Bhun Sa made a face. 'This Scotman place must be a more holy land than I thought. To have someone steal your land and not kill him requires great piety – or perhaps they are cowards,' he added provocatively.

'I wouldn't say that to a Scotsman.' Sawyer grinned and Bhun Sa laughed.

Bhun Sa poured Sawyer another cupful of whisky. He made a motion for Sawyer to drink and waited till Sawyer had finished and wiped his mouth with the back of his hand.

'And what would one say to a See-ah-ay man?' Bhun Sa asked, watching Sawyer like a snake.

It was a thing Sawyer had been expecting, still it made him weak in the knees to hear it. He remembered the bodies by the gate and knew that if he mispoke now, it was all over.

'Before we speak of business matters, there is the matter of two killings to be settled: those of the Kachin and the Akha. These were necessary for my mission and the protection of the woman, who is here to speak for the army of Mith Yon. But if there is payment due for these, then it is better done now, before enemies share rice and pretend to be friends,' Sawyer declared, looking straight at Toonsang and wishing to hell that he had a gun in his hand.

Bhun Sa smiled lazily, showing all his teeth like a big yellow cat. 'If these were Shan who died, men of the SUA, you would be begging this one for death even now. But for an Akha, or the Kachin, mai pen rai,' he shrugged. 'The loss is to this one,' indicating Toonsang, 'and perhaps no loss since I have purchased his ridiculously priced opium and now there are fewer for him to share with.'

Toonsang smiled back, all friendliness. 'The Lord of the Shan is wise. There is no loss, younger brother. The Kachin was becoming presumptuous. The Akha was of no matter. Had I known the Lord of the Shan was desirous of speaking with you, I would have slit their throats myself to safeguard your sleep,' he declared impudently.

Bhun Sa turned towards Toonsang. 'Wisely said. To kill one's customers is bad business.'

Toonsang flinched under Bhun Sa's unblinking gaze. Sawyer was reminded of the old Cambodian saying that only the gods and the dead never blink.

'This one never considered an act of such monstrous rashness. By the phi, may the Lord Buddha doom this one to a hundred lifetimes as a castrated pig if this one ever . . .'

'Do not add blasphemy to your earlier stupidity,' Bhun Sa snapped angrily.

Toonsang's smile grew sickly, as if he could already feel the sharpened point of bamboo penetrating his belly.

'Now leave us, before I turn you into a castrated pig in this lifetime,' Bhun Sa growled, the scar on his cheek deepening along its uneven crease.

Toonsang hurriedly wai'd and scuttled away. Bhun Sa's own men, recognizing the signs, crept quietly out of earshot, as did Suong, her face an expressionless blank. Only Sawyer and Bhun Sa were left. They watched the sway of her hips as she made her way up the path to the cave.

'She is Mith Yon's woman or yours?' Bhun Sa asked, still watching her.

'Mine — and no one's,' Sawyer said, a warning in his voice.

'She has claws and teeth,' Bhun Sa agreed. 'Any woman is a danger, but that one moves like a tigress.'

'Toonsang wanted her. It was the cause of much difficulty,' Sawyer admitted.

'Yet you suffered him to live.'

'Had the Lord of the Shan not attacked the village when you did, he would even now be with the neak ta.'

'By the nats and phi, that is a slippery one. He is like the hanuman snake, yellow-eyed and green as the leaves that hide it till it drops down on its victim from the trees when least suspected, and its bite kills in seconds,' Bhun Sa observed, watching Toonsang.

'Yet the Lord of the Shan suffers him to live in this world of dust and sorrow,' Sawyer said carefully.

'As the beekeeper suffers the bee to keep his stinger, for without it there is no honey. Does our honoured guest wish his death?'

Sawyer spat, but inside his stomach was turning over. On the road to the camp Bhun Sa had had the Kuomintang officer who had led the attack on the village tied by his wrists to the Land Rover's rear bumper. After an hour on the road, the officer's hands were the only things still recognizably human. Sawyer wondered if Toonsang was enough of a danger to test Bhun Sa's good will.

'Is it offered?'

Bhun Sa considered, thoughtfully rubbing his scar. Then he smiled broadly like a merchant about to quote what he knows is an outrageous price. 'In exchange for additional arms, many things are possible. The Golden Triangle is a dangerous place.'

Sawyer shook his head. The water was getting too deep for him. Bhun Sa had let Toonsang ride next to him in the Land Rover. Who could say what their relationship really was? Someone in that Lisu village had acted as a spy so that the trap could be sprung on the KMT. Toonsang maybe?

'Mai pen rai. Let it be as the Lord of the Shan wishes,' Sawyer shrugged. 'We have more urgent matters to discuss.'

'That is good. And men such as Toonsang have their uses,' Bhun Sa declared, offering Sawyer a white Burmese cheroot and lighting one for himself. Although Sawyer no longer smoked, he was too wise not to light up. He considered what

Bhun Sa had said. It was as close to admitting that Toonsang was his spy as he was going to get.

'Then the Lord of the Shan must have known of my coming,' Sawyer said, trying to contain his excitement and make his voice sound rueful. If true, it meant not that only did the buyer want to buy but that the seller wanted to sell.

'The Lord of the Shan hears more in the hills than the call of the toktay,' Bhun Sa agreed, sending a big puff of smoke to heaven like a signal.

'You have the morphine base, not opium?'

'The white man seeks the "white powder". This is known. Also, in these quantities – ' He paused. 'Does our honoured guest know how much of the opium it takes to make the morphine base?'

Sawyer shook his head, although Harris had briefed him. Never show them up was a cardinal rule with Asians.

'It requires two thousands of poppies to produce one kilo of the opium. Ten kilos of the opium make one of the morphine. Who could transport such an amount in opium form?'

'It is said Bhun Sa owns all the opium of the Three Lands,' Sawyer said, flattering shamelessly. He remembered something Harris had said a long time ago, after coming out of a meeting with a certain Secretary of State known for his ego: 'You cannot over-flatter the really powerful. It cannot be done.'

Bhun Sa looked sharply at Sawyer, who could feel a bead of sweat trickle down the length of his spine. 'Not all, honoured guest. But enough.'

'How much?'

Bhun Sa bent forward and motioned Sawyer to lean closer. 'Three thousands and nine hundreds of kilos of the purest morphine base.'

Sawyer whistled to himself. Barnes hadn't been exaggerating. That was worth about a billion dollars wholesale anywhere in the world. Add acetic anhydride and you had an equivalent amount of pure heroin, worth two to three times that in the US or Europe.

'Where is the morphine? Here?'

Bhun Sa smiled. 'Not here.'

'But it is ready for delivery?'

'All ready. Is Yuessay government also ready? Long time ago I send word to See-ah-ay man, Barnes-khrap. Tell your President Carter the Shan wish to be free peoples. Tell him we trade opium for guns and we kill plenty Birmans, plenty communists. But the President Carter has no interest. "The Yuessay government is not in the opium business," they say. So now I say, is Yuessay ready to do serious business?'

Sawyer shrugged and made a Thai gesture that to Buddhists suggested that the past no longer existed.

'The current President sees things differently. He is not bound by old decisions. My orders come from him through my superiors in the See-ah-ay, as you have discovered.'

'The See-ah-ay has bought the morphine and heroin from us before, in the days of the war in Vietnam.'

'Oh, yes,' Sawyer smiled. 'There are those who believe that making money is always in the national interest.'

Bhun Sa brought out the big catalogue. He tapped the cover with his finger. 'I have looked at these pictures with much interest. Are all here available?'

'We'll trade arms for morphine, as we discussed. M-16 rifles, M-60 machine-guns; "thumpers" – M-79 grenade launchers; LAW 66-millimetre rockets; claymores; mortars – 60s, 81s; jeeps, quad-50s; Prick 25 radios; artillery – 105-millimetre howitzers, 175-millimetre self-propelled guns; slicks – UH-1 Huey helicopters; Stinger missiles, MAs – all kind of mines, some looking like rocks, some to put into streams; all the bullets in the world. Give you any goddam thing you want. The store is open.' Sawyer shrugged.

'Gold?'

'How much gold?'

Bhun Sa pretended to think for a moment. 'Ten millions Yuessay dollars' worth. Five millions deposit in my account in Hong Kong bank. Rest delivered with the arms.'

'That's a lot of gold,' Sawyer said doubtfully, rubbing the bristle on his cheek. 'We'd have to buy it in the open market in London or Zurich. People see such things and questions can be raised.'

Bhun Sa looked unblinking at Sawyer. 'Gold is also a weapon,' he said finally.

Sawyer nodded. 'What about Kampuchea? We need men to use these arms against the Vietnamese dog-eaters. For guerilla actions and to lay mines and MAs, booby-traps, along the border. Can you do this?'

Bhun Sa puffed thoughtfully on his cheroot. 'We fight the KMT, the Thais and the Lao army for the opium trade. That is the way of things. But our war is with the Birmans to free the Shan lands. We have no quarrel with the dog-eaters.'

'With the arms we can give you, the KMT will be a memory in the Golden Triangle, even as it is in Yunnan China. You can defeat the Birmans. A pro-Western state on the Thai border would no doubt receive American recognition and with recognition comes much – not the least of which is money.' Sawyer grinned.

'What of the gold now?'

Sawyer hesitated like a fly fisherman watching a trout lip at the bait 'As the Lord of the Shan says, gold is also a weapon,' he said carefully.

Bhun Sa studied the ash at the end of his cheroot as if wondering when it would fall off. He blew on it and it fell. He blew on it again and the tip glowed bright red.

'Mines and traps can be laid,' he agreed. 'That requires only a few hundreds of men and it will be good training for when we use these devices against the Birmans. But for the real fighting against the dog-eaters, we have agreed to supply one-third of all the arms to the Khmer Rouge. They will,' he shrugged, 'need little encouragement to use them against the dog-eaters.'

'Before the monsoon ends?'

Bhun Sa crushed out his cheroot on the log. He held out his hand, palm up. 'First the arms and gold – here,' he said, tapping his palm.

Sawyer nodded. 'You'll get them.'

'How will you deliver?'

'By plane to Chiang Rai. Then by truck to any place with paved-road access that you designate.'

'What of the Thai airport authorities and border-patrol checkpoints?'

'They will see only what they have been ordered to see. The crates will be stamped "Farm Machinery". The papers will be in order and the officers will be alerted not to examine further. What of the morphine?'

'By mule from its present location to a place where it can

be loaded in big trucks and covered with sacks of rice. From there to rice barges that will bring it down the Chao Phraya to Bangkok, at which point you may make your own arrangements.'

'We will need co-ordination between us and the Khmer Rouge that we all attack the dog-eaters at the same moment and in the agreed sectors.'

'What of the other Cambodian groups? The KPNLF, the Hmong and Mith Yon's group?' Bhun Sa asked.

'We will handle these. When all is ready, we will signal you on the radio which we will give you. The signal to attack will be one word, "Dragonfire", which will be repeated until you signal back that the message has been received.'

Bhun Sa looked curiously at Sawyer. 'Tell me, So-yah-khrap. You have confidence in this plan?'

Sawyer's stomach went queasy. For all that he was a primitive war-lord, he had seen that Bhun Sa had an instinctive talent for military strategy. Or maybe it was that the question had aroused doubts within himself that he hadn't wanted to think about.

'Why does the Lord of the Shan ask?'

'Does the See-ah-ay truly believe that these mosquito stings will chase the dog-eaters from Kampuchea?'

Sawyer didn't say anything.

'Perhaps,' Bhun Sa ventured, 'you think to keep the dog-eaters from crossing into Thailand and make children's stories of a free Kampuchea only for such as the woman who speaks for Mith Yon.'

Sawyer hesitated. Darkness had come. He could not see Bhun Sa's face, only his silhouette against the light from the cave. 'More guns for Bhun Sa means more dead Birmans,' he said softly.

Bhun Sa hawked and spat. In the silence of the shadows, it was as loud as a pistol shot.

'But suppose you make a success, So-yah-khrap? Have you thought what is your coalition? My war is in Burma and the Golden Triangle, not Kampuchea. As for the Khmer resistance groups, the Khmer Rouge and the others are like the tiger and a litter of kittens. If the dog-eaters withdraw, who will the tiger feed on next?'

'Not the Shan,' Sawyer said stubbornly.

'Perhaps not today,' Bhun Sa agreed. 'But who can say what a hungry tiger may do? The kittens will be gone in one bite. Thus!' he said, snapping his jaw shut so his teeth clicked loudly. 'And then . . . it is said that once the tiger tastes of human meat he prefers it to any other.'

'I have heard this,' Sawyer admitted.

'The Yuessay people have given much to Asia peoples. But their gifts bring only sorrow, So-yah-khrap. You gave arms and gold to the Vietnamese, yet the communists win. You gave arms and gold to the Lao and it brought them war and the Pathet Lao. You gave arms and gold to the Kampucheans and it brought them war and the Khmer Rouge. Truly, your gifts are most expensive, So-yah-khrap. And now you wish to give arms and gold to me?'

Sawyer spat. When those geniuses in Langley were brainstorming this beauty, they hadn't figured that a backwoods bandit could have seen through the whole thing because he didn't have a thing ready to say. Bhun Sa had put his finger right on it. They were reaching to grab the tiger's tail and, once they grabbed it, they couldn't let go and there was no telling where it would lead. If the Khmer Rouge were ever to win again, they'd begin right where they left off. How many millions more do you want to see die? he asked himself. But if he didn't pull Dragonfire off, the war might engulf all of South-East Asia.

Hobson's choice.

Time to vote.

Sawyer made as if to stand up. 'If you are not interested in beating the Birmans – or ten millions in gold . . .' He shrugged, bluffing like crazy.

'Neh, neh,' Bhun Sa said hurriedly. 'Mai pen rai. Rice is, how you say, rice. And a man must eat, neh?'

Sawyer grinned. 'As it is said, "Rice gives strength even to the king," ' he said.

Bhun Sa grunted and poured out the last of the Johnny Walker. They drank.

'I have one question, So-yah-khrap,' Bhun Sa brought out delicately. 'A matter of some curiosity, but of a personal nature. May one speak?'

'There is no offence when so presented among peu-uns, Bhun Sa-khrap.'

Bhun Sa put the bottle down with a clink. He watched it roll a few inches before stopping against a twig. 'How did you come to lose your eye?'

'A mine. During the war in Vietnam.'

Bhun Sa nodded. 'Then you were fortunate to have lost no more.'

'Yes, though it was not I but a peu-un who stepped on the device. Had it been otherwise, your humble servant should not be here,' Sawyer said, a shade too pompously. All at once the whisky had hit him hard.

'But this covering over the eye. Is it not of a great handicap in your profession? Who can fail to spot a one-eyed man?'

Sawyer laughed. 'Sometimes it is of great value in my profession for one to be easily recognizable. Other times, no, in which case – ' He tore off his eye-patch.

Bhun Sa took Sawyer's chin in his hand and turned it towards the light from the cave. 'By the phi, there is no blemish!' Bhun Sa declared.

'The eye is glass. The skin took numerous surgeries,' Sawyer said. 'So, you see, those told to look for a one-eyed man will not observe me, though I stand in front of them. Also, the fact that my right eye is still good means that I can use a gun.'

'By the phi and all the nats, this is most rare. But if the eye of glass is such perfection, why wear the covering at all?'

Sawyer frowned. It was hard to explain, even to himself. 'Call it a romantic impulse.' He shrugged. Then, seeing the lack of comprehension on Bhun Sa's face, he grimaced and put the eye-patch back on. 'At first, after the war, I wore it as a thing to thrust in people's faces. To remind them of the war because they treated us like lepers when we came home.'

Bhun Sa's brow furrowed. 'Who would treat a warrior so?'

'Many did so because we fought at all. Others because we lost. It seems strange, yet it was a common thing in those days.'

'We say defeat is a child without parents.'

'We say the same,' Sawyer smiled.

'So this covering of the eye was not a thing of vanity, to say to men, "I was there. I was a warrior and you were not," ' Bhun Sa observed shrewdly. In the light from the cave his face looked like a profile on a frieze, a barbaric chieftain from an age when men became legends.

'It *was* vanity. I wore it to say to men, "I am more of a man than you," and to say to women, "Here is a mystery," for they love riddles better than food and drink,' Sawyer admitted, his tongue growing thick from the whisky.

'And did the farang women flock?'

'Some,' Sawyer bragged. 'There was a time when I wanted to fuck every pretty woman I saw. Somtimes I would follow one in the street, fantasizing how she would look, her ingyi opening to bare her breasts and how I would raise her longyi and bend her over. I would contrive to meet her if I could. Yet no sooner did I have her than I wanted to be away and find another. After a time I came to see the pointlessness of such a quest. I was no more than the animal that puts his injured paw in his jaws in order to bite the pain.'

'Why? Do not the farang women know how to give pleasure?'

'Yes, but they wanted something in return.'

'Ah, money,' Bhun Sa clucked his tongue in understanding.

'No, not money. Something else.'

'What then?'

'I never knew,' Sawyer confessed. 'Perhaps they did not know themselves.'

Bhun Sa made a face.

'Pah! I have heard that the farang women are big and pink and yet, despite their size, their female parts are tight and good to give pleasure. But now I see there is no difference. All women want the same.'

'What is that?' Sawyer asked, feeling himself on that high drunken peak below which the world is spread out to view and life is a thing that can be explained.

'I have had many wives of many tribes. And concubines without counting. Yet in this regard they were as one. What women want above all,' Bhun Sa pronounced solemnly, 'is to be envied by other women. Thus they desire most what they think other women have. If it became the fashion for them to stick parrot feathers in their ears, not a bird in the forest would be safe!' Bhun Sa hooted.

They laughed so hard that the others looked up and smiled to see their 'little flight', as happy drunkenness is called among the hill people. As they staggered back towards the cave, Bhun Sa put his arm around Sawyer and pressed his lips to Sawyer's ear as though bestowing a kiss.

'Listen, farang. Your woman-who-is-not-your-woman, she is of another kind. A fire burns in her, but it is a dark fire that gives no light. Perhaps it is she and not that pig Toon-sang who is most like the hanuman snake. For the hanuman is green like finest jade and most beautiful, but its kiss is death,' Bhun Sa said.

Sawyer came awake all at once. The back of his shirt was damp with sweat. There had been no sound, but something had woken him up.

He sat up in the darkness, concentrating the way a blind man does. He listened to the sound of heavy breathing. The Shan who shared the cave slept deeply and he wondered what it was like to be able to sleep that way. He listened to the others sleep and tried to think, and then he realized what had awakened him.

Suong's place was empty.

She had been curled around him, spoon-fashion. She had felt good against him, the whisky making him pleasantly tired with that wonderful feeling that sleep was going to be as easy as closing his eyes. He touched the depression in the blanket where she had been. It was still warm. She couldn't have been gone long. She probably slipped out for a night call, he thought. She'll be back in a minute. Or maybe she's out there praying to that crazy shrine of hers, whatever the hell that is about. Before this thing was over he told himself, he'd have to get to the bottom of that.

Forget it, his tired brain told him. He had a terrible taste in his mouth from the whisky and just wanted to sleep it off. But there was something that had awakened him. Something bad. Stay awake, the Reptile insisted, the sweat prickling all over his body. Even his hands were sweating.

She had taken the Ingram.

His stomach lurched. He clawed blindly in the darkness, feeling for the M-16. Nothing. He felt all around carefully, so as not to awaken the Shan, his panic growing. Then his hands closed on the familiar metal shape. He started to heave a sigh of relief, then thought he'd better check it.

It was empty. All the clips were gone. He didn't bother to check the pack for more clips. Whoever had done it had been very deliberate. They wouldn't have left him a clip by mistake. Not 'they', the Reptile whispered inside him. She. Even the tanto knife was gone.

Sawyer got up slowly. What was it his Recondo instructor at Nha Trang used to say? 'The successful infiltrator moves as if he does not disturb even the air.' He glided out of the cave on the balls of his feet like a shadow.

Outside a wet mist had settled over the camp. Trees loomed like indistinct dark shapes only when they were close enough to touch, and he had to go warily so as not to trip. The ground was covered with wet pine needles, making it spongy underfoot and muffling the sound of his footsteps. It was like walking through a black cloud. It smelled of wet earth and smoke and yet was like nothing he had ever experienced except in dreams.

He moved smoothly, silently, through the camp, remembering what they'd taught him. Remembering the Vietnamese sapper who coached him to move like the butcher's knife in the story of Chuang Tzu. It was said the knife never needed sharpening because the skilled butcher always guided it through the spaces between the joints, so that it separated the bones without ever touching them.

The mist swallowed him up like a sponge. He saw no one, yet there were thousands of men all around. In a way it was good not having a weapon, for no one would question him even if he were spotted. He would just say he'd had to make a night call and had got lost in the mist. But he felt defenceless without a gun all the same. The very fact that whoever — say *she*, admit it, he told himself — had gone to the trouble of depriving him of it was a pretty good indication that he might have need of it.

Something made him stop. He reached out his fingers and touched a branch, its leaves glistening with moisture. Another step and he would have blundered into it. He was lost, not quite sure where he was going, except that he had kept moving up the slight incline and to the left, where he believed Bhun Sa's command cave was.

He felt his way around the tree. Suddenly he saw a gauzy glow shining in the mist like a marsh light. Bhun Sa's cave.

A crack of light was peeking from the edge of the Shan blanket hung over the entrance. She was there, Sawyer thought, feeling anger and jealousy flare up inside him. He didn't know how he knew, but he was certain of it. Where else would she be?

Was she selling him out to Bhun Sa? Or was Bhun Sa trying to cut a separate deal with her? Hatred for both of them came easily. Fucking gooks! he thought. No – stop! Jai yen yen, heart cool, cool, as the Thais say.

There was a sentry seated in the lotus position by the cave entrance, a rifle across his thighs. Sawyer froze. He listened intently. Was there some sound? He could hear nothing, but he could see the sentry turning his head to listen to something happening inside the cave. His stomach tightened like a fist. Suong and Bhun Sa! He had to get to her.

He might be able to circle around and take the sentry from the side away from the entrance, he decided. It could work if the sentry was still eavesdropping on whatever was happening inside the cave. He had to hurry, but with each step he would have to take care not to make a sound and to be sure that his silhouette always blended into a dark background. He began mentally to step his way and had almost worked it out when the swish of a twig sounded behind him. He started to turn. A dark figure with a long knife loomed out of the mist.

Toonsang.

For the briefest instant Sawyer saw the piggy eyes narrowed, the lips drawn back in a killing snarl, and then there was no time for seeing. Toonsang was very fast; he had already adjusted for Sawyer's sudden turn. His blade thrust straight at Sawyer's throat.

Sawyer threw up his right forearm to block, the blade slicing through like fire. Sawyer held the block sideways for an instant, then, still with the right hand, clawed at Toonsang's throat. He grabbed Toonsang's shirt and yanked him forward in the same direction as the thrust, adding to his momentum, while bringing his right knee up in a high side kick. His knee slammed solidly into Toonsang's chest. Toonsang grunted like a pig. As he stumbled over Sawyer's right leg, Sawyer, still adding to Toonsang's forward momentum, put everything he had into a left hook to Toonsang's kidney.

Toonsang sprawled face-down on the wet ground. Yet he still had enough left to slash back at Sawyer's exposed right leg with the knife.

Sawyer just managed to dance out of the way with a quick half jump to the right. The instant his right foot jarred on the ground, Sawyer raised his left knee high and kicked savagely down, his left heel smashing into Toonsang's face. He felt something crunch under his foot. Toonsang's jaw hung slack and twisted like a shoe with the sole half ripped off.

Sawyer reached down for Toonsang's knife. The action saved his life. The crack of a shot sounded in the air where his head had been. Out of the corner of his eye he saw the dark bulk of the sentry closing. Only one chance, Sawyer thought, his hand gripping the knife. He whipped the knife sideways at the blurred figure coming at him in the mist and dived beside Toonsang.

Two shots cracked the silence in quick succession, one of them drilling deep into the muddy ground only inches from Sawyer's hand, the other thudding into Toonsang, who groaned and stirred, even though unconscious.

The smell of earth and blood was thick in Sawyer's nostrils and he cringed, waiting for the sentry to come and finish him off. His only luck had been that the sentry's rifle must have been on semi-automatic and in the excitement he must have forgotten to switch it over. Come on, Sawyer thought irritably. Get it over with!

There was a sound but no shot. Sawyer cautiously raised his head, expecting the blinding explosion of a bullet in his head, but nothing happened. The sentry was seated on the ground not fifteen feet away. His eyes were wide open, but not on Sawyer. He was staring stupidly down at the handle of the knife sticking out of his belly. He plucked it out and it was like turning on a tap. The sentry watched the blood pour out of the wound as though it were a curiosity of nature that had nothing to do with him. He put his fingers to the wound to stem the bleeding. He watched the blood flow over his hand and never saw Sawyer at all.

Sawyer heard sounds of stirring all around in the mist. There was nothing to be seen, but he could feel the darkness coming to life. The sentry's shots must have roused the whole camp. There wasn't much time.

He started for the sentry's rifle, lying on the ground, when he heard a woman's muffled cry coming from the cave. He raced for the entrance. That bastard! he thought, whipping aside the blanket.

The cave was lit by a single lamp on a table that cast the struggling shadows of Suong and Bhun Sa high on the cave wall as though it were a battle of giants. They were fighting for the Ingram, twisted in someone's hand between them. Suong's face was terrified. Her shirt had been torn open. Sawyer could see her breasts, white and heaving, mottled red by angry finger marks.

Bhun Sa's face was scored by bleeding furrows from Suong's nails. His face was grim, a cruel light in his eyes. He had been forcing the muzzle towards her chest at the moment Sawyer entered. Yet his instincts were remarkable. Despite the intensity of the struggle, he had somehow heard Sawyer enter and had already started to turn.

There was no time. The only move Sawyer had was a chop to Bhun Sa's neck, but it was a killing blow. It would mean the end of the mission. Suong looked desperately at him. There were sounds outside.

The Ingram rang out loudly in the confined space. The shots pinged as they ricocheted off the cave walls. They had just missed Suong. Bhun Sa again forced the muzzle against her chest, at the same time swinging her around to put her between him and Sawyer when Sawyer let go a slicing right hand edge-on to the Adam's apple. Sawyer felt something give in Bhun Sa's throat. Bhun Sa collapsed like a thing made of rags, a ghastly strangled sound coming from his throat. His body began to twitch. His heels drummed against the ground for a few seconds and stopped.

Sawyer grabbed Suong with one hand and the Ingram with the other. She looked down with a kind of fascination at Bhun Sa and Sawyer had to yank her towards the cave entrance. He didn't look back. He didn't have to.

Bhun Sa was dead.

CHAPTER 17

The wind blows beneath heaven.
The prince shouts his orders
to the four winds.
A strong and wilful woman;
do not embrace her.

She watched the young man enter the room. His hair was
short and dark. He had knowing eyes and a handsome
mouth. He was strongly built for a Thai, every muscle
perfectly sculpted. His naked body was magnificent. It
gleamed as though oiled in the low light, sending a shiver
through her.

She stretched languorously, feeling the caress of the gold-
coloured satin sheet against her skin. She watched herself in
the mirrors on the ceiling and walls, her sleek body white
against the gold of the sheet. The mirrors gave a hundred
reflected images of her. She was woman, containing multi-
tudes of selves, she thought. She liked watching herself,
turning her firm white thighs this way and that, now
concealing, now revealing the cleft hidden between them like
a secret. She put a finger to her lips, wetting it, then touched
the finger first to one nipple, then the other, stirring them
erect. She shuddered, breathing deeply of the scent of
jasmine. The soft, discordant yet strangely stirring pi-nai
music seemed to smooth out time like an iron pressing cotton
wrinkles.

He turned her over easily, as if she were a child. He raised
her gold curls away from the nape of her neck and nibbled
softly at her neck and ears. Then he poured the warm oil
smelling of sandalwood into his palms and began gently

214

working on the sides of her neck down to her shoulders, his touch somewhere between a massage and a caress.

His hands glided strongly yet lightly over her body, the sensation warming and exquisite. He smoothed away the tension in her back, trailing his fingers around and under the shoulder blades and down the spine to her buttocks, pulling and kneading them till they were tingling, then down the back of her thighs and calves to the soles of her feet. He massaged her toes, one at a time, and when they were done turned her on her back and began on her breasts, moving in circles spiralling inwards towards the nipples growing hard as iron under his touch.

He dipped his handsome face to the soft mound of her belly, kissing and licking his way down into the dense triangle of hair and beyond to the inside of her thighs. She sighed as her thighs parted, and she shivered when his tongue found the entrance, an exquisite warmth spreading from that thrilling point of contact throughout her body.

Now she wanted him inside her. Hard and strong and all male. As she started to reach down for him, she felt a weight around her head. She gazed up at a second man, strong and lean and sporting a magnificent erection. She reached and took him hungrily in her mouth. A wave of sensation coursed like electricity between her upper and lower lips. She gasped as the first man entered her and she clutched him to her, wanting him as deep as he could go, her nails digging red crescents into his buttocks.

She had them both inside her now and she wanted them everywhere. The feeling came stronger and stronger, and just as she was about to go over the peak, they turned her over on her hands and knees, one of them in her mouth, the other in her from behind, building it in waves even stronger than before.

Her pulse pounded in her ears like the surf. Her breathing grew harder, faster. She began to go wild with the over-powering presence of the two men inside her, gnawing at the one as the other pounded against her squirming buttocks. And then she was spinning out of control and it was good, good, so very good. She felt them spurting into her, hard and hot, wet and salty to the taste, and she took it in greedily, only wanting more and for it never to end.

And the old man watching it all through the peep-hole felt the ancient stirrings as the lithe young girl at his feet, half a century younger than he, lapped like a dog at his semi-erection. He crooned softly with pleasure as she proudly held up for him the fruit of her labour, a tiny drop of sperm gleaming like a seed pearl at the tip of his penis.

Through the peep-hole the old man watched the woman sprawl back on the gold satin sheets in utter, delicious exhaustion. He pressed a button and the soft lights in the mirrored room slowly dimmed into darkness. After a moment, he pressed it again and they slowly brightened to a gentle glow.

The two young men were gone. In their place were two pretty young women, both naked, who began to wash the woman gently from head to foot with scented soap. As they sat her on a stool and towelled her with big fluffy towels, the woman looked up at the hidden peep-hole and smiled sardonically.

'Well, Vasnasong-kha. Did you enjoy the show?' she called out in a husky voice that had a world of cigarettes and cocktails in it.

Vasnasong pressed a button and spoke into a microphone. 'More than ever, Lady Caroline. It is great regret for me that you leave Bangkok.'

'And for me, old friend. London has its pleasures, of course, but I find them not sufficiently – Oh, bother! What's the word I want?' Lady Caroline said, lighting a cigarette.

'*Raffiné*,' Vasnasong suggested.

'Yes, that's it!' she brightened, concentrating as though memorizing it for a quip at a future cocktail party. '*Raffiné*.'

She got up and slipped on a sheer white silk peignoir held up by one of the women as she stepped into soft white slippers held by the other woman, kneeling at her feet. She walked with long, purposeful strides, through a mirror that swivelled open at her touch, into Vasnasong's private room.

The young girl was gone and Vasnasong was already dressed and waiting. He was seated in a silk and blackwood chair in front of an exceptional black-lacquer Chinese screen inlaid with ivory. He gestured for her to sit in the facing chair, carefully positioned on a large, red Tientsin rug, its intricate pattern and colours complementing the spare

216

elegance of the matching Chinese blackwood table, and invited her to partake of iced gin-and-tonic and sogo. She drank greedily.

'Christ, I needed that,' she said.

'After such exquisite performance, it is well earned,' he smiled.

'Well, if you enjoyed watching half as much as I enjoyed doing it, then you bloody well had the time of your life, you old fart,' she retorted with a grin.

Vasnasong laughed easily, his ample belly bouncing under his folded hands. 'Bangkok won't be the same without you, dear lady.'

Her face turned thoughtful, moody. 'All because of that Yank bastard, Sawyer. A pity too. He was damn sexy. Even with that bloody eye-patch.'

Vasnasong raised his eyebrows. 'You found his eye-patch exciting? How interesting.'

Lady Caroline smiled. 'Don't go all bloody Asiatic on me, Vasnasong-kha. You're not a woman. He was damn sexy. That thing gave him an untamed look, like a wild hawk. Pity we couldn't turn him,' she said, biting her lower lip as if she wanted to say more but wasn't going to.

'Mai pen rai. Who will not dip into the common bowl will have to go without,' he shrugged.

'Unlike those of us who have learned to share. Haven't we, darling?' she murmured, her eyes sparkling.

'Parting gifts?'

'How wise you are, old friend. That's something else I shall miss about this place: having one's desires understood without even having to ask. The man who could do that all the time could have any woman on the planet,' she said, laughing at herself. It was a good sexy laugh that pealed clear as a bell.

Vasnasong raised his glass to her. 'Wisdom bows to beauty, dear lady. Cha Yo,' he toasted.

'Cha Yo yourself, you old fraud,' she said warmly and drank. Her face was flushed. It made her look not merely attractive but pretty. For a moment he could see how lovely she must have been as a young woman.

Vasnasong put down his drink with slow deliberation. 'I

take it London is not so much unhappy with Sir Geoffrey, despite his recall,' he said carefully.

'Not at all, darling. There's even been some grumbling among the inner circle over the Americans being so heavy-handed about it. Lots of "What can you expect?" and hand-wringing. And now, especially with Geoffrey's last little coup, our final gift to "the Cousins" ', using the MI6 term for their CIA counterparts, 'it makes them look very foolish indeed.'

'A coup, you say,' Vasnasong murmured, not bothering to conceal his interest.

'Don't worry, darling,' she laughed, tossing her hair out of her eyes. 'That's my parting gift to you. From Beijing via our Hong Kong network. The latest on the Vietnamese mobilization. Fifty-five thousand additional troops are being moved to the Thai border. The invasion is scheduled to coincide with the Loy Krathong Festival of the Floating Lights at the end of the monsoon season. Despite "the Cousins' " bloody-mindedness, Downing Street feels we've made a contribution.'

'Ah, that is most interesting,' Vasnasong said, in a tone that indicated the exact opposite.

'Really, darling. I thought you'd be a good deal more impressed,' Caroline pouted.

'No, no. Independent confirmation will no doubt be much appreciated in Washington,' Vasnasong hurriedly assured her. 'It is only my parting gift to you which renders your news less of a surprise.'

'Will it secure our position?' She pounced greedily, deliberately leaving vague whom she meant by 'our'.

'Oh, assuredly,' Vasnasong smiled.

She curled up on her chair like a cat. She licked her lip as though there was cream on it. 'Come on, you sly puss. Don't be such a bloody fanny-teaser,' she purred.

Vasnasong leaned forward. So did Lady Caroline. Their faces were within inches of each other.

'Most interesting refugee arrived in Bangkok yesterday. I got all details myself only last night,' he began.

'A solid source?'

'Ah, yes. You see the refugee – his name is Pich – was the Khmer Rouge's top agent in Samrin government, the

218

Vietnamese puppet regime in Cambodia. Apparently he was senior Khmer Rouge cadre who defected to Vietnamese with Samrin clique but who actually go along under secret orders from Son Lot himself. When the Vietnamese conquered most of Cambodia in '79, he became primary source for Khmer Rouge pipeline to Beijing. The Vietnamese began to suspect him, so Khmer Rouge brought him "out of the cold", as you Brits say, though I would have said it was really getting too hot! So you see, it all ties together.'

'Is that the gift? A saved Cambodian mole?' she asked, her face falling.

Vasnasong shook his head. 'Fortunately, this Pich was foresighted enough not to come empty-handed. Otherwise,' he shrugged, 'his Khmer Rouge comrades maybe just leave him in Tuol Sleng.'

'Did he confirm the Vietnamese mobilization?'

'Ah, yes, but there is information of even more interesting nature,' he smiled.

'Bhun Sa's morphine,' she breathed.

'Ah, yes, but it seems that Son Lot is now partner in the affair. Morphine for arms against Vietnamese. That was the Americans' game. Only they needed an intermediary, Bhun Sa, and a, how one says, "façade" to be able to claim, if it ever came out, that arms were going to non-communist resistance in Cambodia, such as the KPNLF, Sihanouk and even Mith Yon's faction. Only Son Lot took first American, Parker, and now, according to this Pich, he also has the morphine.'

'So Son Lot means to squeeze Bhun Sa out. Is that it?'

'Once your sexy one-eyed American, the So-yah, arrives on the scene, Bhun Sa's position becomes most precarious,' Vasnasong agreed.

'But will the Americans actually do a deal directly with the Khmer Rouge, the perpetrators of the holocaust in Cambodia?'

Vasnasong picked up his drink and swirled it in his hand. The tinkle of the ice cubes made her think of temple bells. When he spoke his voice was without emotion.

'In my experience, dear lady, nations do not have moralities, only interests,' he said. 'If So-yah does not wish to deal with Khmer Rouge, Son Lot will no doubt find a way to persaude him.'

Even though she hated Sawyer for how he had treated her and Barnes, the thought of what persuasion by the Khmer Rouge might mean sent a chill through her. She shook her head to clear it. What happened to the Americans was no affair of hers, she reminded herself.

'Is that all?'

Vasnasong smiled like a hostess springing a surprise dessert. 'Not quite. According to this man Pich, Vietnamese also know about morphine,' he said softly.

'My God!' she murmured.

'But they don't know where it is! They think they will find it on Thai-side when they invade. Only by then it will be in our hands!' Vasnasong declared gleefully.

'How?' she asked, forcing a nervous smile. He smiled back, at that moment looking every inch a ruthless Mandarin of some ancient Chinese court, despite his Western-style silk shirt and slacks.

'Among my various shipping interests is old freighter, name *Siam Star*, vessel of Panamanian registry.' He shrugged. 'She is one of those ships that arouses no attention in any port and appears to be held together primarily by rust but is actually quite seaworthy. The crew, except for the captain, who is Swatowese, like my mother's people, are mostly Philippino scum.

'Because of my Thai connections and also the useful information I was able to supply from MI6, thanks to our connection,' inclining his head in her direction, 'I convinced new CIA station chief, a certain Harris-khrap, that the *Siam Star* could transport the morphine with the kind of discretion required for such a delicate affair.'

'Just don't forget our share in this,' she said.

'Ours?' Vasnasong smiled.

'Yes, ours, Geoffrey's and mine, as you bloody well know,' she snapped.

Vasnasong laughed, holding his hand on his stomach as though it hurt. 'Ah, my dear lady. Bangkok is going to be so very boring without you.'

'Well, then,' she said, slightly mollified.

'Well, then,' he teased. 'Once morphine has been loaded,

Siam Star will leave Bangkok and head south into the Gulf of Thailand to swing well clear of Cambodian and Vietnamese waters. It is possible she may even go a bit too far south, to the waters off Songkhla. Who knows what can happen there?'

'Pirates?'

'It is said the men of Songkhla are fishermen when their nets are in the water,' he smiled.

'And the ship?'

'It is insured. The CIA will no doubt make sure insurance companies do not inquire too deeply into the nature of her cargo,' he shrugged.

'And I get ten per cent, as we agreed, you sly puss,' she said, reaching over and cupping his sex in her hand.

'As we agreed,' he nodded complacently, taking a deep breath. 'But you are already so wealthy, dear lady. What will you do with so much?'

Her gaze was level and absolutely sincere. 'Really, darling. Money is always useful,' she said.

CHAPTER 18

The wind blows above the earth.
The worshipper has washed his hands
but has not yet presented the
    sacrifice.
He examines his own life.

A temple bell sounded the end of meditation and, just like that, Utama was back with them. For hours he had sat in the lotus position without movement. All at once his eyes were twinkling and they could see him breathe once more. He smiled at Sawyer, draped in the yellow robe of a naga aspirant, and Suong, dressed in peasant black. Around them were the sounds of bare feet on stone as the other monks in the uposatha wai'd to the golden Buddha on the altar and exited through the door that led to the hall of the achan.

'Why do you meditate?' Sawyer asked.

'Why do you Christians pray?' Utama replied.

'For God's help, I suppose,' Sawyer shrugged, thinking that he was hardly qualified to speak for Christianity.

'Pah!' Utama said, waving the thought away with his hand. 'That makes of God a celestial telephone operator. "Yes, you may have that new phasin." "Saw at dee! So sorry! Tomorrow your father must die of cancer." "Hello. You want to kill your enemy. This morning he ask my help to kill you. So, so. You win today. But in two weeks your little girl will step on mine and lose her legs. Bye-bye." You make of God a great stupidity. Once I studied in a Christian mission school in Chiang Mai, but they say many so foolishnesses I wonder how the European manages to survive in this world.'

'We manage,' Sawyer smiled. 'And you haven't answered my question.'

Utama smiled back, the wrinkles making deep furrows around his eyes, buried deep in his face like almonds pressed into dough.

'One meditates to clear the mind, my brother. Always there is so much noise in one's head. Chitter-chatter. Chitter-chatter. Even at this instant there is a voice in your mind repeating every word I am saying, though there is no need, for it is I who am speaking, not you. One meditates to get rid of this chitter-chatter. Only when the lake is calm does the water reflect the sky. When the mind is quiet, one can see things as they really are. Then one's life can be purposeful and not of those who are, as the Enlightened One said, "pushed and pulled this way and that like a twig in a drainage ditch".'

The smell of incense tickled Sawyer's nose. He didn't know how to respond to Utama's oblique reference to the hash he had made of things. Suong sat beside him like an ikon. She had said little in the hours since their escape. There were moments when he thought he caught a look of fear or pleading in her eyes, but when he tried to say something her eyes went blank. She had 'gone inside', as the Asians say.

'You mean like me,' Sawyer said.

Utama only smiled. 'Your karma brought you here. Perhaps so we could talk. Tell me, how did you escape from Bhun Sa's camp?'

Sawyer shrugged wearily. He was very tired. 'We walked out. The mist was heavy outside Bhun Sa's cave and we were able to pull the sentry's body inside without being seen. Bhun Sa's men had heard the shots, of course, but by the time they found Toonsang and dared approach Bhun Sa's cave, knowing his standing orders not to be disturbed, we were able to get our packs and were well away. With the KMT out there somewhere and the night so dark and misty, they probably decided to wait till dawn before coming after us. The mist saved our lives.'

'So you came here.'

'So we came here,' Sawyer agreed.

Utama got stiffly to his feet and beckoned them to follow. He led them to the vihara temple for lay people. The vihara dormitory hall was lit by flickering oil lamps. They were alone, though there was room on the floor to bed perhaps a hundred people. Along the walls were murals depicting parables from Buddha's teachings.

'I can give you sanctuary for one night, no more. This we do for anyone and also because I think your escape was most arhat-like, simply to walk out of the camp of your enemies. It is surely karma. But after dawn you must not be here, for we cannot take sides,' Utama said.

'The Buddhists in Vietnam take sides.'

'And look at Vietnam,' Utama replied.

Touché, Sawyer thought and wai'd, Suong wai-ing with a deep bow.

Utama's face was working. He had something more to say. Finally he brought it out. 'There is a thing between the two of you that is festering in silence. It poisons not only your peace but the space around you. There will be a half moon tonight. Perhaps by its light. . . .'

Sawyer frowned. He had prided himself on being a better actor than that. He peered deeply into the monk's eyes.

'We will talk again, afterwards,' Utama said and was gone.

Suong and Sawyer looked at each other in the empty hall. The sound of a heavy tropical downpour drummed on the roof. A young naga came in with two bowls of rice. As he padded out on bare feet, they sat down and began to eat in silence.

After the rain the brightness of the moon came as a surprise. It wore a halo of clouds but was bright enough to cast a shadow. The hills were dark and featureless. Somewhere out there Bhun Sa's men were hunting them but here, in a grove of betel palms outside the temple bot, Sawyer felt safe somehow. There was a whisper of wind in the palm fronds. It stirred the bamboo chimes hanging near the vihara gate to music.

'What do you accuse me of?' Suong asked. She had loosened her hair. It fell loose to her shoulders, framing her face, cameo-white in the moonlight.

'Have I accused you of anything?'

'With words, no. But in your heart, yes.'

'Do you feel guilty? Is that it?'

Suong looked down at the ground. She didn't say anything.

'Why did you go to Bhun Sa?' Sawyer asked finally.

'He summoned me,' she said, not looking at him.

'Why didn't you wake me?'

She took hold of a palm frond and tugged it.

'And the gun. Why did you take it?' he asked.

'Oh, So-yah,' she said. The light of the moon glimmered in her eyes.

'What are you hiding?' he demanded, the softness of his voice only accentuating his anger.

'He wanted me alone,' she said, looking down at the crumpled leaf in her hand. 'The way he looked at me was the way you all look at me. Do you think I have not seen it before? I took your pistolet-mitrailleur so you would not do a foolish thing. For then he would surely kill you. I thought if I showed him the pistolet-mitrailleur, he would think you harmless and let you live. But he spat and said he could sell the morphine anywhere and that the Americans were fools to believe he would risk his men to fight the dog-eaters so far from the Shan mountains when his real war was with the Birmans.'

Sawyer put his hand to her cheek. She pushed it angrily away. She looked up at him defiantly, silver sparks of the moon in her eyes.

'I thought the pistolet-mitrailleur would frighten him, but he only laughed,' she went on. 'He said if I was not his, he would give me to his men. He said they would chain me like a dog to a tree for the use of any who passed by, that the last female so used had spent six months that way, raving and talking to herself. Then he called for Toonsang and sent him to kill you as you slept. I tried to kill him with the pistolet-mitrailleur, but he was too fast for me,' she shrugged. 'The rest you know.'

She looked at the leaf remnants in her hand and threw them away. Sawyer turned and walked to a rise near the edge of the palm grove. From here he could see the dark humps of the hills in the moonlight all the way to the valley of the Nong Lom and, in his imagination, even beyond, to the Mekong. The wind came up and he listened to the sound of the chimes and the noise of the fronds, not idly but with intent, as a sailor listens to the sound of canvas. He sensed her behind him. He turned and they were in each other's arms, kissing passionately. Her lips were warm and sweet and it was the best kiss he'd ever had.

'And now? What now?' she asked finally.

He made a face. 'It's over. Finished. Without Bhun Sa . . . ,' he began.

She shook her head. Her hair flared in the wind. A shadow passed across her face. He looked up. A cloud had covered the moon. It started to rain again, suddenly as someone turning on a shower. They stepped under a tall palm and listened to the rain on the leaves.

'Bhun Sa didn't have the morphine,' she said. Her voice seemed to come out of the night itself. It had the sound of rain in it.

That was right, he thought. With so much else that had gone wrong, he knew that that part at least was right. If the morphine had been in Bhun Sa's camp, Bhun Sa would have shown it to him – and the camp's internal security would have been tighter. Bhun Sa might have been acting, but all his people couldn't have been acting too.

'Who does?'

'Son Lot. The Khmer Rouge. With your arms they could stop the Vietnamese,' she whispered.

'How do you know?'

'Bhun Sa told me. He bragged about it. He was going to betray the Khmer Rouge to the Vietnamese and sell the morphine to them for Russian arms. Less trouble to him and he needn't to risk his men inside Kampuchea. He was a snake, this Bhun Sa. For him you Americans were merely, how one says, des astuces pour gagner, counters to use in his bargaining with the Vietnamese.'

'Plots within plots within plots. It's getting all mixed up,' Sawyer murmured.

Suong wiped the rain out of her eyes with the back of her hand. 'This is Asia, my So-yah. Here nothing is as it appears.'

'If only we knew where Son Lot has the morphine,' he muttered.

'Why? Would the CIA deal directly with the Khmer Rouge? That is the question.'

'I don't know,' he admitted.

'You could ask.'

'But without knowing where the morphine is. . . .' He shrugged.

'But we do know,' she said, smiling a secret smile.

'How?'

She showed him the crude map she had taken from Bhun Sa's pocket while Sawyer was dragging the sentry's body back in the cave. Rain splattered the map as she indicated the markings in Bhun Sa's own hand by the flare of a matchlight. The light revealed her clothes moulded to her body by the rain.

'Inside Cambodia,' he whispered, unable to take his eyes off her.

She began to unbutton her blouse. 'In the ancient place of the gods,' she murmured, the warm rain glistening on her skin as she pulled him down to the soft wet earth.

'How goes it with the woman?' Utama asked.

They were sitting in his tiny cell. A single candle burned on a low table. It created a close tent of light around them. Sawyer knew there were mosaics on the wall, though it was too dark to see them. The smell of incense permeated the air. Its sweetness was almost strangulating.

'Better,' Sawyer said.

'But still. . . .?' Utama suggested.

Sawyer made a face. It was all falling apart in his hands like rotten cloth and he wasn't sure what was true any more. 'This is Asia. Here nothing is as it appears,' she had said.

'Women,' he replied, the way men do among themselves to indicate the impossibility of the two sexes ever seeing eye to eye.

Utama laughed. 'Nonsense. You Europeans always see things in terms of success and failure, winning and losing,' he said cheerily. 'I win my lover. I lose my lover. I give you this much love, but you only give me that much. So maybe I give you less so that I am not losing. Everything is a contest. You even have to defeat death. So silly.'

'Why silly?'

The darkness around the cocoon of candlelight created an odd intimacy. Sawyer felt as though he were talking to himself.

'Because it is not practical. Your thoughts make you what

227

you are. If they do not help you in a most practical way, they are of no value. For instance, the mission priest told us that your Jesus of Christ raised a man from the dead. But of what value is that to you when your own wife or brother dies? Will Jesus come back and raise them too? Of what value then is such thinking? Or must you believe they have gone to live in a celestial Land of Bliss which you yourself have never seen and for which there is not the slightest shred of evidence? This the Enlightened One would never accept. Only what your reason can accept, only what you yourself experience, unclouded by emotion or wishful thinking, only this partakes of truth. This is what Buddha meant when men came to him and, recognizing that he was a different order of being from other men, asked him not "Who are you?" but "What are you?"

' "Are you a god?" they asked. "No." "An angel?" "No." "A saint perhaps?" "No." "Then what are you?" Buddha answered, "I am awake." '

'What would Bhudda have done?'

'A young woman named Kisagotami came to the Enlightened One hugging the dead body of her infant son to her breast,' Utama related. 'She begged him to raise the child from the dead. "This I can do," the Tathagata told her, "but the special medicine I need requires mustard seed from a house where no relative, servant or friend has died." So Kisagotami went begging for the mustard seed from house to house, but nowhere could she find a place where death had not visited. Only then did she understand that all that lives dies; there is no permanence to things. Some lights in the village go out; others come on. It is not a contest. It is the way things are. She became, as we say, "enlightened" and was able to bury her child in the forest. Which approach do you think more practical?'

'And I, how am I to be enlightened?' Sawyer asked hoarsely.

The darkness seemed to press close around them. Utama sat cross-legged, his pale skin almost translucent in the candlelight. Sawyer could see the veins crawling under the skin of his ancient skull like blue worms. Utama blinked like one waking up.

'Mai pen rai, my brother. You have the one eye and can

see much more than those who are blind. It has taken you this far. Yet without two good eyes you cannot see things as they really are. Then who does your action help, yourself or your enemy?'

'What is it that I should see, holy one?'

Utama reached up and pulled off Sawyer's eye-patch. He regarded Sawyer's glass eye with a kind of clinical appreciation, the way a surgeon might. The candle flame could be seen in it, as in a mirror.

'You don't need this any more, my brother. Besides, the men of Bhun Sa will not find you so easily without it. As for the path you should take, remember that your karma has brought you this far. It will take you to the place where you will see the whole truth. Though for you, I think, it is a dark place, lit by a dark fire,' he said uneasily.

'And then?'

'And then you must choose, like all men, even as your bowels turn to water with fear. And worlds will hang upon your choice,' Utama said.

CHAPTER 19

The marsh has risen over the earth.
The superior man puts his weapons
in order and prepares for
    unforeseen emergencies.
Confer with the great man.
Success
as long as you are willing to pay
    the price.

Like slow-motion dancers, the two elephants raised their
right front feet in unison and, with an almost feminine deli-
cacy, rolled the long, heavy, teak log forward a few feet.
Their mounted mahouts lightly tapped the massive shoulders
with short bamboo sticks and the elephants repeated their
dance, pushing the log along the ground until it rested against
the pile being loaded on to a big flat-bed truck. The loading
of the logs created a temporary roadblock across Highway
107, and a line of gaudily painted trucks and carts had settled
down to wait. One enterprising driver had even slung a
hammock from the bumpers of two tractor-trailer rigs and
had settled in for a nap. Other drivers were reading or eating
beside the road, the hot scent of red Prek-kk-noo peppers
shimmering in the steamy midday heat.

It was an ordinary enough sight in rural Thailand, but
Sawyer was instantly watchful. Any roadblock was
dangerous, but there was something about this one that
didn't feel right.

It was too late to turn back. They'd already been seen by
a small group of truck drivers sitting in the shade of an
alocasia and gossiping over a shared bottle of Amarit beer.

Not that there should be anything worth noting, Sawyer reassured himself, about a monk in a worn saffron robe, his hair cropped close, his body shaved smooth and hairless as an Asian's, his skin stained with berry juice, and a young peasant boy of the Lisu, grimy from the road. Suong's breasts were strapped down, her hair was pinned under a straw hat and no one should have given them a second glance. But Sawyer's Reptile was wide awake as they approached the line of trucks, and he could feel the sweat prickling all over his body. His hand tightened on the Ingram, concealed inside the furled black umbrella he carried, like many monks, against both sun and rain.

There was something wrong, the Reptile was telling him. It was like one of those 'Can You Tell What's Wrong?' picture puzzles. At first you don't see anything until finally your eye catches the cloud that actually turns out to be a fish in the sky. They walked past the driver on the hammock and the drivers sitting in the shade eating and there was nothing. One of the drivers wai'd to Sawyer, but he remembered to ignore the wai the way a real monk would. He knew their disguises wouldn't stand up to much scrutiny, but they ought to get them through any casual situation. Bhun Sa's men were looking for a one-eyed white man and a beautiful female, not a two-eyed Asian monk and a Lisu boy. It was just an ordinary rural scene, the stalled trucks baking in the sun, except that his Reptile was getting very jumpy. There was a fish in the sky somewhere. But where?

Suong trudged beside him, head bent as though weighed down by the packs on her back and the steamy afternoon. Then he had it.

The driver lounging in the hammock had positioned it so he was in the boiling sun, something no Thai would have ever done. His position was perfect for covering the road but not for resting. Of course, the sun might have moved, but there were plenty of shady places where he could have strung the hammock. And there was something else. Sawyer let his memory reconstruct the image without forcing it, which always creates distortions in memory. He didn't dare turn around and look back. That would have blown the monk cover there and then. Yes, he had seen it. The driver's shirt had been open at the neck and he had seen part of a Shan tattoo.

It was a trap.

Sawyer's eyes darted around, measuring the distance to the high grass and palms alongside the road. He could fire the Ingram through the umbrella and, once in the high grass, they could make a break for it. His heart pounded. Should they go for it? So far they hadn't been challenged. What were the chances of bluffing versus running, he wondered. Lousy either way. Go for it, he thought. Better to die moving. His legs tensed. The only question was how quickly Suong would react. Then he changed his mind.

Bhun Sa's men were lounging in the shade under the flat-bed truck, covering the road with automatic weapons. They had no choice. They would have to bluff.

Sawyer's skin was shiny with sweat. He hoped to God it wasn't making the stain run. If only the men under the truck had never seen them before, they might have a chance. He felt Suong tense up beside him. She had made no sound or movement, but he felt it. The sun baked down on them. Sawyer felt exposed as though the sun was an eye in a giant microscope peering down at them. He risked a glance out of the corner of his eye and was immediately sorry he had. He didn't recognize any of the others, but Timber Wolf and his M-1 was staring right at him.

The Ingram grip felt slippery in his hand. They were passing within ten yards of the flat-bed. He didn't dare look, but he could feel Timber Wolf's eyes burning on the back of his neck. Just then there was a loud sound and Sawyer almost jumped out of his skin. The flat-bed shuddered and Bhun Sa's men looked up. An elephant had dropped a big teak log from its trunk on to the pile on the flat-bed. The animal smell was overwhelming. The elephant began to urinate. It splattered on the road with the force of a fire hose and Bhun Sa's men laughed raucously as they scrambled out of the way. Sawyer forced an enigmatic Buddha smile, like Utama's.

They plodded on in the burning heat. At every step he expected to hear a shout for him to stop, but it never came. Only after they had rounded the next bend and were out of sight did Sawyer and Suong both sink to the ground at the same instant, as though it had been planned. They managed a feeble smile between them. Their legs were trembling, too weak to carry them any further.

'Dragonfire' was the code intro and Sawyer didn't have to go into a bunch of counter-sign bullshit because he'd have inserted the word 'weather' into the first sentence or two if he were calling under duress. There was no need for security at this end, since Suong was outside the noodle shop keeping watch and this was the only phone in Tha Ton, a tiny village on the banks of the Kok river. From inside the shop Sawyer could see the hang-yao they had hired. It was tied to a wooden plank that served as a pier. The driver squatted in the stern, eating a bowl of noodles slowly, as though he wanted to make it last.

The shopowner, a hill Thai with flat features, stared goggle-eyed at the monk making the call, but there probably wasn't anyone within fifty miles who could manage more than five words of English, and a simple conversation code was more than adequate. The only real danger was bugging at Harris's end, but after the fiasco with Barnes Sawyer figured he'd have that covered.

'What happened?'

Even through the godawful Thai telephone connection he could hear the tension in Harris's voice, waiting for the bad news. A field agent doesn't call his case officer from the red zone to wish him a happy birthday.

'It's our friend from the hills.' He couldn't afford to use Bhun Sa's name.

'What about him?'

'He bought the farm.'

Sawyer could hear the sudden intake of air through the earpiece. But Harris kept it under control. Maybe Harris was better than he had given him credit for, Sawyer thought. By rights he should be cursing Sawyer up one side and down the other.

'How?'

'A field decision.'

'I see,' Harris said quietly.

Sawyer waited, letting the implications sink in. He wanted Harris to see the whole mission dissolve before his eyes

233

before he threw the son-of-a-bitch a lifeline. Because he wanted them to understand, really understand, before they made the decision. Then it would be out of his hands. Then he would just be following orders, he lied to himself, knowing it was a lie.

'No, you don't see. It was necessary.'

'Of course,' Harris said, his tone clearly implying that of course it wasn't.

'It doesn't matter. He didn't have it.'

'You mean the "coconuts"?'

Jesus, Sawyer thought. 'Yeah, the goddam coconuts,' he said. He looked into the face of the shopkeeper, and the Thai had the kreng chai to look away. He looked outside at Suong, who never took her eyes off the Fang road. If there was any trouble, it would have followed them up that road.

'Where are they?'

Sawyer could hear the desperation in Harris's voice. He was grasping at straws.

'Our friend from the hills stashed them with another old friend of ours – from the Parrot's Beak,' Sawyer said, hoping Harris would understand the oblique reference to Pranh, alias Son Lot, in the case file.

'Our *double*-jointed, rather famous friend,' Harris said carefully.

He wasn't stupid, Sawyer thought. Whatever else you might think about the son-of-a-bitch, at least he did his homework.

'That's a ten-four.'

'Where?'

'Where do you think?'

'Inside Cambodia,' Harris sighed. The implications were beginning to sink in. Sawyer could have taken him the next step. It was obvious what they had to do not to abort the mission. But he wanted it to come from them, dammit. He didn't want it to be his idea. Let it be karma.

He saw Suong straighten up outside. She was motionless, utterly concentrated.

'Could we,' Harris began slowly, 'implement Dragonfire using our Parrot's Beak friend?'

'In theory, I suppose.'

'And in practice?'

'Who knows? They shoot on sight over there.'

'But could you?' Harris pressed.

There it was.

'Is that what you want?'

Suong stood up. She had seen something.

Harris's voice was dry, matter-of-fact. 'If it can be arranged,' he said.

'Jesus!' Sawyer exploded, talking openly and suddenly not caring who heard him. 'You know who these people are! You know what they'll do if they win. It's murder, for Chrissakes!'

Harris didn't say anything. They must think he had finally 'gone Asian' to care about a bunch of gooks slaughtering a whole bunch of other gooks when there were important things like careers to worry about, Sawyer thought bitterly. He looked outside. He couldn't see Suong. The sky was ominous. Thunderheads were bundled over the grey river.

'It's murder if you don't. The Vietnamese have moved fifty-five thousand more troops into Cambodia. We've had more input,' Harris said. He told Sawyer about Pich and the data from MI6.

He wouldn't have done it if he hadn't needed to talk me into it. They must be going crazy in Washington, Sawyer thought. And then, God forgive us for the crimes we commit for our country.

'If I don't make it back. . . ,' Sawyer began.

Harris's response was immediate. 'Don't give me that crap! The good ones never talk that way.'

'Good? That's a funny word to use on this one.'

Harris didn't answer. He was smart enough not to pick it up. He was probably wondering just how spooked his agent really was at this point. Plenty, Sawyer thought. He shouldn't have brought it up. When it came to Asia, most round-eyes just couldn't understand. It was like trying to explain colour to a blind man. The receiver crackled in his ear like a nest of insects. Sawyer waited. That was something Asia had taught him: how to wait.

'Anything else?' Harris asked. From his tone Sawyer could tell he was anxious to get on the horn to Langley.

Sawyer hesitated. He had more but his Reptile was working overtime. Where was Suong? He had to go. He eyed the bamboo curtain over the opening at the back of the shop. Whatever it was, it was coming. He should just hang up and go, except he had been damn lucky to find a phone and get through to Harris down in Bangkok somewhere.

And it wasn't clear. All he had were vague suspicions, nothing solid. If he'd presented them in a CTP case study, he'd have been laughed out of the room. But there was something there, all right. No smoking guns, but brick by brick, something was getting built.

'What is it?' Harris asked quietly. He was smart enough to know that not only do an agent's feelings and hunches matter but sometimes they are all that matters.

Sawyer told him.

'I'll check it out. Talk to that Cambodian resistance guy,' Harris said wearily when Sawyer finished.

'No, I will.' Sawyer didn't want to mention Mith Yon's name on an open line.

'I take it you'll be passing through the same place,' meaning Aranyaprathet, where they'd met the last time, 'on your way into – '

Just then Suong came bursting into the noodle shop, carrying both packs. Her eyes were rolling like a crazed animal's.

'Sawyer! Saw– ' Harris's shout was like an insect chirp as Sawyer slammed down the receiver and grabbing his pack, leaped through the bamboo curtain.

He landed in the muddy ground outside the shop and began sprinting for the river bank and the waiting hang-yao. Suong pounded at his heels. Her breath came in sobs. She was trying to say something but couldn't get it out.

Shots rang out. Automatic fire. A lot of it. Coming from the direction of the Fang road. He could see small figures in a Land Rover bouncing over the rutted village street, racing to cut them off from the river. Bullets drilled into the mud around their feet. Suong started to dive to the ground. A natural instinct he had to fight in himself.

'No!' he shouted, yanking her arm with one hand as he fired the Ingram through the umbrella with the other. They were in open ground; hitting the dirt would be suicidal. He began to zig-zag like a rabbit, firing back blindly and suddenly changing direction without pattern. After an instant's hesitation, Suong broke away and did the same. They were two separate, erratically moving targets.

But the shots were getting closer as the Land Rover started to come within range. Sawyer could see it careening wildly through a flock of crazed chickens, the Shan barely hanging on as it cut across the muddy track towards the wooden pier. One of them leaned far out and, balancing precariously, took dead aim at Sawyer's chest. Still running, Sawyer ripped away the umbrella handle and squeezed the trigger.

Nothing happened. He squeezed again, then the sickening realization that the clip was empty hit the pit of his stomach. He ducked and the shots sounded very close. His breath came in great, painful heaves, but he ran on even faster, Suong beginning to fall behind.

He yanked out the empty clip and reached into the pack for another. His hand closed instead on a grenade. For an instant he debated throwing it for a diversion, anything to slow down the Land Rover, but with everything moving it would take a miracle to even get near the vehicle. He was almost at the river bank, but the Land Rover was getting closer. It would be a near thing.

He blinked the sweat out of his eye. Christ! The hang-yao driver had dropped his bowl and was watching the chase wide-eyed. Sawyer could see the Shan in the Land Rover clearly now. They were grinning with betel-blackened teeth at the excitement of the hunt. They knew they had Sawyer and the girl dead to rights. Except the one next to the driver with the devil's eyebrows and bandages around his mouth and one arm.

Toonsang!

That must've been what Suong was trying to tell him. They had been recognized back at the roadblock all right. It was just that Toonsang wanted the pleasure of finishing them off himself.

Sawyer's hand found another clip just as he reached the plank. He shoved it home and fired half a clip. There was a yelp of pain and the Land Rover swerved aside. Toonsang's men jumped out and started to run towards him. They were less than fifty yards away.

Suong ran out on to the plank and jumped down into the hang-yao. Sawyer fired the Ingram again and, for a precious second, Toonsang's men hit the dirt. Sawyer jumped down into the bobbing prow of the hang-yao. He pointed the Ingram at the terrified driver.

'Go! Lee-oh! Now! Dee-o nee, you son-of-a-bitch!' he ordered.

It seemed like an eternity before the driver got the rusty little engine to turn over. Thunder sounded loudly, as though it were right overhead. Sawyer threw the Ingram to Suong. She fired blindly over the top of the bank. Sawyer's head was level with the plank. He pulled the pin on the grenade. He grabbed a handful of mud from the bank and flung it on top of the grenade at the edge of the plank. Bullets smacked into the water around them. The second the engine caught he released the spoon on the grenade and ducked.

'Dee-o nee!' he screamed, pushing Suong down as she fired the last of the clip.

Toonsang came up on the plank as the hang-yao started to pull into the fast-moving current. They were too close to shore for him to miss. His eyes were wide in anticipation. He winced slightly as he raised his AK-47 and, just as the rain came pouring down, a deafening explosion hit the side of the boat like a battering ram. Hot metal fragments whizzed around them. One of them took away a piece of the driver's neck. He watched the blood pouring down his side, the rain washing it away as fast as it poured out. It soaked down to the bilge, turning the water in the bottom of the boat a dull pink. The driver leaned over sideways, as if he were going to lie down for a nap, and toppled out of the hang-yao.

Sawyer peeked over the gunwale. The plank was gone, There were things bobbing in the water, but the rain was like a curtain and it wasn't clear who or what they were. Someone was still firing from the bank, away from the plank, but the current was pulling them downstream very fast and the visibility was too poor for the shots to get that close. A good thing too because the boat was turning in spirals, across the current. Sawyer reached up and grabbed the long-tail tiller, fighting to bring her around and headed downstream.

Suong sat up. Her hair was plastered to her head like a black helmet. She reached into the pack and put a fresh clip into the Ingram. She looked up at him and smiled. It was a wonderful smile.

At that moment, in spite of everything, perhaps because of it, he was happier than he could ever remember being in his whole life. He smiled back. She placed the Ingram where he could reach it and, grabbing a bent tin can, began to bail.

The hang-yao raced down the river. Along this part of the Kok the banks were high and rocky. The teak forest came to the edge of the river, the trees emblazoned with wildly coloured orchids. The greens of the forest and the colours of the flowers, almost electric, were intensified by the warm rain. The beauty caught at his throat and stayed there.

The water was grey – grey as the sky and the rocks. It was choppy and pocked with millions of tiny craters from the rain except where the submerged rocks were. They made the water smooth as glass above them and, with the current running this fast, he kept a wary eye on them.

He watched Suong bail. The wet clothes clung to her body like a second skin. He watched the muscles in her back, delicate yet strong. She was just keeping even with the rain. The pinkish bilge water sloshed around their ankles. There were supposed to be rapids coming up. Most were OK, but they might have to pull in and portage around the really bad ones near Keng Luang. If they could get past the white water, they ought to make Chiang Rai in about five or six hours, he thought. From there they could make connections to anywhere in Thailand. He could change the image, get back into Western clothes. They had to be careful, of course, but the Thai army was strong in that area. None of Bhun Sa's men would normally dare venture into Chiang Rai.

So getting to Chiang Rai wasn't the problem. Cambodia was what worried him. Ever since the Parrot's Beak it had scared him like nothing else. It scared everyone. Just thinking about it made his throat go dry, despite the water soaking him from head to foot. He tilted his head back, opened his mouth and drank the rain. It was warm and clean. It tasted of wet earth. But, no matter how much he drank, it didn't wash away the dryness.

Since the war, Cambodia had become the Land of Death. No one ever came back from there.

PART THREE

Dragons battle in the wilderness.

CHAPTER 20

The lake in the volcano.
The superior man looks inward
and cultivates his virtue.
Remain on friendly ground
and avoid hostile territory.

The market was already bustling when they got to Sisophon just an hour or so after dawn. The main street was lined with stalls selling black-market goods smuggled across the border from nearby Thailand. Although the sun was still low, it was starting to get hot and most of the stallkeepers had their umbrellas and cloth awnings up. Dogs prowled the dirt street for scraps. A goat settled in a patch of shade provided by an old motor-cycle piled high with baskets of oranges. Suong had gone off to try and find a kong dup to take them the twenty-five miles or so to Siem Reap.

Sawyer stopped at a money-changer's stall to convert some Thai baht into the new Kampuchean riels. Then he went across the street to a café consisting of a few crude tables under a coconut palm. It smelled of buffalo manure and dust and the sweet fermented smell of home-brewed daom thnot, sugar-palm beer. The proprietor, who seemed very young, stood behind a wooden table lined with bottles that looked as if they'd been buried in the earth for a hundred years. For decoration he had hung a cracked mirror with a peeling Byrrh advertisement on it from the palm tree.

Two young soldiers in green uniforms with RPK emblems on their caps were sitting at a table. They looked up guiltily when they saw Sawyer and saluted. It surprised him because he was in civilian slacks and short-sleeved shirt. He hesitated

243

for a second, then returned their salute. They both got up and, slinging their AKMs over their shoulders, walked quickly away, leaving their bottles of daom thnot half finished.

Sawyer watched them go. They were very young. In fact, now that he thought about it, everyone that he had seen on this side of the border was young. Maybe it was only the young who had managed to survive the Khmer Rouge, he thought.

'What was that all about?' he asked the proprietor in French.

'You Russki?'

Sawyer shook his head. 'International Red Cross representative.'

'Nye Russki?' the proprietor asked doubtfully.

Sawyer shook his head again. 'Canadian.'

It was always good cover for an American. The Canadians didn't have so many people in the world angry at them and the accent was virtually indistinguishable from American, except for the double diphthong on words like 'out'. But the proprietor still didn't look convinced.

'Not French, not American?'

'Canadian.'

'The Party says the Americans are imperialist enemies of the people. Americans, French, very bad.'

'We Canadians have had some problems with them ourselves,' Sawyer remarked.

'Where is Canadian?'

'Far away near the top of the world, where there is much snow and cold.'

'Like Russki. You want vodka maybe?' the proprietor asked suspiciously.

'Beer. Thai, if you have it.'

'Only Amarit,' the proprietor said mournfully.

'Amarit is fine,' Sawyer said.

The proprietor rummaged in a wooden box and brought out a dusty bottle. He opened it and poured it into a glass fogged with fingerprints. It was warm and flat as bath water. Sawyer drank it anyway, and the proprietor watched him with interest, as though drinking Thai beer was an exotic skill. It tasted stale. Sawyer wondered how long it had been in the bottle.

'Why'd they run off like that?' he asked.

The proprietor sniffed contemptuously. 'They think you are Russki officier. They are not supposed to be drinking during the hours of service. They have fear you will report them.'

Sawyer wondered what there was about him that made them take him for a Russian. He looked at himself in the Byrrh mirror. Maybe it was because he'd cropped his hair so short for the monk disguise. It made him look younger, thinner, but it also made his nose stick out more, like a bird's beak. He didn't like the way it made him look. His glass eye stared fixedly back at him. He glanced away. Maybe they just assumed he was Russian because Soviet advisers to the Heng Samrin government were virtually the only foreigners allowed in Cambodia.

'You want woman?'

Sawyer smiled. 'It's too early in the morning.'

'Never too early. You make baisage in morning, you feel good all day,' the proprietor said with great seriousness.

Sawyer just smiled.

'Young girl. No clap. You no like, I get you other one.' The proprietor leaned confidentially across the table.

'Some other time,' Sawyer said.

'No. No other time. You not want woman. I see you come with pretty woman. Maybe you need papers, cross border.'

Sawyer put the glass down. 'What kind of papers?'

The proprietor poured the rest of the bottle into the glass. 'All kinds. RPK. KR. Even Thai. Also, if you need to cross border, you will need guide. Many mines. Many objets piégés. Very dangerous.'

That was true enough, Sawyer thought. The night crossing from Aranyaprathet through the jungle to the road near Poipet had been harrowing. The border was heavily mined and there were vine and pungi traps on all the trails. It had brought back 'Nam with a vengeance. He remembered the call of 'Lock and load' and the terrible reluctance at every step to put your weight down on your foot because of the mines, until the green stink and heat finally wore you down and that's when it happened. This time he had done it in

245

darkness, following one of Mith Yon's teenage guides as he moved cautiously through the underbrush, while Suong and Sawyer had tried to follow exactly in his footsteps. Sawyer brought up the rear, one hand touching Suong's pack like a blind man, sweat pouring into his eyes and feeling graceless as an elephant.

Suong had thought that Mith Yon and his men would be crossing with them, but after Sawyer had spoken privately with Mith Yon, he had reluctantly agreed to wait in Aranya-prathet for the time being.

'What makes you think I'm heading for the border?' Sawyer asked, taking another sip of the beer.

'Your Omega,' the proprietor said, indicating Sawyer's watch. 'Only high officers and contrabandiers wear Omega. You are not Russki, so you have problem on every side. From RPK, Vietnamese youn, KR. Business never easy without friends.'

Damn! He'd have to get rid of the watch, Sawyer thought.

'I don't need papers or a guide. We're going to Phnom Penh,' Sawyer said loudly, in case anyone else might be listening. He finished the beer.

'By train or road?'

'Train,' Sawyer lied.

'Train better,' the proprietor agreed. 'The road near Siem Reap is very dangerous.'

'Khmer Rouge?'

The proprietor looked around. He wet his lips. 'Many dangers. No person goes there. And in the villages are the Old People.'

Sawyer had heard the term before. The Old People were the peasants favoured by the Khmer Rouge. The New People were those tainted by Western ideas. The Khmer Rouge had slaughtered the New People by the millions.

'Do the Old People still support the Khmer Rouge?'

The proprietor began cleaning the table with a rag. 'The Party denies this, so it cannot be so.'

'No,' Sawyer agreed, wiping his lips with the back of his hand. An ox cart rumbled by, its big wooden wheels squealing loudly. The peasants purposely never greased them so that the noise would frighten away the evil spirits.

Sawyer watched the dusty street. A young woman with a

baby at her breast haggled over a brightly coloured length of cloth. A small band of barefoot children noisily chased a partially deflated soccer ball in between the stalls. The sour taste of warm beer too early in the morning was already backing up in his throat.

It was worse than he had thought and not just because he stuck out like a sore thumb, Sawyer decided. If half of what the proprietor said was true, it meant that Angkor and the area around Siem Reap and even the villages were crawling with troops from every faction. It sounded like a no-man's-land where every peasant in a rice paddy might be an informer and where they were all running scared and trigger-happy. And no matter who they ran into, even if they survived the first encounter, they would be treated as enemies.

And then there was Suong. Just thinking about her started that tingle at the base of his groin. He had never wanted a woman so much and yet, ever since they had gotten together, he had been on the defensive, always reacting, never initiating. Somehow, whether with Toonsang or the Akha or Bhun Sa, it was always her forcing the issue.

All right. Maybe it was always for the good of the mission and she had been proven right time and again. And whenever he ordered her to do something, she obeyed instantly. Maybe it was just masculine pride, he admitted to himself. Perhaps that was it. But he was still uneasy. All he knew was that they had run out of options. There was no time left and he had somehow been manoeuvred into dealing with the one person he wanted to face least in the world. Pranh, who called himself Son Lot.

The memories started to come and he pushed them away. He had learned how to do that a long time ago. That was then, this is now, he told himself. He was thinking so hard that at first he didn't notice Suong standing under a sugar palm down the street, waiting for him.

He handed the proprietor one of the new riel bills.

'Remember. If you need a friend. . . ,' the proprietor began. He really couldn't have been more than fifteen, Sawyer thought.

'Friends are always good to have,' Sawyer agreed, getting up.

The proprietor cleared away Sawyer's bottle and glass and wiped off the table. 'The dog-eater soldiers come to the market at ten every morning to check papers,' he whispered, not looking up.

Sawyer put another bill on the table. 'My papers are in order, but I thank you for your concern.'

'A thousand pardons, oun. I thought only for your convenience,' the proprietor said, slipping the money into his pocket.

'For the convenience then,' Sawyer said.

He walked down the street to where Suong was waiting. He could feel eyes on him as he passed the stalls and shoppers. The sun heated the air into shimmering waves. Although it was still early morning, it had to be at least a hundred and ten degrees already, he thought. He could see the tiny beads of perspiration on Suong's face as he approached. He heard a rooster crow and it was like a warning. He took a deep breath. The air was hot and rank with the scent of mud and vegetation and spices. Asia, he thought. It gets us all in the end. But before it got him, he'd get the truth out of her if he had to tear it out.

Suong fell into step beside him. 'I found a kong dup. But the driver is very frightened. He wants three times the normal rate, and even then he will take us only part of the way to Siem Reap,' she said.

Sawyer nodded. He was going to get control of this mission if it killed him. And the first thing he was going to do was to get inside that goddam black box of hers. His blood boiled. Love wasn't enough. He wanted her very soul.

Suong looked at him, concerned. 'So-yah. Are you OK?'

'I'm fine,' he said. 'Everything is fine.'

CHAPTER 21

The teeth of the lightning
illuminate the majesty of the
  thunder.
The man bites through dry meat;
he encounters something rotten.

They shot the young boy in the rain. From where he was
hiding Sawyer could see the whole thing. They had emerged
from the pointed arch of the Lokeshvara, the high stone
tower surmounted by the giant faces of the Boddhisattva.
There were four faces, each staring out in one of the four
cardinal directions, all identical. In the Bayon temple alone
there must have been more than fifty such Lokeshvara
towers, all of them with the same face, repeated over and
over, wearing the same unending smile for all eternity. The
heavy stone slabs of the columns and arches were carpeted
by green mould, and vegetation sprouted in the crevices. A
silk-cotton tree grew out of the Boddhisattva's head, sending
its white roots deep into the stone structure. Sawyer had
watched the small black-clad figures come out of the shadow
of the arch one by one, like ants emerging from a crack in
a wall. They crept out cautiously, turning their heads from
side to side, looking more like a patrol in enemy territory
than a firing squad.

They pushed the boy against a carved wall. All along the
wall bare-breasted devata goddesses stood in graceful poses,
their feet pointed sideways in a style characteristic of a civilization that had not yet perfected frontal drawing. Rain slid
down the carvings in tiny rivulets. There were fallen palm
fronds and puddles all around the ancient courtyard, and

they had to walk some way along the wall to find a place where they wouldn't have to stand in a puddle to shoot him.

The boy wore black pyjamas like the others, but his hands were tied behind him. Sawyer squinted to see him better. He was very young, perhaps ten years old. They were all young, but the boy looked extremely young. Sawyer didn't want to watch what was about to take place, but he didn't know how not to watch it. The boy's eyes bulged from their sockets as if he couldn't believe it was happening to him.

At one point he tried to run away. Two of them clubbed him to the ground with their rifle butts and this time tied his feet together before they marched him back to the wall. He had to hop to keep up with them and some of the others laughed. They left him swaying in the rain in front of the devatas, and he started to shout something in Khmer in a high childish voice till the volley of shots blew him off his feet.

Some of the bullets knocked chips of stone off the carvings. For a lark one of the boys fired again at the wall, the shots mutilating the stone breasts of one of the devatas. Then another shouted an order and the one who had fired just shrugged. Sawyer watched them go back the way they came. They left the body behind them, lying in the rain. After they had gone Sawyer discovered that he had clenched his fists so tightly that his nails had left deep crescents in his palms.

Sawyer crept over the tumbled rocks back to Suong. When he had left her to reconnoitre, she had been sleeping. The shots must have awakened her, he thought, moving silently and with great care. The rocks were slippery with the rain and the slightest noise could be fatal. Khmer Rouge troops were all around the area. And the crevices between the rocks were favourite hiding places for snakes.

Why'd they do it? Sawyer wondered as he scrambled over a fallen column. What possible crime could a ten-year-old have committed that warranted death? Why shoot a fucking wall, for that matter? Why do anything?

He remembered an argument between Brother Rap and Major Lu the time they had found the mutilated bodies of an entire family killed by the Viet Cong.

'What kind of a mother-fucker would do something like

this?' Rap had demanded truculently, as if he were looking for an argument.

'Oddly enough, they are men just like you and me. They laugh, they cry, they love their families,' Major Lu had replied.

'No way, man! Don't you lay that gook jive on me, mother-fucker! They ain't no way the fuckers who done this are like me, man,' Rap had raged, his eyes rolling white in their sockets.

But Major Lu had simply looked calmly up at him. 'You have not been in Vietnam long enough,' he had observed mildly. 'You do not yet know what you yourself are capable of, what you yourself may do.'

When Sawyer crawled back to the dark niche inside one of the myriad temple corridors he was surprised to find Suong still asleep. He had thought she would have heard the shots. He listened intently. The air inside the niche was dank and dead, as though it had been there for centuries. He couldn't hear the rain. Maybe the sound couldn't penetrate the thick stone walls, he thought. Maybe.

He looked around at the walls in the dim grey light filtering from chinks in the outside corridor roof and wall. They were covered with intricately carved bas-reliefs of an army of dvarapala, the immortal guardians of the temple. He hoped they were keeping watch because Christ knew he didn't want to get caught unawares by the Khmer Rouge. Still, they should be all right here, he thought. The Angkor Thom complex was a vast maze overgrown with heavy vegetation. An army could comb the place for months and not find them as long as they were careful.

He watched Suong. She slept like a child, curled on her side. But it wasn't an easy sleep. He could see her fingers and toes twitch every once in a while. She must be exhausted, he thought. He wasn't feeling so great himself. He couldn't get the execution out of his mind. And now he had to find a way to get to Pranh before *they* got to him and convince him to do the deal. And if he made it, if he actually pulled it off, he would have succeeded in putting some of the best weapons in the world into the hands of those animals who'd just killed a ten-year-old for no goddam reason.

You better not think about that, Sawyer told himself.

That's not your job. Leave that to Washington. Sure, he answered himself. Only how do you not think about it?

He watched Suong's deep, regular breathing, the rise and fall of her breasts. What are you going to do about her? the Reptile whispered. Remember what Bhun Sa said. She was like a hanuman snake, beautiful and deadly. And now Bhun Sa was dead because of her. And you're alone in KR territory. Shut up, he told the Reptile. Just shut up. But what are you going to do?

'Find out the fucking truth once and for all,' he said out loud, digging the black box out of her pack.

He set it on a rock that had once been part of a column plinth. It was a rectangular box about six inches square, made of lacquered black wood and secured with a simple lock. He took out the tanto knife, slid it into the crack near the lock and hit the knife handle with his hand. The lid came open with a loud snap. He heard Suong stir behind him, but he didn't care.

Shoes. Just a pair of toddler-size shoes, for God's sake. And a stump of candle. There was nothing else in the box. His eye hadn't deceived him back at the clearing. He started to examine the box more closely when he heard her suddenly sit up. He whirled and grabbed her, the knife at her throat.

'Don't say it! Don't say anything! I'm tired of this shit! Ever since we met everything's gone wrong, and I can't afford any more mistakes,' he hissed.

'Oh So-yah,' she said. 'Couldn't you wait?'

'No. No more waiting. They kill kids here. What do you think they'll do to us?'

'I know what they do,' she said softly.

'I want it all. Now,' he said, pressing on the knife. The point made a dimple in the skin of her throat.

'Put away the knife, So-yah. There's no need for it any more,' she said, a terrible weariness in her voice.

'I was married before,' Suong began. 'My husband's name was Khieu Phat. He was a colonel in the Cambodian army. We had a little boy, my chouchou. I named him Jean-Pierre after my father, but that was before the Khmer Rouge came and made the having of a farang name a crime. How could

I know when I named him for my cher papa that this would some day be a bad thing, So-yah? How?' she paused.

Sawyer didn't say anything. What was there to say?

'When the a khmau, the soldiers of the Khmer Rouge, came, we said his name is Little Khieu. At night we would coach him and tell him that we make a game to call him Little Khieu and that he must never tell anyone his real name. But he insisted on being called Jean-Pierre and we had to spank him very hard. I will never forget him crying, "I sorry, maman. No more Jean-Pierre. Little Khieu be good boy. Jean-Pierre bad." But sometimes he would forget and not turn around when someone say, "Little Khieu," and it would make a blue fear for me that he would say his true name. But all that comes much later, when it was already too late.'

'Where was this?'

'In Phnom Penh. We had a villa there. It was very pretty. The garden was shaded with banana palms and there was jasmine and bougainvillaea that made the evenings sweet as in the Land of Bliss, where the thewada are said to dwell.

'We did not always live in the villa. It was the war that made us rich and, even then, only late in the war before we could afford to move. Before that we lived in a flat near the Pochentong Market, in a building owned by my mother.

'I believe my husband loved me, for he did not maintain a putain in a separate apartment later, when he could afford one. Although I believe he also married me because my father had left me a little money and also, through my mother, I was related to Sirik Tamak, who later helped Lon Nol oust Prince Sihanouk. You see, although my husband came of good family, he was the eighth son and he had not the money to buy himself a high rank. But my mother told me, "Khieu is a good man, also very shrewd, which is better sometimes than money. And he will put your interests and those of your sons, if the Lord Buddha smile, before his own." And so we wed.

'It was good for us, as my mother foretold, though Khieu advanced so slowly in the army that it made a pain inside him, though he rarely spoke of it. Then Lon Nol and Sirik came to power. And with them came the Americans. And the war.

'And with the war came Khieu's opportunity at last.

253

Through our connection to Sirik, he was given command of a brigade. And this made us rich, for with the Americans came a river of money. It would have taken a Boddhisattva to resist, for the wealth of the Americans overflowed like the Tonle Sap in the time of the monsoon, so that even fools could not help becoming rich. And Khieu was no fool.

'Like nearly all of Lon Nol's officers, he came to command battalions that did not exist and put the pay for thousands of men into his pocket. He made his ball of string, as the French say. But even here he showed integrity, for he did not – though some brother colonels called him a fool for it – keep also the pay of the soldiers he did command, so they must steal food from the peasants. Nor did he sell to the Khmer Rouge the guns and tanks the Americans gave him, as many others did, so that often a battalion was wiped out by its own guns in KR hands.

'Yet, the higher he rose, the sadder he became. The lines in his face became deep and bitter. He would sit for hours staring at nothing, ignoring the baby, and at night, in bed, I could give him no comfort.

' "We came too soon or too late to the war, for we have not the knack of it," he would complain to me sometimes. "Our soldiers bicycle to the front straight down the highway into ambushes. They march with flags in front as though it were the nineteenth century, and many do not even know how to switch off the safety. The artillery stops for lunch and dinner precisely on the hour, even in the middle of a battle, and among the sergeants it is whispered that the enemy can set their watches by the timing of our attacks."

' "The Americans will save us," I told him. That was the common belief in Phnom Penh in those days. He made a face.

' "That is what Lon Nol and Sirik Tamak say. That is what the Americans tell them. But they are all fools if they believe the American is willing to die forever to save Asians from each other. The President Nixon promises much, but every day there are fewer American soldiers in South Vietnam. And some day here also the Americans will get tired and go home, and there will be no one left but these incompetent weaklings and the Khmer Rouge. Then who will stand between us and what is to come?"

'I told you he was no fool. The American B-52s came and dropped many bombs till the land was cratered like the face of the moon, and yet each day it was not Lon Nol's army but the Khmer Rouge forces who advanced.

'We spoke of fleeing the country, but at that time we were not so rich yet. Also Khieu did not like this idea.

' "Where would we go? L'Amérique? La France? Where is there a place in the world where the stranger of a different race is not despised in the heart, no matter what governments may say? And for this we forsake our ancestors? Is this my heritage to my son, to make of him a refugee? We are Khmer. Where is a Khmer to live if not in the land of the Khmer? Who is to save Kampuchea if we do not?" And he told the old Ramakien tale of the fish in the sea who lived in terror of the shark. One day a cobra on the shore overheard their cries of despair. "Why not come up here on the land where the shark cannot get you?" the cobra asked. The fish thought this a most excellent idea and started to swim for the shore. Then the Fish King noticed the cobra's sharp poison fangs and the hungry gleam in his eye. "Mai pen rai. We will stay in the sea," the Fish King said. "If life is so difficult for us in the water, which is our natural element, how much more so will it be on land, which is alien to us?"

'Also my mother was ill then and I did not want to leave her. So we stayed on in Phnom Penh. Perhaps Khieu was a fool after all because afterwards, when we might have thought of getting out, it was too late.

'All that week he did not say much, except to complain bitterly over the stupidity and corruption of Lon Nol's men. A new American "adviser" had joined his unit and had told him, in the casual way of a conversation banale, that most American peoples did not even know they were fighting a war in Cambodia. To Khieu this came like a thunderclap.

' "I was right," he told me that night in bed. "If a government keeps such a matter secret from its own people, it means they fear what the people will say if the truth comes out. Such a government will not save us if the wind should shift. Whereas the Khmer Rouge will fight on if it takes a thousand years." He paused. "Perhaps it is they who have the Will of Heaven, after all."

'And then he said a strange thing. "When I was a boy in

French Catholic school, I was like a brother to Ieng Pranh, who now calls himself Son Lot and sits at the right hand of Pol Pot."

'I believe it was at that moment that he decided to become a spy for the Khmer Rouge.

'But of this he told me nothing for a time. Now he no longer complained of corruption and failure. He moved through the days with purpose. He believed, I think, that he had found a way to save his family. He began to teach me of the Revolution and the angkar in secret. It was a new language he taught me. The ideas were most strange. Buddha was only a man long dead who spoke in useless riddles. Forget Buddha. Forget the neak ta. Do not speak the Français. Enemies were "CIA spies" and "imperialist lackeys". The peasants were the "tools of the Revolution".

' "Does my husband believe these thoughts?" I asked him.

' "When the time comes, we must make others believe we believe it," he whispered, his eyes big in the night.

'Perhaps he believed a little. He wanted to, I think. Also it was easier for us as Buddhists of the Little Raft. For the object of angkar and of Buddhism was in some way the same: the annihilation of one's own selfish desires. Yet there was a difference. At the core of Buddhism is the eternal; at the core of the Revolution was hate. But we did not see into the core.

'When he thought me ready, I became a courier. I would leave messages hidden inside a fish wrapped in newspaper with a sullen peasant who had a shack on the mudflats along the Bassac river. The peasant never said a word to me, but his eyes watched me as though I had come to steal something. Although I trembled inside on these trips, no one ever questioned me. Who would suspect a senior officer's wife with a small child? Meanwhile we buried more gold every week in a secret place under the house.

'By the spring the fighting had come so close that sometimes people would stop what they were doing and children would stand in the middle of the playground to listen to the distant rumble of the guns like dry-season thunder. Then they would go back to what they were doing but with a strange hesitancy, as if what they were doing no longer mattered.

256

'Sometimes a rocket would hit a house. But there was little panic in the city, for it happened too quickly. It came out of the empty sky without warning and afterwards passers-by would look away because the craters and smouldering ruins left behind had an air not of war but of misfortune. Bad karma. Such a thing may happen to anyone and it is best not to arouse the interest of the phi. At night you could see white flashes in the sky, like an electrical storm. It was strangely interesting, and sometimes I would sit and watch for hours.

'Then one night, not long before dawn, Khieu came home directly from the front, an M-16 in his hand. We spoke in the darkened kitchen, for he had warned me not to turn on the lights. His face was dirty and grey with exhaustion, and his uniform was stained and smelled of sweat.

'I stared at him. He was my husband, yet like a stranger almost. I was not used to seeing him like that because he had always been so fastidious about his clothes. We spoke in whispers. His eyes were shining as with fever and I did not know if it was from excitement or fear or both, peut-être. Maybe it was something else. In Paris, as a girl, I read a poem by a Greek, I think. Catafy or Cavafy, some such name. There was something about waiting for the barbarians to take a city and people being disappointed when they did not come because the barbarians were some sort of solution. So perhaps what Khieu felt was a kind of relief that the storm he had built a dike for was no longer threatening but had broken at last.

' "The hour has come," he told me. "At dawn the forces of the Revolution will attack Neak Luong. From there Phnom Penh will be under constant artillery bombardment. The city cannot hold out. You must leave."

' "When?"

' "Tonight. Now."

' "I'll get Jean-Pie – Little Khieu."

'He grabbed me by the hair and twisted till it hurt. His face was contorted and ugly. I had never seen it so and fear stabbed at my heart like a knife.

' "Never say that name again," he hissed. "Never! French is dead. Phnom Penh is dead. Anything that ever happened before tonight is dead."

' "What of my mother? She has only the old woman to take care of her."

' "Mother is dead," he whispered. "You must choose between the old one and our son. I have a jeep downstairs waiting. I will drop you off on this side of the Tonle Sap. A comrade will row you across. Go on foot, you and the little one, on Highway Four towards Kompong Speu. The *a khmau* will stop you within two or three kilometres. Say at once, 'Chevo Yotheyas! Long Live the Liberation!' Say, 'Greetings to Comrade Son Lot from Comrade Khieu,' and tell him I will bring him a present at Neak Luong. Tell them to guard well the family of Khieu or Comrade Son Lot will put them with the *sambor bep*, the fat cats, when we take the city."

' "What should I take?"

' "Dress yourself and the Little Mouse in black peasant garb, krama and sandals. Take a small sack of salt and rice. Nothing else. If you are seen, say nothing to anyone."

' "Should I take identification papers? Money?"

'He shook his head.

' "What of the gold?"

'He gave an odd laugh. It sounded almost like a cough. "Take nothing!" he hissed again. "Leave the gold in the ground from where it came. It will be a long time, if ever, before it sees the light."

'His words made a blue fear in my heart and I trembled. What kind of a world is it where money and gold have no value? I touched his grimy cheek as a small child touches a mirror to see if the image before him is real.

' "Where do you go?" I whispered.

' "Back to the front. I am bringing a gift that should secure our future, if anything will," he said grimly, his eyes shining like a beacon. And suddenly I had an inkling of how terrible it was for him and also how dangerous.

'At that moment I had never loved anyone so much as I loved him. He was our saviour, which is the most thing a man can be, and I threw my arms around him and clung desperately to him. I trembled like a leaf in the dry monsoon and I thought how wise my mother had been in advising me to marry him.

'He caressed my hair and for the first time in our marriage I felt I was utterly his.

' "Why do you tremble? To show fear now is very dangerous," he said at last.

' "Yesterday our neighbour Sath Chung was cleaning and a bat came flying out of the closet screeching and attacking. Sath Chung hit it with a broom and killed it. And when she picked it up she saw that a baby bat had been suckling at its breast and it was also dead. That is a terrible omen."

' "It means nothing any more. Superstition is illegal under the new regime," Khieu said, an odd expression on his face. He kissed me one last time.

'Later that night, because Khieu was as good at being for the Khmer Rouge as he had been against it, he succeeded in surrendering his entire brigade intact to Son Lot. This left Neak Luong's flank open on the river side. The Khmer Rouge took Neak Luong and the non-stop bombardment of the city, swollen with refugees to more than two millions, began.

'When the city was taken at last there were white flags fluttering at every window and then a big celebration with people shouting, "Vive la paix!" and "Vive la Révolution!" or so we were told, because by then Khieu and I were manning a barricade on Highway Five leading north from Phnom Penh. The poor fools! How could they understand, when even with Khieu's teaching I myself did not understand? Because at first I tried to keep my Little Mouse with me. A cadre, a young man with lips thick like they were pumped full of air, snatched him from me and sent him marching into a field with the other children. Jean-Pierre started to cry and it tore at my heart.

' "But he is my son,' I started to say.

'The cadre screamed at me in a voice as shrill as anything I have ever heard. "You must cease such revisionist thought. He belongs to angkar, not to you!"

'I looked to my husband and saw a look in his eyes I will never forget.

' "Forgive this woman, Comrade. The closeness of these filthy sambor bep," pointing at the endless line of people on the road, stopped by the barricade, "has confused her," Khieu said smoothly. "But she knows her duty. Comrade

Pol Pot has said that only unflagging energy will root out counter-revolutionary tendencies."

' "I know what Comrade Pol Pot says as well as you,' the cadre said sullenly, looked across the barrier for someone to take out his frustration on.

'He spied a young man in a nice shirt and slacks, who looked like a bank clerk, and a pretty girl. They were holding hands and the cadre screamed for them to make room at the barrier. The young man looked puzzled. There were too many people for him to move even a centimetre. "Make room, sambor bep!" the cadre screamed and clubbed the young man with the butt of his rifle. The young man fell to his knees, his eyes stunned, and then the cadre was all over him, pounding his head with the rifle even after he lay dead on the ground.

' "Sok!" the girl called the boy's name. She started to cry and the people pressed away to make room for the cadre.

' "Shut up, city whore!" the cadre screeched. "You find new boy to" – here he say something very vulgar – "in country."

'I did not want to see this. I looked over at the field where the children were drilling, the small ones running to keep up with the bigger ones, looking for my little one. A terrible feeling caught at my heart when I saw him marching with the others, all of them like tiny, clumsy soldiers. This feeling was not to leave me, waking or sleeping, ever again.'

'What was happening at the barricade?' Sawyer asked.

'The barricade was a kind of tribunal. We were judges, Khieu and I. There were others, perhaps ten of us, at a table to check identity papers, and around us and all along the road many a khmau, all heavily armed, with hand-grenades hanging all over them like green mangoes on a tree. Every now and then one of the a khmau would shoot his gun, sometimes in the air, sometimes at the crowd, for no reason and a few more bodies would fall. People would step around the bodies, not daring to look, for there were many bodies scattered all along the road. In one place many soldiers still in the uniform of the Cambodian army had been shot with their hands tied behind them.

'It was a thing not to be imagined, my So-yah. For as far as the eye could see were people and carts jammed along

260

Highway Five. Some had water buffalo or oxen to pull the carts through the heat and dust, for the heat was terrible and the dust was in your nostrils at every breath. Some people pulled carts like beasts. The carts were piled high with belongings and sometimes old people or children, hanging precariously to the top. Others pushed rickshaws or velo-cabs and once I even saw a whole family pushing a Toyota crammed with furniture and even a television, for it was forbidden to drive. Others just walked, often carrying babies or sick relatives.

'There were all kinds of people. City people in smart clothes now wrinkled and caked with dust, ragged refugees, Buddhist bhikku in their orange robes, army deserters in city clothes, children still in school uniform. There was no end to it. The procession went on forever. I did not know there were so many people in the whole world and still they came.

'And yet there was an eerie silence, despite the presence of so many. You could hear the babies crying and crying and sometimes a dog barked, but that was how it was, heat and dust and crying babies.

' "Where do they think they are going?" I asked the cadre sitting next to me. He was short, smaller than I, and plump, with a smooth face like a young girl's, and he spoke with a pursing of the lips, comme un pédé, tu comprends? But he had three ballpoint pens in his shirt pocket, which was a sign of high rank among the cadre. Khieu also had three, I one.

' "They have been told that the Americans are coming to bomb Phnom Penh," he said. "After they will be permitted to return to their homes. Look! Who would have believed it? The city has been emptied."

'It was true. The entire city had been turned inside out like a shirt for the laundry.

' "But will any be allowed to return?" I asked.

'He pursed his lips disapprovingly, touching his tongue to his lip like a woman checking her lipstick. His eyes showed plainly that he thought my question a stupid one.

' "Why for? The sambor bep of the city produce no rice; they devour it. Without cities, angkar gains twofold," he went on, as though reading something from a poster. "No city people means there is none to exploit the peasants and steal their rice. Thus less consumption. Also by turning the city people into opakar, field workers, there is more production," he said, motioning the next applicant to come forward.

'With horror, I saw that it was Monsieur Van Sophan, my old Lycée teacher of the mathematics. He recognized me at once and started to say something, then seemed to think better of it. He stood straight like a soldier, as he always had at the blackboard, but his eyes had dark circles under them and his shoes that had always been so brightly polished were scuffed and covered with dust. Mathematics was my most bad subject and I failed my examination. All my friends were going on to the next grade and I pleaded not to be left behind. So he gave me the chance to take the examination again. For a week he came every night to tutor me. I could not understand the fractions, so every night he would bring me cakes and cut them up into the fractions and when I would finally solve one problem, he would applaud and we would both cram the pieces of cake in our mouths, giggling like small children, and my mother would come in and say, "Fine lessons!" but she would be smiling and would then have a piece of cake too. He was a bachelor and lonely, I think, and after my lesson, he and my mother would talk over tea. But he was always most correct, no roublardise, and I think he made the second examination easy for me and I passed, though I never became very good at the mathematics.

'Now he stood there looking as if he had not slept in days. The cadre next to me asked him his name and Monsieur Sophan told him.

' "Identity card?"

'Monsieur Sophan looked at me and I managed to shake my head the most small bit to indicate no. The cadre must have noticed something because he darted a glance at me. But I ignored him and motioned a woman with a child and a crying baby to come forward. She had her identity card ready and I pretended to busy myself with it. I overheard Monsieur Sophan tell the cadre that it had been lost in the shelling. There was a trembling in his voice.

' "No matter. Angkar will give you a new one," the cadre said smoothly, reaching for a blank card.

' "What is your profession?"

'Monsieur Sophan looked again at me and I smiled because our orders were to be firm but reassuring, but my eyes were not smiling. I put fear into them, hoping he would see and understand, but the other cadre was watching and all it did was make Monsieur Sophan to hesitate.

' "Do not be afraid," the cadre said, now smiling reassuringly himself and looking at me with approval. "Angkar is in desperate need of the skilled and the educated. We are fighters, yes, but have no experience as administrators. There are many opportunities for those with the right skills and the willingness to work."

' "I have always worked," Monsieur Sophan said, with a touch of pride.

' "Excellent," the cadre beamed. "At what please?" His pen was poised over the new card. I could not look any longer and motioned the woman with the children to go through the gap in the barrier and past the a khmau in jeeps with machine-guns mounted on them.

' "I am – was – a teacher of the mathematics," I heard Monsieur Sophan say and my heart plummeted.

' "Tant mieux, Monsieur le professeur!" the cadre declared heartily and pointed Monsieur Sophan towards a nearby field already filled with thousands of people squatting in the heat like cattle among their bags and possessions. Some had already been waiting for many hours, but when one of them had gone up to a guard to ask for water, the guard had shot him on the spot and screamed at them to be quiet. After that, there was little talking there.

'Monsieur Sophan looked back hesitantly, clutching his new identity card in his hand as if it were a winning lottery ticket.

' "Go on! Those will be the first to be allowed to return to the city," the cadre said, waving the next one forward. It was a hatchet-faced man who claimed to be a construction worker, but his hands were soft and the blisters on them too new. The cadre called over the guards. They shoved him into a jeep and drove him away.

'As for those sent into the field to wait, they were marched away in small groups and no one saw them after that. Yet new ones were continually added, so that the field never emptied but was like a rice paddy filled and drained by water ditches of the same size. Some remained there for days, living without shelter and staring mindlessly into space, like the animals in the Phnom zoo, where I used to take my Little Mouse, until they too were taken away. When I asked Khieu at night what happened to them, he told me, "Do not ask. You do not want to know."

'But two nights later I was eating and I saw one of the guards come to the communal pot for rice, but his face was sick and he went away without taking any. I sat beside him. He was very young. They were all young, but this one looked too small to carry his gun. His uniform was far too big on him and he wore his cap with the brim tilted up, the way children sometimes do. He looked as though he wanted to run away.

' "To e na bong? Where do you go, little brother?" I asked him. He would not look at me.

' "Do you want rice?" I asked. A spasm passed across his face.

' "I cannot eat," he whispered. I could see sweat trickling down his face. A cadre with one pen sat down on his other side.

' "Are you sick?" I asked.

'He shook his head. "I have never killed anyone before," he said in a guilty voice. "It makes a sickness in my stomach, Comrade."

' "You will get used to it," the cadre said.

'The boy swallowed and nodded, but he did not look convinced. Two more guards, older boys, came over. I knew one of them. His name was Mam and he wore two watches, an Omega that had stopped on one wrist and a woman's diamond-studded Piaget on the other, though he told time by the sun like everyone else. These boys were not like any Khmers I had ever known before. They liked to wave their guns about and would grab for each other's privates when they rough-housed.

' "It would be easier with guns. I am too little for the hoes," the boy offered hopefully.

'The cadre's face was smooth. His eyes were like black stones. "Bullets are precious. Angkar will not waste arms

264

needed against imperialist foreigners and their dog-eating Vietnamese lackeys on such as these sambor bep."

' "I like the hoes, though it is tiring. There is a sound when one hits the head just right that is most satisfying," Mam volunteered. "Like a coconut, though the inside of the head is grey, not white."

' "Try the iron bars," the other guard suggested. "With these one needs only a single blow on the back of the neck, while with the hoes two or three may be required to make them stop jiggling and sometimes these are thrown in the pit still moving."

' "What difference if they are still moving?" Mam shrugged.

' "The iron bar is better," the other insisted. "Did you see me hit that sambor bep with it today? The one who wet his pants with fear and Chhung laughed and say he must be spanked for such naughtiness. We pulled his pants down and used bamboo sticks till his buttocks bled and all the time the sambor bep's face is more and more red and tears are coming from his eyes, though he is not saying anything. Then Chhung says, 'You learn your lesson good, sambor bep?' He shake his head, the tears still coming, and then I hit him with my iron bar and he is finished. Only the one time," he sneered to Mam.

' "It was a most excellent hit," Mam agreed. "Though Chhung was funny about the lesson," he said, turning to us. "You see, the sambor bep was a professor of the mathematics," he explained.

' "Try iron bars tomorrow. Once you get the way of it, it is as easy as breaking eggs," the other guard advised the boy.

'The boy's face had gone white with the telling. I could see he had witnessed it all. I was glad they were looking at his face and not at mine.

' "If only the enemy looked more like an enemy. They look like us. They might be anybody,' the boy whispered.

' "Do not be fooled," the cadre warned him harshly. "These are what Comrade Pol Pot calls 'Khmer bodies with imperialist minds'. These were whoring with the American murderers while we were suffering in the jungle for the Revolution. Now eat the rice. Tomorrow you must do better."

'The boy smiled weakly and managed to swallow a few mouthfuls of rice as though it were dog-meat, while over his head the cadre and Mam exchanged a glance.

'The boy did not come back from the fields the next evening.

'Meanwhile the endless parade went on in the broiling sun, day after day. I was watching my life pass by, for I saw almost everyone I had ever known. Some looked at me with sudden hope when they recognized me, for by then everyone had seen enough to be always in fear. Others could not keep the contempt out of their eyes.

'Such a one was Keo, an old army friend of my husband. Khieu always said that if Lon Nol had had only twenty like Keo, the Khmer Rouge would have been of no greater matter than the evening mosquitoes in our garden. But when Keo saw my husband his face fell momentarily. As he looked up the certainty of his own death was in his eyes. He straightened, droit comme un piquet, and when he spoke, it was as one who has decided to die.

' "I would have believed this of any before you," Keo said.

'Seeing that Keo had condemned himself with his own words, my husband leaped to denounce him. "It is you who speak with the jaw of traitor!" Khieu cried, pointing an accusing finger at Keo.

' "It was impossible to save him. Better to use his death to secure our position," Khieu told me late that night. But his eyes held a shame in them and he would not look at me. But at the time he accused Keo, his eyes were blazing with revolutionary fervour.

' "Comrades! Here is one of the worst of the sambor bep, cowardly trying to escape the justice of the Revolution!"

' "If you are going to shoot me, do it. But kindly do not insult my intelligence with such merde," Keo said, looking disgustedly at Khieu.

' "We will not shoot you," the plump cadre next to me said. There was a silky quality in his voice, like the touch of a spider thread, that made me shiver.

'The a khmau grabbed Keo and staked him out on the highway, where their trucks would go. The trucks drove over him for hours till Keo was nothing but a red smear perhaps forty metres long.

'And still they came. All except my mother. Most of the sick ones never made it that far. Each time I saw one I knew, I trembled inside at the contempt I thought must be in their minds. But none reproached me and I even managed to save some of my old neighbours and family by giving them new identity cards that said they had been lowly workers and passing them through. Only once did someone challenge me. Sath Buth, a girl I had known at school.

'She stood there, her make-up caked with dust, a large Louis Vuitton handbag slung over her shoulder as though she were on her way to tea at the Hotel Phnom. Her identity card identified her husband's profession as "Fonctionnaire publique", but when I tried to give her a new card saying she was a seamstress, she lashed out at me.

' "Don't you dare write such a thing! It is you and your husband who are the true parvenus. Ever since we were in school, you have been jealous of me," she sniffed.

'I could see the plump cadre looking curiously at me. If I did not close her mouth, her imbecile vanity would condemn me too.

' "It is you who lie and claim to be an honest worker. Go there with the others of your kind!" I screamed, tearing her card to bits and flinging the pieces at her.

' "You will never be anything but a petite bourgeoise," she snapped triumphantly, as she gathered her skirt and stepped to the side of the road, her Louis Vuitton clutched in her hand like a weapon.

'It took weeks before the endless procession became a trickle and then it stopped, comme ça. The cadres and guards broke up the camp. Nothing remained but some bodies scattered here and there along the road, slowly turning black in the sun. As a reward for his good work and because of his friendship with Son Lot, Khieu was allowed to return to Phnom Penh as the new commandant of Tuol Sleng prison. What went on there Khieu would not say. But in this time we call the peal chur chat Kampuchea was the worst place on earth and it was said that Tuol Sleng was the worst place in Kampuchea. Nor could Khieu do anything to improve conditions. For Pich Sam, his second-in-command, was a spy, planted there by Pol Pot for no other reason than to report on Khieu himself.

267

'Save for a few fonctionnaires and senior cadres of the angkar, Phnom Penh was utterly empty. There was a strangeness to it that cannot be told. Abandoned cars and overturned kong dup littered the streets, so you would have to pick your way around them. Bodies had been left to rot and there were streets where you could not go because the smell was so bad. Weeds began to sprout in the cracks in the sidewalks and sometimes you would come upon piles of now worthless paper riels, swirled like leaves by the wind. You could walk the main boulevards for hours and hear nothing but the sound of your own footsteps. You would pass the places you knew – the park by the Phnom where I used to take my Little Mouse to play, the Tuol Tumpoung market, the shops on Monivong, the Monorom near the station, where Khieu would sometimes take me for drinks, many places – and there would be only silence.

'But the silence was not blank space. It had a presence like the silence of an empty theatre, and you found yourself talking very loudly as a way to fill it. We were like ghosts in a graveyard, unable to touch the world. The city had become so unreal that it was we who felt unreal.

'We lived in an apartment house with other fonctionnaires. There was no electricity or running water, but we were well off compared with most. In the first days after the barricade, and at Tuol Sleng, Khieu said little. But he no longer reached for me in the night.

' "I cannot now. The things I have seen are before my eyes. They take the desire away," he confessed.

' "Mai pen rai," I told him. "You are a man of strength and it will be with us as before."

'But it never was. Each day there was less and less between us. His eyes grew hard and when he spoke it was in the slogans of angkar, as into a loud speaker. Perhaps he slaked his desire at the prison, for there were female prisoners whom the guards would use for pleasure or torture as they pleased. I know not. Only this do I know, So-yah: if you give one human too much power over another human, it will end with neither of them being human. This happened to Khieu.

'But at night sometimes I would see something in his eyes. It reminds me of the eyes of one who wears the monkey mask in the Khon dance. The face is the face of a monkey,

268

but the eyes trapped in the mask, the eyes are human. So with Khieu. The face was the face of angkar, but his eyes in those moments were full of fear.

' "Tell me your heart," I begged him.

' "Soon it will be our turn," he said. "At first at Tuol Sleng there were those of the Lon Nol régime. Then any of the intelligentsia or those singled out for special punishment. But these are long gone, though they all signed confessions and, at the very sight of the electric wire, they would invent even more hideous crimes to confess. But now almost all of our prisoners are traitors from within angkar itself. The Revolution has become like the snake that swallows its own tail. Bite by bite we consume ourselves."

'And then later, as I lay there listening to him be awake, I heard him say. "If I do not get Pich Sam, he will get me."

'One day he came home in great excitement. "We have captured four Americans in a sailing boat off the coast. They claim they are yachtsmen, but Pol Pot wants them to confess their CIA plotting."

' "Are they CIA men?"

'The look on his face was the look of the new Khieu. It frightened me. His voice was the voice of angkar. "Without a signed confession, we will not let them die so easily."

'Weeks later Khieu reported that Pol Pot himself had been pleased with the Americans' confessions, but Khieu himself seemed disappointed.

' "What is the matter?" I asked him.

'He made a face. "The Americans died badly. They screamed at the electrics like neang instead of men. I used to think them so powerful. They came among us like gods, telling us do this and that, but without their machines and their dollars they are as crying babies. I expected more of them."

' "What did you expect? When they use the wire, everyone screams."

' "A Khmer dies better. He knows there is more to the world than his own khwan. But now I see the Americans are only poseurs."

' "What matters that to us?"

' "Because poseurs could never have saved us and now

269

nothing can save us. The tiger begins to devour his own cubs," he declared and would say no more.

'In the days that followed there was the feeling that time was running out for us. One morning I passed a shoestore and, on an impulse, walked inside. The shop had been smashed, of course, they all were, but still sitting on the counter was the most beautiful pair of blue children's shoes. They were the perfect size for my Little Khieu. I looked around to make sure no one saw me, though that was silly because there was no one to see, and slipped the shoes into my sack. There was no reason for it. All the children had to wear rubber sandals. But the shoes tugged at my heart, like a memory of all that had been.

'Meanwhile we were having trouble with Little Khieu. He was running away from his indoctrination classes. In my heart I was proud of him. He is only a little boy, I longed to tell them. He is too bright and full of life to sit for hours listening to your endless deadening lectures. But I pretended to be angry and scolded him. When that didn't work Khieu slapped his face many times. Our Little Mouse no longer laughed. He grew sullen and began to watch us silently from corners like a wary animal.

'The food situation, even for cadres, was becoming very bad. The rice harvest was disastrous, and Pol Pot secretly shipped almost all the rice that was harvested to China, to trade for arms for our war against the Vietnamese. Once more you could see fresh bodies in the main boulevards as a khmau suspected of being spies for the youn (as the Vietnamese were contemptuously called) were shot down like dogs. Our next-door neighbours got so desperate, they took to making fires in deserted villas to smoke out the bats, who would tumble dizzily to the ground. Then we would all have bat soup.

'One by one, families began to disappear. No one would speak of it, but Tuol Sleng grew more and more overcrowded, and each night the lines in Khieu's face grew deeper.

'He had, he told me, enjoyed the great pleasure of seeing Pich Sam being tortured by his own subordinates. But Khieu's triumph was short-lived. A week later we were arrested and taken to the school. Our son had denounced us for sometimes speaking French at home. Also for hoarding food, which we did, of course. Everyone did.

'At the school Khieu acted outraged. He accused the boy of running away from indoctrination class and making these pretexts to cover his own guilt. The senior cadre hesitated.

'I watched horrified, not knowing which was worse – if they were to believe my husband or my son. I felt like I was being torn apart.

' "That is true. Little Khieu is always running away. We will fix him so he does not run away again," the senior cadre said. He motioned for them to take Little Khieu away. They grabbed him. One of the guards was carrying an axe.

'The other children stood and watched. They had no expression. They were angkar's children. One or two even smiled.

'I looked desperately at my husband. The ghastly monkey look was in his eyes. But he said nothing. The look of angkar was painted on his face.

' "No!" I wailed. Someone grabbed me.

' "Maman!" came Little Khieu's cry.

' "Little Khieu!" I shouted and I felt a blow. I fell to my knees, the world spinning around me. But I saw Little Khieu break away and stand alone in the schoolyard for a moment.

' "No! I am not Little Khieu!" he announced in a loud, clear voice. "I am called Jean-Pierre!"

'A sickly smile came to my husband's face. Then they grabbed him and my little Jean-Pierre too and marched them away. I never saw either of them again.

'Two days later I was sent north to a work camp near Siem Reap. I managed to take the little blue shoes with me. When the Vietnamese youn attacked I escaped from the camp. Mith Yon saved me and we made our way to the mountains called the Oder Mean Chey, the Way Beyond, and into Thailand.

'Now every night I pray to my Lord Buddha for a kindness. That the shoes my little one never got to wear on earth he can to wear in the Land of Bliss.'

Sawyer tried to swallow and couldn't. He reached out his hand to touch her, but it fell into his lap as though the gravity of Jupiter was pulling on it. He leaned his head back against the stone wall and closed his eyes. They burned, and he saw veins of white in the blackness and kept them closed. He heard the swish of her moving and felt her pulling his head to her breast. His ear was against her chest and he listened to the beating of her heart.

'Rest now, my So-yah. You need rest. I will keep watch. Later we will find Son Lot and finish it,' she soothed. He thought it was odd that she was comforting him. It should be the other way around, he thought. And yet it was right somehow. It was what they both needed, he thought, drifting off.

He heard shooting, automatic fire, faint and far away. He wasn't sure if he were dreaming or if he really heard it. He opened his eyes. The niche and the temple corridor were empty. He heard nothing. It must have been a dream, he thought. His eyes were burning from lack of sleep. He couldn't have been out for more than a few minutes. He felt for the Ingram. It was gone.

Then he remembered. Suong had taken it when she went on watch. He started to relax when he heard footsteps scraping over the stone paving of the corridor. More than one person, coming fast towards the niche. Christ! he thought, grabbing the knife. It hadn't been a dream!

Suddenly there were three shadowy figures in front of the niche. He raised the knife to the throwing position. A flashlight clicked on, almost blinding him.

'Drop it, Jack!' a voice snapped in English. It was familiar. He had heard it before. He could see that two of them had SKS carbines aimed right at him. The knife clattered on the stones.

'Put your hands on your head,' the same voice ordered.

'Get that fucking light out of my eyes,' Sawyer said.

'Of course,' Pranh said, coming nearer and pointing the flashlight down at the floor. Flanking him were two young Khmer Rouge. They kept the SKSs pointed at his head. Their eyes showed nothing, like the eyes of the dead.

CHAPTER 22

The earth contains and sustains;
the qualities of a mare.
The dew has frozen.
Winter approaches.
The sack is tied up.

They walked atop the stone wall of the great baray. The ancient reservoir had long since dried up and become overgrown with jungle. Sawyer had to step across thick vines reaching out over the wall from the dense greenery below, like octopus arms from a Grade B horror movie. He had to be careful not to trip and couldn't use his hands to steady himself. They were tied behind his back. The sun was brilliant and the heat was becoming unbearable.

'Water,' Pranh said, indicating the overgrown baray. 'That was the secret of Angkor. By building the baray with dikes and canals above the level of the surrounding plain, our Khmer ancestors could use the force of gravity to irrigate the land during the dry season. This enabled them to grow two or three rice crops a year instead of one, and with the surplus of rice came trade and the ability to support armies and a great civilization. Once this,' he said, with a sweeping gesture that took in the ruins and the vast sea of vegetation, 'was the capital city of a great empire. The population of the city alone was well over a million. All this when London was a mud village and Paris a squalid fortress town confined to the Île de la Cité.'

'Pranh, I'm hot and tired and history bores me, so if you want to play tour guide, I'd just as soon wait in the bus,' Sawyer said, running his tongue over his dry lips. He was very thirsty but knew better than to ask for a drink. A request from a captive is a lever for the jailor; it always puts the captive at a greater disadvantage.

Pranh stopped. 'I am called Son Lot now,' he said.

'You're called a lot of things now.'

Pranh looked at Sawyer. His face was still handsome and unlined. He had an air of power, despite being dressed like the others in black shorts and shirt. His hair was neatly combed and parted. He hadn't aged a day in all these years, Sawyer thought. His eyes were yellow, like a lion's eyes, and he still moved with the grace of a big cat.

'You haven't changed, Jack.'

'You have.'

'No,' Pranh shook his head. 'You just never really knew me. You foreigners never knew us at all.'

Sawyer didn't say anything. It was true. They stood in the sun blazing so high overhead they barely cast a shadow, staring out at the crumbling ruins snared in tendrils of advancing vegetation like long-dead flies in a vast green spider web. One guard stood near Pranh, his eyes never still. The other stood behind Sawyer, his finger on an SKS's trigger. A leather thong had been tied from Sawyer's hands to the muzzle, so that if he tried to run or jerk the weapon, it would automatically fire into his back.

'You should care,' Pranh said.

'Why?'

'Because this is where it all began.'

Pranh nodded to Sawyer's guard and they began to walk again along the wall and down huge stone steps to a road unevenly paved with big sandstone slabs. Sawyer could feel the heat of the stone even through the soles of his sandals.

'Comrade Pol Pot came here when he was young. It fired his imagination. In Paris, where he went to study radio mechanics, they treated him as an inferior, comme tous les Asiatiques. For Kampuchea to regain la gloire perdue, we had to return to the ways of Angkor. One leader: like the Buddharaja. One religion: the Party. One goal: rice.'

'But you failed.'

'We have had a setback,' Pranh conceded.

'You were too ruthless.'

Pranh's reply sent a shiver down Sawyer's spine. 'No. We were not ruthless enough.'

He looked into Pranh's yellow eyes and saw what he had never seen before and it terrified him. Pranh was insane.

'What about Suong? What have you done with her?'

Pranh whirled suddenly, his hand raised as if to slap Sawyer. The front guard pushed his SKS at Sawyer's face till the muzzle touched his forehead. Sawyer tensed. He could see the desire to pull the trigger in the guard's eyes.

'That is none of your affair! You are not to mention her!' Pranh shrieked.

Sweat trickled into Sawyer's eyes, but he didn't dare blink or look away. His eyes were locked with Pranh's. Sawyer licked his lips. They were already beginning to dry and crack.

'What about Parker?' Sawyer croaked.

Pranh looked at him sharply. A faint smile hovered on his lips. 'You will see him soon enough. We will have a, how you say, big reunion, de touchantes retrouvailles.'

'Where are we going?'

'That too you will see, very soon.'

They passed through a Lokeshvara gate, the shade under the arch a momentary relief from the blazing heat. There were soldiers in black shorts and shirts lounging around the gate until they saw Pranh and snapped rigidly to attention. Even their eyes were rigid. The open area beyond the gate was swarming with Khmer Rouge. They had set up hootches and cooking fires among the fallen lingams and broken statuary. It was a combat lager. They went through the camp and through another Lockeshvara gate.

Beyond the gate was another ruined temple. It had a long, high central staircase surmounted by the remains of what must have been a tower. The temple was very old, the design of it more primitive, less ornate, than the Bayon. It was surrounded by Khmer Rouge dug into positions facing the temple.

Pranh motioned to one of the guards, who handed him a canteen. He sat down on a giant stone head of Buddha staring straight up at the sky. It might have tumbled from the clouds, for there was no headless statue near by that it could have come from. Pranh took a long swallow. He looked at Sawyer for a moment, then pulled out a knife and motioning Sawyer to turn around, cut his hands free. He handed Sawyer the canteen.

'You see how it is. We have to do business, you and I. That is why we treat you so well,' Pranh said seriously, not conscious of any irony.

Sawyer drank the tepid water greedily, never taking his eyes from Pranh. This was a man who shot ten-year-old kids for nothing, he reminded himself.

'Where is the morphine?'

'In there,' Pranh said, tilting his head to indicate the temple.

'We trade arms for the morphine. You co-ordinate an attack on the Vietnamese with the other Cambodian resistance forces. The Viets have moved their troops to the Thai border. We both know you couldn't hold this area if they hadn't. You can hit them from behind. They'll be caught between you and the Thais. It's a classic hammer and anvil operation, but the timing is everything. It must occur as soon as you have the bulk of the arms, before the end of the monsoon. That's the deal,' Sawyer said, rubbing the ache out of his wrists where they had been tied.

'The monsoon is better for us. It makes it more difficult for them to use their tanks.'

'We'll give you all the anti-tank weapons you need.'

'Good. That is our understanding, too. And one thing more –'

'What?' Sawyer asked nervously. The fact that he had been expecting something didn't make it any easier.

'We naturally expect the USA government to recognize us officially as the only legitimate government of Kampuchea.'

This was the part Sawyer hated. He hated all of it, but this was the part he really hated. Fuck Harris, he thought. Fuck all of them.

'Those are my instructions,' he said.

Pranh smiled. It was the same eerie smile that the Boddhisattva wore. You couldn't get away from it in this place.

'Then there is no problem. Your morphine is there,' gesturing at the temple with the canteen. 'Take it.'

Sawyer could hear the water slosh in the canteen. He shook his head. He wasn't ready yet. 'Why did you take Parker?'

Pranh's smile broadened to show perfect teeth. He really was very handsome, Sawyer thought.

'Ah, Jack. You want more than morphine for your guns. You want wisdom, too,' Pranh said.

Sawyer stuck his hands in his pockets and just stood there, head cocked to one side. At that moment, he looked very American.

'Why? That's all I want to know.'

Pranh's eyebrows went up. 'So little. Only that. That is only a little wisdom,' he mocked.

'You didn't do it for fun. You had to come into Bangkok to do it. That was a big risk for you. Why was it so important?' Sawyer insisted.

'So we could deal directly with the Americans, of course,' Pranh said, as though it were perfectly obvious. 'We had to find out first how serious you were. When Bhun Sa said the USA government now wished to buy morphine, naturally we were sceptical. Also, to eliminate Bhun Sa.'

'Why?'

'Bhun Sa was hors de propos, you understand. He was no longer needed, so why should he have a share? We do the fighting. We have the morphine. You should deal directly with us. By taking Parker we bring you to us. By questioning him we find out your true intentions.'

'He didn't know our true intentions, dammit. They don't tell field agents everything,' Sawyer said, trying to suppress the anger in his voice.

'Unfortunately, it took a great deal of questioning before we were able to ascertain that,' Pranh said, a bland expression on his face.

You bastard! Sawyer thought. You miserable bastard!

'When I leave, he goes with me,' Sawyer said, keeping his voice under tight control.

'As you like, Jack. C'est du pareil au même. Only neither of you is going anywhere until the arms have been delivered. We have the radio from your pack. The one disguised as an electric razor. Once you have explained all your codes to us, we will allow you to call your people to arrange the delivery.'

Sawyer leaned against the Buddha head and looked at Pranh. He had to squint in the strong sunlight. 'I guess I did you a favour by taking Bhun Sa out, didn't I?' he observed.

'Most people in this world are necessary only to themselves. We were not sorry to hear of his death, but it has left us with one little problem.'

'Ah,' Sawyer said, like an Asian. Pranh's brows beetled and Sawyer smiled inside. He had gained a little face on the bastard.

'Inside the temple is a squad of Bhun Sa's men. The morphine is wired to explosives. If you cannot convince them to surrender, they will . . . pouf!' Pranh said, throwing his hands into the air.

'Me!'

'Who else?' Pranh shrugged. 'For some reason they will not believe us.'

'I can't imagine why not,' Sawyer said.

Pranh climbed down off the Buddha head. His men tightened in expectation of orders.

'Do not fail to persuade them, Jack. For if there is no morphine, then there are no arms, no attack on the dog-eaters and no reason to keep you and Parker alive,' he said.

Sawyer just looked at him.

'Tou!' Pranh ordered. 'Go ahead!'

Sawyer turned and started to walk towards the temple. Pranh called him and he turned back.

'Eh bien, Jack. Why don't you just say it?'

'Say what?'

'Whatever it is that is going on behind your forehead.'

Sawyer stood there, sweating. He wondered if he should tell the truth. Then it struck him that it didn't matter. Pranh was an utter pragmatist. He could say anything he liked.

'I'm sorry we're on the same side. I'd prefer you as an enemy,' Sawyer said.

'Because of the Parrot's Beak.'

'Because of a lot of things.'

'Poor Jack,' Pranh said, lighting a cigarette. 'You always were a sentimentalist.'

The air inside the temple was hot and stale. It was air with the oxygen taken out of it. They had taken him to a storeroom somewhere in the centre of a maze of narrow passageways. Stacked against the walls were thousands of wooden boxes covered with red Thai and Chinese Lettering. They had made no attempt to hide the plastique and wires placed around the boxes. Sawyer almost gagged on the smell of chemicals and unwashed bodies confined for too long in a narrow space. There were candles burning on boxes all around the room, giving it an almost church-like feel. The room was bright with their light and hot as a sauna. Stalactites of wax dripped from the base of the candles down to the stone floor. It made Sawyer nervous, so many candles so close to the plastique, even though in theory he knew it should be safe enough.

One of them, a fat, bare-chested Shan, his tattoos stretched over a bulging belly and pointed, womanish breasts, motioned Sawyer to sit with a rusty ·45 Automatic that looked as if it hadn't been cleaned since World War Two.

'The khrap will take cha,' the fat Shan said in Isan Thai, pouring Sawyer a tiny cup of jasmine tea. It was not a question.

'A thousand of thanks, Khob khun khrap,' Sawyer replied, taking a sip. It was very sweet and good, despite the heat.

The fat Shan took a sip and smacked his lips loudly to show appreciation. He put his cup down.

'So now they send a farang to try to persuade us,' he said, speaking not to Sawyer but to the other Shan in the room. The others did not respond but only stared blankly into space.

'You mean you do not burn with the desire to put yourselves into the hands of the Khmer Rouge?' Sawyer asked facetiously.

The room exploded with laughter. The fat Shan slapped his thigh loudly as a pistol shot. 'By the nats and phi, this one is a jokester!' he wheezed when he could catch his breath. He put the ·45 down on a wooden case as if to signal that he was ready to talk, nevertheless being careful to place it out of Sawyer's reach. 'No, jokester-khrap. Though we have had no orders from Bhun Sa, yet we have no great trust of the Khmer Rouge.'

'What have they told you?'

'That Bhun Sa is dead, but we do not believe.'

'Bhun Sa is dead,' Sawyer said.

The fat Shan looked away. No one met his glance. When

279

he looked back at Sawyer, his eyes showed that he believed Sawyer but that he didn't want to believe it.

'How do you know this? Have you seen the body?'

'Yes,' Sawyer said, wondering what it was that made them believe him. Then he realized what it was. 'You haven't been able to raise Bhun Sa's camp with your radio, have you?' he asked.

The fat Shan didn't answer. All at once a cunning light came into his eyes. Somehow he had guessed.

'Did you kill him?'

The room was deathly still. Sawyer wondered, if he told the truth, whether they would kill him. He remembered Utama. It was karma, whatever happened.

'Yes,' he said.

A breath of air entered the room as though the temple itself had sighed. The fat Shan tapped his thick fingers on the butt of the ·45 as though trying to decide whether or not to use it on Sawyer.

'We are dead men,' the fat Shan said.

No one spoke. There was no answer to that.

'We have orders . . . ,' one of them said, coming forward. He was tall for a Shan.

'Of what value loyalty to a dead man!' a thin-faced Shan broke out.

'How do we know this? On the word of a farang?' the tall Shan objected.

'And this of the radio? Does this one presume that is no proof? Or that we hear nothing from Bhun Sa? That too is nothing?' the thin-faced one demanded.

'Radios can malfunction. This is known. This one's mother's sister's son bought a radio at the market in Kengtung and within a ten of days it made only noises like the crackling of burning wood.'

'That was a different kind of radio, imbecile!'

'A radio is a radio,' the tall Shan insisted.

'And a fool is a fool.'

The tall Shan started to say something, then thought better of it. He paused at the doorway, drawing himself up. 'My brother is a good man, but he knows nothing of the modern mechanics,' he declared impressively and walked out.

The fat Shan looked at Sawyer as he sipped his tea. His

hand was as big as a ham. The cup disappeared in it. 'Son Lot says he will let us keep our arms and all the morphine we can carry. He says he will guarantee our safe passage out of Angkor. That is what he says,' he said.

Sawyer sipped his tea. Behind him he could hear the thin-faced Shan snort in disgust.

'Can we believe him?' the fat Shan asked.

Christ, what do you do with that? Sawyer thought. How the hell should he know? And why should they believe him? It was their lives balanced against the mission. The goddam mission. And who made him judge and jury? And maybe it didn't even matter what he said. They would make their own judgements. There was no answer. There was only karma.

'I don't know,' Sawyer said.

The fat Shan nodded as though Sawyer had told him exactly what he needed to know. 'I think he will kill us. The Khmer Rouge kill everyone, even their own. I think they will kill us too. That is what I think,' he said.

'What shall I say to Son Lot?'

The fat Shan looked up. 'Tell him we stay. If we go outside, we die. If we stay here, we die. So we might as well stay here.'

'Inside, outside. What difference? We are dead all the same,' the thin-faced Shan snapped.

'Mai pen rai. There is no difference,' the fat Shan shrugged. 'I prefer to die fighting. It is a man's way to die, that is all. But there is no difference.'

The sunlight was very strong and it made him blink coming out of the temple. The walk down the ancient stairway seemed to take a long time. Pranh was waiting for him, crouched behind a battered army deuce-and-a-half truck that he kept as a shield between him and the temple, though no shots had been fired on either side. Pranh looked expectantly at Sawyer as he came around the truck.

'They're not coming out,' Sawyer said.

Pranh's handsome face twisted with sudden, violent hate. 'It is you who failed!' he screamed, struggling to pull his pistol out of the holster on his hip.

Something exploded inside Sawyer too. 'No, it's you they

don't trust! You! You! You!' he shouted back, jabbing his index finger towards Pranh as though it were a gun.

'Now you die! Is finished!' Pranh shouted, freeing the pistol. He pointed it straight at Sawyer's head and cocked the hammer.

A voice cracked out of the truck cab like a shot. 'Wait!'

Pranh froze like a machine when the plug has been pulled.

'I am sure So-yah oun can be persuaded to try again,' Suong said, leaning her head out of the truck cab, her long hair falling to one side like a black cape.

Sawyer looked, unbelieving, from Suong to Pranh, then back to Suong.

All at once everything was crystal-clear.

CHAPTER 23

The sun sets behind the earth.
He enters the belly of the dark
   regions.
The dark times of Prince Chi.
He ascends above the roof of
   heaven;
He will descend below the crust
   of the earth.

He couldn't stop shaking. His mind bounced off the inside
of his skull like a ping-pong ball, finding no place to rest.
The thing he had feared most in the world had finally
happened. He was blind. They had sewn the lid of his good
eye shut.

She was smiling as she ordered them to do it. She, not
Pranh! She was the stronger. She who guessed his most secret
fear. What could be hidden from her? They had all felt it
and obeyed her instantly. Her bronzed face glowing in the
sunlight, its beauty still tugging at him, had been the last
thing he had seen before they wrestled him to the ground
and blotted out the sky.

That and the image of her next to Pranh, the two of them
like mirror images of each other. A blind man could see they
were brother and sister.

No, he told himself bitterly. A blind man sees nothing.
How fitting that he should see nothing, he thought. Because
he had seen nothing all along, even though from the first
he'd had the feeling he had seen her before. Utama had been
right. If you can't see, who do your actions help, your enemy
or yourself?

A groan escaped him. He put his fist in his mouth and bit the knuckle to stop it. Oh, Christ! He had loved her! He felt polluted, as though she had infected him with a venereal disease. But it was worse than that. There would be war now. No way to stop it. And those two would feed off the carnage like hyenas. No wonder Pranh had outsmarted them all. No, Pranh, the great Son Lot, was a front. *She* had outsmarted them all! First she eliminated Parker. Then she got him to eliminate all the other players one by one, Barnes, Vasnasong and the Brits and, finally, Bhun Sa and Toonsang, till there was no one left to pick up the pieces but her and Pranh. And Pol Pot.

She must have been in constant touch. The shoes! Those baby shoes – and the nightly prayers, always alone! He should have torn that black box apart long ago, but every time he got close she had suckered him. How it must have galled her to have to feed him that story about the shoes when she was so goddam close to home. Christ, what an actress! They were all actors. That's what agents were. But she was in another league. She could win an Oscar with her hands tied behind her back. That story about the kid and the Khmer Rouge – she couldn't have made all that up. No one could. A chill passed through him.

She hadn't invented that stuff about the killing fields and her son. It had all happened. It was like an optical-illusion puzzle where all you see is a rabbit and then you somehow look at it another way and see that it's a nude. She had told the truth, the way the best liars do.

Except for one thing. She wasn't an unwilling participant in angkar's reign of terror. She was one of the perpetrators.

And if he completed his mission, she would do it again.

And if he didn't, there would be another Vietnam war.

The old monk had foreseen it. What was it he had said? That Sawyer would have to choose. And that worlds would hang upon his choice. And that he would be afraid. That was true too because, oh, Christ, he was scared. He couldn't stop shaking. And they had sewn his eye shut just for openers! He lay on the hard floor of the pit or whatever place they had thrown him in. It smelled of wet earth and something rotten. Something had died in here. His hands were tied behind him. He tried to get himself under control, but he couldn't. A whimper escaped him. He couldn't help it.

'Jack? Is that you?'

A voice groped in the dark for him like a blind man's hand. At first it startled him. And then he realized that he had heard it before, a long time ago.

'Mike? Mike?'

'Yeah, it's me. Can't you tell?' Parker croaked. His voice was weak and Sawyer could hear the pain in it.

'They blinded me. I can't see.'

'Is it really you, Jack? Or am I talking to myself again?' Parker's voice faded away.

'It's me, Mike. Harris brought me in after they snatched you.'

Sawyer waited. Parker didn't say anything. He wondered if Parker had passed out. He sounded bad. Talking when you are blind is like tapping out a telegraph message, he suddenly realized. Until someone responds, you're never sure if the message has been received.

'Mike, you still there?'

'So she got you too, huh?' Parker croaked.

She. Not Pranh. Not they. She. What was it Bhun Sa had said? The hanuman snake is beautiful and its bite is fatal.

'Take it easy,' Sawyer said.

He heard a curious sound. It sounded like Parker was choking or gagging.

'Mike? Mike?'

The sound got louder, wilder, and then he recognized it. Parker was laughing, but it was like no laughter Sawyer had ever heard before. It sounded insane. It tapered off with little hiccoughs of sound like an arpeggio.

'Of all the fucking agents in the whole fucking Company they had to send you, you one-eyed son-of-a-bitch,' Parker said, the laughter starting up again. Only now it degenerated into something else, a kind of deep-throated gasping, and all at once Sawyer understood. Parker was crying.

'You got to help me, Jack. You got to,' Parker blubbered, unable to keep an awful whine out of his voice.

'All right, Mike. All right,' Sawyer said, the lie sticking in his throat like a bone. He couldn't even help himself. Talk about the blind leading the blind! He almost laughed aloud

285

himself before he caught it. Jesus, what was happening to him? Was insanity contagious? He didn't know. He didn't know anything, except that unless he held tightly to something he would be as lost as Parker. Then it hit him. That was what she was counting on. That was why she had put them together. She had to break Sawyer without physically incapacitating him in order to use him to get the morphine. Clever little Suong!

He wouldn't let her do it. That was what he could hold on to.

'Don't bullshit me! I know what you're thinking. You're thinking Parker can't hack it. Parker fucked up!' Parker lashed out, his voice breaking.

He was going off the deep end, Sawyer thought. He had to do something, but he didn't know what. And then he understood what the monk had been trying to tell him. When you're up against the wall, the only thing that works is the truth.

'Maybe you can't hack it,' he said quietly into Parker's tirade.

'Oh, Christ! Christ! Christ! I can't take it any more! It's my feet, Jack. Look what they did to me.' Parker's voice degenerated into that awful whine.

'I can't see, goddammit. What did they do?'

'My feet are killing me,' Parker whined.

'I'll help you, Mike. I swear,' Sawyer said. He knew what he had to do. He just had to get Parker to co-operate.

'Help me, Jack,' Parker pleaded, a crafty note creeping into his voice. 'You know how.'

'No,' Sawyer muttered in a strangled voice. They had sworn never to speak of it again.

'You promised,' Parker's voice sulked like a child.

'I didn't promise that, goddammit. Don't you understand? The mission is over. Everything is over. We lost. The buzzer has sounded. It's over. There's nothing left except for us to try and save our own asses. That's all. We're getting out, man. We're gonna get out of here. OK?'

At first he thought Parker was coughing. Then he realized he was laughing again, laughing hysterically.

'You blind son-of-a-bitch! You don't understand a

286

goddam thing! Christ! You think Langley will ever understand this? Do you?' Parker said.

Parker was right about that, Sawyer thought, summoning up Langley in his mind. The big square buildings, white as sugar cubes in the sun, white inside and out, sterile as a hospital with its endless cubicles and computer terminals and everyone with their little badges clipped to white shirt pockets. Langley was an enclosed, rigorously ordered world and the view out of the windows was of other white buildings, identical amid the greenways and the parking lots. Langley could no more understand the reality of a pit in the Cambodian jungle than it could admit to a belief in witches and dragons.

'Fuck Langley,' Sawyer said.

'I'm not leaving here. I can't,' Parker whispered.

Parker was pushing all the buttons, Sawyer thought. He was bringing it all back now. The Parrot's Beak and the Twelfth Evac and Zama. Out of habit, he slammed the door shut in his mind, the way he had learned how to do it. Tell him anything. Just get it going, Sawyer thought.

'All right, Mike. But I'll need your help.'

'You know how,' Parker insisted sullenly.

You gutless bastard! Sawyer thought. You always were a gutless bastard.

'I'll need my hands free,' he said.

'Try to get over here and turn around. I'll use my teeth,' Parker said. He had obviously been thinking about it.

'Where are we? Describe it,' Sawyer said, struggling to his feet. He used Parker's voice to find him.

'We're in a pit about ten feet deep. Dirt floor and walls all around. They got bamboo bars over the top like the tiger cages back in 'Nam.'

'Are we open to the sky?'

'Yes.'

'What time is it?'

'Almost dark. If it wasn't so cloudy, you could see the first stars.'

'What about guards?'

'Yeah. There's always one. They look in during the day, but it's pretty dark down here at night, so they don't bother much. Be glad you don't have the midday guard.'

'Why?'

'He likes to piss down on my head,' Parker admitted, starting to cry and then it changed to a laugh and then they were both laughing.

'Hey, remember Brother Rap always said Asia was a fucking toilet,' Sawyer managed to wheeze. They laughed harder and for an instant they were on the same side again.

'Yeah, Brother Rap,' Parker said finally, and they both stopped laughing.

'When do they change the guards?'

'They already did. We're OK for now. There's only one up there, and half the time I think he's sneaking in a nap.'

'Won't they hear us talking?'

'Sure, but it doesn't matter. They don't know English and anyway they're used to me screaming and talking to – Aaaah!' Parker screamed.

Sawyer had bumped into something.

'Don't hit me any more. Please, I'll tell you anything. Please, please,' Parker whimpered.

'Hang on, man. Just hang on,' Sawyer urged.

'I can't.'

'You're better than you think. Now just shut the fuck up and use your teeth for something useful,' Sawyer said brutally.

He waited, listening to Parker's whimpers. Listening to him try to fight it. The smell was very bad by Parker. It was almost overpowering.

'It'll take a while. It's pretty tight,' Parker managed to get out.

'That's OK. We've got all night.'

Sawyer felt a tug and then a series of tiny jerks as Parker began to gnaw at the rope binding his wrists. It felt like a fish mouthing a baited hook. He could hear wet, chewing sounds behind him. He tried to stand utterly still and get himself under control. 'Yeah, Brother Rap,' Parker had said. There was nothing to do except stand there and try not to think, only the door-shutting trick wasn't working this time. This time there was no way not to remember. No way at all.

They were coming out of the jungle. Thousands of them,

288

crawling into the rice paddy like black worms. They'd been expecting it, but still it was spooky to see it in the ghostly light of a flare. Sawyer glanced around the lager, sensing the ARVNs stirring along the Night Defensive Perimeter. They wouldn't hold this time, he thought. Ever since the firefight earlier, he had known it was only a matter of time.

Pranh had led them all the way into the jungle, insisting that the real VC headquarters, COSVN, wasn't 'the City', uncovered by American troops in the Fish Hook, but was in the Parrot's Beak. Since he was supposed to be S-2 for Cambodian intelligence, and since the enemy kept melting into the jungle ahead of them, Major Lu had gone along. They kept marching deeper and deeper into the Parrot's Beak, seeking a COSVN that was becoming increasingly mythical, like Spanish conquistadores seeking El Dorado. Then – was it only yesterday morning that it all happened? – Brother Rap had laid it on him.

'Pranh's di-di'd, man.'

'What are you talking about?'

'I mean the mother-fucker di-di'd. He's gone, man.'

A queer feeling came over Sawyer. 'Maybe he bought it. Maybe . . .'

'Forget it, bro. The LP saw him go out through the NDP wire. They asked him what he was up to and he gave them some slope jive about "LRRPing" it. That fucker never even touched a gun before. It's a fucking trap, man,' Rap said, squatting next to Sawyer. He bent his head forward as if he were praying and his love beads swung free.

'We've got to get out of here,' Sawyer said.

'Hey, tell me about it,' Rap agreed.

'What about Major Lu?'

'He called it in and HQ told him to stay put. They say they ain't no Charlie worth worrying about in the Parrot's Beak anyways. Lu's called in a slick. He's gonna debate it with 'em face to face.' Rap grinned, spitting in little squirts through the spaces between his teeth.

They both looked out at the terrain. The lager was on a rise that overlooked the rice paddies down to a stream bordered on the far side by the jungle. The sky glowed with the milky light that comes before the dawn, and the trees beyond the stream had begun the change from shadow to green. A veil of mist lay over the fields. Soon the sun would come to burn off the mist and reveal the emerald-green forest that stretched to the rim of the world and it would be light enough to light a cigarette.

Sawyer shook his head. 'That won't work,' he said. 'MACV's already called the Parrot's Beak a big goddam victory without hardly a shot being fired. How in hell are they going to allow us to retreat?'

'Yeah,' Rap agreed, shaking his head dubiously, as though getting screwed was what life was all about.

They waited all morning for orders, the air shimmering in the rising heat. It wasn't until they finally heard the slick coming in that the VC opened up with rockets and mortars. Brother Rap started shouting at the ARVNs, trying to organize return fire. Parker was with the RTO, a small ARVN named Phuoc whom everyone called 'Fuck', trying to call in air support. Someone screamed, 'Incoming!', the cry that got to you like nothing else, and Sawyer hit the dirt. The ground seemed to slam him in the face as an 82-mortar exploded nearby, and in the sudden glare he saw a head soaring in a high arc through the air like a punted football. Parker! Sawyer thought and started running.

Parker's arm was bleeding. The upper part of Phuoc's body was gone and the radio was a twisted piece of smoking metal, though as a shield it had probably saved Parker's life.

'It's OK, Mike. It's a beauty, man. No real damage and free drinks in the bars when you get back to the World,' Sawyer said.

For a moment, Parker clutched at Sawyer's arm with his good hand. 'Tell me the truth, Jack. I can take it.'

'I wish it was me,' Sawyer said, hauling Parker to his feet, half-dragging him to the slick as the chopper dropped to the ground, blue-green tracers from an RPD machine-gun disappearing into the dust storm churned up by the rotor.

They saw Major Lu scramble on board. The slick started to pull up. RPD machine-gun bullets were hitting the ground all around them and Sawyer thought he was going to go crazy. He heaved Parker into the hatch.

'This ain't no Dust-Off. We got no −' a crewman screamed, his eyes wild with fear.

'Take him, or I'll shoot you myself,' Sawyer screamed

back, aiming his M-16 at the crewman as the slick pulled heavily into the sky with an incredible clatter.

Sawyer was already on the ground. He watched the chopper go, resisting a sudden panicky impulse to call it back and jump aboard, as though it was his last chance. He watched it fly above the stream of tracers into the sun, the door gunner still working his M-60 on the tree line. A rocket exploded nearby, bringing him back to his senses. He headed for the NDP in a jerky but rapid four-legged lizard crawl.

After about an hour the firefight began to die down, but it wasn't until weeks later that he learned that, although the slick had made it safely back to Division, Major Lu had also disappeared without ever having made a report. They settled down for the night, still waiting for orders that never came, knowing that the VC would hit them seriously after dark and that without the radio they couldn't even call for help. They were utterly cut off.

They could feel it coming. Everyone had his weapon switched to automatic. The grenadiers loaded their M-79s with canisters. Sawyer went along the line, warning them to be sure the claymores weren't turned around before using them. The ARVNs just looked at him with despairing eyes, but the safeties clicked off their weapons as he passed.

'Now I know how Custer felt – and I always used to root for the Indians,' Rap tried to joke, but his grin was unreal, like the smile painted on a doll's face.

They hunkered down to wait. Knowing it was coming made the night pass very slowly. Still, when it actually came, it was a surprise. An RPG rocket exploded somewhere off to the left. RPDs and AK-47s opened up. A flare went off and the paddy was swarming like an anthill in the harsh white light. A few M-16s started to return ragged fire, though Sawyer shouted at them to wait. A nervous ARVN set off a claymore prematurely and blew himself into bits of wet confetti. VC sappers had turned it around in the night. Suddenly Brother Rap was beside him.

'They ain't gonna hold, man,' he whispered, his hand jiggling the sling on his M-16, too nervous to keep still. Sawyer shouted, 'Fire!' and the intensity of firing got very heavy. It was like a wind, all long bursts and no breaks.

Sawyer had never been so afraid. The VC were coming

through the wire. He screamed at the ARVN for them to use grenades, not the claymores, but it was too late. The claymores went off, tearing holes in the NDP where two-man ARVN teams had been. The claymores had all been turned around. That was what set it off. The ARVNs broke. Screaming in panic, they began to run. The LZ was a mass of confusion, dark figures running everywhere.

Sawyer and Rap were running too. Shadows rose up from the ground near the far paddy dike. Sawyer didn't know if they were ARVN or VC. He heard shouts over the roaring in his ears. He fired, cutting down three of them. The shouts became screams. Rap was firing too and then they were running again. Somehow they made it over the dike and into the jungle and the endless night.

They gathered up the remnants of the ARVN Ranger battalion in the morning. They barely made up two squads. Lieutenant Qui was the only ARVN officer left, and they agreed the only chance they had was to try and walk out through the bush, avoiding the trails as much as possible. The afternoon sun was a blinding glare that filled the sky with a blue-white haze. Rap took the point and Qui the slack as they made their way through a band of razor-edged elephant grass. Sawyer brought up the rear, spending half his time walking backwards, because that was where the VC would most likely hit. The exhausted ARVNs crashed noisily through the elephant grass like a band of apes. The noise made Sawyer cringe, but shouting at them would only make more noise and, worse, if they didn't obey him because they were that far gone, it would have meant that nobody would follow orders any more.

Drops of sweat stung Sawyer's eyes and he blinked to clear them. Up ahead he could see Rap emerge from the elephant grass up-hill into a clearing. He was carrying his M-16 across the back of his neck, both arms wearily draped over the carbine, his head lolling with fatigue and the heat. He looked like a Black Christ with his arms like that, and Sawyer was stabbed with a sudden pang of fear. He better take the point himself, he thought, getting ready to call a halt. The line of ARVNs shuffled wearily, like pilgrims on an endless journey, as they made their way across the clearing back towards the jungle.

'Oh, God, I'm on it!'

Sawyer heard the sudden anguished cry and was torn with the realization that it was Rap's voice even before he hit the ground.

'Freeze, dammit! Freeze!' Sawyer screamed as the ARVNs hit the dirt, the sudden silence deafening as an artillery salvo.

'Jack! Where's the EOD? Where is the mother-fucker?' Rap screamed in a high, thin voice and Sawyer knew Rap must have panicked because the Explosive Ordinance Disposal, an easygoing sergeant named Minh, had been wounded by a booby-trap two weeks earlier and hadn't yet been replaced. Sawyer raised his head, but couldn't make his legs support him. He was terrified. He finally managed to shout.

'Rap, is it pressure or a Bouncing Betty?'

Because if it was a Bouncing Betty there was no way to get off it without setting it off and all you could do was pray that the explosive charge got bounced up high enough to finish the job.

'Jesus! I can't tell! Jack, help me! Please help me!' Rap wailed.

And then, without knowing how or why, because it wouldn't do any good, Sawyer was running towards Rap. And all he could think of was that he couldn't let Rap die thinking that no one even tried to help.

'Coming,' Sawyer shouted, his voice quavering as he pounded towards the clearing. He could see Rap balanced like the ball on a seal's nose, the sweat pouring down his brown face in rivulets. Only a few more yards, Sawyer thought.

'Oh, shit, it's a Betty,' he heard Rap whisper.

And then it went off.

You know how, Parker had said. And Sawyer was back in the hospital ward in Japan. He remembered the hospital smell of disinfectant that somehow couldn't disguise the stink of the factories and the polluted river nearby. But Sawyer couldn't see them. His eyes were bandaged. Only one was gone, but they had bandaged both. Something about sympathetic nerves or something.

Zama Army Hospital. And the night on the ward when

Parker, his arm still in a sling, found him and took him to see Brother Rap.

Parker led him down endless corridors. It appeared to take a long time. Sawyer wasn't sure if it seemed so far because he was blindfolded or because the hospital was so spread out. 'All army hospitals are spread out in case of attack,' the ward master, a lifer, had told him.

'Why? I thought we were in Japan. Or are the Japs after us too?' Sawyer had said.

If he had known how bad it was, he would have let Rap die out there. That's what he always told himself, although even now he didn't know if he would have gone through with it. The medic had given Rap some morphine and albumin and maybe Rap would have just died there in the clearing if the Dust-Off hadn't spotted them and the desperate ARVNs hadn't waved it in. At the time Sawyer remembered thinking that it was good luck.

Brother Rap was awake, Parker said. That was the worst part. He was looking at them, although Parker wasn't sure he saw them. Rap's eyes were squinted to slits with the pain. His face was untouched. Except for the bandages around his waist, his upper body appeared to have escaped injury, Parker whispered in his ear.

'How is he?' Sawyer asked.

'He's bad,' Parker said.

'How bad?'

'He's bad, Jack. Real bad.'

'Take the bandage off my right eye. I can still see with that one.'

'You're not supposed to. The doctor said – '

'Fuck the doctor!'

'It's the regs, man. If they catch us – '

'Take the fucking thing off!'

'All right, Jesus, just keep it down, will you? You'll get the night nurse in here,' Parker hissed.

'Jack. Is that you, man?' Rap called out.

'I'm coming,' Sawyer said, pulling the bandage off his eyes. Although it was night and the only light came from a single, dim night light, he was almost blinded by it. He squinted his good eye, desperately trying to see.

They were in a small surgery-recovery room. Rap was

hooked up to so many tubes he looked like something from a science-fiction movie. His upper body seemed unmarked, but the white cotton sheet covering the lower part of his body was flat below the hips. Sawyer winced at that. Although the left leg was gone below the knee back in the clearing, the right leg, though covered with blood, had still been attached and he had hoped they could save it.

He glanced down at the chart at the foot of the bed. It was as thick as a small-town phone book. It was all unreadable medical gobbledegook, though words like 'nephrectomy', 'ureterostomy' and 'traumatic amputation' leaped out at him. Then he noticed that Rap's arms were strapped to the bed. They looked very black against the white of the sheets and the bandages.

He could see Rap's lips moving. He motioned Parker over to the door to watch out for the night nurse. As he approached, he could feel the heat from Rap's body. It was like standing next to a hot stove. Rap's eyes were glassy with fever and pain. Sawyer felt sick to his stomach. He bent over till their faces were almost close enough to kiss.

'I tried to kill myself. Pulled out the tubes. The fuckers stopped me,' Rap croaked.

'Can't they give you something for the pain?'

Rap grimaced. 'They give me so much fucking morphine and Demerol now, in Bedford Sty' the junkies be sucking my blood like Dracula if they could.'

'And the pain's still that bad?'

'Oh, man,' Rap whimpered.

'Oh, shit, man. Oh, shit,' Sawyer murmured, not knowing what to say. He watched the blood drip one drop at a time from a hanging bottle into a catheter inserted into the back of Rap's good hand.

Rap closed his eyes tight and Sawyer watched him struggle with the pain, his hands clenched into fists. Sawyer was supposed to say something, but he didn't know what.

'It'll get better, man. They got all kinds of shit now. Artificial limbs you wouldn't believe, all kinds of stuff,' Sawyer said.

'They ain't got anything.'

'Yeah, they do. And you'll be getting plenty of money from the Army. Maybe get a new Mustang with one of those special hand controls they got. Drive the chicks crazy, man. So you won't be a hot shot at the discos. So what? Men dancers are all kind of faggoty, anyway,' Sawyer babbled, conscious of how inane he sounded.

'I ain't a man no more,' Rap said.

Sawyer stopped. He felt like throwing up. He could hear someone groaning down the ward, but just from the sound he couldn't make out if it was pain or a nightmare. Vietnam was portable, he realized for the first time. You could take it with you wherever you went, whether you wanted to or not.

'I didn't know,' he said.

Rap managed to raise his head an inch from the pillow. His neck tendons were like ropes; the liquid in his eyes looked like it was about to boil.

'You gotta help me, man. I can't go back. Not like this,' Rap whispered.

Sawyer shook his head. 'Come on, Rap. Come on, man.'

'Look at me, mother-fucker! Look at me!' Rap raged, his voice barely a whisper. 'I got no insides any more. I be hooked to machines forever, man. No way to take care of myself. And what for? I ain't anything any more, 'cept somethin' in pain that even morphine can't help. Can you picture me like this in a fucking Brooklyn tenement, man? Don't do this to me, Jack. For Chrissake, man.'

Sawyer looked helplessly at him. 'I . . . ,' he began and then he saw it come into Rap's eyes. Don't say it, he thought. For God's sake, don't say it.

'You owe me, mother-fucker. You the one who talked me into going back,' Rap said, not looking at Sawyer.

That's when it hit him: the picture of Brother Rap sitting in a wheelchair by a window in his mother's apartment in Brooklyn. Only he wasn't Brother Rap any more. He was back to being Harold Johnson. He was hooked up to some kidney machine and staring out at the grey street, at the battered cars and the dudes jiving to a ghetto-blaster and the girls in their short skirts, cheap and tight and hot with colour. And Harold just staring, his eyes glazed with boredom and drugs. He was only nineteen. The doctors were good. They were very good. They might be able to keep him alive like that for a long time, Sawyer thought.

He put his hand on Rap's shoulder, then he went over to Parker, near the door. Parker's face was terrified.

'You're not going to listen to that, Jack. He's crazy. The fever's put him out of his mind.'

'He's right.'

Parker started to back away, shaking his head. Sawyer grabbed his hospital robe near the throat.

'It's wrong, man. Don't do it. And besides,' Parker said, his eyes darting around suspiciously, 'if they caught us, it's murder. They'd crucify us.'

'Look at him. Just look at him, for Chrissakes!' Sawyer hissed, hauling Parker to the side of the bed. 'Can you see him back in the World? Can you? What are they keeping him alive for? To suffer? Because they're scared shitless to kill him. They weren't scared to send him out to get his legs and balls and cock blown off! They weren't scared to do that!'

Parker squirmed in Sawyer's grasp. He tried to look away. Sawyer grabbed a handful of hair and forced Parker to look into his good eye.

'I can't, Jack,' Parker whispered.

'What if we were still in 'Nam? Still in Indian Country. What then?'

'We're not in 'Nam. This is Japan, man. It's all nice and clean here. They don't understand anything here.'

'Uh-uh,' Sawyer shook his head. 'The hospital may be in Japan, but we're still in 'Nam. You don't believe me, just look inside the head of every poor fucking grunt in this whole fucking place. We're in 'Nam right now.'

Rap stirred behind them. 'Sweet Christ, hurry! I need another shot,' he said.

Parker blinked. He looked straight into Sawyer's eye and Sawyer could see him remembering. Maybe he was seeing Sawyer picking him up, heaving him into the slick. Sawyer and Rap staying behind, diminishing to the size of ants as the slick rose into the burning sky.

'If they catch us, we've had it,' Parker managed, his mouth dry.

'Nobody'll catch us if you watch by the door and keep your fucking mouth shut,' Sawyer said, shoving Parker towards the door.

Parker crouched by the door. They heard footsteps approach and he signalled with his good hand. Sawyer knelt by the bed, listening. He recognized the ward master's tread by the slight shuffle of one of the feet. Blind people learn how to listen, he thought. If someone comes in, he wouldn't have to do it, he thought, not sure if he wanted to be stopped or not.

The footsteps receded down the corridor. Parker looked across the dim room and nodded. His face was white as a sheet. Sawyer knelt over Brother Rap. Rap's breathing sounded loud and harsh. Sawyer could hear the congestion rattling in his lungs.

'You gonna do it, honky?' Rap whispered, his eyes wet with pain.

Sawyer nodded.

Rap took a deep, rasping breath, then another. 'OK', he said, closing his eyes. 'OK.'

'I'll take the watch. You go to sleep,' Sawyer said, leaning over Rap, a pillow in his hand.

He felt the rope start to loosen even before Parker said anything. Parker spat out a mouthful of something and then it was only a minute or two before it was loose enough for Sawyer to pull free.

He felt Parker slump against him and turned to support him. Then he felt the ropes holding Parker up, and the bad feeling he'd had when Bhun Sa had dragged the KMT officer behind the Land Rover came back.

'You OK?' he whispered.

'No, I'm not OK,' Parker whimpered.

Sawyer felt his way down Parker's body. Parker had been tied in a sitting position so that he was held upright even if he slept. They had seated him on a block of stone that couldn't be knocked over. As soon as Sawyer touched Parker's thighs, Parker screamed.

'Shut up!' Sawyer hissed.

He quickly slid his fingers down Parker's legs till he encountered something metal. Parker gasped with a sudden intake of air as he tried to stifle his scream. Sawyer touched the metal. It was round and smooth and felt like brass, with a round opening and a wide lip. The shape was like an old-fashioned spittoon, maybe that's what it was, and then he felt the crudely sawn piece of wood. Parker screamed again and Sawyer had to wait till it became a groan before he could talk. The bastards! he kept repeating to himself. The bastards!

'How'd they break your feet, Mike?'

'What?' Parker's voice was small and far away.

'Your feet. What'd they use?'

'An iron bar. On a rock. They smashed them again and again. I begged them. I begged them. They were like bloody rags and they kept hitting them,' Parker's voice broke.

'Take it easy. Just take it easy,' Sawyer said, feeling the twinges in his own feet. He could see it now in his mind. They had broken Parker's feet and jammed them into a brass pot, forcing him to sit there as his feet swelled against the sides, the pressure creating an incredible agony. But that still wasn't enough for Pranh. He'd wedged in a two-by-four for them to pound any time they wanted to raise the pain a few decibels.

There was still something he had to find out. He would have to hurt Parker to do it. He prodded Parker's legs with his fingers. Parker groaned. The flesh was hot and soft and held the impression. He could smell the rot. It was like sticking his fingers into thick oatmeal mush. The mushiness extended all the way to above Parker's knees. At every touch, Parker screamed.

Sawyer slapped him hard across the face. 'Shut up, for God's sake! Just shut up!'

'You fuck! You lousy fuck!' Parker said suddenly, quite distinctly.

'I'm sorry. I had to see what it was,' Sawyer said. He gave a short, sharp laugh, harsh as a cough. He could see nothing. He moved around Parker and began plucking at the knots that tied Parker's hands behind him.

'Jack? Jack?' Parker whispered into the darkness. His voice was very weak.

'Yeah, Mike.'

'I can't move. I'm a liability. You can't get me out.'

'I know.'

Parker hesitated.

'If you leave me here, you know what they'll do to me.'

Sawyer could hear the fear in his voice. 'I know that too.'

'I can't take it any more, Jack. Please. You promised. Like Brother Rap, OK? OK?'

'Don't beg, Mike. Just don't beg,' Sawyer muttered.

If only he could see! And then he felt it, working on Parker's hands. Parker's fingernails hadn't been clipped for a month, maybe more. They were long and sharp as claws, he could use one of them to cut the stitches that sewed his eyelid shut. It would probably infect, but that didn't matter. He needed to see now, not later.

He knew what he was going to do. It was a war all right, but it had nothing to do with America or Cambodia or Vietnam any more. It was down to just him and Pranh.

And the bitch.

CHAPTER 24

A tree on the mountain.
The wild geese reach the desert.
The husband leaves on an expedition
but will not return.

The wind came and blew out the moon as though it were a candle. Sawyer could hear it moving in the trees with a continuous murmuring sound like a fast stream over rocks. When the first drops of rain came he had looked up in terror and fury, thinking that the night guard was pissing on him, but it was just the rain. It wasn't a heavy monsoon rain but the light rain that just goes on and on until you think it will never end.

It was a good omen, he thought. Not even the Khmer Rouge liked sitting out all night in the rain, and it would help give him cover. He wasn't sorry about losing the moonlight either. He needed the dark and at least he wouldn't have to look at Parker any more. He didn't have to. The image of Parker, made black and white by a single ray of moonlight, re-tied to keep him erect, his head slumped down on his chest, his swollen legs primly tied together with the feet inside the brass pot, was seared in his brain as though put there by a branding iron.

You know how to do it.

Don't beg, Mike. Just don't beg.

And then the agony of Parker plucking out the stitches and he could see. His eye stung like crazy, but he could see. Parker was worse than he had imagined. If Sawyer had passed him on the street he might not have recognized him. Parker looked like an old man. There were black streaks running up his legs and his calves were swollen to the size of thighs.

'Spend my share, Jack. Have the biggest goddam blowout the bastards ever saw,' Parker croaked.

'What share?'

Parker went dead-still.

'What share, Mike? Barnes and the morphine?'

Parker sighed. It might have been relief. 'Yeah. And Vasnasong and Harris. You didn't really think they were gonna just destroy all that lovely valuable skag, did you?'

'Harris too?'

Parker bit his lip. The pain was getting to him. He wouldn't be able to hold it much longer, Sawyer thought.

'Ask Barnes.'

'Barnes is dead.'

Parker turned away. In profile in the moonlight his face looked like the head on a silver coin. He looked almost the way Sawyer remembered him. They'd been friends once and he changed his mind about pushing Parker on Harris. It didn't matter any more. He had quit the team. They just didn't know it.

'Asia,' Parker mumbled. 'Fucking Asia.'

Sawyer got up and started to re-tie Parker's hands. He didn't want to hear any more.

'She gets us all, Jack. She lifts her skirt and you think it's gonna be a quickie, but once you're in, it's like a tar baby and you can't ever get unstuck. You're the last one, Jack,' Parker gasped over his shoulder, the pain harsh in his voice. 'You better di-di or it'll get you too, man.'

'Go to sleep, Mike,' Sawyer said, the echo of Zama loud in his ears.

'Hurry, man,' Parker whispered.

Sawyer put his left forearm at the back of Parker's neck and locked it on his right bicep, the right arm coiled around the throat.

'Jack! Jack!' Parker whispered.

'Yeah, Mike.'

He could hear Parker swallow in the dark.

'Don't tell them how it really was with me, Jack.'

Sawyer felt as though he had just stepped into something left by a dog on a pavement. Why'd he have to do that? he thought. He remembered Parker in his Class As on hospital leave in Japan, wearing every ribbon he had, including the little bullshit ones that even the REMFs got, like the Vietnam Service Ribbon and the National Defense Ribbon. You pathetic bastard, Sawyer thought, feeling sorry for Parker and hating him for making him feel that way.

'They wouldn't understand,' Parker mumbled, only making it worse.

It was a lousy way to go out, Sawyer thought, and felt ashamed for both of them. He wished he didn't have to be such a self-righteous son-of-a-bitch. All he wants is his version of extreme unction, he told himself. You're in the wrong business. You're too good for this world. You should have been St Francis in a cave. And then he realized the joke of it all.

'Don't worry, Mike. You're a fucking hero. They'll put your name on a corridor in Langley. There'll be a whole new generation of CTP shitheads who'll bust their balls to try and live up to the standards you set.'

'Thanks, Jack,' Parker sighed, completely missing the irony.

Let it go, Sawyer thought. For Christ's sake, let him keep something. Maybe their believing he was a hero will make him one. Maybe that's what heroes are.

'Don't mention it,' Sawyer said, tightening his grip relentlessly like a vice.

The rain was heavier now. He stood on Parker's still warm lap and, slipping the wooden pin, cautiously raised the bamboo lattice. He could see the black silhouettes of the palms and a crumbling temple wall against the dark clouds. It was still dark, but the sky had begun to acquire the faint glow that signals the pre-dawn.

The sentry was dozing against a sugar palm just a few feet away. He kept jerking his head up to try and stay awake. Sawyer waited, debating whether to let the sentry fall asleep or get him closer. A look at the sky decided him. Once it became light enough to see, he wouldn't stand a chance. He needed to bring the sentry closer, but how? He had ignored their voices all night. Then he thought of a sound that would wake any Asian in a second.

Sawyer hissed softly like a spitting cobra. The sentry jerked upright like a marionette. He got up cautiously, his eyes glued to the ground as he walked step by step to the edge of the pit.

Sawyer moved. In a single motion he threw open the bamboo lattice and yanked the rifle muzzle down, toppling the sentry head first into the pit. Sawyer jumped down after him, right hand raised shoulder-high for a killing blow, but there was no need. The sentry lay in the kind of uncomfortable sprawl unique to death, his head twisted sideways, at an impossible angle, against the dirt wall.

Sawyer checked the rifle in the dark. It was an SKS, and going over it brought back Nha Trang and the times they had to do it blindfolded, Sergeant Willis screaming in his ear, 'Come on, turkey. It's not a tit. Don't diddle with it!' Now it was starting to come back. Simonov SKS. Chinese-made 7·62mm semi-automatic carbine. He checked the clip and magazine. Safety off. All right.

He stood on Parker's lap again and slid the SKS, butt first, up on to the ground. He eased the bamboo lattice open, grabbed a handful of wet grass and swung himself up and over the edge.

He stopped, listening, the SKS ready. He was in a small clearing between a carved temple wall and dense jungle. He could see the outlines of things, but it was still too dark to distinguish details. The rain cut the visibility further, plastering his clothes to him. The rain felt good on his eye. It still stung, but he could live with it. After all, it wasn't anything compared with what Parker had gone through.

He heard something. It wasn't coming from the temple area, where the KR defence perimeter had been set up, but from the jungle. A sound of branches scraping and the Reptile was wide awake. Christ, what was happening?

He waited till the sound faded, then scuttled on all fours into the dense foliage. He found the track only a few yards in. It had all come back now. He didn't have to think about how to do it any more. He found a muddy heel mark. It was deep, water already pooling in it. So whoever they were, they were heavily laden. There were no scraps, cigarette butts or garbage of any kind. So they were probably far from their base and were porting everything they needed. They were good, leaving nothing behind and that also meant they would be setting up MAs and ambushes. Further on he found more footprints. A lot of them. They were fresh, superimposed upon each other. It was a patrol in force.

He fingered a broken twig speculatively. It was chest high, so they were holding their weapons at port arms, ready for combat. Further down the trail he found a few ripped thorny tendrils, about mid-section high. It suggested that they were carrying AKMs or AK-47s because the AKs are long and the banana clip had a tendency to catch on vines. Just underneath he found a faint circular imprint in the mud, where someone had set down what was probably the base of an RPG-7 to rest for a moment. All Soviet arms, Sawyer thought. He'd done this before. He knew who they were.

North Vietnamese regulars. Charlie.

He moved carefully now, one step at a time. About twenty yards down the trail he found the first one. A vine about eight inches high stretched across the trail. He followed it into the undergrowth to a claymore aimed at anyone coming up the trail from the direction of the temple complex.

He'd found his war. The one the Company wanted him to start. Only the Khmer Rouge wasn't going to attack the Vietnamese. It was the other way around. The Vietnamese had surrounded the Cambodians. They were in a trap.

Basing his calculation on the size of the lager and the perimeter Pranh had showed him, Sawyer figured Pranh must have at least three thousand men with him. The NVA had to have a full division, maybe more, to pull it off. There was no way Sawyer was going to be able to walk out through a whole damn army. He was trapped right along with the KR.

Parker had been right, he thought. Asia always gets you in the end. There was only one thing left for him to do. Karma. He wondered if he'd ever really had a choice. He got ready. There was damn little time left. The NVA couldn't stay undetected by Pranh's patrols for ever. They would probably attack at dawn. He would have to hurry.

He made his way back towards the temple complex. It would be faster going there, with little likelihood of mines and booby traps within the defence perimeter.

He came to the edge of the tree line and froze, scarcely breathing. He had heard something. He waited, watching the temple wall and the eternally smiling face on a Loveshvara gate. Then he heard it again. Conversation. It was somewhere off to the left. A Khmer Rouge two-man listening post.

He moved away from them, careful not to make a sound. 'Combat is a misnomer,' Sergeant Willis used to say. 'The idea is not to confront the enemy but to evade him. The whole thing is to get around the bastards. You don't want to fight 'em, just to kill 'em. Preferably by surprise from behind. If you have to fight the fuckers, that means they have a chance to get you too, and nobody ever won a war by getting killed.'

The rain was easing by the time he made it to the outside temple wall. There wasn't much time left. He crouched low beside a long line of spear-carrying warriors carved on the wall. I've done this before, he thought. Everything twice, like the fool who had to climb Mount Fuji. Cambodia twice. Charlie in the jungle twice. Having to terminate my own twice. 'All this meditating and incarnations, how long do you have to do it?' he had asked Utama. 'Until you get it right,' the monk had replied. He heard something and whirled, but it was just a hawk rising over the trees.

He crept closer. There was sure to be a sentry covering the Lokeshvara gate, but he couldn't spot him. Take your time, he cautioned himself. The guys who bought it in 'Nam were the ones who lost patience, who didn't make sure. He tried again, quartering the area and using the side of his eye, because peripheral vision is better than straight-on in bad light. He worked his way up, starting at ground level, and still couldn't spot him.

'Come on, turkey,' Sergeant Willis used to snap on the 'boom-boom' course. 'You'd find it fast enough if it had a triangle of hair above it.'

There was just the tip of a muzzle sticking out of the foliage on top of the wall to one side of the arch. The first time he had mistaken it for a twig. Avoid confrontation, he reminded himself. He looked along the length of the temple wall, away from the hidden sentry, till he found what he was looking for. He slipped through the foliage alongside the wall till he came to the silk-cotton tree whose roots had already begun to push the stones apart and breach the wall. He slung the SKS over his shoulder and was about to climb

306

the tree when he stopped and looked around. Something had changed in the landscape.

The rain had stopped.

He climbed the tree, then, using the uneven handholds and footholds, climbed down on the other side of the wall. The Khmer Rouge camp was just beginning to stir. He would have to go quickly now.

Langley doctrine. Worst-case situation. When you are where you don't belong and don't have adequate cover, act as if you own the joint. He unslung the SKS and began to walk openly across the bivouac area, past the hootches and the smouldering cooking fires, the massive pyramid of the temple ruin now clearly visible against the reddening sky.

A soldier in black pyjamas came out of a hootch, yawning and stretching. He stopped when he saw Sawyer. He stood there, watching Sawyer cross right in front of him. Sawyer acted as if the soldier didn't exist. He felt the soldier's eyes burning holes in his back, but he kept moving till he saw what had to be Pranh's CP tent, still shielded from the entrance to the temple ruin by the deuce-and-a-half truck.

By now others were beginning to watch him. He kept going. A Khmer Rouge officer and a squad of men approached diagonally from his left. The officer shouted something at him. Sawyer ignored him and kept his eyes straight ahead. It was all happening very fast. He saw the uneven paving stones of the ancient courtyard, the weeds sprouting in the cracks, the fallen stone carvings and the giant head of Buddha still staring up at the empty sky and, at the edge of his field of vision, the KR officer and the squad cutting him off from Pranh's tent. He wasn't going to make it.

The officer shouted again. The carbines were pointing at him now and, like a man in a dream, he turned slowly towards them, the SKS coming into firing position as though it were a part of his hand and Pranh's still closed tent just out of reach as if it were on the other side of a border.

The whistling sound was the sound that could still snap him bolt-upright, sweating in the night, even after all these years. He flung himself to the ground even before he consciously identified it as the sound of an incoming artillery shell.

The KR never got the chance to fire. The blast rolled over Sawyer, hot and smelling of cordite, and then the rockets and mortars began to explode all around. Big ones, he thought, 122s and 82-mortars. And then everything went crazy. Small-arms fire and black pyjamas running everywhere. As Sawyer started to get up, he saw the KR officer struggling to point a heavy RPD at him. Sawyer dropped him with a single shot from the SKS.

He ran to the tent, expecting to get hit by a fragment at any second. He threw the flap open and had just an instant to take it all in. Suong was sitting up on a cot, her breasts exposed, her eyes dominating her face like the eyes of a starving child. Pranh, brow furrowed, was jumping naked from the cot for his pistol. And Sawyer thinking, her own brother! She even did it with her own goddam brother! He was so stunned he actually waited till Pranh started to turn. Pranh's eyes, black as a snake's, were fixed on his as Sawyer fired. The first shot hit Pranh in the shoulder, spinning him around. The second opened a hole in his back, the blood immediately starting to trickle out of it. Sawyer's third shot smashed into the back of Pranh's head even before he toppled to the ground.

'So-yah, no!' Suong screamed as he pointed the SKS at her. 'I did it for you, So-yah. I had to. It was the only way to save you. The only way!' she cried.

Sawyer pointed the muzzle at the valley between her heaving breasts. He could hear the explosions and fighting outside, but none of that mattered. His war was here.

'You lied!' he said through clenched teeth. 'You always lied. You lied about Parker. You delivered him to Pranh on a silver platter. You lied about how you found me at the warehouse. That was you and Vasnasong. You got to him because you didn't want the buyer killed off. And me, the big jerk, I was so glad to be alive, I didn't look too closely at how you found out about the warehouse. Then you killed the Akha to force the issue with Toonsang because you knew he was a thief and you couldn't afford to let anyone see what was in your pack, could you?'

She shook her head wildly, but Sawyer wasn't paying attention.

'Then you got us captured by Bhun Sa's men because you

308

didn't want me cutting any separate deals with Bhun Sa, and when that didn't work you went to see him that night. Then you lied about Bhun Sa. He wasn't trying to kill you. You were trying to kill him! So you could have it all. Cobras don't share, do they? And you lied about Bhun Sa's map. You had it in your pack all the time, didn't you? Then the shoes. There was a radio hidden in them, wasn't there?'

Her head hung down, sleek black hair shrouding her face.

'Wasn't there?' he shouted.

'No, I told you! They were my Little Khieu's,' she cried, tears starting down her cheeks.

'Little Khieu's, my ass. That's how you were able to stay in touch with Pranh all the time. That's what made him so fucking smart and that's what you couldn't let Toonsang find. Or me.'

'No, So-yah, you . . .'

'No wonder everything went wrong on this mission, with Little Miss Fixit sabotaging it every step of the way,' he shouted, spittle flying.

Outside the crump of rockets began to die down. The rattle of small-arms fire grew closer. The Vietnamese were moving in. The tent canvas trembled like a sail in a rising wind.

'By then I had begun to suspect, so I connected with Mith Yon in Aranyaprathet. But I wasn't sure, so I took you along, figuring that, worst case, you might be a link to Pranh once we got here. But you fooled me again with that fairytale about your kid and husband.'

'I was married! I did have a baby!'

The shooting was getting closer. He didn't have much time left.

'And who betrayed them to angkar? Who? Who?'

She looked at him in utter horror. Her mouth dropped open. There was no mistaking the truth written on her face. Her naked breasts rose and fell rapidly, as if she couldn't get enough air.

'I had to,' she whispered. 'Pol Pot himself ordered me. He made me marry Khieu in the first place.'

'You're a mole. Just a lousy mole. You've been one all along,' he accused. 'Only I was getting too close, so you signalled Pranh to come and get me. I thought I'd heard shots. Pranh! Your own brother! Look at you! You even fuck your own brother!' he screamed.

'Pranh and I are —' she faltered, 'were one. From birth we were one. The world is very old, my So-yah, and these are things you know nothing of,' she said, her perfect chin jutting out like the prow of a boat.

'Tell me one thing. Just one,' Sawyer said, coming closer, the muzzle of the SKS almost grazing her nipple, strangely erect.

'The killing fields. Why the killing fields?'

Her face twisted, almost in contempt. 'Ah, So-yah. Don't you kill for your country? I too. What difference?'

'There's a difference.'

'No difference, So-yah. My Lai. Kampuchea. No difference.'

'There's a difference,' he insisted.

'So what now? You kill me now? Pourquoi? Who will fight the Vietnamese for you?'

'Fuck the Vietnamese!'

'Look at me, So-yah! Look at me!' she cried, throwing off the sheet. She lay naked on the cot, tracing the exquisite curves of her body with her long, expressive fingers. She trailed her fingernails across her breasts and ribcage to the swell of her belly and down to the silky black hair where her middle finger disappeared.

'All this is yours, So-yah. Yours! Why destroy?' she breathed, parting her legs to give him a better view.

Sawyer's finger tightened on the trigger.

The shock wave and debris from the explosion hit the tent like a hurricane.

CHAPTER 25

The man stands alone amid conflict.
Something approaches;
a pig covered with mud;
a carriage full of ghosts.
He draws his bow then relaxes it;
It is not an assailant,
but a close relative.

'You will want this back,' the Vietnamese officer repeated, raising his voice. He handed the electric razor with the transmitter concealed inside to Sawyer.

'Yes,' Sawyer said, looking at it as though he had never seen it before. His ears still rang from the explosion.

They walked around one of the numerous square pillars that had once supported a corridor roof. The temple roofs had been made of wood and had decayed into dust centuries ago, but the stone pillars remained. The Vietnamese paused to study a bare-breasted relief of Lakshmi, the royal consort of Vishnu, carved on one of them.

'Exquisite,' the Vietnamese murmured, as though talking about a living woman.

'Too fat,' Sawyer shrugged.

'Like me,' the Vietnamese said, looking down and ruefully patting his bulging stomach.

'That's what happens to conquerors. They get fat, Major.'

'General, s'il vous plaît,' General Lu reproved Sawyer gently. 'I'm a general now.'

They began climbing the steps to the vast stone terrace carved with images of elephants on the walls and railings. Even the banister supports were carved to look like elephant trunks. The sun was high and very hot, throwing sharp-edged shadows across the crumpled courtyard below.

'You've come up in the world.'

'We all have.'

'No. Not all of us,' Sawyer replied, pausing on one of the steps.

General Lu nodded. They continued up the stairway to an elevated platform that allowed them to overlook most of the temple complex. In the distance smoke was rising from the burning thatched roofs of a village to the north, almost hidden in the green carpet of jungle.

'Your men?' Sawyer asked, indicating the smoke.

General Lu shook his head.

'Some of the escaping Khmer Rouge. They probably grabbed everything they could carry and then set the fires as a warning to the other villages, comme d'habitude.'

'Some got away, then?'

'Ah, yes. No operation ever goes perfectly.'

A rattle of machine-gun fire echoed from a jungle clearing. Sawyer felt the old tightening in the pit of his stomach. Christ, how he hated Asia. It was difficult to swallow and he had to force down some saliva in order to be able to speak.

'You're taking no Khmer Rouge prisoners?'

General Lu looked at him as though he didn't understand the question. 'Whatever for?'

Sawyer looked away. For a time he stared at a wall carved with ancient battle scenes, myriad limbs wielding spears and swords, without seeing it. Then he realized what it was. The old monk had been right, he thought.

'Plus ça change . . . ' he murmured.

'What?'

'Nothing,' Sawyer said. *How long do you have to do it? Until you get it right.* 'So you'd call it a success?'

General Lu's brown eyes twinkled and his smile had nothing of the mystery of the Buddha in it.

'Ah, yes. Two thousand and five hundred enemy dead. Son Lot, the Khmer Rouge's ablest commander, killed. A good ten per cent of Pol Pot's effective force destroyed in a single morning. A success is certainly what I shall be reporting to the Politburo.'

'You couldn't have done it without me. I handed it to you on a silver platter, didn't I?' Sawyer said bitterly.

'You were, one might say, invaluable,' General Lu agreed.

'Who tumbled me? The café owner in Sisophon?'

General Lu nodded.

'After you were spotted in Sisophon, we stopped every train heading south to Battambang and set up roadblocks on Highway Five. But I had a hunch about Highway Six because we'd had reports of increased Khmer Rouge activity near Siem Reap. So we left it open, and when you didn't show up elsewhere we moved in on Angkor during the night.'

'I should have waited. Taken the café owner out.'

General Lu shook his head. 'It would have made nothing, Jack. You were seen by others. Also you would have had to surface for the rendezvous with Son Lot. You cannot keep an entire army and four thousand kilos of morphine hidden forever. It was the reports that Son Lot had been spotted in the area that first alerted us in any case. Also we made the time very short. If you force the timing, the enemy must expose himself.'

'So you won again. Just like the Parrot's Beak. Is that why they made you a general?'

'C'est la guerre, Jack. In the end we were all of us involved in the espionage: you, I, Parker, Pranh. Ho Chi Minh once said that a spy in the right place at the right time is worth ten times ten divisions. That is why we all do what we do.'

'But in the Parrot's Beak you and Pranh actually worked together to sucker us in, didn't you?' Sawyer said, squinting into the sun to look at General Lu. He rubbed his eyelid where it had been sewn. They had put antibiotic ointment on it, but it still hurt.

General Lu looked out at the stony temple spires poking out of the endless foliage like Aegean islands in a bright-green sea.

'There was a brief moment when the NVA and the Khmer Rouge actually worked together,' he admitted.

'And so you and Pranh became generals and Brother Rap got his balls blown off,' Sawyer said. He hawked and spat over the railing. 'Tell me, as a matter of historical curiosity, where was the Viet Cong COSVN anyway?'

'Ah, you Americans,' General Lu said, shaking his head.

'What arrogance! You always see the world in your own image. Because you had a Pentagon, you assumed we must have one too. We were never that sophisticated. COSVN never existed. It was a myth, like these gods and goddesses,' he said, vaguely gesturing at the ruins all around. 'Like the myth of this very temple, about some Khmer king who mated with a she-dragon. What nonsense! C'est une bêtise!'

Sawyer thought about Suong and didn't say anything. He stared at the blackened ruin, amazed that so much of the temple had survived. There were new fissures running down the pyramidal sides, and a big jagged gap, like the opening to a cave, had been blown in the main stairway leading up to what was left of a tower that had vanished in some other invasion, centuries ago. It was the blast from that gap that had blown away the tent.

He watched a long line of Vietnamese soldiers going in and out of the gap, trying to salvage what was left of the morphine base. So far it looked as though they had found barely a dozen of the wooden boxes intact.

'Why'd they blow it?' Sawyer asked.

General Lu took off his officer's cap and wiped his sweating brow on his uniform sleeve. He watched the soldiers working on the ruin with his lips pursed, as though they were performing an act of great stupidity.

'When the shooting started, they probably thought the Khmer Rouge were attacking them. They had no hope of escape . . . et voilà. Now no person gets Bhun Sa's treasure. If you can take the satisfaction, that part of our operation was not a success,' General Lu said, turning to Sawyer.

'Would you have really sold us the morphine?'

'Of course,' General Lu snapped, peering shrewdly at Sawyer. 'I thought surely you would have guessed by now what our operation was all about?'

'Most of it. There's not a damn thing wrong with my hindsight. God knows, it's better than my foresight,' Sawyer said, shaking his head to refuse a cigarette. General Lu lit one for himself. The smoke drifted out over the ruins as the machine-gun opened up again. Neither said anything. They waited for the sound to stop so they could resume their conversation, the way people do when a jet plane passes overhead.

'American,' Sawyer commented.

'Quoi? The cigarette? Ah, yes. You addicted us to them. You addicted us to more things American than you ever knew. After the war we found whole warehouses of American cigarettes at Tan Son Nhut and Bien Hoa. For a time the Cholonaise used them for currency until we could get them to accept the dong.'

'Money,' Sawyer said, with a little snort of laughter. 'The mother's milk of politics. That's what it was all about.'

'We are a poor country, mon cher Jack. And while our Soviet allies, towards whom we feel great gratitude and the strongest of fraternal socialist ties, have been most generous,' General Lu recited, glancing around as though he feared he might be overheard, 'just between you and me, the Russians are what the bar girls used to call "cheap Charlies".'

'That's tough,' Sawyer said, without conviction. He leaned on an undulating stone balustrade carved to represent a giant serpent. The old Khmers had mixed it all together, he thought. Ancient tales of dragon goddesses and Buddhism and Hindu myths about a giant snake who churned up the Sea of Milk to create the world. The stone was hot under his forearms. He watched the soldiers piling up white chunks of morphine, crumbling like cheese, on the stone paving below. At least the machine-gunning had stopped for a while.

'Yes, it is, how you say, tough,' General Lu agreed carefully, watching Sawyer intently out of the corner of his eye.

Sawyer turned and looked sharply at the Vietnamese. 'Are you saying what I think you're saying, Lu?'

General Lu smiled happily. 'I told them you were good. If you were not good, it would have been a disaster. It was like the jiu-jitsu, you see. It is the enemy's own strength which defeats him.'

Sawyer's face twisted. 'We made the one crucial error. We just didn't know there was another player on the field. You,' Sawyer said.

General Lu smiled and it reminded Sawyer of a snapshot Pranh had taken of them all in a jungle clearing a long time ago.

'Tell me. This Cambodian – what was his name?'

'Pich, I believe. A certain Pich Sam,' General Lu said.

Sawyer sighed. It was Khieu's second-in-command. The

one Suong could not afford to let Khieu terminate, so she turned in her own husband. It all fitted.

'This Pich. Was he a "double" or just a "mole" that you were feeding disinformation to?'

'A "mole", as you Americans so colourfully put it,' General Lu smiled. 'He thought he was passing the good information. He was a True Believer. It was much better than to try and "turn" him. We made great efforts to supply corroborating evidence. It was essential that he be believed about our invading Thailand.'

'Who'd he pass it to?'

'A true "double", as one says. One of the so-called Old People. A peasant living in a shack on the river who was really one of ours. That was how we first got on to Pich. We knew it was the kind of thing the Khmer Rouge would surely pass on to their allies in Beijing. From there, one way or another, it was inevitable that it would eventually reach the Americans.' General Lu shrugged.

'All right,' Sawyer nodded. 'Here's the scenario. There never was going to be a full-scale invasion of Thailand. Maybe just a few raids on Cambodian resistance camps. But the satellite confirmed mobilization and lots of troop movements. Where'd you really send them?'

'Against our real enemies,' General Lu said, his lips tightening.

Sawyer whistled silently to himself. 'North, then. To the Chinese border,' he said.

General Lu nodded again.

'OK. Our operation was to forestall an invasion that was really never meant to happen. But your operation had at least two objectives: to bring Pranh, alias Son Lot, out into the open so you could nail him, and to grab Bhun Sa's morphine for yourselves to acquire good old Western hard currency.'

'Exactement,' General Lu agreed. 'You see, in Cambodia we found ourselves in a position somewhat similar to the situation you Americans had in Vietnam: fighting a guerrilla war in a country where the masses, although we ended the "holocaust" for them, would be happier to see us go home. It is a racial problem. We consider the Cambodians slow-witted and backward, the way some of your white Southern

316

officers used to talk about les Noirs, while they secretly call us "youn" and "dog-eater".

'However, we were determined not to repeat your errors. Pranh was a tiger on his own home ground. If you want to kill a tiger, you don't go beating around in the bush, for that is his game. No. You tether a goat in a clearing and wait for him to come,' General Lu said.

'And Bhun Sa's morphine and the chance to sell it to the Americans for arms was the goat to tempt Pranh into the open.'

'Just so. It was the rumour about Bhun Sa's opium and a possible connection between Bhun Sa and Son Lot that first gave us the idea.'

'So you fed Pich the story about Thailand, figuring it would get back to us.'

'How did it?'

Sawyer shrugged. It didn't matter now what he told Lu. 'The Khmer Rouge, Pranh, sent the information to his friends in Beijing. They deliberately let it slip, possibly to a "double" of their own, who got it to Hong Kong, where the British MI6, which is strong there, picked it up and passed it to their American "Cousins". Because it was Sir Geoffrey's network, he got the credit for passing it to London,' Sawyer said.

'Fascinating.'

'That set us in motion. You were counting on us somehow getting through and leading you to Pranh and the morphine. You didn't hunt the tiger; you trapped him. So your operation was at least half a success. Ours was a total failure,' Sawyer said, making a face.

'Pas du tout, Jack. Your job was to stop our invasion of Thailand, and you performed it brilliantly. You may even get a medal, mon vieux. There will be no invasion.'

'Only because you never intended to invade in the first place. What a joke! What a stupid joke!' Sawyer said.

He watched the soldiers coming empty-handed out of the gap in the temple stairway. They were standing around, waiting for orders. There was obviously nothing more to salvage. A pile of about thirty kilos' worth of morphine lay on the hot paving stones. Some of the boxes were covered with rust-coloured splotches. Blood, Sawyer thought. The Shans had stayed Shans to the end.

'You know, Lu, there's enough there to keep us both in comfort for the rest of our lives,' Sawyer said, gesturing at the pile.

'And go where?' Genral Lu smiled.

Sawyer shrugged, his hands in his pockets. 'Switzerland. Hong Kong, maybe.'

'Neh, Switzerland. What would one do? Watch them make the cuckoo clocks?'

'And yet half the putains in Asia have a poster of the Alps over their beds.'

'A fantasy,' General Lu observed. 'Haven't you yet learned that the worst thing you can do with a fantasy is try to make it come true? Besides, they get the posters free from the airline offices,' he added, putting out the cigarette and carefully field-stripping it.

'And Hong Kong?'

General Lu looked seriously at Sawyer. 'No Vietnamese ever feels comfortable surrounded by Chinese.'

The two men began to walk down towards the Lokeshvara gate Sawyer had bypassed only that morning. Far down the long stone pathway a dark puddle shimmered like black silk. A heat mirage, Sawyer thought. It's just a heat mirage.

'I'm leaving the woman, Suong, with you. Call it a gesture of good will,' General Lu said.

'Don't bullshit me, Lu,' Sawyer said, stopping. 'North Vietnamese good will is like a present of mangoes with a hand-grenade hidden in the basket.'

General Lu's smile broadened. 'Eh bien, mon vieux. Let us just say that I prefer not to execute her and risk making her a martyr of the Kampuchean cause.' His smile faded. He lightly touched Sawyer's arm. 'She was the Madame La Farge of their Revolution, vous comprenez. She has the blood of millions on her hands.'

Sawyer didn't say anything. After a moment they resumed walking, their shadows stretching ahead of them.

'But I say this in all seriousness, Jack. You will deliver our very unofficial offer to the American government, eh? That is why I let you live,' General Lu said, poking Sawyer with his pudgy fingers, knowing Sawyer didn't like it, to emphasize his point.

'Now we're getting down to it. The real reason for your operation, eh, General? Pranh was just a sideshow, icing on the cake, n'est-ce pas?'

General Lu nodded. 'This invasion was a threat. To let you know what we could do. Next time it might not be a feint, Jack. Next time we might really do it.'

'Oh, for Chrissakes, Lu! Just say what the fuck you're after,' Sawyer spat out.

'We want help, Jack. Aid. Also trade. We're broke. We need money. This occupation of Cambodia is very dear for us.'

'Then go home, Lu. We did.'

'Mais oui. And what did you leave behind? Killing fields and concentration camps. Tell me. How can you still support these people? How?'

Sawyer looked away.

'You do business with plenty of communists, Jack. The Russians, the Chinese, even the Khmer Rouge. Why not Vietnam?' General Lu insisted. He stopped walking.

Sawyer walked on.

'You owe us, Jack! You owe! Our whole country was devastated. Children still die from mines you left behind. You have an obligation!' General Lu shouted, his voice rising at the end.

Sawyer stopped and turned back. He looked at General Lu and thought of the Parrot's Beak. Of Brother Rap and Parker and a black wall in Washington.

'We already paid,' he said.

They passed a Lokeshvara gate and down a long lane bordered on either side by giant stone heads, one after another. Each of the faces was identical.

'These faces. Always the same. Pah!' General Lu grimaced in disgust.

'It's supposed to be the face of God.'

'Yes, well, the Khmer God repeats himself. It is boring.'

'The Khmers aren't the only ones who keep repeating themselves,' Sawyer said.

They walked down the aisle of great stone heads that cast shadows across the road, so that they kept alternating between shadow and sunlight as they went. The hot sun had bleached much of the blue from the sky, and in the distance an island of grey monsoon cloud floated over the jungle.

'The Caravelle still going strong in Saigon?' Sawyer asked.

'It's called Ho Chi Minh City now,' General Lu corrected him.

'How about the old "Continental Shelf" on the other side of Lam Son? Do they still sit there over beers and watch the girls bicycling by in their tight ao-dais?'

'One supposes,' General Lu said gloomily. 'I have not been back in some time. But the bars on Tu Do down by the river are closed now. Some are cafés. That at least is better, Jack. More Vietnamese. Eh bien, I have been in Kampuchea for too long now.' He stopped. 'Pranh was right. We had a reunion. No good, Jack. We're all that is left, you and I. We've been at war too long. Too long.' Lu looked around suddenly at the ruins and the soldiers and the jungle. 'I do not like Kampuchea,' he said.

For a time they walked side by side without talking. They passed Vietnamese soldiers clearing the area, preparing to evacuate. They came to the place where the giant head of Buddha had fallen facing the sky. Suong was seated on the giant forehead, guarded by two Vietnamese soldiers. With her long black hair and her hands tied behind her, she resembled a hawk on a perch, its wings folded. Her eyes were hooded, like a hawk's. She didn't look at either of them, yet they sensed her watching.

'How does this rasoir-machine march?' General Lu asked, gesturing at Sawyer's electric razor.

'If I release this button, open the head, raise the antenna and turn this screw, it sends out a "squirt", a compressed transmission which will be picked up by an SR-71 Blackbird somewhere up there, too high to see or hear,' Sawyer said, pointing at the sky. 'Once it's received, they'll home in on the location and there'll be a chopper here in two to three hours to pick me up.'

'So you don't need to talk.'

Sawyer shook his head.

'Suppose someone else were to take it from you and use it?'

Sawyer grinned in a way that reminded General Lu of long

ago. 'If anything else is pressed or opened, it sends another "squirt". Within a couple of hours the location will be hit with an air attack, followed by the Delta Force. That's a little something for *you* to watch out for next time.'

General Lu looked warily at Sawyer, the smile frozen on his face. 'You had this, how you say, in the pocket all the time! If the Shan had not destroyed the morphine, either Pranh or I might unwittingly have called in a strike and you would have gotten the morphine anyway!'

'Why bother?' Sawyer shrugged. 'There never was a real invasion. That was a very dangerous lie, General. A good lie but a dangerous one.'

General Lu once more took off his cap and wiped the sweat from his face with his sleeve. His hair was beginning to thin, Sawyer noticed. When Lu looked back at Sawyer, his smile was Buddha-like, indifferent. No, Sawyer corrected himself. To Asians the smile of the Buddha is compassionate; it's only to us Westerners that it seems indifferent. General Lu put his cap back on and straightened his uniform.

'That makes nothing, Jack,' he shrugged. 'You lied to us. We lied to you. Your failure was that you also lied to yourselves. This we did not do. That is why we won,' he hesitated. 'Allez. Call in your helicopter.'

Sawyer looked around at the soldiers. 'Will two hours be enough time for you to get all your men out of here?'

'But yes. And you will report our interest in US assistance, will you not? An invasion can still be mounted,' he added ominously.

Sawyer spat in the dust. He still had enough saliva for that. 'Haven't you had enough fighting?'

'We've been at war for over forty years now, mon vieux. It's all we know.'

Sawyer grimaced. 'I'll tell them,' he said. 'They won't believe me, but I'll tell them.'

'Why not?'

'They won't go for it, Lu. You don't understand us any more than we do you. We haven't paid blackmail since the days of the Barbary pirates.'

'But it is more logical. And also pour l'humanité – and so much cheaper than a war in Asia.'

'OK, have it your way.' Sawyer made a face. 'That's none of my affair. Politics is out of my line.'

'Mon cher Jack,' General Lu laughed, holding his quivering belly, 'you are still lying to yourself. What do you think you have been involved with all this time if not the politics?' Then more seriously, looking over at Suong, 'What will you do with her?'

'I don't know.'

General Lu looked into Sawyer's eyes. The glass eye had turned slightly so it stared off to one side. It was very disconcerting. It made Sawyer look as though his thoughts, like a madman's, were always elsewhere. General Lu forced himself to concentrate on Sawyer's good eye. He decided that Sawyer was lying, as usual.

As his men were getting ready to leave, one of them brought Sawyer's Ingram over to General Lu. He handed it to Sawyer who checked it over to make sure it was working and loaded.

'With that one, you may need this,' General Lu said, indicating Suong.

Sawyer pointed the Ingram at the sky and fired a few rounds to make sure it was working. At the sound of the shots, the soldiers froze. Even the jungle birds were silenced momentarily. Then there was a clang of metal as someone picked something up and everything went on as before.

'Don't forget, Jack. For us Asians, America is like a rich, somewhat vulgar, uncle. Better that he hate us than that he ignore us – and even what he throws away as garbage is of value to us,' General Lu said.

Sawyer nodded, then turned and scrambled up on the head of Buddha, across from Suong. General Lu's aide came up and Lu barked the order for them to pull out. The rumble of truck engines filled the hot afternoon. General Lu looked back one last time as his truck pulled down the dusty road, bordered by those endlessly smiling stone heads. He watched the two figures shrink in the distance.

That was how he left them. Sawyer and the woman. They were still sitting facing each other on the tumbled head of an ancient god, nothing between them but the Ingram submachine-gun, waiting for the Americans.

322

CHAPTER 26

Heaven within the mountain.
The superior man stores within his mind
the words and deeds of history,
in order to know what is right

There were two of them. They were dressed in black, which
made them almost invisible in the darkness. They were good,
moving cautiously down the rain-deserted wharf, using the
stacks of rice bags for cover. From his vantage behind a
capstan on the freighter's deck Sawyer watched them
approach. They didn't look behind them and that worried
Sawyer because there should be more of them, and if one of
Mith Yon's men opened up too soon. . . . Don't think about
that, he told himself.

He blinked the rain out of his eye and lost them for a
moment. They had disappeared behind a big rice stack near
the gangplank. He eased the safety off on the Ingram. He
had to force himself to breathe slowly, praying that some
trigger-happy ape didn't open up too soon. They had to let
them come on board first and signal that it was clear. He
had gone over and over that with Mith Yon. They had to
wait at least until Vasnasong was on the gangplank before
they opened up. That way whatever additional men Vasnasong had brought would be boxed in. If it worked, even if
they missed, the shooting should drive Vasnasong on board,
straight into Sawyer's field of fire.

The heavy monsoon rain hammered on the metal deck. A
tall palm swayed as the wind swept the rain along the wharf
like a giant broom. Drops skimmed across the slick deck.
The air smelled of wet rice. Sawyer scanned the wharf for

more of them, but all he could make out was the outline of the warehouse on the quay. The rain made the surface of the river choppy, shattering the reflections of the city lights into a billion fragments.

'Why are you doing this, sir?' Captain Henderson of the Delta team had asked him when Sawyer put the Ingram to his head on the ride in from U-Tapao air base.

'Just get the goddam message to Harris,' Sawyer had replied.

'I don't believe you'll shoot me,' Henderson had said.

'I will,' Sawyer said, cocking the Ingram.

Henderson looked into Sawyer's eye. It was red-rimmed and bloodshot, and whatever he saw there, Henderson ordered his sergeant driver to pull the car over. Sawyer left the two of them standing on the side of the road just outside Chon Buri. The two Army jeeps that had been following them in convoy immediately took up the chase, but it wasn't that hard to lose them in the traffic detouring through the slums around Bangkok.

'What you do with me now, So-yah?' Suong had asked him just before she made the call to Vasnasong.

He held the receiver in one hand, the Ingram in the other. 'No mistakes this time. Tell him you have the morphine and to meet you tonight aboard the *Siam Star*. Tell him I'm dead.'

'Maybe he not want to come.'

'Make him come. You know how to make men do things.'

'Oh, So-yah. You not understand.'

'Understand what?'

'You my country now,' she said, her eyes shiny like the lights of the city in the rain.

Sawyer glanced back up at the bridge, but he could see nothing of the Swatowese captain or Mith Yon's man, crouching out of sight, his gun aimed at the captain's back. The rest of the crew were tied up in the aft hold. From here on deck Sawyer could see only the rain slanting through the golden haze cast by the freighter's running lights.

The rain was so loud that he sensed the weight of them stepping on to the gangplank before he heard them. They were moving faster now, the gangplank their point of greatest vulnerability. The metallic scrape of footsteps seemed very near as they came on board. He could see them clearly. They looked young and tough, crouched over their Uzis. One of them passed on the other side of the capstan, close enough for Sawyer to hear his breathing. Sawyer tried to shrink inside the shadow of the capstan.

The Ingram's magazine grip was wet in Sawyer's hand. He was sure it was going to slip the second he pulled the trigger, but there was no way to wipe it dry. His clothes were soaked anyway, and he couldn't afford to make the slightest sound. He could sense that the man on the other side of the capstan had stopped and was listening intently. The man said something in what sounded like Cambodian and the other flicked on a flashlight. He signalled to someone back on the wharf, and a bulky shape that could have been Vasnasong, followed by two others, emerged from the shadows. Vasnasong carried something that looked like an umbrella. The others had guns.

It's going to work, Sawyer thought exultantly. He took a long breath to clear his mind, reminding himself to make sure of the first shot when all hell broke loose.

There were sudden flashes all over the wharf as heavy gunfire erupted from Mith Yon's positions.

It's too soon, Sawyer agonized. Too soon!

Vasnasong's men hit the ground as Vasnasong himself scuttled behind a rice bale. The two Cambodians on deck whirled and, ducking behind the railing, began firing back at the muzzle flashes. Sawyer saw one of Mith Yon's men topple from the top of the warehouse down to the wet concrete wharf.

It would be easy to take the two men on deck, Sawyer thought. They had their backs to him and probably wouldn't hear him in all the commotion till it was too late. But then he would have revealed his position to Vasnasong and it would all have been for nothing. Gritting his teeth, he forced himself to hold his fire, hoping to God he didn't get hit by a stray shot from one of Mith Yon's men.

Suddenly he saw Vasnasong peering up at the freighter from behind the rice bale. Vasnasong hesitated for the briefest instant, trying to decide which way to break. Come on, you bastard, Sawyer prayed. It's nice and quiet on the ship and your own men have signalled that it's safe. Come on, come on, said the spider to the fly.

Bullets stitched into the bags of rice near Vasnasong's head and he ducked back. Rice poured out of the bags. Sawyer watched it form a tiny mountain that, even as it formed, was washed away by the rain. For some reason it reminded him of Pranh talking about water and the ancient Khmer rice harvests. He stared blankly at the firefight and the warehouse and its big sign: 'South-east Asia Rice and Trading Company'.

His breathing was coming fast now. Maybe because he had almost died in that warehouse, where Suong . . . 'My father was French rice merchant' . . . Or maybe. . . . All at once he remembered sitting in Vasnasong's office, looking at the picture of Vasnasong being greeted by Chou En-lai behind the desk. Christ! What an idiot he had been! It had been staring him in the face all the time. He had been right to get away from Henderson's Delta team and out from under Company control. If only Vasnasong – come on, you bastard!

As if he had somehow heard Sawyer's thoughts, Vasnasong peeked out once, then broke for the gangplank. The two men on deck gave him covering fire, but there was heavy shooting from the direction of the warehouse. Ricochets pinged off the railing. Arms flailing, Vasnasong went down on the gangplank. There was no way to tell if he had been hit or had fallen. All Sawyer could do was wait. Not now, he thought, barely able to restrain himself from an insane try for the gangplank, when Vasnasong suddenly crawled on to the deck on all fours and rolled heavily behind a big metal storage box bolted to the deck.

One of the men on deck started over towards him, but Vasnasong, chest heaving, waved him back. The man turned and fired his Uzi again at the wharf.

Now, Sawyer thought, now, moving out from behind the capstan and getting set in the squat position, no longer conscious of the rain or his breathing or anything except telling himself to make it slow and sure. His first burst caught the man farthest away full in the back. The man hadn't even time to arch his back before Sawyer was firing at the second man, already whirling around, the Uzi sweeping towards

Sawyer. There was the briefest instant when their eyes locked, and then the Ingram's bullets smashed into the side of his face and the Cambodian went down.

Sawyer ran towards Vasnasong, almost falling on the rain-slick deck. Vasnasong was fumbling with something caught in his umbrella. He wasn't going to make it, Sawyer thought. But Vasnasong couldn't free the umbrella. He looked up just as Sawyer raised the Ingram. With a grunt, he smashed the Ingram into Vasnasong's head. Vasnasong fell to the deck.

A savage joy flooded Sawyer. It felt so good hitting Vasnasong, it took every bit of will he had to keep from pounding the man's head to mush. Instead he twisted the umbrella out of Vasnasong's hand and flung it into the river. He hauled Vasnasong to his feet and, using the Ingram as a prod, marched him up a ladder on the river side and into a small mess room. Sawyer slammed the heavy metal door behind them, shutting out the rain and the sounds of shooting. He had to hurry. There wasn't much time.

The cabin stank of diesel oil and fish. It was lit by a single, dangling bulb. Sitting, tied up in a corner, was Suong. The three of them just stared at each other. Sawyer tried not to look at Suong's face because every time he did he could feel his throat tighten as though a big hand was squeezing it.

'I was right, Sawyer-khrap. You are dangerous man,' Vasnasong managed, panting to catch his breath. He steadied himself with the table. There was a red welt on the side of his face where Sawyer had hit him.

Sawyer popped a new clip into the Ingram. The sound of it slamming home was very loud in the small cabin. Sawyer gripped the Ingram with both hands. At this range it was impossible to miss.

'No, So-yah, no,' Suong cried out, squirming desperately in the corner.

'You make terrible mistake, Sawyer-khrap,' Vasnasong wheezed. His face was waxen in the smoky yellow light.

'Not this time,' Sawyer said, gritting his teeth so tightly they could see the line of his jaw throbbing.

'We are on same side, Sawyer-khrap,' Vasnasong gasped.

Sawyer pointed the Ingram straight at Vasnasong's belly. They could see his face working, trying to hold the rage in.

'How?' Sawyer managed to say. 'When the Khmer Rouge

was running things in Cambodia, how did they manage to get the rice from the killing fields to Red China?'

Vasnasong didn't answer. His mouth twisted. He looked as if he was about to throw up. Suong was barely breathing.

'The Khmer Rouge traded rice to China for arms to use against the Vietnamese. The land routes through Laos and Vietnam were controlled by the Vietnamese, so they would have had to ship it by boat. Maybe even this very boat,' Sawyer said, his eyes darting back and forth between them. He didn't wait for an answer. It was written plainly enough in their faces.

'Suong's father was a rice merchant,' Sawyer went on. 'She didn't just call you. You were in the same business. You knew each other all the time. I should have guessed from that picture of Chou En-lai in your office. You're the link with China, Vasnasong-khrap. And Suong was your pipeline to the Khmer Rouge. This whole thing,' Sawyer gestured vaguely with the Ingram, 'was being run from Beijing.'

A gleam came into Vasnasong's eye. His fleshy lips worked as though he was about to eat something. 'Do you see, Sawyer One-Eye? Do you finally see?'

'And all that bullshit about the British. MI6 only thought they were using you. In reality, you were spoonfeeding them. Christ, you must have strained a gut pretending you didn't know anything whenever Countess Dracula came calling.'

'Sometime very difficult. I must use most incompetent agent in Hong Kong to follow MI6 men to convince London of authenticity of coded messages without interfering with information getting through,' Vasnasong admitted.

'And the men you sent against me were all Khmer Rouge. That's why they didn't know how Buddhists behave. Under angkar, religion was outlawed in Cambodia. My God,' Sawyer shook his head, 'thanks to you and Suong, everyone was dancing to Beijing's tune and didn't even know it.'

Vasnasong straightened. His face had begun to lose its waxy look. 'So you see you cannot kill me, Sawyer-khrap. We are on same side. America and China allies on this.'

'What about her? What about the killing?' Sawyer demanded, gesturing towards Suong with the Ingram.

Vasnasong splayed his pudgy fingers in a helpless gesture. 'She did it for her country.'

'So did Hitler.'

'She is for you, Sawyer-khrap. Can you not see?'

A look passed between Vasnasong and Suong. There was something very intimate about it and Sawyer's throat tightened. Vasnasong was just trying to save her, Sawyer told himself, wondering why Vasnasong didn't try to sacrifice her to save himself. Unless. . . . There was more in the look than that. It was the kind of look. . . .

'You seduced her, you bastard,' Sawyer hissed, aiming the Ingram almost point-blank at Vasnasong's face. 'You knew her father, didn't you? Maybe you even ran him. How old was she when you fucked her? How old?'

Vasnasong's mouth opened, but nothing came out. He looked sick.

Sawyer turned towards Suong. 'He forced you, didn't he? How old were you?'

Her eyes brimmed over. She shook her head wildly. 'Please, So-yah. It was so long ago. It makes nothing now.'

Sawyer whirled back to Vasnasong. 'You forced her, you miserable bastard. She was only a little girl and you raped her.'

Vasnasong looked at him strangely. 'I fear you not understand women after all, Sawyer-khrap. I was not always old. Before twenty years I was handsome man. Rich. Powerful. And Suong no ordinary young girl.'

'So?'

Despite the fear, there was contempt in Vasnasong's face. 'I did not seduce Suong. It was she who seduces me.'

Sawyer didn't have to look at Suong's face to know it was true. Then he did look at her and it burst out of him.

'Jesus! Is there anybody you haven't fucked?'

The Ingram hung lifelessly down at his side. Vasnasong brushed himself off and started confidently for the door. Sawyer looked at him.

'I go now. There is no more here. We are allies, yes? You do not have to love your ally, Sawyer-khrap, only not to kill him,' Vasnasong said.

'You're forgetting Parker. You set him up,' Sawyer said. His voice was toneless. It might have been a dead man talking.

Vasnasong stopped. He looked back at both of them.

'Your Parker was stupid, greedy man. He was warned of danger.' Vasnasong shrugged. 'In Asia many die. Asia is most dangerous place,' Vasnasong said, turning towards the door.

The first rounds of the Ingram took off the back of Vasnasong's head. Vasnasong sprawled face-down on the metal floor. The cabin smelled of gunpowder and the faint salt scent of blood. Sawyer came close to Suong. Her eyes were black as death.

'Why you do this? Now you will be stranger in your own country,' she whispered.

His face worked. He was holding himself together the way a wounded soldier trying to make it back to his own lines holds himself together.

'We were friends in Vietnam,' Sawyer said. 'After a while, that was all that mattered. Not big words, not bullshit about God and Country, just each other. I never really liked Parker that much, but he was all that was left. At that, he died better than he lived, so maybe there's hope for the rest of us yet. There's got to be something.'

Suong pressed her breast against the still-warm muzzle of the Ingram. Sawyer jerked it away as though she had touched it with a torch.

'There is something, my So-yah. I know what men really want. Their deepest desire,' Suong said, pressing her thighs together as if imagining him between them. Her voice with its strange three-in-the-morning timbre caught at him. His throat tightened. 'I do anything for you, So-yah. We are both without country. I make you my country. You will be everything for me. I will bring you other women and we will do such things. Nothing is forbidden. Nothing!' she whispered.

'No,' he said, backing away from her.

'You want me. I know you want me.'

Having her hands tied behind her made her breasts more prominent. He watched them heaving, the nipples poking against the fabric of her blouse, as she came closer.

'Touch me one last time. My hands tied. I can't stop you. Please,' she said, kneeling at his feet. He could feel her breath, warm on his wet trousers. 'You know you want to.'

'No,' he lied, feeling himself harden like steel.

She looked up at him. He couldn't stop looking at her, at

330

her breasts and the line of her chin where it came under her ear, at the shining black sweep of her hair, at her eyes and the way her lips parted. She was so beautiful it hurt to look at her.

'Then what you do with me. So-yah?'

'I don't know,' he whispered, the tightness in his throat almost choking him.

'Don't be fool, So-yah. Most emotion never truly felt. Most time we only pretend to feel, even to our-self. But with us is no pretend. If you lose me, you not feel again. We both know this, my So-yah. Destroy Suong, destroy you-self.'

The door burst open. Mith Yon came in, gun first. His eyes still had the unfocused look that comes with killing. He almost stumbled over Vasnasong's body and just caught his balance against the bulkhead. He looked at both of them. Wind whipped the rain into the room. Water streamed down Mith Yon's face to drip into the puddle of blood spreading on the floor.

The floor began to tremble. Raindrops danced along the floor as a loud rumble filled the silence, followed by a sensation of motion. The *Siam Star* had begun to move.

'What you do now, my So-yah?' Suong whispered, her eyes catching the light like black diamonds. 'What you do now?'

EPILOGUE

On the night of the full moon after the monsoon rains have ended is the festival of the Loy Krathong. As darkness falls, the people gather on the banks of rivers and klongs throughout Thailand to sail tiny boats made of banana leaves. Every boat carries a single burning candle and there is great excitement, especially among the children as, one by one, each member of the family launches his boat. Wide-eyed, they watch the current carry their boats away to join the thousands of flickering lights already floating in the darkness.

The Loy Krathong is a happy time, and there is much singing and dancing, and the night resounds with firecrackers along the shores. No one knows the origin of the festival, for it comes from the time of the ancients. There are those who say the floating lights are an offering to the river dragons. Others say it is a celebration of the end of the monsoon waters that have ensured the fertility of the land. Among the common people it is believed that they are casting their sins upon the waters. Some more cynical types suggest that the lights are a way of apologizing to the Mother of Waters, as the Chao Phraya river is known, for all the pollution the people pour into her. Whatever the origin, everyone knows that most of the waters of Thailand feed into the Chao Phraya and that the view of the river at midnight, with its galaxies of candles floating by in the darkness, is spectacular.

In Bangkok, where the spectacle is at its height and the klongs and riverbanks are noisy till dawn with merrymaking, it is generally conceded that the most prestigious place for viewing is from the upper terrace of the Royal Palace, where two men stood apart from His Majesty's other guests, gazing down over the parapet at the myriad dots of light moving down the klongs and the river, delineating them like iridescent veins in a vast, dark body.

The two men were utterly dissimilar in appearance. One was tall, fair-haired, obviously a Westerner. He wore a superbly cut, light tropical suit with an air of casual elegance that professional models have to work a long time to perfect. The other was small, bent, Asian. He was very old. He wore a gold-braided black military uniform that sagged and wrinkled and seemed several sizes too big for him. Seen from behind, they looked like a man and his pet monkey. Yet it was because of the little Asian and not the tall Westerner that no one, even from the Royal party, dared approach the two men.

'So the Vietnamese never intended to attack. Only to trap Son Lot and perhaps the opium of Bhun Sa also,' Bhamornprayoon said.

'And to send us a warning, your Excellency,' Harris replied.

The old man gazed shrewdly at Harris. 'Interesting. That you see the threat but not the offer, Harris-khrap. You of the West are most curious.'

Harris made a gesture of dismissal. 'The offer is meaningless, Excellency. No President could ever approach Congress to ask for aid to communist Vietnam in present circumstances. That Sawyer even mentioned it shows how politically naïve he was.'

'And the opium of Bhun Sa?'

'Destroyed, it seems. It was all for nothing.'

The old man looked up suspiciously, his sharp eyes almost disappearing in a nest of wrinkles. 'Is this certain?'

'It seems so, Excellency.' Harris sighed. 'In any case, we have no way of ever finding out for sure. Unfortunately, this agent, Sawyer, has managed to give our people the slip.'

'Has he?' Bhamornprayoon said in a tone of voice that left little doubt in Harris's mind that he'd already heard about Sawyer's disappearance from his own sources.

There was nothing to say to that, so Harris just looked out over the city and the countless lights twinkling on the river. Behind him the gold-covered spires of the chedis and mondhops and the phallic golden prangs of the Royal Palace glowed in the floodlights set up for the festival like a fairytale castle. In Chinatown an enormous dragon's tail of firecrackers went off. It sounded almost like a machine-gun. There were loud cheers in the streets that could be heard even up here.

'What happened to the woman? This Suong?'

'He took her with him,' Harris said, an edge in his voice.

'They were lovers, then?'

'I don't know what they were,' Harris snapped, unable to conceal the bitterness. There were lines around his handsome mouth and, all at once, Bhamornprayoon was able to see very clearly what Harris would look like as an old man.

'You blame yourself?' Bhamornprayoon asked quietly.

'Sawyer was out there alone too long. It was my mission. I should have seen it. He suckered us all the way,' Harris said sternly.

'Mai pen rai.' The old man shrugged. 'Why must you Americans see all things only as success or failure? There is no invasion. There will be no war for this year. That is at least something. It has fallen, as the proverb says, on one horn of the buffalo but not the other. The rest,' he shrugged again, 'is karma.'

'It couldn't have happened if Sawyer hadn't slipped one over on us. That one-eyed bastard pulled a gun on the way in from U-Tapao, and the next thing we knew, they had both gone to ground. It wasn't until later, after the Bangkok police fished Vasnasong's body out of one of the klongs, that we were able to piece together what happened.'

'Who killed Vasnasong? Sawyer?'

'Don't you know?' Harris asked, elaborately affecting an air of surprise.

'Vasnasong play many sides. In Bangkok, Hong Kong, many sides. Our eminent Chief Police have theory maybe Vasnasong killed by Western drug smuggler. The men of the drug trade are said to be of desperate character.' Bhamornprayoon smiled.

'No doubt that is what happened.' Harris smiled back.

'But we forget the woman. What of her?'

A furtive look came into Harris's eyes. At first Bhamornprayoon thought that Harris was about to lie and then he saw that it was something else. Harris was confused, almost fearful. For a man like Harris anything other than absolute certainty had to be a special kind of purgatory, Bhamornprayoon thought.

'Somehow Sawyer managed to spirit the woman Suong on to this rusty old freighter Vasnasong had waiting to take the morphine cargo. One of the Cambodian resistance groups, headed by a certain Mith Yon, had taken over the ship, and they all sailed south into the Gulf of Thailand. Apparently, Sawyer had suspected something and set it up with Mith Yon even before he went into Cambodia. The son-of-a-bitch was good, you know. I told you he was good.'

'But you say the morphine destroyed. Why he do this?'

Harris looked at the wizened old man, at the deep fissures under his cheeks that made him look both sad and wise, the broad Asian nose, the black buttons that were his eyes. He didn't know how to explain it to Bhamornprayoon. He didn't know how to explain it to himself.

'It wasn't about the dope for them. For Sawyer and Mith Yon. It was about her. Suong.'

'I am not understand.'

'She was, together with Son Lot and Pol Pot, one of the guiding spirits of the Khmer Rouge and their death camps in Cambodia. Mith Yon and his followers were her victims. Don't you see?' Harris said in a hushed voice. 'He was bringing her to trial.'

'What happen?' Bhamornprayoon asked gently. From Harris's tone he could tell they were almost there.

Harris's shoulders slumped. He suddenly looked smaller, less sure of himself.

'We've got two versions from two separate sources. But they're almost the same,' he whispered, as though he was ashamed of something. 'According to one, Sawyer turned the woman over to Mith Yon, telling him they could do anything they wanted but not to spill even a single drop of her blood. That all sounds a bit too Shakespearian for me,' Harris said, making a face.

'It is an old saying here. But mai pen rai, only say what is known,' Bhamornprayoon ordered, his eyes searching Harris's face as if he were trying to see Sawyer's behind it.

'The other version is simpler. Sawyer just turned the woman over to the Cambodians and took off when the ship was somewhere off the coast of the southern peninsula. Or maybe it was one of the islands. I don't know,' Harris shrugged. 'Nobody's seen him since.'

'And the woman?'

'Yeah. The woman. It seems they anchored or drifted, who the hell knows, out into the middle of the Gulf. I don't know if they had a trial or what. But they didn't spill a drop of her blood, if that matters.

'Anyway, I can't get the picture out of my mind. The bunch of them on this rusty old hulk, drifting nowhere on an empty blue sea under an empty blue sky, the sun blazing down on them. You know what the sun is like in those latitudes. It's unbelievably hot here in Bangkok, but down there, my God!

'There was a big iron box on deck. Maybe it was used to store tools or something at one time. They locked her inside it. It must have been unbelievably hot, worse than an oven,' he said, going faster now. 'But that wasn't enough. They got aluminium foil or strips from somewhere and made reflectors around the box. It must have been hundreds of degrees in there. They say her hammering and screaming went on for two days.'

From across the river on the Thonburi side they could hear the crash of gongs and the whining tones of festival songs.

'She must to go insane after some hours like that,' Bhamornprayoon said finally.

'Probably,' Harris agreed. 'Most probably.'

Behind them the soft murmur of conversation gave way to 'Oohs' and 'Aahs' as new arrivals crowded the parapet on the far side of the terrace near the Royal Box.

'What was she like, this woman?'

Harris paused. 'I never met her. They say she was very pretty.'

'Ah,' Bhamorprayoon said, as if that explained a great deal. He looked up at Harris. 'A terrible death,' he said, clicking his tongue. 'No matter what she did. To be burned alive like that.'

'No! Don't you understand?' Harris said suddenly, a sick look on his face. 'She wasn't burned. She was cooked! They said when they finally took the body out, the meat was so tender it literally fell off the bones!'

336

The two men looked away from each other. They stood there for a long time. They looked down over the millions of lights shining on the dark water and just watched and didn't say anything at all.

Below them the Chao Phraya flowed on in the night, a river of stars carrying the sins of men to the sea.

Bestselling Thriller/Suspense

☐ See You Later, Alligator	William F. Buckley	£2.50
☐ Hell is Always Today	Jack Higgins	£1.75
☐ Brought in Dead	Harry Patterson	£1.95
☐ Maxwell's Train	Christopher Hyde	£2.50
☐ Russian Spring	Dennis Jones	£2.50
☐ Nightbloom	Herbert Lieberman	£2.50
☐ Basikasingo	John Matthews	£2.95
☐ The Secret Lovers	Charles McCarry	£2.50
☐ Fletch	Gregory Mcdonald	£1.95
☐ Green Monday	Michael M. Thomas	£2.95
☐ Someone Else's Money	Michael M. Thomas	£2.50
☐ Black Ice	Colin Dunne	£2.50
☐ Blind Run	Brian Freemantle	£2.50
☐ The Proteus Operation	James P. Hogan	£3.50
☐ Miami One Way	Mike Winters	£2.50

Prices and other details are liable to change

ARROW BOOKS, BOOKSERVICE BY POST, PO BOX 29, DOUGLAS, ISLE OF MAN, BRITISH ISLES

NAME ....

ADDRESS ....

....

....

Please enclose a cheque or postal order made out to Arrow Books Ltd. for the amount due and allow the following for postage and packing.

U.K. CUSTOMERS: Please allow 22p per book to a maximum of £3.00.

B.F.P.O. & EIRE: Please allow 22p per book to a maximum of £3.00.

OVERSEAS CUSTOMERS: Please allow 22p per book.

Whilst every effort is made to keep prices low it is sometimes necessary to increase cover prices at short notice. Arrow Books reserve the right to show new retail prices on covers which may differ from those previously advertised in the text or elsewhere.

Bestselling Fiction

☐ Toll for the Brave	Jack Higgins	£2.25
☐ Basikasingo	John Matthews	£2.95
☐ Where No Man Cries	Emma Blair	£2.50
☐ Saudi	Laurie Devine	£2.95
☐ The Clogger's Child	Marie Joseph	£2.50
☐ The Gooding Girl	Pamela Oldfield	£2.95
☐ The Running Years	Claire Rayner	£2.75
☐ Duncton Wood	William Horwood	£3.50
☐ Aztec	Gary Jennings	£3.95
☐ Colours Aloft	Alexander Kent	£2.95
☐ The Volunteers	Douglas Reeman	£2.75
☐ The Second Lady	Irving Wallace	£2.95
☐ The Assassin	Evelyn Anthony	£2.50
☐ The Pride	Judith Saxton	£2.50
☐ The Lilac Bus	Maeve Binchy	£2.50
☐ Fire in Heaven	Malcolm Bosse	£3.50

Prices and other details are liable to change

ARROW BOOKS, BOOKSERVICE BY POST, PO BOX 29, DOUGLAS, ISLE OF MAN, BRITISH ISLES

NAME ....

ADDRESS ....

....

....

Please enclose a cheque or postal order made out to Arrow Books Ltd. for the amount due and allow the following for postage and packing.

U.K. CUSTOMERS: Please allow 22p per book to a maximum of £3.00.

B.F.P.O. & EIRE: Please allow 22p per book to a maximum of £3.00.

OVERSEAS CUSTOMERS: Please allow 22p per book.

Whilst every effort is made to keep prices low it is sometimes necessary to increase cover prices at short notice. Arrow Books reserve the right to show new retail prices on covers which may differ from those previously advertised in the text or elsewhere.

Bestselling SF/Horror

Prices and other details are liable to change

ARROW BOOKS, BOOKSERVICE BY POST, PO BOX 29, DOUGLAS, ISLE OF MAN, BRITISH ISLES

NAME ....

ADDRESS ....

....

....

Please enclose a cheque or postal order made out to Arrow Books Ltd. for the amount due and allow the following for postage and packing.

U.K. CUSTOMERS: Please allow 22p per book to a maximum of £3.00.

B.F.P.O. & EIRE: Please allow 22p per book to a maximum of £3.00.

OVERSEAS CUSTOMERS: Please allow 22p per book.

Whilst every effort is made to keep prices low it is sometimes necessary to increase cover prices at short notice. Arrow Books reserve the right to show new retail prices on covers which may differ from those previously advertised in the text or elsewhere.

Bestselling Fiction

☐ Hiroshima Joe	Martin Booth	£2.95
☐ Voices on the Wind	Evelyn Anthony	£2.50
☐ The Pianoplayers	Anthony Burgess	£2.50
☐ Prizzi's Honour	Richard Condon	£2.95
☐ Queen's Play	Dorothy Dunnett	£3.50
☐ Duncton Wood	William Horwood	£3.50
☐ In Gallant Company	Alexander Kent	£2.50
☐ The Fast Men	Tom McNab	£2.95
☐ A Ship With No Name	Christopher Nicole	£2.95
☐ Contact	Carl Sagan	£3.50
☐ Uncle Mort's North Country	Peter Tinniswood	£2.50
☐ Fletch	Gregory Mcdonald	£1.95
☐ A Better World Than This	Marie Joseph	£2.95
☐ The Lilac Bus	Maeve Binchy	£2.50
☐ The Gooding Girl	Pamela Oldfield	£2.95

Prices and other details are liable to change

ARROW BOOKS, BOOKSERVICE BY POST, PO BOX 29, DOUGLAS, ISLE OF MAN, BRITISH ISLES

NAME ....

ADDRESS ....

....

....

Please enclose a cheque or postal order made out to Arrow Books Ltd. for the amount due and allow the following for postage and packing.

U.K. CUSTOMERS: Please allow 22p per book to a maximum of £3.00.

B.F.P.O. & EIRE: Please allow 22p per book to a maximum of £3.00.

OVERSEAS CUSTOMERS: Please allow 22p per book.

Whilst every effort is made to keep prices low it is sometimes necessary to increase cover prices at short notice. Arrow Books reserve the right to show new retail prices on covers which may differ from those previously advertised in the text or elsewhere.

A Selection of Arrow Bestsellers

☐ Live Flesh	Ruth Rendell	£2.75
☐ Contact	Carl Sagan	£3.50
☐ Yeager	Chuck Yeager	£3.95
☐ The Lilac Bus	Maeve Binchy	£2.50
☐ 500 Mile Walkies	Mark Wallington	£2.50
☐ Staying Off the Beaten Track	Elizabeth Gundrey	£4.95
☐ A Better World Than This	Marie Joseph	£2.95
☐ No Enemy But Time	Evelyn Anthony	£2.95
☐ Rates of Exchange	Malcolm Bradbury	£3.50
☐ For My Brother's Sins	Sheelagh Kelly	£3.50
☐ Carrott Roots	Jasper Carrott	£3.50
☐ Colours Aloft	Alexander Kent	£2.95
☐ Blind Run	Brian Freemantle	£2.50
☐ The Stationmaster's Daughter	Pamela Oldfield	£2.95
☐ Speaker for the Dead	Orson Scott Card	£2.95
☐ Football is a Funny Game	Ian St John and Jimmy Greaves	£3.95
☐ Crowned in a Far Country	Princess Michael of Kent	£4.95

Prices and other details are liable to change

ARROW BOOKS, BOOKSERVICE BY POST, PO BOX 29, DOUGLAS, ISLE
OF MAN, BRITISH ISLES

NAME ....

ADDRESS ....

....

....

Please enclose a cheque or postal order made out to Arrow Books Ltd. for the amount
due and allow the following for postage and packing.

U.K. CUSTOMERS: Please allow 22p per book to a maximum of £3.00.

B.F.P.O. & EIRE: Please allow 22p per book to a maximum of £3.00.

OVERSEAS CUSTOMERS: Please allow 22p per book.

Whilst every effort is made to keep prices low it is sometimes necessary to increase cover
prices at short notice. Arrow Books reserve the right to show new retail prices on covers
which may differ from those previously advertised in the text or elsewhere.